Hushed into Silence

Smoky Mountain Secrets Saga,
Book 2

Jeanne Hardt

CHAPTER 1

Lily bent sideways, doing all she could to stretch and relieve her body of its aches and pains from the long trip. The hot July weather didn't help. She wished she'd had room in her bag for the heavy winter coat she kept draped over one arm, making her even warmer.

She'd been impressed by the fancy buggy she'd arrived in, driven by a man simply known as *David*. After two weeks traveling across land and water, she'd never gotten his last name. He hadn't been at all talkative, but honestly, she didn't care. She hadn't felt like carrying on a conversation.

No matter how elegant the vehicle had been, its fine cushioned seat eventually got uncomfortable—the reason for her sore backside and aching bones. On the bright side, she'd experienced other luxuries that weren't quite so painful. Fine hotels and food she'd never tasted before.

Yet she couldn't bring herself to *enjoy* any of it. Every mile took her away from her son and everyone she loved.

Once they arrived at their destination, David had helped her down from the seat of the buggy, then hopped back in and rode away before she could thank him. Luckily, he'd remembered to set her knapsack on the ground.

For an instant, she feared he might've left her at the wrong address, but that was a silly notion. After all, the man had been paid by her aunt, and Lily doubted anyone would purposefully cross her.

Regardless, Lily was in a strange place and butterflies fluttered in her belly, confirming she felt lost, alone, and completely out of sorts.

Some of her worries faded when she saw the name, *Clark*, scrolled in wrought iron over the top of the metal entrance gate. The gate's swirled design looked like thin branches with leaves interwoven here and there. A chest-high rock wall encircled the property and stretched a full block, but she couldn't see a house. Had she not been so downhearted, she'd probably appreciate the fineness of the elaborate setting.

The gate stood open wide, so she sighed, grabbed her bag, and headed down the stone pathway.

Though abundant, unfamiliar maple trees surrounded her. They were nothing like her beloved birch and pines from the cove. Not only had she been forced to leave behind her loved ones, she ached for the place she'd always known as *home.*

She spotted a man on his knees digging around in a bed of flowers. He lifted his head, briefly smiled, then kept working.

He ain't my uncle, that's for sure.

For one thing, he appeared much too young, but more than that, she knew her uncle would never do that kind of work.

The path turned and she passed a thick grove of trees. She jerked to a stop and gaped.

Lawdy . . .

The two-story house stretched so far from side to side, she had to crane her neck to see all of it. Made of white brick, it was unlike any house she'd seen before. More fancy black wrought iron encased every window. A long, covered porch with sculpted pillars led to the front door.

If they had the kind of money to afford something this magnificent, why on earth hadn't they helped her family through their hard times?

Uncle Stuart must truly be a miser.

Lily glanced down at her simple dress. The best one she had, but she doubted it would do.

I don't care. Let 'em think poorly of me.

Her life couldn't become any more miserable than it already was.

She drew in an enormous breath of courage and stepped onto the porch. Chairs with fine-stitched cushioned seats faced outward. She ran her hand over the woven material the chairs had been made from. It felt like wood, but looked more like hardened straw.

Amazin'.

Nothin' like the furniture back home.

For the briefest moment, she considered sitting down and taking it all in, but she needed to get the introductions over with.

She raised the heavy gold knocker on the door and rapped several times. Her heart thumped hard, right along with it.

The door inched open.

A tall, slim, sharply-dressed man nodded at her. "May I help you?"

So proper.

"Uncle Stuart?"

"Heaven's no. I'm Gerard, the butler."

She'd read about men like him. "Oh. Well, I'm Lily. I reckon they're expectin' me."

His face puckered like he'd tasted something sour. "You *reckon*?" He said the word as if it disgusted him.

"Yessir. Aunt Helen fetched me. That is, she hired some man named *David* to do it. I just got here an' I'm mighty tired. Is she home?"

"Yes. Mrs. Clark is having tea. I'll alert her to your arrival."

"Thank you. Can I come in?"

"No. Wait here." He pointed at one of the porch chairs.

What a welcome.

Lily gingerly sat on the seat indicated. It surprisingly held her weight and was oddly comfortable. She folded her hands atop her lap and waited.

Minutes passed.

Lily picked at her dress, then lifted the skirt and studied her worn-out shoes. Maybe if she was lucky, Aunt Helen would buy her a new pair.

The door opened and Lily held her breath.

The woman who stepped out and faced her looked nothing like what Lily expected. Her royal blue gown fell in layers to her feet, with rows of black lace that also lined her sleeves. The dress fit her tight at the waist, but full through the hips. The neckline had a row of tiny black buttons all the way up to her chin. A matching hat perched on top of her gray-haired head.

She's gotta be burnin' up in that dress.

Lily jumped to her feet. "Aunt Helen?" She had a similarity to Lily's ma around her mouth and eyes, but lacked any kind of warmth.

She jutted her nose skyward, then took Lily in from head to toe. "My, oh, my. It's worse than I ever believed." She raised Lily's skirt and exposed her legs. "No crinolines?"

"Huh?" Lily felt like a piece of livestock being examined for purchase. If she checked her teeth, she might have to slap the woman.

Her aunt's upturned nose wrinkled. She let go of the dress, but fingered Lily's sleeve. "How *old* is this garment?"

What happened to how was your trip, or I'm glad you're here?

"Um . . ." Lily fanned out the skirt. "Reckon it's goin' on four years or so. I'm lucky I didn't outgrow it. It's one a my best."

"A four-year-old dress is one of your best?"

"Well, I ain't got nothin' fine like what *you're* wearin'." Lily crossed her arms and frowned.

"*Ain't*," Aunt Helen grumbled, then took Lily's chin in her hand and turned her head from side to side, studying every detail of her face. "At least I have something to work with. You're a pretty girl."

"Thank you." Lily stared downward. Though she'd been complimented, it didn't feel good.

Aunt Helen gestured to Lily's bag. "Is that all you brought?"

"Yes'm. Don't got much a nothin'."

"You *haven't* got much of *anything*."

"That's what I said."

The woman grunted. "Not exactly. Do you have something in that bag for me from your mother?"

"Yes'm." Lily bent over and dug around in the bag until she found the box, then handed it to her aunt.

"Thank you." Aunt Helen smiled for the first time and untied the strings that held the package together.

Lily's ma hadn't told her the contents. Only to make sure her sister got it. She assumed it was some sort of gift, but thought it odd that Aunt Helen expected it.

"Just as I remember," Aunt Helen whispered and lifted a gold necklace from the box. "Mother's necklaces." She drew out a second chain—one bearing a gold cross—then held both close to her chest.

No.

They'd been the only things of value Lily's grandma had given specifically to her ma. "Why'd she give you those?"

"It was part of the bargain. I agreed to take you in, but insisted on having these. We'll be spending a great deal of money on you. Mother's jewelry is the least Rose could do. Truthfully, it was *all* she could do. She has *nothing* thanks to that pitiful excuse of a husband she married."

"Don't talk 'bout Pa like that!" Lily scowled at the hateful woman.

Aunt Helen returned her glare, accompanied with a finger in Lily's face. "That's the last time you'll raise your voice to me. Understood?"

Lily took several labored breaths, standing practically nose to nose with her aunt. They'd not started off well, but it was hard to care for a woman who'd never shown her or her family any love.

She swallowed hard. "Yes'm. I understand."

"Good. Now follow me." She opened the door and went inside.

Lily trudged after her.

Her aunt glanced over her shoulder. "Are your shoes clean?"

"Clean as can be."

"Regardless, wipe them on that rug." She pointed at a mat beside the door.

Lily wiped her feet, then stepped onto the polished wood floor. It gleamed with a shine brighter than sparkling water on a cloudless day.

There ain't never gonna be no chickens runnin' 'round inside this *house.*

When she scanned the rest of the entryway, her knees nearly buckled. A large stairway fanned out in front of her, with dark-stained wood railings. The carpeted steps narrowed as they reached the second floor.

A large portrait of Aunt Helen, and whom Lily assumed to be her Uncle Stuart, hung on the wall's center at the top of the stairs. Both were dressed in the finest of clothes. Lily's mouth dropped as she gazed at the nearly life-sized painting. "Wow," she muttered. The artist had made them appear *real.*

"Never gape," her aunt said and motioned upward. "Your room is on the second floor at the far end."

"How many folks live here?"

"Six, including you." Aunt Helen ascended the stairs, and Lily followed.

"Who else? I hate bein' nosy, but Ma said you don't have no children. Do Uncle Stuart's folks live here or sumthin'?"

"My goodness, child. I wish you wouldn't speak so much. I can hardly *bear* to hear your crude attempt at the English language."

Lily would *not* be intimidated. "I don't have the schoolin' you did, but I ain't stupid. Reckon I can do a lot more than *you* can."

"I doubt that. However, when I'm through with you, I'll allow you to prove yourself."

"Through with me? What do you aim to do?"

They reached the second floor and Aunt Helen kept her fast pace down a long hallway. Closed doors lined the walls on both sides.

"You'll be instructed in proper English, etiquette, and style. Once you no longer sound and look like a backwoods ragamuffin, I'll introduce you to society, as well as our church. The new building was just finished last year. Stuart and I were present when they laid the cornerstone. The church is magnificent."

"What kind a church is it?"

"By *kind*, I assume you mean denomination?" She looked down her nose. "It's Lutheran. Stuart's mother was German and insisted her children be brought up in the faith. It's nothing like the Baptist church you're accustomed to, but you'll get used to it."

"Lutheran? Will I hafta be baptized again?"

"No. But, you'll need to learn our ways. The Lutheran church is liturgical."

Lily screwed her mouth together. "Liturgical?

"Of course you wouldn't know what that means. We have particular prayers we say and words we sing every week professing our faith. Rituals, so to speak, which is part of the beauty of our denomination. But, we're getting ahead of ourselves. None of that will matter until you can properly verbalize. Once you've mastered *that*, you may attend."

Aunt Helen pushed open a door at the end of the hallway. "This is your room."

Lily held a hand to her heart. The room was twice the size of the one she'd shared with Violet. The walls were covered in the finest paper. Two-tone purple flowers swirled against a lattice-like background. The lavender covering on the bed matched the lightest shade in the paper, and the bed itself was much taller than Lily's old one.

She pointed at it. "How many mattresses are on that thing?"

"That *thing* is called a bed. It's well-cushioned so you can be assured a restful night of sleep. I had Evie dress it with fresh linens. As for bathing, we have a room specifically for that purpose on the first floor. When you wish to bathe, let Evie know and she'll prepare your water."

"Who's Evie? One a the six people what live here?"

The woman grunted. "Yes, and she happens to be human. Thus, a *who*, not a *what*. She's my housemaid. Her quarters are on the first floor behind the kitchen. And since you previously asked, the others who reside here are Gerard, whom you met, and Mrs. Winters, our cook. But you mustn't bother them. They have jobs to do and are substantially paid to perform them."

"Well, if I ain't s'posed to pester Evie, how do I ask for bath-water?"

"Don't get sassy with me." Aunt Helen stood primly straight. "Drawing baths is part of her responsibility. She will also change your bedding and wash your clothes. Though I'm quite sure we'll destroy everything you brought with you, including that pathetic dress you're wearing."

"What'll I wear? I'm sure you don't want me runnin' 'round naked." Lily couldn't resist saying it. After all, she'd just been insulted. *Again.* She made a point to keep a straight face.

Her aunt's eyes widened. "Such a *vulgar* girl." She huffed. "I can only hope Mrs. Gottlieb can manage you."

"Who's she?"

"A refined woman who will teach you manners."

"*Ma* taught me manners."

"Not the kind you'll need to find a proper husband."

Lily gulped. That was the last thing she wanted.

A satisfied smile covered Aunt Helen's sour face. "As for your clothing, now that I'm aware of your size, I'll purchase appropriate dresses and undergarments. As you can see, the style in St. Louis is nothing like it was in Cades Cove."

"Yes'm." Her heart wrenched simply from hearing the name. She'd give anything to be back there again. But since she had nothing more to give, returning would be impossible.

Her aunt gestured to a wooden stand against the wall. "You'll find fresh water in that pitcher. There are washcloths in the cabinet beneath it. Freshen up. If you'd like to nap before dinner, you're welcome to. We'll eat at six o'clock sharp."

Lily nodded and set down her bag. "Aunt Helen?"

"Yes?"

"Where's the outhouse?"

"The *facilities* are behind the main house. Do you require them now?"

"Yes'm."

"Very well. Follow me."

The way the woman huffed, Lily could swear her simple request had inconvenienced her. Though folks here *dressed* differently, they had the same bodily functions. It would trouble everyone a lot more if Lily didn't know where to go.

Even the outhouse was fancy. It had two seats, which made no sense. She doubted two people would go in together to use it.

When she came out, her aunt had vanished.

Lily made her way back inside and up to her room. She'd freshen up, then try to rest. If not for her heavy heart, she'd want to explore the entire house. Yet all she wanted to do was sleep and hope to forget how much she hated what her life had become.

CHAPTER 2

Violet lay in bed and stared at the open window. A breeze blew in and helped cool the small room, but nothing could motivate her to get up. She'd been having a hard time sleeping with Lily gone. Her sister had always been by her side, and it didn't feel right having her so far away.

They'd received a telegram stating she'd arrived safely in St. Louis. Short and to the point. Since telegrams charged by the word, it made sense. Her uncle spent as little as possible. From Violet's understanding, the man didn't like to let go of his money.

Lily *had* to be miserable in Aunt Helen's care. The woman's letters had been torturous enough. Living with her would be like hell on earth.

Ma an' Pa shouldn't a sent Lily there.

"Violet!" Her ma knocked on the bedroom door. "Get up an' do your chores. Sun rose thirty minutes ago!"

"Yes'm." She swung her legs around and stood, then quickly dressed.

With Lily gone, more responsibility had fallen on Violet's shoulders. But it wasn't the reason she missed her sister. Lily was her best friend, and her absence left no one to confide in.

Violet had just celebrated her eighteenth birthday. Though no fuss had been made over the event, her ma had given her a new dress. Blue with tiny white flowers—perfect to wear to church on Sunday. If only she had someone to impress.

Without even acknowledging her ma, Violet rushed out the door and headed to the barn. She grabbed the milking stool and pail and set to work.

As she milked Sadie, she couldn't help but ponder how Lily had spent *her* eighteenth birthday, tangled up with Caleb Henry.

Violet jerked a bit too hard on Sadie's udders and received a reprimanding maw.

"Sorry, girl." She patted the cow's side.

Whenever Violet thought about Caleb, she became angry. Lily might still love the man, but Violet had no respect for him. Any man who'd bed a woman then marry someone else didn't deserve forgiveness. Because of him, Lily had to give up her son and pretend she'd never birthed him. Caleb had been none-the-wiser. He didn't know she'd had their child. Even so, he should've come back and done right by her.

Now her folks were raising sweet little Noah, pretending he was their own. Her ma had gone so far as to stuff a pillow under her dress for months leading up to the birth. They'd kept Lily hidden away, so no one would know. Surprisingly, they'd managed to keep her pregnancy a secret from Violet's younger brothers, who believed Noah was simply another sibling.

Her folks might've protected the good Larsen family name, but doing so had ruined Lily's life. She'd left the cove broken-hearted.

It ain't fair!

"You tryin' to yank them udders off?"

Violet jumped, startled by her brother, Lucas. At least she hadn't spilled the milk. "Don't sneak up on me, Lucas."

"I didn't sneak. You just wasn't payin' attention. What you so mad 'bout anyways?"

"I ain't mad."

"Tell that to Sadie. *You're* a girl. You should know jerkin' so hard on them things wouldn't feel too good." He smirked and folded his arms.

"Don't be talkin' like that."

He sat down atop a bale of straw, then picked out a piece and stuck it in his mouth. "Why? I know how things work. I know lotsa *other* things, too."

"What's that s'posed to mean?" She paused from her work and kept her eyes on him. "You're up to sumthin'."

"Not yet." He sniggered and twirled the straw through his lips. "You need to come help me pick blackberries. Ma wants as many as we can get."

"That's *your* chore. I got plenty to do here. You can take Horace an' Isaac with you."

"They eat more than they put in the bucket. 'Sides, your chores is done once you take the milk an' eggs to Ma."

Violet returned to milking. "No, they ain't. I hafta do laundry."

"It can wait. You're gonna help me get berries."

"Why should I?"

"Cuz if you don't, I aim to tell our secrets to everyone in the cove. You're gonna do whatever I say."

Her heart pattered harder, but she wouldn't be threatened by a fourteen-year-old. "What are you gonna tell? You let on 'bout Callie, an' eventually folks is gonna know *you* killed that captain."

He chuckled as if she'd told the funniest joke ever.

She leered at him. "Lucas, this ain't no laughin' matter."

"Sweet, sweet *Callie*." He stood and wandered close, then crossed his arms over his chest and gazed down at her. "The captain's murder ain't the secret I'll tell. I know 'bout Noah."

Her heart raced. "What 'bout him?"

"You was in the room when he was born. You saw where he came from, an' it sure as hell weren't Ma."

Violet gulped and shifted on the stool to face him directly. Though inclined to fuss at him for cursing, she had to address the more serious insinuation. "How do you know that?"

He stood tall, grinning. "I heard Lily yellin', squeezin' out the thing. I'd know her voice anywhere. Ma moans and groans different. An' before I shot that captain, I seen Lily an' Caleb kissin' in the barn. When I asked her if they'd done more than kiss, she slapped me." He smirked and shook his head. "That told me more than anythin'. It was like she'd admitted her guilt right then an' there. An' lastly . . ." With the same sly grin, he bent at the waist and looked her in the eye. "Noah looks just like Caleb. He ain't my brother, he's Lily's bastard."

Violet's hand shot out like it had a mind of its own. She slapped him hard. "Never say that again!"

He straightened up tall, scowling. "Do that one more time, an' I'll hit you right back."

"Do, an' I'll tell Pa!"

"I don't care. I know enough 'bout this family to make even *Pa* do what I say. How do you think folks would treat him if I told 'bout all his drinkin', an' how he covered for Caleb? Or what 'bout him almost killin' that other soldier by whackin' him over the head with a shovel? Then, he went an' blamed it on *you*. There's so many lies in our family, they could fill this here barn."

She stood and looked up into her brother's eyes. He'd grown nearly as tall as their Pa, and almost as strong. "You're part a this family. Why would you wanna hurt us?"

"Cuz I'm tired a playin' second fiddle. First, I had to do whatever Lily said. Now, her little brat gets all a Ma an' Pa's attention. They don't care 'bout me. They only want me to work my tail off cuz Pa can't do nothin'. He shoulda died in that war instead a gettin' his arm hacked off. Then Ma coulda found another husband an' I wouldn't have to do everythin' to keep up the farm. I wanted to go off an' fight, but I was too young. Now the war's over, an' I hafta stay here. How'd you like to be forced to do sumthin' you hate for the rest a your life?"

Violet wanted to slap him again so badly, her hand twitched. "You should *wanna* help. I don't understand why you're so full a hate. I swear, if anyone's not my brother, it's you. You're nothin' like the rest of us. The way you act is sinful."

He grabbed her wrist and squeezed. "Least *I* tell the truth. Seems to me I'm the only one in the family who *ain't* sinnin'."

"You killed a man!"

"I protected Lily!" His hand wrenched tighter.

Violet whimpered and he let go. Her red wrist throbbed from the imprint of his fingers.

"After breakfast," he said stone-faced, "meet me on the front porch. We got berries to pick." He strode out of the barn without another word.

Tears threatened, but she wouldn't cry. She sat on the stool and finished her work.

Lucas knew too much. Now more than ever, she had to watch over Noah. She wouldn't put it past her hateful brother to hurt him. His jealousy had made him crazed.

One thing was certain. Regardless of being threatened by Lucas, she had to tell her folks he knew the truth about Noah. Their pa would never let Lucas run the household. As well as Violet knew her pa, her defiant brother was likely to get a boot in the rear.

She lifted the pail and walked toward the cabin.

The only bad thing about telling would be the possibility of Lucas taking it out on Noah. Maybe she'd give Lucas a day or two to calm down before she said something.

She handed the pail to her ma, then headed back to the barn with a basket to gather eggs.

Since they no longer had to fear having the soldiers come in and take their chickens, her pa and Lucas had put together a decent coop, surrounded by a good-sized pen. They had six hens and a hellish rooster.

Of all her chores, she wished she could pass this one off to Lucas. But, he'd never agree to it. He thought it was funny that she had to fight the rooster for the eggs.

She entered the pen, hastened to the coop, and felt for eggs. No sooner than she'd gotten a hand under a hen, and the dad-blamed rooster started pecking at her legs.

"You hateful bird!" She carefully used her foot to push it away. Honestly, she wanted to snap its neck and have it for supper. "I'll be bruised for sure!"

She was rewarded with a hard peck that pierced her skin. Her gentle shove afforded the rooster access to her leg. He scratched her with one of his sharp spurs.

"Ugh!" Violet placed three eggs in her basket and quickly left the pen. The rotten bird strutted around victoriously.

Free of the threat, Violet lifted her skirt and peered down to assess the damage. A tiny amount of blood trickled down her leg.

She looked around, expecting to find Lucas, laughing, but he was nowhere to be seen. *Thank goodness.*

She went inside and set the basket on the kitchen table. "The rooster got me again, Ma. Look at my leg!" Once again, she exposed her bare skin and pointed at the damage.

"Heaven's sake, Violet." Her ma gave it a brief glance then started cleaning the eggs. "You act like that bird wants to *kill* you. It's just a little blood. Go wash it."

"What if it gets infected? I could lose my leg."

Her ma set aside the eggs and faced her, scowling. "You ain't gonna lose a leg. You shouldn't even say such silly things. You know full well there's men what lost limbs in the war. Your pa included. Fightin' a rooster ain't nothin' in comparison."

"Yes'm." Anytime any of them complained about an injury, her ma always brought up her pa's lost arm. Maybe Violet *had* overreacted.

She got a clean rag and went to the basin. She wiped away the blood and dabbed at the tiny cut in her skin. Regardless of whether or not she'd overreacted, she hated fighting the bird. He scared the fire out of her.

"Violet?" Her ma's expression had turned somber.

"Yes'm?"

"It ain't just your pa I want you to be mindful of. Harriet Quincy told me the Myers' boy has finally come home."

Violet's heart pattered a bit harder. "Gideon?"

"Yep. After the war took their other boys, everyone thought Gideon was gonna die, too. He was in a hospital for quite a spell, then moved into some kind a charitable boardin' house. Seems he was too ashamed to come home."

"Ashamed? Why?"

Her ma wiggled a finger at her leg, now free from any trace of blood. "He lost part a *his* leg. They cut it off right below the knee. Harriet says he's been withdrawn. Lays around all the time doin' nothin'."

"I can understand why. It'd be almost impossible to do much a anythin' with only one good leg."

"The boy has two strong arms. He can work, if he'd get his mind right."

Noah let out a squall from his crib.

Without waiting to be asked, Violet hurried to him and lifted him into her arms. "He needs changin'. I'll see to it." She headed for her folks' bedroom where all the diapers were kept. She grabbed one, then stopped and listened. Aside from the baby, the house was far too quiet.

Holding both the baby and the clean diaper, she returned to the kitchen. "Where's Pa an' the boys?"

"Your pa's takin' a walk. Horace an' Isaac are with Lucas. They went out to check the blackberry patch. I told Lucas they need to be picked."

A better opportunity to speak her mind might not come again anytime soon. Though she wanted to tell her pa first, her ma also needed to know. "Lucas told me I hafta help him pick the berries."

"That boy don't got a lick of sense. You have laundry to do." More so than ever since Noah had arrived.

"I told him, but he said if I didn't do whatever he says, he'll tell everyone our family secrets."

"Do what?" The poor woman's face paled.

"He knows 'bout Noah, Ma."

She grabbed onto a chair and plopped down hard. "How?"

Violet pulled out her own chair and sat, cradling her eight-month-old nephew. "He said he saw Lily an' Caleb kissin'. An' when Noah was born, Lucas could tell it was Lily yellin', while pushin' him out."

"You didn't affirm it, did you?" Her eyes widened, and she twisted her fingers together.

"I didn't have to."

"*What?*"

"He was hateful, Ma! He called Noah a bastard. I got mad an' slapped him."

Her ma covered her face with her hands, then smacked them against the table. "You shoulda lied. Swore you saw *me* birth him."

Violet glanced at the Bible that always rested on the tabletop, then looked directly at her ma. "I'm tired a lyin'. The truth is so messed up 'round here, I can't remember every story. Someday, I just know it's all gonna come back an' bite us on the tail."

"Violet!"

"Well, it will, Ma. You used to tell us to be truthful—said you hated lyin' worse than most anythin'. Yet now, it's all we do."

"You know very well why we done it."

"Yes'm, I do. To protect our family's good name. But I sure don't see much good here anymore." Tears once again threatened. "I miss Lily. How could you send her away to that horrid woman?"

"That *horrid woman* is my sister. She's family, and I trust her to do right by Lily." She jutted her chin high. "Mark my words. The next time you see your sister, she'll be a proper lady."

Violet wiped a tear from her cheek. "I want Lily back. I loved her the way she was. An' just cuz Aunt Helen is blood-related, it don't mean she's decent. Lucas is proof that not every member of this family is kind an' good."

"Don't speak 'bout your brother that way." Her ma shook a rigid finger at her.

Noah fussed louder. "I best be changin' him. As for Lucas, you an' Pa better do sumthin' 'fore he goes blabbin' to everyone in the cove."

Violet stood, then carried Noah into her room and laid him on the bed to put on a fresh diaper.

As she cleaned him up and secured the clean diaper, she listened to her ma grumble in the kitchen.

Violet bent close to Noah's ear. "Don't worry. I'll make sure nothin' bad happens to you."

His big brown eyes blinked slowly.

"I love you, Noah," she whispered and kissed his cheek.

If only Lily could raise him. The poor baby shouldn't be in the middle of such a messed-up family. She studied Noah's features, and Lucas was right. The boy looked exactly like his pa. Too bad Caleb would *never* see him.

CHAPTER 3

For a moment, Caleb just stared at his sobbing wife, then he pulled her into his arms. She'd been crying too much. And though this time it was because of something *she'd* done, he still blamed himself for her tears. No matter how hard he tried, he couldn't fully put his heart into their marriage.

"I'm sorry I burned the chicken," Rebecca mumbled into his shoulder, then raised her tear-streaked face. "We've been married more than a year. You'd think by now I'd know how to cook. I wish we could move back to the hotel. I know you'd eat better there."

She had a good point. But he'd gnaw on countless pieces of charred meat, rather than leave the farm. "Your cookin' ain't so bad. Your pies make up for anythin' you overcook."

Avery wailed from her crib and added more tears to the situation.

Rebecca's chin quivered faster. "I thought she'd sleep a little longer an' give us some time to ourselves. My blubberin' must've woke her up."

Smoke from the burnt meat hovered around their heads and stung the inside of Caleb's nose. He gently released his wife. "I'll get Avery. Don't fret over the chicken. We'll just eat them beans an' taters."

Without saying a word, Rebecca returned to the stove.

Caleb went into the baby's room and lifted her from the crib. "Hush now, sweetheart."

She patted his face, grinned, and her tears instantly dried. "Pa-pa."

"That's right. I'm your pa." He kissed her cheek, then carried her to the kitchen.

The smoke made her cough, so he set her on the floor to put more distance between her and the offensive air.

She'd been capably walking for two months. She toddled around, curious about everything.

Almost immediately, Rebecca scooped her up, put her in her highchair, and scooted it close to the table. All the while, the poor woman sniffled.

Caleb opened the back door to let in some fresh air, but he doubted it would help his distraught wife. Today's incident only added to others. He swore she cried at least every other day. His plan to take care of her and make her happy hadn't worked out as he'd hoped.

Avery seemed oblivious to her ma's pain. The sweet baby girl giggled and slapped her hands against the table.

Caleb bent down to her level. "Are you hungry?"

She bobbed her head and pointed. "Ma."

"Yep. Your ma's fixin' you some food. Want some taters?"

"Taters." Her limited vocabulary was as cute as her.

Rebecca put some mashed potatoes into a bowl and set it in front of Avery. Though she placed a spoon within the girl's reach, Avery gave utensils little regard. She dug her fingers into the bowl and put a fistful of potatoes in her mouth. Within moments, they covered most of her face and dotted bits of white through her dark hair.

The sight tickled Caleb, and he laughed, but Rebecca didn't show even a slim smile.

He took her into his arms once again. "Sumthin's wrong, ain't it? Worse than the burned meat."

"I don't want to talk 'bout it right now. Not in front a Avery."

He glanced over his shoulder at his daughter, then focused on his wife. "She's too little to understand much. You can talk to me 'bout anythin'."

"No, Caleb. She might not comprehend everythin', but when I talk 'bout this, I know I'll cry more. She doesn't like seein' me upset."

"But you're *already* upset." He drew his fingers through her hair, then tapped the end of her nose. "I miss your smiles. Ain't you happy with me no more?"

She stared into his eyes, then eased out of his arms. "Like I said, I don't want to discuss this in front a Avery. All right?"

"Fine." He pulled out a chair and sat beside his daughter.

Rebecca filled two plates with mashed potatoes and green beans. She set one in front of Caleb, then put the other in the spot across from him and silently sat.

Caleb speared several beans with his fork. "Don't forget, Ma wants us to come to the hotel on Sunday for supper."

"I haven't forgotten. Honestly, I've been countin' the days till I know you'll have a decent meal." Again, she sniffled.

Caleb set his fork down. "Becca. That's enough a all that. Your cookin's fine. It's easy to get distracted when you have a child to tend. I reckon there's plenty a women with young'uns who burn food."

She'd been sitting without moving, but lifted her head and met his gaze. "I only have one child. I thought by now we'd be well on our way to more, but you spend so much time workin', you're always too tired."

"Becca, I—"

"Maybe it's for the best. After all, if I burn a meal with only one baby to tend, I might very well put the whole house aflame if we have more."

Her dismal mood was *completely* his fault. He rarely made love to her and used being worn out as an excuse. It was partially true. If he wasn't in the fields pulling weeds and chasing off varmints, he was working on the house and the barn, and tending livestock. He had more than enough to keep him busy. A farm this size usually had more than one set of hands to manage it.

Lily.

If *she'd* been his wife, she probably would've toted the baby to the field and been by his side at every turn. Rebecca, however, had never worked the land, nor had she tended any kind of animals. She'd never done much more than bake. And though he knew all that before he'd married her, the reality hit harder every day. They weren't at all well-suited.

He loved her, but wasn't *in* love with her. Had he been, it wouldn't have mattered how tired he was when he crawled into bed beside her each night. He'd want to have her regardless. Yet, he felt more at ease keeping his distance. As hard as he'd tried, he couldn't let go of the memories he'd made with Lily.

Even things she'd said still haunted him. Especially what she'd professed after they'd made love in the burrow.

Once we're married, we'll do this every night.

If she was the one lying next to him at night, he'd want to. Not a day had passed that he hadn't wondered if she was all right. He ached to see her again. Hard work was the only thing that kept his mind off what he'd never have.

"Caleb." Rebecca's tone sounded almost *harsh*.

"What?"

"I've been talkin' an' you haven't been listenin'. Can't you at least give me your attention at the supper table?"

"I'm sorry. What was you sayin'?"

"Nothin' important." She frowned and her shoulders slumped low. Her food hadn't been touched.

"You should eat, Becca. You're lookin' a little peaked."

Avery threw a handful of potatoes onto the table. "Taters."

Caleb chuckled. "Them's for eatin', not tossin'. Right, Becca?"

His beautiful wife sadly sighed, then pushed her chair back, stood, and left the room.

Caleb handed Avery a bean. "Eat this, sweetie."

She took it in her tiny hand, studied it for a mere second, then put it in her mouth. He expected it to be spewed out, but she chewed it up and swallowed it. At fourteen months, she had enough teeth for the task. Even so, she'd been known to spit out any kind of greens.

"Good girl!" Caleb hugged her, then gave her another.

He wanted to go after Rebecca, but Avery needed him more right now. Once they finished eating, he'd check on his wife. Maybe some time alone would help her.

He sniffed. Something other than the chicken was burning.

"Becca! You got sumthin' in the oven?"

She raced into the kitchen and flung open the stove door. Smoke billowed out. "I can't even bake a decent pie anymore!" She grabbed a dishtowel, removed the burnt pie, then set it on the stovetop. "I give up!"

Avery clapped her hands. "Pie!"

Rebecca glanced their way, burst into more tears, and again fled the room.

Caleb ran a hand over Avery's head. "No pie t'night. But you an' me need to do sumthin' to cheer up your ma. Okay?"

Avery nodded, yet he doubted she understood. Then again, she was a smart baby. She probably knew more than he realized.

They finished eating, then he dampened a rag and cleaned her up. The potatoes in her hair gave him some difficulty, but he managed to remove them without making her cry.

He carried her to her room and set her down in the crib. "Play with Moo-Cow till I come back." He handed her the stuffed toy his ma had given her on her first birthday. "I'm gonna check on your ma."

Avery cuddled the cow close and plopped down onto her rump.

Caleb heard her babbling at the toy as he walked down the short hallway to the bedroom he shared with Rebecca.

She lay on the bed, facing the wall.

Seeing her this way constricted his heart.

I hafta do better.

He climbed atop the bed and lay down, then scooted himself as close as he could get to her. "Becca?" He pushed her hair aside and dotted her neck with kisses. "Please don't cry."

She rolled onto her back and stared up at him. Her puffy eyes searched his face, and he gazed back intently. Why was his heart keeping him from fully loving this kind, beautiful woman?

She lifted her hand and ran a single finger across his cheek. He smiled and closed his eyes to her soft touch.

"So handsome," she whispered. "When we got married, I thought I'd never have another sad day in my life. Yet, all I do is cry anymore. I don't understand what happened, but sometimes I think you don't love me."

"Becca, I do. I swear it."

"But that's just it. You shouldn't have to swear to sumthin' like love. I should be able to feel it—see it in your actions. Do you realize you've *never* initiated our lovemaking?"

"What?" That couldn't be right.

"You see? You're not even aware of it. I thought men wanted women all the time. But you only have me when *I* push for it." Though she didn't cry outright, tears spilled onto her cheeks. "Don't you find me desirable?"

"Course I do." He gently wiped her tears, then kissed her.

She pushed against his chest. "Don't kiss me out a pity."

"I ain't."

Her eyes narrowed. "Don't lie to me, Caleb."

"I'd never lie. 'Specially 'bout sumthin' this important. Sure, I feel bad you're cryin', but I kissed you cuz I love you. I'm sorry I ain't been the kind a husband you expected. But there ain't nothin' wrong with you. It's me. I want this farm to be successful. I wanna be able to provide a good life for you an' Avery. Can you forgive me for havin' my mind so focused on other things, I forget what's most important?"

Her expression softened. "Which is . . .?"

"You, of course."

She smiled for the first time in a great while. "You mean that?"

"Yep." He grinned. "Avery's gonna start to fuss soon. That cow can't talk back, an' I think she gets bored with it. She'll want our attention. But, when she falls asleep tonight, I aim to show you exactly how much I love you."

Rebecca yanked him down and kissed him with longing. They hadn't coupled in weeks, and he had to admit, his body craved it.

Her mood had completely changed. She practically purred and squirmed on the bed. "I wish we could carry this further *now*."

"So do I." Heat coursed through his veins. He kissed her, stronger and deeper than before.

She grabbed hold of him and rolled him atop her. "Maybe there's time."

Avery let out a wail, and their sensual mood vanished.

He gave Rebecca a quick peck on the lips, then moved off her and rose from the bed. "Keep thinkin' 'bout it, Becca, an' we'll finish what we started later t'night."

"Promise?"

"You better believe it. I want you so bad, it hurts." He wasn't lying. Grinning, he readjusted himself in his trousers.

Rebecca giggled. "You best *stop* thinkin' 'bout it, or you'll be miserable till I can satisfy you."

He leaned over the bed, kissed her again, then stood erect with his arms folded over his chest. "I think I should start carin' more 'bout satisfyin' *you*. I wanna keep that smile on your face."

She sat up and sighed. "Another baby would help."

"You sure?"

Grinning, she nodded.

"Well, then. I reckon I got my work cut out for me." He winked, then headed for Avery's room.

His confused heart pumped hard. He prayed that for once, he could love on his wife without thinking about Lily. At least he had a few hours to get his mind right.

CHAPTER 4

Lily's eyes fluttered open. For the briefest moment, she forgot where she was. Then the softness of her bed brought her back to reality.

When she'd first seen it, she couldn't understand why anyone would have more than one mattress. But without a doubt, it was the most comfortable thing she'd ever lain on.

A tiny tug gnawed at her heart. This was the kind of bed she wished she could share with Caleb.

Of course, the instant she thought of him, her thoughts turned to Noah and tears formed.

"No," she mumbled. "I gotta let them go." Why keep herself miserable, longing for what she could never have?

A rap at her bedroom door startled her, and she gasped. "Yes?"

"May I come in, Miss Lily?"

Miss Lily?

Though definitely a female voice, it wasn't her aunt. Whoever stood on the other side of the door sounded young and . . . *nice*.

Lily sat up and put her feet on the floor. "Sure. Come on in."

A young woman stepped into the room and held herself perfectly straight with her hands primly folded. "I'm Evie. I came to let you know dinner will be served in fifteen minutes." She nodded toward the bed. "You've been sleeping, haven't you?" Her lips formed into a pleasant smile that lifted Lily's heart.

Maybe she could make a friend here—whether or not the girl was the hired help. Lily believed they were about the same age.

"Yep. I slept like a hibernatin' bear. I was plum tuckered out."

Evie laughed. "You truly aren't from around here, are you?"

"Nope. Ever heard a Cades Cove? Up in the Smoky Mountains?"

"Only from what your aunt told me. She said you were a mountain girl, but I don't know what that means." Evie lowered her eyes and stared at the floor.

Lily stood and tried to smooth out the wrinkles in her dress, but it did no good. Her appearance must seem wretched to Evie, who was wearing a crisp white dress, covered partially by a pale blue apron.

Regardless of how she might appear, Lily decided to be herself and not put on a false front. If Evie couldn't accept her that way, then a friendship would be out of the question. "I'm a mountain girl cuz I know how to skin rabbits, gut a deer or most any kind a wild animal, an' grow enough food to feed a family." She splayed her hands wide, showing her rough skin. "I'm not afraid of a hard day's work."

"Oh, my. That doesn't sound pleasant." Evie's head lifted and she met Lily's gaze. The girl had beautiful green eyes and the blackest hair she'd ever seen. She'd rolled it in a curious-looking braid.

"It's actually right wonderful. There ain't nothin' like the beauty of the Smokies. Livin' there made it worth all the difficult chores."

Evie tipped her head to one side. "Then why are you here? Why leave someplace you love?"

Lily's mind spun. How much did Evie know about her? If Lily said more than she should, it wouldn't set well with her aunt.

"Aunt Helen was kind enough to offer me a place to stay. Ma wants me to learn how to be *proper*."

"Then you've come to the right place. Mrs. Clark insists on *all* things proper. I'm sure you'll be meeting Mrs. Gottlieb soon. She helped me when I came here."

"How long you been here?"

"Two years." Evie's shy eyes once again looked downward. "I was in an orphanage. I'd been there since I was thirteen. I doubted anyone would want me. They would've put me out at eighteen, but your aunt came for me just before my sixteenth birthday. Though she had no intentions of adopting me, she gave me a place to live and work. I was happy to come here. It's much nicer than the orphanage, and the Clarks have been kind. I want for nothing."

Hmm. Maybe there's good in them after all.

Lily slowly nodded. "How did Mrs. *Gottlieb* help you?" *Such a strange name.*

"She specializes in etiquette. You know, social mannerisms. How to walk, talk, dress—"

"Lawdy! I ain't no *baby*."

Evie covered her mouth with one hand, hiding what Lily thought was an enormous grin. "Of course, you aren't a baby, but things are done differently here. I doubt I'll ever have the opportunity to use a lot of what she taught me, but you will. Your aunt mentioned she'll be grooming you for marriage."

The thought sickened Lily, so she chose to keep the conversation about Evie. "Why can't *you* use what she learned you?"

Evie giggled. "Mrs. Gottlieb is going to love you." She immediately sobered. "Forgive me, I didn't mean to laugh, but I've never heard anyone speak quite the way you do."

"Pay it no mind." Lily waved a hand. "But, ain't *you* bein' *groomed* for a husband?"

"No. I don't get out much. It's hard to find a beau when I'm working every day."

Lily's thoughts of her aunt and uncle rapidly spiraled downward again. "*Every* day? You mean, you hafta work Sundays, too? A day meant for *rest*?"

"Yes. On Sundays, there's still plenty to do." She glanced over her shoulder. "We best be going to the dining room. I'm sorry there's nothing else for you to wear. Mrs. Clark said she'll be shopping for you tomorrow. For now, you'll have to wear *that* to dinner." She pointed at Lily's dress.

It seemed even the help disliked her clothes. "I don't mind. Been wearin' this here dress a long time. It keeps me covered an' decent."

Evie eyed her from head to foot. "Will you allow me to do your hair tomorrow?"

"Do my hair?"

"Yes. Fix it up stylishly. It's a lovely color and wonderfully thick. Have you ever worn a chignon?"

"Huh?"

Again, Evie giggled. "I'll show you. It'll be beautiful. I'll fix it similar to the way mine's done." She twisted her head around and gave Lily a better look at the way she'd rolled her hair into a braid. It practically floated atop her shoulders.

"All right. Reckon I'm gonna hafta get used to all this fancy stuff."

"*Reckon* you will." Evie grinned. "I've never said that word before." She gestured to the hallway. "I'll walk down with you, but then I'll need to help Mrs. Winters in the kitchen."

"I can help, too."

The poor girl's eyes popped wide. "No. It's not your place. The Clarks would never allow it."

"Oh." It didn't feel right *not* helping and would be difficult to get used to, but she'd do as she was told. Even if it happened to be *nothing*.

She rested a hand on Evie's arm. "I'm glad you live here. I need someone to show me what I can an' can't do. I was afraid I wouldn't have *no one* to talk to."

Evie stared at Lily's hand, so she pulled it away. Maybe folks here weren't supposed to touch each other.

Her eyes rose to meet Lily's. "I'm glad you're here, too. I have a feeling I can learn a lot from *you*."

"Got any rabbits need skinnin'?" Somehow, a grin emerged from Lily without thought. The first time she'd smiled in weeks. Though it seemed foreign, it truthfully felt good. She'd always embraced life, and even with a broken heart, she wasn't ready to give up. Someday, she'd surely see her son again. When that happened, she wanted to be whole.

Evie laughed and shook her head, but didn't answer. "I'll show you to the dining room."

Lily finally felt more at ease. Of course, now she had to meet her uncle. If he was anything at all like Aunt Helen, Lily was bound to be studied like an infectious disease that had arrived to plague their home.

At least she'd found a friend. No one would ever replace Violet, but it helped having Evie in the house.

She silently followed the girl and fully took in her surroundings. Being here seemed more like a dream than reality. Everything around her was spotless. Probably Evie's doing.

Every trinket atop end tables had been positioned perfectly centered. Or if there were more than one, each was arranged like a well-thought-out design. Balanced and proportionate. Lacy doilies lay beneath them, similar to the crocheted pieces Lily had seen at Mrs. Quincy's home. They'd likely been put there to keep the glass from scratching the wood. The numerous pieces of glasswork would never survive at Lily's cabin in the cove. The boys would surely break them. Isaac would think the figurines shaped like animals were toys.

As they descended the stairs, she gave a quick glance to the portrait of her aunt and uncle, then focused on her footing. If she took a tumble, she'd make an even worse impression. On her relatives *and* the floor.

They passed many rooms that drew her interest. The library excited her more than any of the others. Bookshelves lined three walls and covered them from floor to ceiling. She'd never have time to read them all, but she planned to try. If she wasn't allowed to work, maybe she'd be given permission to read.

Wonderful aromas surrounded her, and her stomach growled. A sign her appetite had finally returned. Violet had insisted she take care of herself and start eating better, so Lily would do it for her. Appetizing food would make it easier.

Evie stopped and faced her. "You go in through there." She pointed at a large open archway. "I'm going to the kitchen."

"Thank you."

"Oh, by the way, would you like to bathe this evening?"

"Reckon so."

"Very well." She gave a single firm nod. "I'll prepare your bath at seven-thirty. You can have a good soak before you retire for the night."

"You don't mind doin' that?"

"Not at all. I'll come to your room and let you know when it's ready." She curtsied and walked away.

Lily stood without moving and watched her go. Being catered to this way didn't feel at all right. Why should anyone be waited on hand and foot?

I ain't royalty, that's for sure.

Her feet didn't want to budge. She stared at the arched opening as if it would come to her.

A clock, taller than Lily, loudly chimed.

Six o'clock.

If she didn't move now, she'd be late. And in this house, it wouldn't go over well.

She pulled her shoulders back and strode into the dining room.

Oh, my.

A white linen tablecloth covered the dark wood table, which was as big as the entire kitchen back home. Though the table had enough seats for fourteen people, only three places were set, and her aunt and uncle already occupied two of them.

Uncle Stuart sat tall and dignified at the head of the table. He looked exactly like he did in the portrait. White-haired, handsome, and well-to-do. His wire-rimmed glasses made him appear smart, and he probably *was* considering how wealthy he'd become.

Aunt Helen was in the chair to his left, sour as ever. She motioned to the empty seat across from her. "I'm happy you decided to join us." Her words held no joy.

This should be fun.

Lily hastened to the chair and pulled it out, finding it surprisingly heavy. "Evie and me was talkin'. Sorry I'm a little late." She gulped and sat.

Uncle Stuart leaned toward his wife. "You were right. Mrs. Gottlieb has a challenge ahead of her."

Lily stared at her plate and the cloth napkin folded on top of it. A strange place for it to be, if she was supposed to fill the plate with food. She quickly moved it to the side.

Aunt Helen cleared her throat. "The napkin belongs on your *lap.*"

"Oh." Lily leaned sideways and noticed her uncle had a napkin on *his* lap and did as she was told. "You're my Uncle Stuart, right?"

"By marriage, yes."

A strange thing to say. "Thank you for allowin' me to come here. I promise to do all I can to learn your ways."

"I'm counting on it." He lifted his water glass and took a sip.

Lily decided it would be best to imitate whatever they did. It might keep her from making more mistakes.

She took a drink from her sparkling crystal goblet. As she moved to set it down again, the base hit the side of her plate and almost tipped over. At least she didn't break it. She carefully put it where it belonged, but not before splashing water over the side and onto the table. It dampened the linen.

Uncle Stuart closed his eyes and shook his head.

"Don't worry, my dear," Aunt Helen said, patting his arm. "I know she's trainable. Remember how *I* was when we met?"

"Yes, I've never forgotten." He turned and smiled at the woman. It seemed he had a heart after all and was capable of bearing a warm expression. "A beauty then, even covered in dirt." He took her hand and kissed it. "I'm glad I rescued you."

She fluttered her eyes at him, then shifted her gaze to Lily. "You see what kind of man you can acquire if you apply yourself and learn to be proper?"

"But, he chose you 'fore you was *groomed*. Are you sayin' he wouldn't still love you if you hadn't changed your ways?"

Aunt Helen's head drew back. "Well, I . . ." Her face screwed together, completely befuddled.

"I can answer the girl," Uncle Stuart said and turned to Lily. "Yes, I would love her regardless. However, had she not changed, she wouldn't belong in my world. I have important clients to entertain and events which require her attendance as well as mine. If we don't set a proper example of exemplary behavior and status, my business will suffer. Do you understand?"

"Course I do. But why bother with *me*? You got a wife to show off to your friends. As you said, I'm your niece by *marriage,* so I don't understand why you agreed to take me in at all. Makes no sense."

A large, round woman waddled into the room carrying a tray of food. She set it in the center of the table. "Would you like me to serve?" A white scarf covered most of her gray hair.

"Not tonight," Aunt Helen said. "We'll manage ourselves. Thank you."

"Yes'm." The woman, presumably Mrs. Winters, smiled at Lily, then left. Before Lily could take a breath, she returned with two bowls and set them beside the tray.

Lily eyed the food. Mashed potatoes, green beans, carrots, and roasted chicken. Similar to the meals back home, but served in fancy dishes. She doubted the decorative ceramic bowls would improve the flavor.

"It smells wonderful," Lily said to the woman. "Are you Mrs. Winters, the cook?"

"That I am." She stood a little taller. "And you must be Lily."

"Yes'm. Pleased to meet you."

The dear woman lit up with the best smile Lily had seen since her arrival. "You as well."

"That'll be all, Mrs. Winters," Uncle Stuart said and waved her away.

She shuffled off without another word.

If learning how to be proper included being rude to your help, Lily wanted no part of it.

"Everyone has their place," Uncle Stuart muttered, then reached for the potatoes. He scooped some onto his plate and put a mound on Aunt Helen's as well. He then passed the bowl to Lily.

"Thank you." She dipped out her own portion, then put the bowl back in the center of the table.

In the same manner, her uncle passed the rest of the food.

Lily was about to grab her chicken leg and bite into it, when she noticed her aunt cutting the meat off the bone with a knife, while holding it in place with her fork.

There were more utensils beside Lily's plate than she'd ever need. Besides, who in their right mind would eat a chicken leg that way?

Since Lily didn't want to further embarrass herself, she tried to imitate her aunt's actions. All she accomplished was pushing the leg off her plate and onto the table.

Dad-blame it!

She quickly jabbed it with her fork and put it back in its place, but not before hearing a disgusted grunt from her uncle.

"Sorry," she muttered. "Why can't I just pick it up an' eat it?"

"We don't eat with our fingers." He dabbed at his mouth with the cloth napkin, then returned it to his lap.

"What if we was havin' sandwiches?"

"That's different."

"Why?"

He inhaled such a large breath, it lifted his chest. "Meat is greasy and soils the fingers. Once you've mastered the appropriate way to hold your utensils, you'll find eating to be less of a challenge."

Lily did all she could to remove the meat from the bone, but could've eaten it clean if she'd been allowed to pick it up. She decided it was easier to eat the vegetables. *They* didn't fight her.

Mrs. Winters returned with a tray holding three small bowls. She set one in front of each of them.

Lily eyed the yellow substance. "What's that?"

"Dessert," her aunt said. "It's called custard. When you've finished the rest of your food, you may eat it. Use the dessert spoon above your plate."

"Yes'm."

"Don't worry, Lily." Her aunt's lips *nearly* rose into a smile. "Mrs. Gottlieb will teach you all you need to know. When the time comes for your first dinner party, you'll be ready. Tonight, we're eating casually, so you won't feel too uncomfortable."

"Does that mean I can pick up my leg an' finish it off?"

"No." Aunt Helen's eyes pinched into slits. "We may be informal, but we're not barbarians."

Lily knew she couldn't strip off any more of the meat with the fork, so she ate all of her potatoes and vegetables, then waited to try the custard until her aunt and uncle ate theirs.

Mrs. Winters came back and took their plates. As soon as she left the room, Uncle Stuart moved his dessert bowl to where the plate had been.

"What's the brown stuff on top?" Lily asked, while positioning her own bowl.

Her uncle's eyes shifted toward her, then back to his dessert. "Nutmeg."

"Oh." She scooped her spoon into the custard and took a bite. The creamy texture was something she'd never forget. It tasted sweet, and the nutmeg added a unique flavor. "It's delicious." She finished every bit and was tempted to lick the bowl. But knowing that wouldn't be *proper*, she used her spoon to get out as much as she could. "Has my ma ever had this?"

"I doubt it," Aunt Helen said. "Nothing like grits, is it?"

"No'm. Someday, I'd like to make this for Ma. Reckon Mrs. Winters can learn me how?"

Aunt Helen drummed her fingers on the tabletop, but said nothing.

Uncle Stuart sighed and stood. "Are you finished, my dear?" He held onto to the back of Aunt Helen's chair.

"Yes. Quite."

He helped her to her feet, and she linked her arm through his.

"Lily," he said. "I trust you to use great care in our home. Aside from the outdoor facilities, there should be no need for you to wander anywhere but your bedroom and the bathing room."

"What 'bout the library?"

"You can read?"

"Course. Ma taught me to read the Bible when I was four. Been readin' whatever I can get my hands on, which ain't been much."

"Obviously. Your English is lacking."

She jutted her chin high. "Then, let me read from some a them books. It might help."

His brows drew in tight. "As long as you promise not to fold or tear the pages and never eat or drink while reading, then I'll let you peruse some of them. I'll select a few that I feel are appropriate for a young woman."

"Thank you. I'll be careful as can be."

"Good. If you're not, your privilege will be revoked."

"Yessir. I understand." She scooted her chair back, stood, and dipped her head. "I'm goin' to my room till Evie fetches me. She's gonna fix me a bath."

"Very good." He placed a hand atop Aunt Helen's. "I expect to see her in a new gown when we have our dinner tomorrow night. And make certain something is done with her hair."

"Oh." Lily chose to speak, even though she'd not been spoken to. "Evie said *she'd* do my hair."

Her uncle lifted a single brow, then walked out of the room with Aunt Helen attached to his arm.

Lily felt utterly insignificant. What she had to say didn't matter anymore. She'd be told what to do, where to go, when to speak, and how to act. But it bothered her more than anything that she didn't understand why they wanted her here. She'd asked, but Uncle Stuart hadn't exactly answered.

Why groom her for marriage, unless . . .

Maybe one of his highfalutin friends had a son who needed a wife. Yet, if that were the reason, why not marry him off to some upper-crust girl from St. Louis?

With Lily's luck, he'd be ugly and have foul breath. It would make sense a man like that couldn't find a decent girl to marry. Then again, if he had money, most women wouldn't care if he looked no better than a worn-out fence post and smelled like a skunk.

She trudged up the stairs to her room. Her list of unanswered questions had substantially grown.

CHAPTER 5

The supper table was much too quiet.

Normally, Violet's little brothers would talk up a storm, but they silently ate their food. Their frowns and the sad eyes they kept focused on their plates, said more than words.

Lucas had been hateful to them. Violet had succumbed and had gone along with the boys to help pick blackberries. Horace and Isaac had been laughing and popping the plump purple fruit into their mouths, until Lucas smacked the backs of their heads and told them to pick and not eat.

Violet had tried to defend them, but when Lucas shot her one of his hateful looks, she clamped her lips tight. If he told the other boys about Noah, they'd never keep it secret.

Their pa had to set Lucas straight soon, or life at the cabin would be completely miserable.

Her pa cleared his throat. "Violet?"

"Yessir?" He'd broken the silence and the suddenness caused her heart to pound.

"Your ma tells me the rooster's been givin' you trouble. That so?"

Lucas grunted, but Violet paid him no mind. "Yessir. It attacks me whenever I go for the eggs."

"It's a dumb bird," Lucas mumbled. "Stomp on its head an' it'll leave you alone."

"Hush, boy!" Their pa slammed his hand against the table, right in front of Lucas.

Lucas scowled and picked at his food.

"I don't wanna hurt it," Violet said. "But, I'm scared to go near it."

Her pa nodded. "I understand. I've raised my share of protective roosters. He sees you as a threat to his brood. He's tryin' to show he's in charge, but he ain't. You gotta prove you're the boss."

"How? I don't speak *rooster*."

Isaac giggled. A wonderful sound to hear.

"I'll show you after supper," their pa said. "Once you learn the trick, you won't have a bit a trouble."

"Thank you, Pa." She sipped some water and glanced at Lucas. The boy looked as sour as ever. He might not like the life he was given, but someday, he'd better learn to be grateful for all he had.

"As for you . . ." Her pa pointed at Lucas. "When I'm done with your sister, you an' me's gonna have us a long talk. Hear me?"

"Yeah." Lucas folded his arms over his chest, then leaned his chair back slightly and sneered at the man.

"'Scuse me?" In a flash, their pa swiped at the legs of the chair with his boot and Lucas fell backward onto the floor. Her pa glared at him.

Lucas breathed hard and leered back. He jerked his chair upright and sat down hard. His gaze remained locked with their pa all the while. "Yes. *Sir*."

The two just stared at each other, and heat rose in the room. Violet had never feared so much for her family. It felt as if things might explode at any moment. Lily had always been the stabilizing force in their home. With her gone, everything had gotten off balance.

Once they finished the meal, Violet helped her ma clear the table. She was about to wash the dishes, when her ma motioned her out the door. "Go with your pa. Learn how to tame that bird."

"Yes'm."

She followed him outside, then on to the chicken pen.

As they neared it, the rooster strutted closer. "See, Pa? He's already defendin' his harem."

"*Brood*." He chuckled. "What books you been readin' lately?"

"Sumthin' Mrs. Quincy loaned me."

"Hmm." He rubbed his chin, studying her. "I reckon you're old 'nuff for such things. Just don't tell your ma. If it ain't the Bible, she don't take kindly to it."

"Yessir."

He stopped and put his back to the pen. "All right. What you gotta do is make that rooster aware you're bigger an' meaner than him. I know you got a soft heart, but don't let him see it. Hear?"

"How?"

"Challenge him. I want you to go in the pen, an' when he approaches you, flap your wings."

"My *wings*?"

"I'd show you, but I only got one. Not as effective. Just tuck your fists into your armpits an' flap."

"But that's plum silly."

Her pa let out an exasperated breath. "Give it a try. Show me your wings."

She rolled her eyes, then glanced around, praying no one was watching. She did as he told her and moved her arms up and down a few times.

"Flap *harder*!" Her pa gestured with his one hand.

Her cheeks heated right along with her armpits, as she moved her bent arms faster.

"Good!" His face beamed. "Now go on in the pen. When he comes for you, start flappin'. Don't take your eyes off him an' chase after him if you hafta. But whatever happens, don't look away, don't *run* away, and don't turn your back on 'im. Got it?"

"What if he comes at me again with his spurs?"

"Get a stick. Smack him with it if you hafta. Not hard, only enough to show him you're in charge."

She scanned the yard and quickly found the perfect stick. Long enough to hit him and still keep her distance. She hoped she wouldn't have to use it.

Please let this work.

A silent prayer never hurt.

She entered the pen, and the game was on. The horrid bird charged her.

"Flap, Violet!"

She wasted no time and did as her pa said, feeling silly all the while. "Dumb bird! Get on back!" She glared at him and stomped her foot.

He lurched forward, and she flapped harder. "I said, get on back!" She charged *him*.

He hesitated, then came at her again. "It ain't workin', Pa!" Her eyes remained glued to the insubordinate poultry.

"Keep at it. Wear 'im down!"

Instead of flapping, Violet waved her hands in the air and rushed at him. His head jerked back, then lowered. His body deflated and he pecked at the ground. "Look, Pa!"

The man chuckled. "Yep. He's submitted. Go on an' touch one a them hens. See what he'll do."

Violet wandered to the coop and patted a white hen on the back. She glanced over her shoulder at the rooster, who strutted to the other side of the pen.

Violet laughed. "Reckon *I'm* top rooster now."

"That you are. You may have to flap every once in a while, but I doubt you'll have any more trouble from that bird."

She stepped out of the pen and hugged her pa. "Thank you. I never knew you was so smart 'bout chickens."

He tapped a finger to his temple. "I'm smart 'bout many things." His smile vanished into a frown. "But now I gotta figger out how to *tame* your brother. He's gonna learn there's a peckin' order in our *family*, an' he ain't nowhere close to bein' top rooster."

"He scares me, Pa."

"Don't be afraid." He ran his hand over her head. "Anytime you have trouble with that boy, come see me. I ain't gonna let him do nothin' to hurt you or *anyone* in this family."

She took hold of his hand. "Please keep him away from Noah. He's so little. Lucas could easily break him in half."

"I love that baby boy. I ain't gonna let no one harm him."

"How you gonna do it, Pa?"

"You'll soon see. I'm gonna use a mite a *tough* love."

Violet frowned. It didn't sound pretty.

Her pa patted her cheek. "Ain't what you're thinkin'." He smiled, tapped her face again, and walked away.

Ever since he'd sent Lily to St. Louis, Violet had difficulty trusting his ideas of just punishment. Of course, her folks didn't see what they'd done as a reprimand. They'd viewed it as a loving gesture meant to keep their family in good standing.

She loved her folks and would never do anything to hurt them, but a small spark of anger toward them lingered. No matter how hard she tried to snuff it out, it kept on flickering.

She eyed the rooster one more time, then laughed. The instant the bird noticed her looking at him, he lowered his head and went the other direction in a defeated strut.

The front door of the cabin slammed, and Violet jumped.

Her pa and Lucas were on the front porch. She carefully crept behind the house so they'd not see her, but she could still hear them.

"You slammed that door to wake Noah, didn't you?" her pa snapped. Though she couldn't see him, she was sure his eyes shot fire.

"What if I did?" Lucas's voice had the same angry pitch, but it was followed by a loud smack. No doubt her pa had slapped him.

The rate of Violet's heartbeat quickened.

"I won't have you turnin' our lives upside down, just cuz you don't like the way we live." Even from a distance, Violet heard her pa's heavy breathing. "I won't have you threatenin' your sister, or bein' hateful to your brothers. 'Specially Noah!"

"He ain't my brother! He's a bastard!" Another slap. "You gonna keep hittin' me, Pa? That how you aim to make me mind? I ain't a child no more. You can't bully me into doin' what you want. I swear, one more go at me, an' I'll hit back!"

"You ain't got a lick a sense! You're livin' in one a the finest places ever there was, but you ain't happy. Why, boy?"

"I hate it here! I don't wanna be a farmer. I wanted to be a soldier, but now I can't. The war's over an' there's no one left I can rightfully kill."

"You think it's all 'bout *killin'*? Men simply shootin' cuz they *can*?"

"I ain't that stupid." Lucas's voice had calmed a bit, but his anger hadn't subsided. "I know they was all fightin' for what they thought was right, but in war you can pull a trigger with no consequences."

"No consequences? I lost an arm!"

"An' you've been *whinin'* 'bout it ever since! I wish you woulda died! Just like I told Violet!"

Silence.

Violet held a hand to her chest. Her heart thumped so hard, she could feel it against her palm.

"Tell you what . . ." Her pa's voice rumbled low. "You say you don't like livin' here, right?"

"I *hate* it."

"Then, *leave*."

Violet gasped. She slapped a hand to mouth, praying she'd not been heard.

"Huh?" Lucas couldn't have sounded more confused.

"I said, *leave*. Go on an' get your tail outta here. Find out what it's like to make your own way."

She wished she could see their faces right now. This must be her pa's idea of tough love.

"Fine," Lucas said. "I *will!*" Again, the front door slammed.

Violet hurried to the porch and found her pa alone. "Oh, Pa . . . Are you really gonna make him go?"

He slowly nodded. "He's gotta learn to appreciate what he's got."

"But—"

"Hush now. Trust me on this, all right?"

"Yessir."

Lucas came out carrying a blanket and a pillow casing that looked like it held something other than a pillow.

Her pa gestured to the items. "Where you takin' them?"

"Gotta have sumthin' to keep me warm at night." Lucas sneered and lifted a corner of the blanket. "An' I got me some food to get me by till I can hunt. I aim to take Caleb's bow. He *owes* me."

"Them things ain't yours. Leave 'em here."

"No."

Their pa puffed up his chest and towered over Lucas. "I said, leave 'em."

Lucas shifted his eyes to Violet, then bolted with the items held firmly in his arms.

Violet laid a hand on her pa's arm. "There ain't no way we can catch him." He'd always been the fastest runner in the family.

"I know. But he's run off with my words spinnin' in his mind. He didn't stop at the shed to get the bow. It's gonna be tough gettin' food."

"So, are you gonna let him starve?"

"I ain't lettin' him do nothin'. Trust me, the boy'll be back." He smiled—the saddest one ever—then went into the cabin.

Violet stared in the direction her fiery red-headed brother had gone. As much as she oftentimes disliked her brother, she loved him and didn't like thinking of him being alone. Though fourteen, he was still a little boy in many ways.

CHAPTER 6

Warmth embraced Rebecca's body. She'd added some rose-scented bath salts to the water. Caleb had always remarked how he loved the way she smelled, and since she expected him to have her tonight, she wanted to make herself as desirable as possible.

At times, she could swear Caleb must have affections for someone else. When he'd married her, she'd believed wholeheartedly that he loved *her*. But something didn't feel right.

She'd often see him gazing into nothingness, looking so sad it tore at her insides. His behavior reminded her of the way she'd been after Abraham had died. It left a hole in her heart she thought would never be filled, and she hadn't been whole until Caleb returned. But what had caused Caleb's emptiness?

Avery was already asleep, and Rebecca assumed Caleb was finishing up his evening chores, so he could give her the attention he'd promised.

She had no complaints about him as a pa. He'd been wonderful to his brother's baby girl. And though he'd never let on to anyone that Avery was anything but his, Rebecca hoped if the two of them had a child of their own, maybe he'd finally bond himself to her completely.

She set her hands atop her belly.

Please let it happen t'night.

Her bath had cooled, so she carefully stepped from the tub and dried off. She'd tied her hair up high on her head to keep it out of the water, but now she let it fall loose. Caleb seemed to like it that way.

She reached for her nightgown, then stopped, grinning. *Not tonight.* She wouldn't need it.

Dim light filled their house, but it would soon be dark. She crept to their bedroom, not wanting to wake Avery, and lit the lantern on the table beside the bed. With heart-quickening anticipation, she lay back against the pillows and waited.

Soon after, the back door shut and footsteps approached.

Tread softly, Caleb.

As if he'd read her thoughts, he tiptoed into the room. His eyes widened the instant he saw her.

He pushed the bedroom door almost shut. They never closed it completely, fearing they wouldn't hear Avery if she cried.

Caleb approached the bed and eyed every inch of her body. "Oh, Becca . . ." He gulped hard. "I've been thinkin' 'bout this all evenin'."

"Good." She moistened her lips. "What are you waitin' for? Want me to help with your clothes?"

"No. You stay right where you are. I wanna keep that image in my mind till I can do sumthin' 'bout it." He quickly worked the buttons on his shirt, then tossed it aside. His trousers followed just as fast.

She giggled at his eagerness—something she'd not seen in a great while. If ever. But another thing struck her that almost spoiled the mood. Like every other time, he'd not initiated this. Her crying at supper had led to it.

Bare-bodied, he climbed onto the bed. The handsomest man she'd ever known, with a body any woman would desire. Muscular and manly.

She couldn't deny how she constantly craved him. If only she could believe he felt the same about her.

He burrowed his face into her neck. "You smell so good, Becca." His head lifted and he stared into her eyes. "Like always."

"I do it for you. I may be the world's worst cook, but I know how to *love* you. That takes no effort at all." She traced around his lips with her fingertip. "Do *you* love *me*, Caleb?"

"Let me show you."

His lips covered hers. He kissed her in a way he'd not done before. It sparked with a new kind of fire that warmed her everywhere. Their tongues danced together like entwined lovers in their own right.

All the while he kissed her, his hand moved over her body. Excited chills mingled with heated passion. He caressed the insides of her thighs, then touched her more intimately exactly where she wanted him.

"Yes, Caleb," she rasped into his ear.

He rose and peered down at her. "You're so beautiful. Can you ever forgive me for not bein' the husband you need?"

"There's no forgiveness needed. Just love me. That's all I've ever wanted."

He kissed her again, then moved atop her. "Sure you want that baby?"

"Yes." She opened to him, then closed her eyes and savored his entry.

Once he started to move, she reopened her lids to watch the expression on his face. He moved ever-so-slowly, and his soft smile held tenderness and devotion. The lamplight flickered and grew in brightness as the room darkened from the waning sun. She should've never worried about his feelings for her. His features reflected utter love.

"I wanna make it last," he whispered, then bent low and kissed her.

When he rose again, she stroked his chest, all the while moving with him. They were so well-suited; their bodies a perfect fit.

A whimper from Avery stopped him. He hovered above Rebecca, no longer at ease. His brows dipped with worry.

"No, Caleb. She's fine." Rebecca cupped his bottom with both hands and lightly jerked, hoping to get him moving again.

He glanced in the direction of the hallway, then returned his eyes to her. "You sure?"

"Yes."

After looking toward the baby's room a second time, he breathed deeply, then started to move. He greatly increased his pace. Though he smiled, she could tell his thoughts had drifted. They were no longer fully on her.

The fluttering in her belly disappeared. All she felt now were his intense thrusts, as if he merely wanted to get this over with.

If only Avery could've remained quiet.

Rebecca twirled her fingers through the mass of hair at the center of his chest, trying all she could to regain the romantic mood. But Caleb's eyes were shut tight and his face drew together in a grimace. No tenderness remained.

He loudly moaned and thrust a final time.

At least she'd have his seed. Maybe she'd get the baby she wanted. Then again, additional children would require more of her attention. She and Caleb would have even less intimate moments.

Tears formed.

No. I won't cry. Not now.

Caleb had not yet pulled from her, but he lay still, breathing hard. "I'm sorry, Becca. The baby—"

"Shh." She pressed her fingers to his mouth. "I understand. Avery spoiled our mood. But, it's fine."

"No, it ain't. I know you didn't get much out of it."

"You're wrong. Anytime you love on me, it's wonderful. I wish we'd do it more often."

He nodded, but didn't say a word, then rolled off her. "I'm gonna check on Avery."

He stood from the bed and pulled on his trousers, then opened their door wide and walked out of the room.

Shortly thereafter, she heard him talking to the baby. The rocking chair creaked.

He'd done this often. Instead of coming back to bed with her, he'd rock Avery till she slept soundly in his arms. Sometimes, *he'd* fall asleep, too.

He loves her more than me.

Rebecca shook her head to dismiss the silly thought. His love for Avery differed from his feelings for her.

She'd have to work harder to be the kind of wife Caleb needed. For months, she'd been blaming her misery on him, yet perhaps it was her own fault. If she'd help him with the farm, he might not be so tired at night.

They'd *both* benefit.

She covered herself with a lightweight sheet and closed her eyes. Maybe she'd be lucky and he'd return to her sooner rather than later. They could start over and make love a little longer.

Only in my dreams . . .

* * *

Before Caleb sat with Avery in the rocking chair, he checked to be sure she'd not wet the bed. They kept a pot in her room, so they wouldn't have to take her to the outhouse at night, and he tried to get her to use it, but she clung to him, obviously needing comfort.

She hadn't bawled outright, but had whimpered enough to concern him. He knew he'd let Rebecca down, but she had to understand Avery took precedence. Their crying child needed tending.

He'd been determined to love on Rebecca as a proper husband should. And from what he could tell, they'd started out well. He couldn't help that Avery had fussed.

She cuddled against his bare chest, then giggled and fisted a clump of hair.

"Don't pull," he whispered. "You don't wanna hurt Pa."

"Pa-pa." She eased her grasp and laid her head on his shoulder.

"My sweet girl." He got the rocker moving.

Why did he enjoy holding his daughter more so than his wife? The joy he felt with Avery in his arms overwhelmed him. She had Rebecca's dark hair and eyes, but she also looked a lot like Abraham and bore the same deep cleft in her chin.

"Your pa woulda been so proud a you." Caleb made sure to keep his voice low, so as not to disturb Rebecca.

Someday, he prayed his guilt would subside. He thought it would help to marry Rebecca and raise Avery, but it only changed the *focus* of his guilt. Though he still felt horrible for killing his brother, most of his shame lay in the way he'd treated Lily. *She* should be his wife, not Rebecca.

He doubted time would ever heal this wound.

Avery's eyes were shut, but her tiny fingers kept moving. They ran across the scar on his shoulder. Another reminder of Lily.

Stop thinkin' 'bout her!

He couldn't change things now. His life's course had been set, and if Rebecca had her way, they'd soon have more children and be bound together tighter than ever.

Lily had moved on with her life, too. He imagined she'd married some man in the cove who'd come home from the war needing a wife. It sickened him thinking of her lying with anyone but him. Yet, how could he fault her? He'd made love to Rebecca more times than he could count. Even so, by her standards, it wasn't enough.

He'd learned from both Lily and Rebecca that a woman's desires were just as strong as a man's. Something he found oddly surprising.

He stroked Avery's head. "I want the best for you."

A thought wrenched his heart. What if a man came into Avery's life and married her simply to help himself overcome guilt? It wouldn't be fair to her. Especially if that same man had all his thoughts on another woman.

Caleb had made a bigger mess of things than he'd ever thought possible, and he feared it all might end badly.

He slowed the movement of the rocker and held Avery closer. Somehow, he needed to make a change for the better.

Unfortunately, he didn't know how to accomplish it.

CHAPTER 7

Lily found it difficult to sit around the house being waited on. Evie treated her kindly, but not like a friend. Something Lily longed for. It felt as if Evie was afraid to get close to her and talk about things—other than when Lily wanted bathwater drawn or her bedsheets changed. She needed to find a way to get Evie to relax—like she had when they'd first met.

Likely, Aunt Helen had told her not to talk to Lily any more than necessary. If that had happened, it would make sense for Evie to be afraid.

Lily doubted she'd ever get used to her odd relatives. Family shouldn't feel distant, and guilt weighed Lily down over lack of love for them.

Her aunt had bought her three gorgeous dresses, which only magnified Lily's guilt. The gowns didn't come close to filling the large wardrobe, but she would never complain. These alone would be enough for many years to come. They were so fancy, Lily feared putting them on. She certainly didn't want to tear them or worse, stain them with dropped food. But, her uncle had acted a great deal more pleased when she'd come to the dinner table wearing one.

She'd survived three days in St. Louis and was on her way to meet Mrs. Gottlieb. The woman who'd supposedly make her *proper*.

David arrived with a carriage and helped her and her aunt inside. He still said very little, though he greeted Aunt Helen with a smile—probably because she paid his salary.

Once he closed the carriage door, she and her aunt settled themselves on the cushioned seats facing each other. Lily readjusted her position, then smoothed the silky blue fabric of her lovely new gown. Truthfully, the dress had enough material to make *three* garments. The bountiful layers made her perspire. Underneath the enormous amount of fabric, she wore a thin chemise her aunt had said would soak up perspiration, so as not to stain her dress with moisture. The strange crinoline covering her legs made no sense at all—an odd wire-like cage covered in fabric, designed to push out all the layers of material. Why did women choose to torture themselves this way?

Reckon they measure their status by the fullness of their skirt.

"Your hair looks quite fine," Aunt Helen said, sitting tall. She was dressed in bright green with a matching cap hat. "The Clarissa coiffure it very much in fashion."

"Thank you." Lily had no idea who Clarissa was, or what a coiffure might be, but she liked the way Evie had fixed her hair and held it in place with an almost invisible net. "Evie done it for me. I reckon I'll never be able to do it right myself."

Whenever Lily spoke, her aunt's features soured. "Thank goodness we're on our way to your path of redemption. Mrs. Gottlieb *must* do something with the way you speak."

"Don't know why it rubs you the wrong way. Didn't you used to talk like me?"

"Yes. Something I've tried hard to forget." She parted the curtain that covered the small window on the door. "It's a lovely day." She released the fabric, then faced Lily again. "Remember.

Only speak when you're spoken to and do all you're told. Understood?"

"Yes'm." Lily picked at the lace on her skirt.

"And don't fidget."

"Yes'm." Lily let out a long sigh, expecting to be reprimanded for it. To her relief, her aunt didn't say a word. Since Lily didn't feel like talking anymore, she saw it as a good thing. Besides, they never *truly* talked. Her aunt merely fussed over Lily's inadequacies. Lily preferred being silent, so she could ponder her personal misery.

She should be happy having such nice things, but her broken heart didn't care about fineries. She needed to write to Violet and ask about Noah, though their folks would likely keep Violet from telling her much of anything about him. They'd see it as a way to break all remaining bonds between her and her son.

Caleb.

She pinched her eyes tight and forced away every tear.

The carriage jerked to a stop.

Her aunt actually smiled. "We're here." She reached for Lily's hand and gave it a squeeze. "Are you at all excited to meet her?" The woman's cheery behavior was odd, to say the least.

"Reckon so. Is she nice?"

"She's the finest woman I know."

Fine didn't exactly mean *kind*.

David opened the door, then extended a hand to her aunt, who took it and stepped to the ground. Lily followed suit. She caught herself before nervously laughing over the way her skirt popped outward, forced by the crinoline. The strange clothing would take a lot of getting used to.

"Come back for us this afternoon at three," her aunt instructed, then fluttered her fingers at David, motioning him to leave.

Lily gaped at her. "*Three*? We're gonna be here all day?"

"Yes. Nine till three every day until you're a proper lady."

"Are you stayin' with me the whole time?"

"Only for today. Tomorrow, I'll trust you to come by yourself. However, I want to be certain you'll treat Mrs. Gottlieb with the respect she deserves."

"Ma taught me to respect *all* my elders. Mrs. Gottlieb won't be no different."

"Perhaps so. We'll see." With her nose high in the air, her aunt walked up the stone pathway, and Lily shadowed her. The two of them resembled frilly bells floating on air. At least the crinoline kept the fabric from catching on Lily's feet. Her aunt had purchased new shoes for her, and Lily didn't want to trip and scuff them.

What would Caleb think if he saw me like this?

She quickly shifted her thoughts to her surroundings. It was senseless to ponder anything about Caleb.

Masses of ivy covered one side of Mrs. Gottlieb's small house. The shapely green leaves looked pretty against the white wood structure. Flowers filled small beds in front of the place, giving it abundant color. Lots of pink, red, and purple. It felt homier than her aunt's house, and a soothing relief flooded over Lily. Maybe this woman wouldn't be so uppity after all.

They stepped onto the stone porch. Her aunt rapped on the door, then gave Lily a sideways glance. Her eyes narrowed into a *don't embarrass me* glare.

Lily's stomach knotted. She held her breath and waited. Nothing could be worse than how her aunt and uncle had treated her, could it?

A well-dressed petite woman opened the door and smiled. "You're right on time. Please, come in." She fanned her arm and stepped to the side.

"Thank you." Aunt Helen sauntered in—shoulders back and head held high.

Lily followed her, but not with as much enthusiasm. Though uneasy, her discomfort hadn't come from the idea of meeting Mrs. Gottlieb. Every step she took into this unfamiliar world carried her further from herself and her son. If forced to become someone she didn't like, she might never feel comfortable stepping back into Noah's life.

Exactly what Ma an' Pa want.

The thought prompted a more painful one. Not only did her aunt and uncle disregard her wants and feelings, her folks had done exactly the same thing. Their decisions had gotten her into this mess.

Of course, they blamed *her*, but she'd never believe her love for Caleb had been wrong.

The woman led them into a warm sunny room. Large plants stood in every corner, as if some of the outside greenery had purposefully been brought indoors. An odd thing to do, though the plants thrived in front of the many windows. Lily had never seen so many panes of glass in one place. They lined two walls and had no coverings.

Decorative upholstered sofas with detailed floral prints sat below the windows. One on each wall. Pillows embroidered with leafy patterns rested on them. The colors of the fabric reminded Lily of the flowers in the beds at the front of the house. No doubt Mrs. Gottlieb certainly loved nature.

"Please, make yourselves comfortable." The woman gestured to the sofas.

Aunt Helen positioned herself like a queen. Tall and regal.

Lily tried her best to imitate the woman, but her crinolines popped her skirt high the instant her bottom touched the seat. She quickly pushed it down again, hoping she'd not appeared foolish.

The woman who'd led them into the room studied every move she made. "Your aunt has told me a great deal about you."

She smiled and gracefully sat on the seat beside Aunt Helen, across from Lily.

Lily's cheeks heated. "Oh, my. Are *you* Mrs. Gottlieb?" She eyed the small woman up and down. Nothing like what she'd expected. Though older-looking than her Aunt Helen, Mrs. Gottlieb had soft, friendly features.

She lightly laughed. "There's no need to feel embarrassed. Many young women have made the same mistake. Since I open the door, they assume I'm the housemaid. However, I have no need for such luxuries."

"Oh." Lily didn't know what to say or do, so she fidgeted with her skirt. Almost immediately, she realized her mistake. She gulped and shifted her eyes to her lap. The last thing she wanted to do was look at her aunt and receive a glaring reprimand. It was bad enough hearing the woman huff.

"My dear, girl," Mrs. Gottlieb said. "I can see you're uncomfortable. However, when you're in my home, all I ask is that you be yourself. It's the only way I can get to know you and discover what you need to learn. So please, rest easy, and don't be afraid to say whatever's on your mind."

Aunt Helen grunted and received a sharp glance from Mrs. Gottlieb.

Lily watched the unspoken battle waged between the two women. They both awkwardly smiled, and their eyes widened and narrowed more than once. Though smaller-framed, Mrs. Gottlieb definitely had the upper hand.

Aunt Helen faced away from her, jutting her chin high.

Mrs. Gottlieb sat taller. "Helen, dear, I'd like to get to know your niece. Yet, I sense your presence is causing her some discomfort."

"Well, I—"

"You should take a stroll in the garden. I'll speak privately with Lily, then you may join us for tea."

Aunt Helen slowly stood. "It's rather warm outside."

"No more so than in this room." Mrs. Gottlieb smiled up at her, undisturbed by her reluctance to leave. "We shan't be long."

Without looking Lily's way, her aunt left the room. In mere seconds, a door shut *hard*. Not quite the forcible slam Lily used to hear from Lucas back home, but loud enough to make a point. Her aunt didn't appreciate being removed.

"Now, then . . ." Mrs. Gottlieb inched over on the sofa and took Aunt Helen's spot, closer to Lily. "Tell me about yourself."

Lily met the woman's gaze. Her silvery blue eyes sparkled and she wore a genuine smile—much kinder than the one she'd shown Aunt Helen.

Evie had said Mrs. Gottlieb had taught her what she needed to know, so maybe this woman could truly help Lily—answer all the questions her aunt and uncle avoided.

"What do you wanna know?"

"Everything." Another gracious smile.

No, you don't.

Lily lowered her eyes and once again stared at her lap, unsure what to say. There'd been a time when she'd spill out all she'd ever done and not give it a second thought. But family lies and secrets had changed everything.

Mrs. Gottlieb's small hand moved atop Lily's. "Whatever you tell me will stay between us."

Maybe so.

No matter, Lily would keep some things hidden forever. "For-give me, ma'am, but I don't know you. I ain't comfortable tellin' you much of anythin' just yet."

"I understand." She withdrew her hand and sat erect, smiling. "So, tell me what you *are* comfortable with. Perhaps something about your family?"

"My family?"

"Yes. Your aunt mentioned you have a number of siblings."

Lily swallowed hard. "Yes'm. One sister, an' three brothers. There were more, but they died."

"Only *three* living brothers?"

"Yes'm."

"Oh. That's a shame." Mrs. Gottlieb's forehead crinkled. "I assume something must have happened to the baby. I'm truly sorry."

Noah . . .

Lily's cheeks warmed. "Silly me. Don't know what I was thinkin'. I meant I got *four* brothers, not three. I ain't used to havin' Noah 'round." She prayed Mrs. Gottlieb believed her blunder. After all, Noah had been in the family eight months already. Long enough to acknowledge his existence.

Mrs. Gottlieb held a hand to her breast. "I understand. I'm relieved your mother didn't lose him. I've known your aunt for many years, and she's shared details of her sister's sad losses. Though I have no children of my own, I can't fathom the heartache of losing a child."

"But you're married, ain't you? Bein' a missus an' all."

"Yes, I am. However, my husband died many years ago. Long before we were able to produce a child."

"So, why not remarry? If it was that long ago, you had plenty a time for a family."

The woman's lips pursed, then she lightly chuckled. "I thought *I* was the one asking questions."

Lily lifted her chin. "You told me to say what's on my mind. Reckon I wanna get to know you, too." Besides, it was easier talking about Mrs. Gottlieb than herself. Especially where Noah was concerned.

"That I did." Mrs. Gottlieb folded her hands atop her lap. "I suppose if I want to know about *you*, I should ask more pointed questions."

"An' if I don't wanna answer?"

"That's up to you." Her head tipped to one side. "Lily, do you *want* to be a proper young lady?"

"I don't know. Folks back home liked me just fine the way I am. But here, I'm a fish outta water. I can't do nothin' right."

"Would you like to remedy that?" She leaned a little closer.

"Reckon so." Lily frowned. "I hafta live here, an' I can't stand seein' Aunt Helen grimace whenever I talk. But . . ." Tears came out of nowhere and pooled in Lily's eyes.

"Yes, dear?"

Lily blinked and a droplet trickled down her cheek. "I used to be strong. *Fearless*. Nothin' 'bout mountain life scared me. But fittin' in here has me terrified. Worse yet, I'm scared I won't like the person y'all want me to be."

Mrs. Gottlieb extended a frilly piece of cloth. "Wipe your eyes with this handkerchief."

Lily took it from her and dabbed at her face, and the dear woman watched with a weaving brow. When Lily attempted to return the finery, Mrs. Gottlieb waved it away. "Please, keep it. You may need it again. Though I'm not fond of gossip, your aunt and I spoke of many things. Most importantly, the reason why your parents sent you here."

Lily tightened her grip on the soft cloth and couldn't utter a sound.

"No need to worry, my dear." Mrs. Gottlieb cast an encouraging smile. "It helps me to know how the war troubled you. It was a ghastly ordeal that ruined many lives. I understand how difficult it must have been for you, fearing for your future and the slim possibility of finding a respectable husband. Especially when so many young men lost their lives."

Lily gulped. "Yes'm." Her tears streamed faster. As Mrs. Gottlieb had predicted, Lily needed the handkerchief again. Much sooner than she'd expected. "I feel plum silly."

"Don't." She tapped Lily's knee. "Tears are never *silly*. I intend to do all I can to help you heal. And please trust me in regard to your training. Teaching you to be proper won't change who you are. You'll still have the same heart, you'll simply carry yourself well and speak in a way that will draw attention and respect." She peered deeply into Lily's eyes. "Do you ever feel unnoticed? As though your thoughts and opinions don't matter?"

"All the time." Lily breathed deeply. This woman understood more than Lily thought possible.

"Wouldn't you enjoy having your voice heard?"

"Yes'm."

The sweet woman clapped her hands a single time. "Good. I know exactly where we must start."

"You do?"

Mrs. Gottlieb stood and extended her hand. "Come with me to the kitchen. We'll prepare tea. I intend to introduce you to the English language. You're about to discover the means to a wonderful end. When I'm through with you, you'll have the attention of everyone around you."

"From my understandin', my uncle just wants to marry me off to someone." Lily placed her hand in Mrs. Gottlieb's and rose to her feet.

The woman patted their joined hands. "My dear, once you're finished with my instruction, I have no doubt *many* men will ask to court you."

Lily forced a smile, but said nothing. She couldn't imagine *anyone* courting her. Not when her heart held onto Caleb Henry. Her love for him tainted any chance she had at happiness with someone else.

CHAPTER 8

Lucas?

Though it had been days since Violet had seen him—and the house had certainly been a lot more peaceful—the sound of his voice eased her heart.

But, he wasn't alone. An older, deeper voice joined his, in a conversation with her folks.

She'd been resting, troubled with womanly pains, but got out of bed regardless. Curiosity over what was transpiring in the other room outweighed her discomfort.

She slowly opened her door, then gasped.

No.

Her folks had their backs to her, but Lucas faced her. And right beside him stood the last man she ever wanted to see. The creak of the door obviously caught his attention, because his eyes immediately met hers. She quickly looked down.

Sergeant Douglas no longer wore a uniform, but she'd never forget his face, or the way he'd inappropriately touched her. It made no sense for Lucas to be with him.

"You remember my sister, Violet," Lucas said in a tone that was anything but nice. "Don't you, Vincent?"

Why's he callin' him by his first name, all cozy-like?

"Of course, I do," Sergeant Douglas said. "It's impossible to forget someone so lovely."

Violet's insides knotted, worse than any female-induced cramp.

Her pa motioned her into the room. "It's all right to come out. He's not here to cause trouble."

Violet trusted her pa, but cautiously inched from the protection of her room and took in their *guest*.

"Yes," the sergeant said. "Not only did I come to thank your mother for proficiently stitching my wound . . ." His eyes pinched into slits. *He still thinks I was the one who whacked him over the head with that shovel.* "I'm here for a specific purpose."

It ain't gonna be me.

"Yep," Lucas said. "An' I'm gonna help him." His remark took away the fear that the sergeant had come for her, but why had he come at all?

Her brother stood tall, proud, and cocky as ever. Seemed their pa's method of teaching him to appreciate a good home life hadn't worked out as it should.

Her folks were by no means at ease. They acted just as nervous as they'd been during the war.

Noah fussed from his crib, so Violet went to him and picked him up.

"That's my little brother." Lucas nudged the sergeant. "Ma an' Pa got busy after y'all left." He smirked as if he'd said something funny. No one laughed, but the sergeant's brows slightly rose.

Violet swayed with the baby. Somehow, holding him gave her comfort and a spark of bravery. She stared directly at Sergeant Douglas. "So, what's this *purpose* you came for?"

Her pa cleared his throat. "He's lookin' for Callie."

A slap to the face wouldn't have shocked her more. "*Callie?*"

"That's right." Lucas's chin jutted upward. "Seems Captain Ableman's widow don't take kindly to a crazed mountain woman murdering her husband. She hired Vincent to hunt Callie down an' execute justice."

Violet eyed her mischievous brother. "After all this time? Callie's long gone. It's been well over a year—"

"When a loved one has been murdered," Sergeant Douglas interrupted, "time doesn't matter. Once I completed my military obligations, the captain's wife employed me. She's a bitter woman who will do whatever possible to find her husband's killer. I was on my way here to further question your folks regarding Callie's whereabouts, when I came across your brother on the road. I asked him about Callie, and he told me he knows where she might be. Seems she sent a letter from Waynesville." His eyes roamed Violet's body, sickening her even more. "I believe Callie might be more inclined to come forward, if she sees someone she trusts. Your brother is willing to accompany me, but since he's not of age, I felt it appropriate to ask your parents' permission to have him join me."

No wonder her ma acted scared to death. The poor woman dropped into a chair at the kitchen table and ran her hand back and forth across the Bible.

Lucas folded his arms over his chest, puffing up with pride. "Pa told me I can go. I aim to find Callie. Sooner or later."

If only Violet could get inside her brother's mind. He was up to no good. And if he implicated Caleb . . .

As bitter as Violet felt toward the man, no one but Lucas should be blamed for Ableman's death. Lucas was toying with the situation—using it as a means to track and scout. He'd be roaming around the country doing anything but a hard day's work.

Noah squirmed and fussed.

"You should go change him," Lucas said. "I can smell him from over here."

Without saying a word, Violet took Noah into her folks' bedroom and got a fresh diaper. While she cleaned him up, she attuned her ears to the conversation in the other room.

"In regard to this letter," the sergeant said. "I'd very much like to read it."

"We ain't got it." Her ma's voice shook. "It was sent to our daughter, Lily. She'd bonded with Callie an' was tryin' all she could to help the poor girl. Callie sent the letter specifically to her."

Violet could swear she heard Lucas snigger. Her heart beat out of her chest. None of this was good.

"I see." Sergeant Douglas's words were followed by complete silence. Violet held her breath, waiting to hear more. "Where's your daughter now?"

"St. Louis," her ma said. "Livin' with my sister, Helen, who wasn't blessed with children of her own. She wanted to give Lily a chance for a better life. Lily'd been deeply affected by the war, an' it brought her spirits down. We all thought a change a scenery might help."

"St. Louis is a fine city. I've been there many times. I'm certain it will afford her great opportunities. As for the letter, can you at least tell me the contents?"

Violet perched on the bed beside Noah. Her heart hadn't calmed one bit.

"The letter didn't say much," her ma muttered. "Callie simply said she was well, but wouldn't be comin' back. *Ever.*"

"Well, we know it was sent from Waynesville. It will give us a place to start. We intend to speak to everyone possible and hope someone will have seen her. If we're fortunate, perhaps she's still there. And although I hate to use your son as bait, as I said before I believe he may be what's needed to draw her out. He told me he and Callie got on quite well."

Violet's nervousness turned to something darker and harsher. How could Lucas be so deceitful?

"See, Pa," Lucas said. "There's things I can do instead a farmin'. Mrs. Ableman's got plenty a money, an' Vincent's gonna pay me to help him. But, that ain't what's drivin' me to do this. You an' Ma always told me to do what's right. Bringin' a murderer to justice is a fine thing. Ain't it?"

Heated anger coursed through Violet's body. Her horrid brother would take money from a widow and lead everyone on a meaningless venture, hunting for a fictitious person.

"Yes," her pa said. "It's a fine thing."

Her ma whimpered.

"Don't worry, Mrs. Larsen," Sergeant Douglas said. "I'll look after your boy. I believe he has the makings of a good man."

Violet bent down and kissed Noah's chubby cheek. "Least he'll be far away from you," she whispered.

She'd always protect Noah, but also feared for her brother. He might think he had the upper hand in this situation, but lies had a way of coming around. Aside from all that, he'd be with a lecherous man. If Lucas aimed to learn from him, his character would be further damaged. But from all she could tell, her folks weren't even *trying* to stop Lucas from going with the sergeant.

She studied her sweet nephew, who grinned and giggled, completely carefree. Such a precious life.

Your ma would be so proud a you.

She needed to write Lily a letter and tell her all that had happened. Maybe Lily could rest easier knowing Lucas wasn't anywhere close to Noah. But if she told her where he was going and *why*, Lily would worry about Caleb.

Violet scooped Noah up from the bed. "Reckon I'll just keep this to myself for the time bein'," she softly muttered. "No need givin' your ma more to fret over."

When she returned to the living room with the baby, Isaac and Horace had come in from playing outside. They kept their distance from Lucas and hovered close to their ma. Lucas seemed unbothered by it.

"Thank you again for allowing Lucas to assist me," the sergeant said.

"Welcome," her pa muttered.

Sergeant Douglas turned to Violet. "It was a pleasure seeing you again."

Violet shifted her eyes to the floor and said nothing.

"As I promised," he went on, "I'll take care of Lucas. And should we have no good fortune in Waynesville, we very well may travel to St. Louis."

Violet's head popped right up and her ma gasped, but quickly covered her mouth.

The sergeant gave her an odd glance, then shrugged. "If your daughter still has that letter, Mrs. Larsen, I might be able to attain something valuable from it that you've not seen."

"But . . ." Her ma swallowed hard. "Why travel so far for a letter she might've thrown away?"

The arrogant man smirked. "Young women rarely discard correspondence. Besides, Mrs. Ableman instructed me to follow every lead. She has the means to afford such a venture. Should we need to go there, I'll send word. I'd like to keep Lucas with me until we've exhausted every possible lead."

Lucas puffed up, grinning. He had an air about him as if he thought himself better than the rest of the family.

Yet, they all knew the truth.

A bad seed becomes darker with time, and Lucas had already lost every bit of light that had ever shone from his eyes. They'd grown cold and no longer reflected a warm heart.

He walked out the door with a man he'd once wanted to kill. Yet now, they behaved as best of friends.

* * *

Violet sat in the rocking chair and softly patted Noah's back. His head rested on her shoulder, and soon he'd be asleep.

The sergeant and Lucas hadn't been gone long, but discomfort still weighed heavy in the cabin. Violet wanted to discuss what had happened, but until she could get her folks alone, they wouldn't elaborate on any of it.

Horace and Isaac sat near her, drawing on their slates. They'd become more at ease with Lucas gone, but their eyes retained anxiety. She found it horribly sad that they feared their own brother. But in many ways, they all did. He'd proven he was capable of anything, no matter how sinister.

Isaac looked up and smiled. "When I was little like Noah, did you rock *me*?"

"Sometimes." She returned his smile. "Lily rocked you more." The instant she said her name, she regretted it.

Isaac frowned. "I miss her. I wish she was here."

Violet glanced over at their ma and received a look of warning she knew well. "Lily's where she needs to be. I miss her, too, but we gotta learn to get by without her."

Horace scribbled across his slate. "How's Lucas gonna lead that sergeant to Callie when there ain't no Callie no more?"

Their ma smacked her hand against the table. "Buck, you'd best talk this out, or we're gonna be in a mess."

The man had been pacing ever since Lucas walked out the door. "Ain't much to talk out, Rose." He wandered close to Violet, then motioned her out of the rocker.

She stood with the baby and let her pa sit. Her ma grabbed a chair from the kitchen table, placed it beside the sofa, and sat with a huff.

Noah had fallen asleep, so Violet laid him in his crib, then she, too, positioned a chair close to her folks. These kinds of family discussions always led to more lies and secrecy. Difficult things for her young brothers to comprehend and retain.

Truth had somehow managed to disappear from their lives. An odd thing to happen to a family who claimed to be Christian.

Violet couldn't contain herself any longer. "Why'd you let Lucas go with that man? I thought you said he'd learn his lesson an' come home."

Her pa's face soured. "He would've if the sergeant hadn't found him on the road." He rubbed his temples and his frown deepened. "Lucas ain't learned nothin' yet. 'Cept how to deceive. I blame myself for that."

"But you shoulda told Sergeant Douglas you didn't want Lucas traipsin' 'round with him. You know full well Lucas is takin' advantage of the situation. An' that poor widow—"

"Is better off without that despicable husband a hers." Her ma cut her off, scowling. "If she knew the truth, an' what he tried to do to your sister . . ." She quickly covered her mouth with her hand.

"What did he try to do?" Horace asked.

Their ma sat tall. "He wanted to hurt her. Callie, too."

Horace's nose wrinkled. "But there ain't no Callie. Just Caleb."

"That's right. An' if Captain Ableman had found out Callie wasn't no woman, he'd a killed Caleb."

"So, Lucas done right killin' him first. Ain't that so?" Horace's head tipped to one side. "He kept 'em both from dyin'."

Isaac's head shifted from side to side as he watched everyone speak. "Won't the sergeant be mad at Lucas if he finds out *he* killed Mr. Ableman?"

"Yes." Their pa nearly growled. "An' that's why all this hasta stay in the family." He pointed a stiff finger at the boys. "You don't speak 'bout this to no one. Hear me? If anyone asks 'bout Lucas an' where's he's gone off to, tell them he's moved away for work. An' if they ask what kind, tell 'em he's helpin' a widow woman. Nuff said."

"Should we say he's lookin' for Callie?" Horace asked.

"No!" Their ma threw up her hands. "Don't mention Callie to no one. An' never breathe a word 'bout Caleb!"

Horace stared at his lap, shoulders slumping.

"Don't be so harsh, Ma," Violet said. "They're too young to understand all this."

The woman's eyes widened, then narrowed into slits.

Their pa let out a long breath. "Don't cross your ma."

"Yessir," Violet whispered. Months ago, she'd never have been so forward. But with Lily gone, someone had to stand up for the boys.

Lily had always told her she needed more spunk. It felt good to speak her mind, despite being reprimanded for it.

"You boys go outside an' play," their ma said. "An' if them Quincy boys come 'round, remember to keep quiet 'bout all this."

"Yes'm," they said in unison, then hopped from the sofa, laying their slates on the table as they raced past it. In mere seconds, the door slammed shut.

Violet sat tall in her chair and lifted her chin. "How many more lies will we have to tell?"

Her pa slowly rocked. "As many as it takes to keep our family outta trouble."

"I don't like it." She couldn't bear to look at the man. There'd been a time she was proud to be a Larsen, but not anymore.

"I don't neither," her ma muttered. "But you can blame your sister for all this. Your pa an' me ain't at fault."

Violet's throat dried and tears threatened, but she pushed them down. She loved her sister too much to place this kind of blame on her. "Ain't you at all worried 'bout Lucas?"

The rocker stopped moving. "Far as I'm concerned," her pa mumbled, "the boy made up his mind. He'll hafta live with the repercussions."

Violet shifted her eyes to her ma, who sat unmoving and expressionless. "You still care 'bout him, don't you, Ma?"

"The son I raised don't exist no more." She stood and wandered to the kitchen.

Violet's stomach churned and her heart ached. She disliked the things Lucas had done, but would never stop loving him as a brother. If only Lily were there to talk to. She'd know what to do.

"I'm gonna lie down for a spell." Violet passed the crib and checked on Noah before going to her room.

Her folks didn't question her need to rest, yet her intentions were for something much different.

She'd made up her mind it was high time to write a letter to Lily. Though she'd have to approach all she intended to say with great care, Lily needed to know what had happened with Lucas and that he and the sergeant might be coming to St. Louis. Figuring out how to mail the letter without her ma finding out was another matter entirely.

CHAPTER 9

The carriage ride to Mrs. Gottlieb's home was a great deal more pleasant without Lily's aunt glaring at her. Lily found herself looking forward to the visit. Anything was better than spending time with her aunt and uncle.

David behaved as distant as ever, though he helped her from the carriage. It could be that he'd been instructed to ignore her—similar to the way Evie treated her.

One day, you'll smile for me, stubborn man.

She dipped her head at him, then paraded up the long pathway to the house. To her surprise, she came upon Mrs. Gottlieb pulling weeds from a bed of flowers.

The woman lifted her head, then stood. "Good morning, Lily." She brushed some dirt from her fingertips and motioned to the front door.

"Mornin', ma'am."

Mrs. Gottlieb folded her hands in front of herself and faced Lily squarely. "First lesson of the day. Calling me *ma'am* is suitable, however you should say, *good morning, ma'am.* Not simply *mornin'.*" She imitated Lily's accent. "So, let's try it again. Good morning, Lily."

Lily cleared her throat. "Good mornin', ma'am."

"Much better. I realize your accent will be difficult to tame, but we can soften the edges. Men admire women who speak with a refined southern *lilt*. Once you master it, you'll be irresistible." She tittered, then motioned Lily inside.

Irresistible?

Nothing could convince Lily that she wanted that kind of attention.

Mrs. Gottlieb peered over her shoulder as they walked down the hallway to the tearoom. "Your dress is lovely. That shade of lavender suits you."

"Thank you." Lily liked the lacy fabric, but especially appreciated that it wasn't as heavy as the other gowns. She could actually breathe in the dress.

Mrs. Gottlieb motioned to a small sofa. "Have a seat while I wash my hands. Though I love working in my garden, I don't like the way the dirt gets under my fingernails."

"Why don't you wear gloves?"

"Strange as it might seem, I enjoy the feel of the soil. Gloves get in the way." The woman poured water from a pitcher into a ceramic bowl, then grabbed a cake of soap and briskly scrubbed every finger. She even had a small brush she used specifically on her nails. She painstakingly glided it across every one, then held her fingers up into the light that streamed in from the window and closely examined them.

Lily remained standing and watched every move she made.

Mrs. Gottlieb peered over her shoulder. "Do you find this entertaining?" She grinned and pursed her lips.

"Sorry, ma'am. I just think it's odd someone like you would want to get their hands dirty."

"Someone like *me*?"

"Yes'm. You wear such fancy things an' all, an' it's your job to learn girls like me to be proper. I'd think workin' in dirt would be highly *im*proper."

Mrs. Gottlieb grabbed a towel from the small table where the bowl and pitcher were kept. She thoroughly dried her hands, then set it aside. "There's nothing improper about doing things we enjoy. I love nature, and I have a special fondness for flowers. As for my occupation, I *teach* girls to be proper. I don't *learn* them." Her brows lifted high, and she peered into Lily's eyes. "Now, have a seat." Again, she motioned to the sofa. "We'll simply chat a while. Does that suit you?"

"Yes'm." Lily carefully tucked her skirt beneath her bottom and sat, then lay her hands atop her lap to keep the crinolines down. Once seated, she crossed her legs at the ankles and pulled them close to the sofa, all the while keeping her back utterly straight.

Mrs. Gottlieb sat in a chair across from her. "You handled yourself well. It appears you retained all I taught you yesterday."

Lily had been made to sit and stand over and over again until both her aunt and Mrs. Gottlieb had been satisfied. "I'm able to learn most anythin'. I ain't ignorant. But why didn't you help me with my speakin' yesterday? You said you was gonna."

"First, there's no need to defend yourself. I'm well aware of your intellect. As for yesterday, I chose to forego your instruction in language, because of your aunt. I love Helen dearly, but I don't care for the way she scowls every time you open your mouth."

"You noticed that, hmm?"

"I'm not blind." She smiled and proudly lifted her head. "I care about you, Lily. I want our lessons to be enjoyable. So, as I demonstrated upon your arrival, I shall be bringing your word usage problems to light as the improprieties occur. It will help you understand what needs to be corrected."

"All right." It didn't sound *too* hard.

"Now then . . . Based on what you said to me moments ago, the simple use of *ain't* will cause those who hear you to question your intellect. Proper speech is an outward sign of a well-functioning brain." Mrs. Gottlieb lightly tapped Lily's forehead.

"What's wrong with *ain't*? Everyone I know uses it. 'Cept folks here."

"Exactly. You're from a region where refined education is lacking."

Though Lily liked Mrs. Gottlieb, she couldn't help but frown. It felt horrible being insulted. "Folks back home is smart. They know how to grow crops and fend for themselves. I even learned how to make medicine from my ma. The Cherokee passed on their knowin's. Reckon you'd say *they're* not very bright, since they don't know how to speak proper. But I'm inclined to disagree."

Mrs. Gottlieb smiled and leaned back in her chair. "You misunderstood. As I said, *I'm* aware of your intelligence and I have great admiration for native Indians. However, those who you'll meet in the city won't give you the time needed to discover what you have to offer, if all they hear are the crude words you speak."

"Crude? I don't use profanity."

"And I'm glad of that. Yet usage of words such as ain't comes across just as vulgar in most circles. So please, trust me. We must weed it from your vernacular."

"My what?" Yesterday's lesson seemed much easier, but Lily wasn't about to give up. She simply needed to understand what was expected of her.

"Your speech patterns." Another wide smile. "For instance, when you said, *I ain't ignorant*, you should have said, *I am not ignorant.*"

Lily inhaled deeply. "I am *not* ignorant."

The dear woman clapped her hands together and beamed like the sun. "Yes!" She leaned close. "You have no idea what a difference it makes. Please, say it again."

Lily sat a bit taller and jutted her chin. "I am *not* ignorant."

"Beautiful. The poise you used saying those simple words came through loud and clear. Even the way you held yourself made me believe you. I knew you had it in you all along."

"Thank you." Her praise felt incredible. Though Lily didn't care whether or not she pleased her aunt and uncle, she wanted to make Mrs. Gottlieb proud of her. In addition, she wanted to prove to herself that she had the ability to do this.

"It's important that whenever you decide to speak, you think through what you wish to say. It will take a while to break the habit of using inappropriate words, but practice will help you achieve it." She cast a large smile, then her expression took a significant change and her brows drew in. "Lily, dear. One of your greatest hurdles will be to restructure not only your words, but the way you put them together and form sentences. Yours are frequently twice negative. Something completely undesirable."

"Twice negative?"

"Yes. For example, if you were to say, *I ain't got no . . .*" She gulped and sighed. "Forgive me. It's difficult to say. Not only is ain't used, but by using it with no—meaning none—you're stating that you don't have none, which means you have *some*. A complete opposite of your intended meaning."

"Huh?" Lily gaped at her.

"*Exactly.*" Mrs. Gottlieb released an exasperated breath. "It tires me just thinking about it, let alone speaking it."

"I can tell Aunt Helen an' Uncle Stuart find my speakin' irritatin', but I never realized it was so *complicated.*"

"Every dialect has its difficulties." She lifted a piece of paper from the small table beside her chair. "I've written some lines for you. These will help you properly form words and sentence structure. You're to take this home and read it aloud every night before bed. As you sleep, the words will continue to roam your mind and become engrained. I'd also like you to read at least two chapters from a selected book every night."

Uncle Stuart had said he'd select books for her, but he'd never offered even one, and Lily hated to ask again. She took the paper from Mrs. Gottlieb's hand and quickly scanned it. "Who's gonna select the books?"

"*I* shall. Your uncle has a vast library, but I'm not certain he has the kind of books I'd like you to read. You're an adventuresome young woman and a wonderful book was released this past year that I feel you'll enjoy. It stretches the imagination, but also uses proper English. I'll loan you my copy, but you must promise to return it."

"Course I will."

"*Of* course you will."

"*Of* course?"

"Yes. Course without the word *of*, is a path or route, which is not your intended usage."

Lily shut her eyes and shook her head. Proper English had made her temples painfully throb.

Mrs. Gottlieb stood. "Let's have some tea. After we refresh ourselves, I'd like you to read the sentences I gave you. Before you leave today, I'll give you *Alice's Adventures in Wonderland* to take home. Rest assured, your imagination will soar—something healthy for the growing mind."

"It sounds nice. But I reckon my mind's bein' stretched awful far as it is." She rose to her feet. If she was lucky, the tea would ease the pounding in her head.

Mrs. Gottlieb held a hand over her heart. "Not to overwhelm you further, but *reckon* is another word we must pluck from your vocabulary. Like weeding the garden, certain undesirables must go."

"Reckon's undesirable?"

"I'm afraid so."

Uneasiness returned to Lily's belly. How could so much of what she said and did every day be so unappealing? Caleb sure seemed to appreciate every part of her.

But he married someone else.

The thought jabbed sorrowful pain into a mix of all her other emotions. She had no choice but to keep moving forward. If that meant plucking every weedy word from her brain, then she'd have to succumb.

* * *

Mrs. Gottlieb walked with Lily to the waiting carriage. David dipped his head at the woman and smiled. When Lily met his gaze, his face instantly sobered.

Maybe she truly was undesirable. At least to men in St. Louis.

Lily firmly clutched the book from her teacher. She couldn't wait to find out what kind of adventures Alice would have. It might help her forget her own misery. "Thank you again for the book. I'll take good care of it."

"I know you will."

David opened the door and Lily stepped inside.

Mrs. Gottlieb rested a hand on the door. "I'm proud of you, Lily. You're progressing quite well."

"Thank you. I'm tryin' real hard."

"Yes, you are. Tomorrow, we shall walk."

"Walk?"

"Yes. There's a proper manner in which to do *that*, as well."

Lily grinned. "Then, let's pray it don't rain."

"We'll pray it *doesn't* rain." Mrs. Gottlieb tipped her head and smiled. "Read your sentences over and over. I promise it will get easier."

"Yes'm."

The dear woman stepped back and David shut the door.

The piece of paper with Mrs. Gottlieb's sentences had been folded inside the cover of the book. Lily withdrew it and studied the words. Though she'd read them aloud several times for Mrs. Gottlieb, she wanted to look at them a bit closer. It was hard to understand why simple words should matter so much. Since she was tired of talking aloud, she read them to herself.

Jane and Richard strolled along the avenue and basked in the brilliant sunshine.

They sounded a little uppity. Maybe Mrs. Gottlieb wanted her to understand the way folks here behaved. There might be a *stroll* in Lily's future.

'Would you like some tea, Mrs. Smith?' Miss Roberts asked.

'Thank you. I would indeed,' Mrs. Smith replied with a gracious smile.

Folks there sure did like tea. She did, too, but she'd never drank it out of such a fancy cup till she'd arrived in St. Louis.

She continued on to the next set of lines.

The ballroom filled to capacity. Gentlemen in fine clothes bowed to their intended partners and the ladies curtsied in reply.

Her aunt and uncle had a ballroom. What if she was being *groomed* to dance?

Her heart pattered harder. A dance in a fancy ballroom would be nothing like the barn dances they had back home prior to the war. Mr. Quincy had played a mighty fine fiddle, but no one had ever bowed or curtsied. Thinking of him pierced her heart. He'd died too soon and in a horrible way. If only things could've stayed the same and not been spoiled by the war. No matter how much she missed the cove and all the people in it, it would never be like it once was. But at least it retained its simplicity. A way of life she cherished.

The world she now lived in couldn't be more foreign.

She stroked the cover of the book, then opened to the first page. Escape to *Wonderland* sounded like a good idea.

CHAPTER 10

A knock on the front door whipped Rebecca's head around. No one but her mother-in-law ever came for a visit, and never this early in the morning.

Avery sat secure in her highchair eating a bowl of oats. She had more in her hair than in her tummy, but her happy demeanor made mealtime enjoyable for both of them.

Rebecca patted Avery's head. "I'll be right back. Someone's come callin'."

Her sweet baby girl blinked, then shoveled another bite of the thick cereal into her mouth.

The second rap on the door resounded a lot louder.

"I'm comin'!" Rebecca wiped her hands on her apron and scurried to answer it.

When she swung the door open, a tall thin man smiled and dipped his head. "Good morning, ma'am. Are you Mrs. Henry?"

She shifted her eyes to a redheaded young man at his side, who wore a questionable smirk. "Yes, I am. How can I help you?" Unease filled her belly.

"Is your husband available?" the older man asked. "We'd very much like to speak with him."

She swallowed hard. "Caleb went out early this mornin' to pick blackberries. I expect him home soon. He didn't have breakfast 'fore he left." She fidgeted with her apron. "Mind tellin' me what this is all 'bout?"

The man casually folded his hands in front of himself. "We believe he might have helpful information regarding a woman we're searching for."

"A woman?"

The redhead's smirk broadened. He seemed to be enjoying her discomfort.

"Yes. A mountain woman who goes by the name, *Callie*. Has he ever spoken of her?"

"N-No, sir." Instinct told her to limit what she said. Of course, not knowing anything made it easy.

"Ma!"

Rebecca jumped at Avery's loud cry. "I need to tend my daughter."

"You have a little girl?" the redhead asked, lifting his chin.

"Yes. She's fourteen months." She hesitated for a second, then decided it would be best to be hospitable. "Why don't you come inside an' have a seat while you wait for my husband? I can get you some coffee if you'd like, or perhaps a glass of water?" She took a small step backward and motioned them in.

"Thank you." The older man entered first, followed by the younger. "My name is Vincent Douglas, by the way, and this is Lucas Larsen. He knows Callie and is helping me locate her."

"Pleased to meet you." She jerked her head in a single nod. "Have a seat on the sofa, while I see to my daughter. Would you like that drink I offered?"

"No, thank you," Mr. Douglas said. "I had my fill at the hotel."

She looked directly at Lucas. "What 'bout you? Are *you* thirsty?"

"Nope. I had my fill, too." He licked his lips in a manner that further disturbed her. She hurried away without any additional formalities.

If they'd been at a hotel, she assumed it was Iverson's. But who had sent them here?

When she found Avery with the cereal bowl upside down and resting atop her head like a hat, Rebecca covered her mouth to stifle a chuckle. Bits of oats ran all through the girl's hair and over her face.

"Silly child." Rebecca grabbed the bowl and set it on the table. "What were you thinkin'?"

"Oats." Avery grinned and smeared the mess across her cheek and into her ear.

"You'll need a bath for sure." Rebecca glanced over her shoulder, then returned her attention to her daughter. "But, we'll have to wait till your pa gets home. We have guests."

She grabbed a washrag and dampened it, then tried her best to clean away the misplaced cereal.

The back door opened.

Caleb walked in, grinning. "I see she's wearin' her breakfast again." He set a large bucket of blackberries on the kitchen counter. "Good thing Ma's comin' by to show you how to fix jam. This'll make plenty." He bent down and kissed Avery's messy cheek, then smacked his lips. "Don't taste too bad." His grin widened.

Rebecca laid a hand on his arm. "Sweetheart," she whispered. "There's men in the other room wantin' to talk to you."

"Men? What men?" He gazed beyond her.

"Vincent Douglas an' Lucas Larsen. Do you know them?"

Caleb gulped and his face paled. The happiness he'd shown before disappeared. "No. Never heard a them." He, too, kept his voice low. "Did they say what they want?"

"Yes. They're lookin' for some woman named Callie."

Caleb wavered and grabbed onto the edge of the table. His color grew even more peaked.

Rebecca grasped onto him. "Do you know her?"

He sluggishly nodded. "I best go talk to 'em."

"Want me to come with you?"

"No." He bit off the word. "Stay here with Avery."

"Caleb?" She searched his eyes for understanding. "Sumthin' doesn't feel right 'bout all this."

"I'll explain later. For now . . ." He stood tall and framed her face with both hands. "Trust me to take care of it. All right?"

He kissed her forehead and walked away before she could answer.

* * *

Caleb did all he could to control his roiling stomach. Questions darted through his mind. The greatest of which was why Lucas had come here searching for Callie. The boy was up to something, and knowing Lucas well, Caleb assumed it to be anything but good.

And who's Vincent Douglas?

Caleb took several deep breaths to calm his pounding heart, then pulled his shoulders back and walked with forced confidence into the living room.

He glanced at Lucas, whose eyes held disdain. Of course, the boy had every right to be angry with him for not coming back for Lily, but still . . .

He looks like he wants to kill me.

The older man stood. "Mr. Henry?"

Caleb gave him his full attention. "Yes. I'm Caleb Henry. An' you are . . .?"

"Vincent Douglas." He gestured to Lucas. "And this young man is Lucas Larsen."

Stone-faced, Lucas slowly rose. He'd not given any indication that he wanted the other man to know they were familiar.

Caleb chose to go along with the ruse. "Pleased to meet you," he calmly said. "What can I do for you? My wife mentioned you're lookin' for someone."

"That's right." Vincent folded his arms over his chest. "We've run into a rather peculiar situation."

Caleb's knees had become weaker by the moment. "Why don't we all sit? It'd make talkin' more comfortable."

The men once again took their place on the sofa, and Caleb sat across from them in a chair. He prayed Avery would keep Rebecca busy, so she wouldn't hear their conversation.

"So." Caleb swallowed hard. "What sort a situation involves *me*?" If only he could read Lucas's mind, or at least get him alone and *really* talk.

Vincent leaned back against the cushions, looking much too comfortable. "My young friend and I are searching for a woman who's committed murder. She goes by the name, *Callie*." He peered straight into Caleb's eyes. "I was told you know her."

Murder?

Though Caleb had only gotten a brief look at the soldier Mr. Larsen had whacked with a shovel, he believed Vincent was that very man. And yes, he'd made a remark that he thought Callie had killed Captain Ableman, so murder made sense.

If the man knew Lucas had pulled the trigger . . .

Caleb shifted his eyes to Lucas. A wry smile curled his lips.

He's enjoyin' this.

"You say her name's *Callie*?" Caleb scratched the back of his head. "Not sure who told you that, but I don't recall knowin' no woman by that name."

"Are you certain?" Vincent leaned forward. "Your mother told us otherwise."

"My ma?" *Could this get any worse?*

"Yes. Mrs. Iverson directed us to her."

"I don't understand." At least *that* was the truth.

Lucas inched to the edge of the sofa. "You don't remember writin' to a girl named Lily Larsen in Cades Cove, Tennessee?"

Caleb didn't think it possible, but his heart beat even faster. "Um . . ." Sweat poured from his brow.

Lucas jutted his chin high. He'd grown a great deal since Caleb had last seen him, but the mischievous boy still remained. "Stop pertendin' you don't know Callie. Your ma told us you wrote that letter for her."

What are you up to?

"At this time," Vincent said. "You're not in any trouble. However, if you're hiding the girl, or helping her in *any* way, I'll see to it you're prosecuted right along with her. She killed a good friend of mine. An upstanding man who served as a captain in the war."

Upstanding?

There was nothing decent about the man, and Caleb wasn't about to be implicated in a crime he didn't commit. His mind raced faster. He had no idea what his ma might've said to them. Every word that left his mouth could get him deeper into trouble.

He stared at his lap. "You're right. I knew Callie, an' I wrote a letter for her." He lifted his head and met Vincent's leering gaze. "But I ain't got no notion where she might be now. She disappeared after I wrote the letter."

The man studied him keenly. "Why did you *lie* when we first asked about her?"

Caleb glanced over his shoulder, then leaned closer to the man. "My wife knows nothin' 'bout Callie," he whispered, then widened his eyes to drive the point.

Vincent's sharp gaze turned into a smirk. "I see." He nudged Lucas. "You told me Callie wasn't bad-looking." He focused again on Caleb. "I understand. I'm sure once we leave, you'll enjoy explaining this to your lovely wife."

Lucas snickered.

Vincent chuckled right along with him. "What did Callie tell you to write in the letter?" He, too, seemed to relish Caleb's discomfort. Neither he nor Lucas could be called, *honorable*.

The pleasure on Lucas's face grew. He knew full well the predicament Caleb was in, and he reveled in it.

Caleb shut his eyes, then inched them back open. "It's been a while, but Callie just wanted to thank Lily for helpin' her, an' to let her know she wouldn't be returnin' to Cades Cove."

"Hmm . . ." Vincent rubbed his jaw. "That's similar to what Mrs. Larsen told us."

Thank God.

Caleb released the breath he'd been holding. "I swear, I didn't know she'd killed someone." He peered into Lucas's eyes, feeling his own disdain. The boy was toying with everyone.

Lucas sat taller. "How'd you meet her?"

Damn you.

The air thickened and Caleb's chest constricted. For the slightest moment, he'd thought he might get through this. His thoughts tumbled, and he formed a story. "I was stayin' at the hotel with my ma." He gazed toward the ceiling. "This is a mite embarrassin', but I ran into Callie when I was comin' from the outhouse."

Vincent chuckled. "I see."

"Though not bad to look at, she was kinda bedraggled an' confused. I offered to get her sumthin' to eat, but she said she was afraid a bein' found." He turned to Lucas and locked eyes with him. "Now I know why. Murder ain't *nothin'* to be proud of."

Lucas huffed and shifted his body, but retained his smugness.

"Then she asked you to write the letter?" Vincent asked.

"That's right. She said she wanted it to go to a family in Cades Cove. An' specifically to . . ." Her name stuck in his throat. He swallowed the enormous lump, then coughed. "To *Lily*."

"My sister," Lucas said. "Callie made a mess a everythin'. Hurt everyone I care 'bout." He kept his cold gaze glued to Caleb's face. "My family tried to help her, an' what she done broke 'em apart. Few weeks back, Lily left the cove, all troubled an' broken-hearted. The war brought her down, but worryin' 'bout Callie made it worse. That letter tore her up."

Every word Lucas uttered further wrenched Caleb's heart. The boy pummeled him into the ground solely by speaking.

Lucas's icy stare turned smug. "The only good thing that's happened for us is my new baby brother. He's just eight-months old now, but growin' like a weed." Lucas's eyes pinched into slits. "You enjoy your baby girl?"

Caleb ached to ask more about Lily, but he couldn't. It would raise too much suspicion. And why did Lucas bring up a baby brother in such a pointed way?

"Yes," Caleb said. "I love bein' a pa. Best thing ever happened to me."

Lucas hadn't shifted his eyes. "Reckon you'd like a *son* someday?"

"Reckon I would."

Vincent loudly cleared his throat. "We've gotten away from the matter at hand. Is there anything more you can tell us about Callie? Did she say where she was from?"

"No. But when she left, she headed east." Caleb's nervousness had vanished. All that remained were painful aching memories and a mountain of regret.

"East?"

"That's right. But you're lookin' for a needle in a haystack. You know that, don't you?"

Vincent stood. "Yes. But we're fortunate to have the luxury of a wealthy employer who's paying our way. However long it takes us and regardless of the distance needed to travel." He gestured for Lucas to get up. "Seems we'll be heading east. St. Louis will have to wait."

"St. Louis?" Caleb asked, also rising to his feet. "What's there?"

"My sister, Lily," Lucas said, grinning. "Vincent wants to ask her 'bout the letter. But it sounds to me like it didn't say much a anythin'. Even so, it didn't help her broken heart. The war ruined her. She nearly died from not eatin'."

Died?

Caleb grasped the back of the chair to keep himself from crumbling. "I'm sorry to hear it." He was more than sorry. He blamed himself for all of it. "But, she's well now? In St. Louis?"

"Reckon so."

Caleb had so many more questions. He wanted to know about *all* of them. Violet, her folks, and especially the boys. But he pinched his lips together and nodded.

Vincent wandered toward the door. "If you think of anything else, we'll be staying at Iverson's for another day."

"All right." If Caleb didn't compose himself, the man would know their revelations had had an effect on him. He might even think he was hiding something, which of course he was, but Lucas was manipulating everything.

Caleb hurried to the door and opened it for them.

Vincent leaned toward him. "I don't envy you explaining our conversation to your wife. I'm quite certain there's more to your involvement with Callie than you've let on. Perhaps a little more than *penning a letter?*" He jiggled his brows and stood erect, then walked out.

Good. Let him think dallyin' with Callie is what's makin' me worried.

Lucas paused in the doorway. "Funny thing." He kept his voice low and shifted his eyes toward Vincent—who was already some distance away—then grabbed Caleb by the arm. "My baby brother looks a heck of a lot like you." He gave Caleb a shove, smirked, and strode away.

Caleb shut the door as fast as he could, then dropped to the floor.

Eight months old.

The math was easy. Without even clinching a fist, Lucas had punched him hard.

Rebecca rushed to Caleb and knelt beside him. "What happened?"

He stared at his beautiful wife, speechless.

"I'll get you some water." She hurried away.

Numbness set in.

He'd not seen this coming. His sixth sense had failed him. By trying to fix the wrongs he'd done, he'd created more.

Lucas had every right to hate him.

And Lily . . .

Oh, God. My sweet Lily.

She'd birthed his son and her folks obviously chose to raise him as their own. But why send her away, and what made them choose St. Louis?

The Larsens were exceptional at creating falsehoods. He'd been a part of more than one. They'd never want the family shamed by exposing Lily's pregnancy.

Lily's aunt.

He recalled the hateful letter Mrs. Larsen's sister had sent from St. Louis. If they'd sent Lily there, she'd be miserable.

What've I done?

He covered his face with both hands and rocked back and forth.

I have a son . . .

CHAPTER 11

Caleb couldn't remember walking to the kitchen table, but he found himself there with his head resting on the hard wood.

"Sweetheart," Rebecca knelt beside him. "Please tell me what this is all 'bout. I've never seen you so out of sorts."

He had to tell her *something*, but a partial truth would have to suffice. He'd never tell her about Lily. "It's . . . *Callie*."

"Oh, dear Lord." Rebecca stood, yanked out a chair, and sunk into it. "There *was* another woman before me, wasn't there?"

"Callie," Avery chirped. Their cheerful child was oblivious to all their troubles.

Caleb managed to smile at her, then reached for Rebecca. "No. It's not like that at all." The pain and worry in her eyes brought him even greater heartache.

She tentatively took his hand. "So, tell me. I can't endure not knowin'."

He gathered his wits and sat upright. "You see—"

A rapid knock at their front door stopped him from going further.

"Well, I swanee," Rebecca muttered. "Who else is goin' to disrupt our lives this mornin'?" She huffed and stomped out of the kitchen.

Maybe Lucas had come back by himself. If he had, he was the last person Caleb wanted Rebecca to talk to. He shot to his feet, glanced briefly at his daughter, then raced after his wife. To his relief, his ma stood in the doorway.

"Caleb Henry," she said, frowning. "You have some explainin' to do."

"I know." He jerked his head toward the kitchen. "C'mon. I was 'bout to tell Rebecca. Best be tellin' you, too."

His ma pushed past them. He couldn't imagine what had been said to her, or how she'd come up with the idea that he'd written the letter on Callie's behalf. Maybe Lucas had guided her into saying the right thing. But why?

"Why does my grandchild have oats in her hair?" His ma picked at the dried-on food.

"She thought her bowl was a hat," Rebecca said. "I washed off as much as I could, but she needs a bath."

"That'll hafta wait." His ma scooted a chair close to Avery and sat.

Rebecca sighed and took her own seat.

The air in the room weighed heavy. Caleb wanted to crawl into a hole, but went back to his place at the table. "'Fore I tell my side a all this, what did you say to them men at the hotel? An' why'd they talk to you at all?"

His ma kept plucking food from Avery's hair, much to the child's annoyance. "Poor Mrs. Iverson was all a flutter. Those *men* —which of course one is truthfully a rather rude *boy*—kept questioning her 'bout the mail sent from the hotel. They asked specifically 'bout a letter to . . ." She glanced at Rebecca, then returned her gaze to him, eyes wide. "Lily Larsen. They said it had come from some woman named Callie. Mrs. Iverson had never heard a her, but told them *you'd* sent Lily Larsen a letter. She suggested they talk to me. Once they questioned me an' left, she came to me all upset. Afraid she'd divulged sumthin' she shouldn't of. She feels just awful 'bout it."

"Ouch!" Avery's face puckered, and she leaned far away from her gramma.

"Ma," Caleb said. "Leave her hair be. Becca can take care of it later."

"Fine." His ma folded her hands atop the table. "So, tell me, Caleb. Who's Callie? You told me you were writin' a letter to the family what helped you heal 'fore you came home. You never mentioned any *Callie*."

"Or *Lily*," Rebecca added. She firmly crossed her arms over her bosom. "Truthfully, you never said much a anythin' 'bout *any* family."

Caleb peered upward, praying for divine intervention, then looked from one woman to the other. "*I'm* Callie."

"What?" Rebecca gaped at him, as did his ma. "Did *you* kill that man?"

"No!" He rubbed his temples.

"Caleb." His ma's tone was one he knew well. "Don't raise your voice in that manner. And please, explain yourself. How in heaven's name could you be Callie?"

His cheeks heated, but not from anger. "It's how I was able to survive an' not be discovered. See . . . I wanted to help 'em with their farm. Figgered it was the least I could do to repay 'em for fixin' me up. But it woulda caused trouble if I'd a been seen. So, I wore a dress an' bonnet anytime I left the Larsen's cabin."

Rebecca covered her mouth, but he could tell she was hiding a grin. "A *bonnet*?"

"It ain't funny." Caleb blew out a frustrated breath. "If them soldiers had found out I was a man, I'd a been killed. It was humiliatin' wearin' them clothes, but I done it to live."

His ma shook her head and leaned back in her chair. "Never thought I'd see the day when one a my boys dressed like a girl."

"You *didn't* see it, Ma. Wish I wouldn't a had to tell you. But I swear I didn't kill no one."

Rebecca's expression softened. She didn't look angry anymore, but rather seemed to pity him and his situation. "Why do they think Callie did it?"

Memories of that awful day rushed in. Ableman's hateful words ground deep into Caleb's mind. "The man killed was a captain in the rebel army. Named Ableman. Lily an' me was . . ." Not a good time to fumble over what to say, but what could be said?

"Go on . . ." Rebecca sat primly straight.

He swallowed hard. If he didn't get his head together, she'd know he was keeping something from her. "We was doin' some work in the barn. Cleanin' it out an' such. Then Ableman came in. He wanted us in a less-than-honorable way."

Rebecca clutched her heart. "Oh, my. But, couldn't he tell by lookin' at you that you were a man?"

"He only seen me from the back. We thought for sure I'd be discovered, then outta nowhere a gunshot went off, an' the captain fell."

His ma leaned over the table. "Who shot him?"

"Lucas. The boy what was here with Vincent Douglas. Mr. Douglas was a sergeant back then. He was there that night, too. He came into the barn after the captain got shot. By then, I'd taken the gun away from Lucas, so Sergeant Douglas seen *me* holdin' it an' assumed I shot the man."

"Didn't *he* see your face?" The intensity in his ma's words grew with every one she spoke.

"No. Mr. Larsen whacked him over the head with a shovel an' knocked him out 'fore he could see or do much at all. Then Mr. Larsen told me to leave. We all knew more soldiers would come. Eventually, they woulda found out I wasn't a woman. I'd a been hung or shot. Maybe worse."

Rebecca jumped up from her chair, raced around the table, and flung her arms around Caleb. "My poor, Caleb!" She kissed all over his face. "It must've been awful for you. An' to think that redheaded boy is at fault. It makes no sense for him to be paradin' 'round the country searchin' for someone who isn't real."

"Actually, it does." He stroked her cheek, then softly kissed her. "Sit back down, an' I'll tell you more."

A painful smile lifted the corners of her lips. She hurt for him, and he didn't deserve an ounce of it.

His ma cast a cautious look his way. No doubt, she feared he'd let on about his feelings for Lily. To ease her, he gave her an encouraging smile. Hopefully, she'd understand and relax.

Avery stretched her arms out to him.

"She's gettin' bored a all this." He took her from her highchair and cuddled her on his lap. "The Larsens were good folk. They patched up my wounds, fed me, an' gave me a place to sleep. I befriended Lucas. He was the oldest of three boys. I reckon he looked up to me, cuz I taught him how to hunt with a bow an' to track in the woods quiet-like. But he has a dark side I don't understand. He enjoys seein' folks hurt. Animals, too. Revels in their pain. He didn't bat an eye shootin' the captain in the back. For once, his doin's turned out to be a good thing. He saved Lily an' me."

"That still don't explain what they've undertaken," his ma said.

"Ableman's widow hired Vincent to find her husband's killer. Lucas is keepin' up the farce to save his own hide. If Mrs. Ableman is fundin' their venture, Lucas is livin' an easy life, stayin' in fancy hotels an' such. He never liked workin' the farm. Only ones who know the truth 'bout what he done are the Larsens an' me. They ain't gonna tell, an' I sure as heck won't. If keepin' Callie alive protects me, I gotta do it."

Rebecca nodded. "Why didn't you tell me all this before? You've held so much inside. It's no wonder you've seemed distant at times. I knew sumthin' was troublin' you."

"I didn't wanna burden you with it." He stroked Avery's hair, still matted with globs of dried cereal.

"I'm your wife. You can tell me anythin'."

His ma lightly kicked his leg under the table. Enough said.

Rebecca ran a single finger across the tabletop. "I'm curious as to why you sent the letter to Lily? She's one a the children, right?"

Caleb nodded.

"Why not address it to her folks?"

Another kick. Any harder, and he'd be bruised for sure. His heart beat faster, just as it had when he knew Lucas had come. How could he explain this?

Then, it struck him.

Please make her believe me.

His ma looked like a frightened rabbit, but Caleb put on the biggest grin he could manage. "I was messin' with the woman what takes care a their mail."

"What?" his ma mumbled.

"The Larsens have an ongoin' issue with Mrs. Quincy. Sadly, her husband died at the hands of some wayward soldiers, but the woman herself is a nosey busybody. Always poked 'round in the Larsen's business. I knew full well that sendin' a mysterious letter to Lily would light a fire under Mrs. Quincy. I'm sure Mrs. Larsen enjoyed puttin' it out." He chuckled, more for feeling proud of himself for coming up with the story than the lark itself.

"Shame on you, Caleb," his ma said, laughing in a manner he knew held its own relief. "You shouldn't toy with folks that way."

"I know. But at the time, it felt good doin' it."

Rebecca barely smiled. "It's not kind. Doesn't seem like you at all." She licked her lips, then wiped at them with her fingers. "So, how old is Lily?"

He shrugged. "Not sure. Sixteen. Maybe seventeen."

"She pretty?"

"Nothin' special to look at. You seen her brother. Lily's similar." Why these lies came so easily, he wasn't sure.

"Oh." Rebecca's mouth screwed together. "I best be bathin' Avery." She stood and reached for her.

Caleb placed her in her arms. "You may hafta soak her head a mite to loosen them oats."

"I know. Since it's nice an' warm outside, I'm gonna fix the tub for her outdoors. She enjoys the sunshine." She headed for the back door, but stopped and faced his ma before going out. "When I'm done with her, she'll likely be ready for a nap. Maybe you can show me how to fix that blackberry jam." Though she'd put on her brave face, hurt lay in her words.

"I'll be happy to." His ma smiled broadly, and Rebecca walked out.

The minute the door shut tight, his ma slumped over the table, then slapped her hands against the wood. "I thought you were done for." She sat erect, shaking her head.

"So'd I. Ma, I hate keepin' things from Becca. You seen the way she acted. It's like she knows there's more to Lily an' me than I'm lettin' on."

"Well, you stumbled over your words at the wrong moment. Even if you hadn't, women can sense these things. But you'd best stick to your story. If she found out you'd been in love with that girl, it'd crush her."

I'm still in love with her.

"I know. I ain't gonna hurt her, Ma. But I reckon I'll go into town an' see if I can get Lucas alone. I wanna know what his plans are. I don't trust him one bit."

"A fine idea, but be careful. That Vincent Douglas is connivin' an' despicable in his own right. Not to mention a womanizer. His eyes roamed over *me* as if I were the evenin' meal. An' from what

I heard, they had a girl in their room last night. *Sickenin'.* If Lucas Larsen is an example of the others in that family, you should be glad to be rid a them."

"You sure 'bout that girl? Lucas is only fourteen."

"Yes, I'm sure. It was another reason Mrs. Iverson was so upset. If they didn't need the income, they'd a tossed both them *men* out in the street. Mr. Iverson runs a respectable business, and he made his wife promise to keep it quiet. Course she told *me.* Now I'm tellin' *you.*"

"An' that's how gossip starts." Caleb stood and paced. If his ma knew everything *he'd* done, she'd never forgive him. Fathering a child, then walking away was inexcusable. She'd probably label *him* despicable, too.

"You go on into town. When Rebecca comes back in with Avery, I'll tell her where you've gone."

He bent down and kissed his ma's forehead. "Thank you. I'm sorry you were put in the middle a this. Somehow, I gotta make it right."

"Why not tell Mr. Douglas the truth? Tell him Lucas killed that man."

"I can't."

"Why?"

"Cuz Lucas saved my life an' kept Ableman from puttin' his hands on Lily." With a wrench in his chest, he headed out the door.

* * *

It could take hours, but waiting behind the hotel's outhouses seemed the most sensible place for Caleb to be. After all, Lucas would eventually show up. And since it wasn't typical for men to visit the facilities together, he'd likely be alone.

Caleb had the benefit of a cluster of trees to hide behind. He made himself as comfortable as he could and waited.

As minutes ticked by, all he could think about was Lily, and of course, the son they'd created. And though he'd already accepted it as true, he wanted to hear Lucas say it. He also had to know Lily was all right. But how could she be? He'd hurt her in a way that couldn't be healed. No poultice would aid this wound. Yet how could she go away and leave behind their baby? It wasn't in her character.

He held his head in his hands, but it didn't stop it from pounding.

Folks came and went. He felt a little like a voyeur sitting there watching everyone. Worse of all, the smell surrounding the small structures churned his insides.

Minutes turned to hours. Luckily, he'd brought along a canteen of water. His stomach growled from hunger, but at least he satiated his thirst.

A familiar chuckle rose into the air. Footsteps neared.

Caleb stood and placed himself behind a large tree, then peered around it. Tall and proud, Lucas strutted toward one of the vacant chambers.

Caleb almost grabbed him right then, but chose to wait till he'd finished his business. If not, being startled could lead to an unpleasant accident.

The instant Lucas exited the building, Caleb nabbed him from behind and placed a hand firmly to his mouth. Lucas struggled, but Caleb easily dragged him backward into the brush.

"Stop fightin' me," Caleb whispered, recalling a similar situation with Lily. "We need to talk." He guided him even farther away, not wanting to risk being seen.

Once they were a great distance from the hotel, Caleb eased his hold, but didn't let go. "Nod, and swear to me you won't yell or run."

Lucas rapidly bobbed his head, and Caleb let him go.

The boy whipped around and faced him, glaring in the same way he had before. "How's that wife a yours?"

"Becca's none a your concern. What are you doin' here, Lucas?"

"I already told you. We're lookin' for Callie." He sneered and stuck his nose in the air.

"You ain't got no sense. Why ain't you home helpin' with the farm? Your pa can't do it alone."

"Why do *you* care? Pa wouldn't be alone if Lily hadn't been sent away. All cuz a you! You ruined everythin'. I *hate* you!"

Though Caleb deserved the boy's anger, his words stung. "You know I never meant to hurt no one. I loved your sister, an'—"

"You loved her real good, didn't ya? Put a baby in her, then ran away."

Caleb clutched his belly. "I didn't know . . ." He dropped to the ground, then sat back hard on his rump.

Lucas knelt beside him, eyes on fire. "That's a lie. You had my sister, an' we both know how babies is made."

"She shoulda told me. I woulda come back."

"By the time she knew, you was already married. Didn't take you long at all to get another woman. Lily trusted you. You said you'd come back after the war, then you sent that damn letter. Lily stopped eatin'. Reckon the only reason she started again was for the baby."

Lucas breathed hard, and his anger clearly came through. "Ma pertended to be with child. Fooled all the neighbors. Heck, even Horace an' Isaac think ma birthed him. My folks sent Lily away, so she'd forget 'bout the baby. She's bein' taught how to be all proper an' such. Gonna get her a rich husband. That should make you happy. No one will ever know 'bout your little bastard."

"Don't call him that!"

"He *is* one. Just like his pa. You're the biggest bastard ever there was."

Caleb clinched his fists, but not to strike out at Lucas. After all, for once, the boy spoke the truth. "I understand why you're angry that I didn't come back for Lily, but why do you hate me? I thought we were friends."

"I did, too. Till you took up with my sister. I couldn't figger out why all of a sudden you ignored me. I didn't matter one lick to you anymore. An' when you left, you didn't say a word to me. All you thought 'bout was Lily."

"Lucas, I'm sorry . . ."

Lucas rolled his eyes, then sat down beside him and casually leaned back on his elbows. "I sorta understand now. 'Bout women an' all." He plucked a long stem of grass and chewed on the end. "Vincent has a way with women, an' he let me in on it. But the kind a women we have don't care nothin' 'bout what's in your heart. All they concern themselves with is how to pleasure a man. I'm fine with that."

"No, Lucas." Caleb turned to face him. "It'll lead to trouble. Trust me. I seen men in the war die from messin' with them kind a women."

"Trust you?" He grunted. "Never again. Vincent knows how to find good clean women who know what they're doin'. I ain't gonna die from lovin' on *them*."

"It ain't love. You said it yourself. They don't care 'bout what's in your heart."

Lucas sat up, grinning. "Exactly how I want it."

There was no reasoning with him. If his folks knew what he was up to, they'd be crushed. "How far are you gonna take this ruse, Lucas? You can't go on forever."

"Mrs. Ableman's got plenty a money. Enough for good food, fancy rooms, an' fine women. I'll ride this ride long as I can. Vincent's enjoyin' it as much as I am, so why spoil the fun?"

"But, it's wrong."

"Wrong. Right. I don't see no difference. I'm havin' a good time. Ain't that what life's s'posed to be about?"

Caleb shook his head. If the boy had a heart at all anymore, it sure wasn't showing. "What 'bout Lily? Are you *sure* she's all right?"

"Right as rain. By now, I reckon she's wrapped up with some uppity man in St. Louis. If not, when Vincent an' me get there, he might decide to give her a go himself. You should be happy knowin' you broke her in good for someone else."

"Keep him away from her!" It was all Caleb could do to keep his fist from flying into Lucas's jaw.

"Vincent won't hurt her. She'd probably like it."

Caleb could scarcely breathe. He wanted to beat the boy bloody, but it would only make things worse. He fought against every violent urge and shifted his attention elsewhere. "What 'bout the baby? Our son? Is he healthy?"

"Spoiled rotten. Violet gushes all over him. Noah will be a sissy for sure."

"Noah?"

"Yep. Ma an' Pa named him. An' I didn't lie when I said he looks just like you. Maybe next time I come here, I'll bring him with me an' show him to that pretty wife a yours."

Caleb leered at him. "Stay away from Becca."

Lucas laughed and got to his feet, then brushed off his trousers. "I gotta admit, you got good taste in women." He returned Caleb's hateful gaze. "She better in bed than my sister?"

Caleb lunged and knocked him to the ground, then straddled his body, pinning Lucas beneath him. He'd taken all he could. "Leave Waynesville an' never come back. Hear me?"

Lucas's eyes pinched almost shut. "What you gonna do if I don't?"

"I'll tell Vincent the truth. That you pulled the trigger on Ableman."

"You do, an' I'll tell your wife 'bout Lily an' Noah."

Breathing hard, Caleb stared at him. No doubt, he'd do it without giving it a second thought. For several long moments, he remained atop the boy, then slowly climbed off him and got to his feet.

Once again, Lucas stood and brushed off his clothes. "Guess we'll *both* keep our secrets. Now, if you don't mind, Vincent's waitin' for me. We're checkin' 'round town to see who's gonna *entertain* us tonight."

"Go home, Lucas. 'Fore it's too late."

Lucas splayed his arms wide. "I *am* home." The boy strutted off, cocky as ever. Not one tiny chink had dented the boy's armor.

Caleb had someone else to add to his list of guilt. In a roundabout way, he'd helped push Lucas in Vincent's direction. It was true he'd not paid the boy as much attention as he should've once he and Lily had professed their feelings for each other. She'd been all he could think about, and that hadn't changed.

Every part of Caleb ached, but at least now he knew for sure. He had a son he'd never be able to see.

Men weren't supposed to cry, yet tears filled his eyes. He gazed heavenward through a cloudy pool.

Are you still punishin' me?

He'd never managed to wash away the memory of being in Lily's arms. Loving on her with every part of himself.

Their love had created a child.

It ain't fair.

All he'd ever wanted was to atone for killing his brother. In doing so, he ruined the life he could've had.

Broken and numb, he trudged toward home.

CHAPTER 12

The bright sun gleamed through Lily's bedroom window. She sat on a cushioned bench and leaned against the wall. Though she gazed toward the outdoors, she wasn't actually looking at anything. Her mind lay elsewhere.

She clutched a cup of tea that had cooled completely. August temperatures were too warm to be drinking hot beverages, but her aunt always insisted on afternoon tea. So did Mrs. Gottlieb.

If only Lily could be with her tutor and not here, but her lessons were only held Monday through Friday, and being Saturday, Lily remained stuck in her room. She'd prefer to *live* with Mrs. Gottlieb, where she felt comfortable being herself without being chided. And even if the woman reprimanded her, it was done in a tender manner. Here—though not as frequently as when she'd first arrived—her aunt scowled in such a hateful way.

Family wasn't supposed to behave like that, yet Lily had given up on changing her aunt's feelings toward her. As for Uncle Stuart, he'd said little more than ten words to her since the first dinner they'd shared.

A light rap on her door brought her out of her dismal thoughts.

Evie poked her head into the room. "May I come in?"

Lily shifted on the seat and faced her. "Of course, you may." After a month of training, the words came easily.

Evie took two steps forward, then curtsied. "You chose the perfect dress for tonight's meal, Miss Lily."

"Thank you." Lily ran her hands over the bountiful blue fabric. The dress might look nice, but she wished she could wear something cooler and not so constricting around her neck.

Evie studied every move she made. "Are you nervous?"

"*No.*" Lily sat tall and folded her hands on her lap. "Should I be?"

"Well . . ." The poor girl appeared a bit befuddled and anxiously wrung her hands. "You're aware how important tonight's meal is, aren't you?"

"Important? Won't it be like all the others? Good food and no decent conversation?"

Evie stared at the floor, then slowly lifted her head. "You don't like it here, do you?"

"I'm lonely. I miss my *real* family. Especially my sister." *An' my baby.* Just thinking about Noah brought on tears, so she quickly shifted her focus. "I'd hoped you an' I could be friends, but you've ignored me almost as much as Uncle Stuart."

"I'm sorry." Evie stepped even closer. "But, your aunt . . ."

"Told you to pay me no mind, right?" Feeling sorry for herself wasn't in Lily's nature, and though she'd changed a great deal, that was one aspect of her life she wouldn't succumb to. She had to remain strong to retain her self-respect, so she pushed down her tears. After all, the world overflowed with many less fortunate people.

Evie fidgeted with her apron. "Mrs. Clark didn't exactly tell me to *ignore* you, but . . ." She nodded at the edge of the bed. "Mind if I sit?"

"Please do."

With a long, loud sigh, Evie perched on the bed. "I *wanted* to be your friend. But you must understand how things are done here. You and I aren't in the same class of people. I'm simply the help, but you're heir to this estate."

"Huh?" The brief slip in Lily's vernacular couldn't be helped.

Evie's face flushed red. "You didn't know?"

"How could I know sumthin' like that? I thought they hated me."

The embarrassment displayed in Evie's cheeks faded. Her eyes widened with fear. "I shouldn't have said any of this. But I thought you were well aware. Tonight's dinner is your final test. If you do well, Mrs. Clark said you'd be taken to Sunday services. You'll likely meet your intended."

Lily clutched her belly. Eating would *not* be easy by any means. "My intended?"

Evie glanced nervously over her shoulder, then leaned closer. "I overheard them talking. There's a young man Mr. Clark has spoken of more than once, who's been trying to find a wife. Archibald . . . something or other."

"*Archibald*?" A name like that alone made him miserable-sounding.

"Yes. I assume he's quite rich." Evie gnawed her lower lip, then smiled. "I envy you. One day soon, you'll have your own fantastic home. And someday, you'll inherit more money than you'll be able to spend in a lifetime. Isn't that wonderful?"

Lily faced the window and carefully considered what to say. Mrs. Gottlieb's training had sunk in deep. "Money's not everythin'. All the gold in the world can't fill an empty heart."

She startled when Evie laid a hand on her shoulder. She'd not even noticed the girl rise from the bed.

"Maybe Archibald won't be so bad," Evie whispered. "Perhaps *he* can fill your heart."

Lily looked up at her, but couldn't speak. A man already resided there, yet it did little good. He hovered in her life like a ghost who haunted her memories. His *physical* being embraced another woman.

"And when you have children," Evie went on, "you won't be lonely at all."

Lily's tears returned with vengeance and trickled down her cheeks.

"Oh, Miss Lily." Evie's brow furrowed deep. "Please, don't cry. I'm sure Archibald is a lovely man." She worked her lower lip, breathing hard. "I should've been smart and kept quiet about all of this."

Noah . . .

Lily mindlessly rubbed a hand over her stomach, and her tears kept falling. Though she gazed toward the window once again, her clouded vision nearly blinded her.

"Oh, dear." Evie inched backward toward the door. "Mrs. Clark will be furious if she knows I made you cry."

Lily wiped her eyes and stood. "She won't know. I'll wash my face an' come down for supper at the proper time." She took hold of Evie's trembling hand. "I'm glad you told me 'bout Archibald, so stop frettin'. I don't know what Aunt Helen an' Uncle Stuart are lookin' for t'night, but I'm gonna be myself. If that's not good enough for *Archibald*, then so be it."

Evie's lips quivered into a smile. "Any man would be fortunate to have you for a wife."

Lily forced her own smile, but doubted it would be convincing. "Thank you." She knew of only one man she wanted.

After a quick curtsy, Evie scurried away.

* * *

With a freshly washed face, Lily strode into the dining room like she belonged there. She walked tall, lifted her chin, and drew her shoulders back.

Aunt Helen was already seated in her usual place. As Lily approached *her* seat, Uncle Stuart pulled out her chair, nodded, and helped her sit by holding onto her arm.

"Thank you," she said, politely dipping her head.

Once Uncle Stuart sat, Lily daintily lifted her napkin from the plate and covered her lap. She then folded her hands atop it and waited to be served.

Her uncle positioned his own napkin. "You look lovely tonight."

"Thank you."

"Yes," Aunt Helen added. "I believe blue is your best color. It goes well with your hair, which I must say is perfectly in place."

"Thank you." Lily felt like one of those birds that only uttered simple phrases. She needed to say something more or she might go mad. "I did it myself. I'm glad you approve." Though she couldn't manage the net without Evie's help, she'd learned how to pin her hair up in a shapely manner.

"Of course, I approve. Otherwise, I wouldn't have made the remark." Aunt Helen's lips pursed, then she nonchalantly sipped from her water glass.

"Truthfully," Uncle Stuart said. "You're stunning. Those earrings add an elegance to your appearance I didn't expect." He broadly smiled, and Lily thought she might faint. Who were these people?

Aunt Helen let out a weird little laugh. "Nothing like the girl who arrived a month ago."

Lily jutted her chin high. "I'm the same girl." She glanced downward, then looked from aunt to uncle. "I'm merely packaged differently."

"That you are." Uncle Stuart's brows rose to his hairline. "Tomorrow, I intend to thank Mrs. Gottlieb personally. Things are most definitely coming together as I'd hoped." He rubbed his hands against each other and grinned. His behavior reminded Lily of how her brothers acted when waiting for a sweet treat.

What *things* was he referring to?

If he truly intended to marry her off to this Archibald person, what was in it for him? A nice pat on the back from the boy's father? *No.* There had to be more to it.

Lily couldn't mention any of what Evie had told her, but she could easily delve deeper into what her uncle had said. "So, you plan to see Mrs. Gottlieb on a *Sunday?*"

Mrs. Winters entered the room and began setting food on each plate. No longer did she place the bowls on the table for self-service. Lily had graduated to being waited on, and she didn't like it. Not one bit. The dear woman rarely made eye contact anymore.

"We see Mrs. Gottlieb *every* Sunday," Uncle Stuart said, utterly ignoring Mrs. Winters. "She attends our church."

"Oh. I wasn't aware."

"That's where I first made her acquaintance," Aunt Helen said. "I'd heard from others in the congregation that she worked wonders with young women. So, once I knew she was a decent Christian, I employed her to help Evie, and then *you.* She's never disappointed me. Especially now. If your mother could see you . . ." She held a hand to her breast, smiled, then scowled at Mrs. Winters. "You overcooked the meat. Take it back to the kitchen and bring me something edible."

"Yes'm." Mrs. Winters speared Aunt Helen's piece of steak and put it back on a large platter.

Uncle Stuart sternly pointed at his, and she took it as well. The sweet woman looked as if she might cry.

Lily glanced at the food on *her* plate. It wasn't overcooked, it was burnt to a crisp. Mrs. Winters never served food this way.

Sumthin' must be troublin' her.

She tried to take Lily's steak, but Lily held her hand above it, smiled, and shook her head. "Mine's just fine. Thank you, Mrs. Winters."

The woman's chin trembled and she bobbed her head, then rushed from the room with the platter.

"Very good," Uncle Stuart mumbled under his breath. He bent toward Aunt Helen. "She passed the final test."

What?

How could her behavior toward Mrs. Winters be part of the *test?*

"Excuse me." Lily bolstered her courage. "What test are you talkin' 'bout?"

He beamed. "Listen to her, Helen. Every trace of that vulgar dialect is gone. She sounds refined. Still southern, of course, but in a desirable way. I find her accent quite enthralling."

And Lily found *his* manner quite *disturbing.*

"Don't become too enamored, dear." Aunt Helen laid her hand atop his on the table. "I may resort to jealousy."

"*Never.*" He raised her hand to his lips and kissed it, then stared at Lily. "You've made me happy and extraordinarily proud. I'll be pleased to present you as my niece."

"An' not just by marriage?" Lily couldn't help herself and *had* to say it.

He laughed and shook a finger. "You're a sharp one. I shouldn't have doubted Helen's judgment. She had faith in you from the start. I, however, had reservations. But now . . ." He splayed both hands wide. "Look at you. You're ripe for marriage."

"Marriage?" *Ripe* didn't set well with her either.

"Yes. Every young woman's desire, isn't it?"

"Reckon—" Lily slapped a hand to her mouth. Aside from *ain't*, reckon was the one word she'd had the hardest time letting go. "That is, I would assume so."

Uncle Stuart laughed even harder.

Lily prodded the meat with her fork. "You didn't tell me 'bout the test. Why did it matter that I kept my food?"

Aunt Helen leaned forward. "In all situations, you must be polite. If you're served something undesirable, you should eat it regardless."

"But, *you* weren't polite."

"No, I wasn't." She sat tall and proud. "I purposefully behaved that way, as did Stuart. We needed to see how you would react."

Lily thought about it for a brief moment. "Not only did it hurt seein' Mrs. Winters so sad, I was raised to eat everythin' on my plate. You may not realize it, but sometimes food can be scarce."

Her aunt said nothing. She merely sat there with her ever-present better-than-thou expression. She was probably thinking about what a poor provider Lily's pa was.

Uncle Stuart turned in his chair. "Mrs. Winters! You may bring out our proper food!"

A sad thing when folks could afford to ruin perfectly good meat, simply to conduct a nonsensical test.

Mrs. Winters bustled in carrying another platter. After removing Lily's burned steak, she set down a perfectly cooked piece on each plate.

Unless Mrs. Winters had lived a life as a stage actress prior to becoming a cook, Lily believed wholeheartedly she'd been deeply bothered by being told to serve inadequate food.

Folks in these parts certainly had unusual ways.

Lily tried all she could to catch the woman's eye to offer a comforting smile, but Mrs. Winters never looked at her, not even when placing her food.

Lily ate slowly, just as Mrs. Gottlieb had instructed. She'd said rapidly devouring one's dinner made a human no better than a savage beast. Women needed to show their daintiness at *all* times, which included while eating.

There'd been artful lessons in all Lily had learned, and what stood out the most was the difference between men and women.

A woman was expected to be delicate and soft, whereas men were to be strong and the providers for the home. Unless a woman became a widow. Sometimes then, she'd have to rely on herself to make ends meet, similar to the way Mrs. Gottlieb had.

Or, as in Rebecca's case, she could only hope to marry another man.

My man.

Lily had made her relatives happy, but maybe it wasn't a good thing. Now she'd be forced to meet someone her uncle intended her to marry. If she didn't care for the man, her life would be even more wretched.

She could only hope she'd meet someone like Caleb.

Handsome. Kind. Giving.

But she wasn't worthy of a man like that. Her chastity had been taken. No man would want her if he knew.

Her ma had told her to remain hushed about the circumstances and keep it to herself. To never tell a soul—especially Aunt Helen. The family shame would be unbearable if her aunt discovered the truth.

Worse yet, marriage meant giving up any possibility of being Noah's ma. Lily would have to live and die with the secret and *without him.*

Archibald something-or-other might be rich, but all the wealth in the world couldn't replace the loss of her son.

CHAPTER 13

It made no sense for Lily to have butterflies in her belly simply going to church. She'd been involved with worship at the Baptist congregation for as long as she could remember—with the exception of the years they'd canceled services during the war.

Fear of the unknown Lutheran practices had to be the reason for her unease, regardless of the fact they all worshipped the same God. *He* was the only being she needed to impress. However, the watchful eye of her aunt and uncle troubled her more than the good Lord.

The stifling carriage didn't help.

Lily rapidly fluttered her hand in front of her hot face, but it did little good.

Aunt Helen pointed at Lily's wrist. "Use your fan, my dear."

"Oh. Yes." She'd forgotten about the gift she'd been given along with another new dress. The delicate fan had a silk strap that encircled Lily's wrist. She slipped it over her hand, then opened the item wide and gently moved it back and forth.

"Much better." Aunt Helen brought out her own fan. "Many ladies in the church use these to cool themselves." She smiled and glanced at Uncle Stuart. "Doesn't Lily look splendid? I told you this shade of blue would suit her just as well as the other."

Uncle Stuart had taken the spot beside Lily rather than next to his wife. Dots of perspiration beaded on his forehead. It wasn't surprising. After all, he'd worn a solid black suit.

He turned his head and scanned her from top to bottom, then placed two fingers under her chin and studied her face. "It softens her appearance. Perfect for Sunday services."

Aunt Helen beamed. "That is exactly what *I* thought."

Lily forced a simple smile. She liked the dress because it was lighter in weight than the darker blue garment. But it still had a high neckline with similar itchy lace trim. She missed the plain comfortable dresses her ma had made.

Uncle Stuart angled his knees toward her and shifted his body. "Now, remember. We'll be introducing you to important people. Say very little, but if they should want to converse, keep your words concise. And please, *think* before you speak."

Lily fluttered her fan a few times, then snapped it shut and smiled. "I always do."

His eyes rested on hers a little longer than she felt appropriate.

Aunt Helen cleared her throat. "We've arrived."

Good.

Lily needed to get out of the carriage and distance herself from her uncle. *If* that was possible.

David opened the door and extended his hand to her. Even that felt out of place. In the past, he'd always helped her aunt first.

Lily set her hand in his and stepped out. Once firmly on the ground, she released him. "Thank you." She gave him her best smile, then nearly buckled when he returned it.

"You're very welcome, Miss Lily."

She gulped, took a few steps back, and waited for the others. Though she'd been determined to make him smile, now that he'd done it, it didn't feel right. Had she changed that much?

Her aunt moved beside her and examined her again. "I'm glad Evie did your hair this morning. The chignon is stunning, yet refined." She cupped her hand under Lily's netted hair. "Excellent."

"Leave the girl be," Uncle Stuart muttered, joining them. "I won't have you making her nervous. This is too important."

"Yes, dear." Aunt Helen snapped her chin high, then headed off without them.

"Shall we?" Uncle Stuart held out his arm and eyed Lily.

She hesitated. "Is it *proper* for me to take your arm?"

"I'm your uncle, and I'm escorting you to services. Nothing more. People will view it as a kind gesture. They'll see that I'm doing what I can to make you comfortable in an unfamiliar setting." His arm remained rigid, waiting.

Tentatively, she linked her hand into the crook of his elbow.

"Good." Uncle Stuart patted the top of her hand. "Now stand tall and walk with me."

"Yes, sir."

He cast a half-grin, then strode up the walkway like he'd won a prize.

Lily finally took her mind off him and studied her surroundings. "Mercy," she whispered. "That's your church?"

"Yes. Trinity Lutheran. Isn't it grand?"

She managed a nod, but couldn't say another word. *Grand* didn't come close to describing the building. It stood twice as high as her small church in the cove and was four times the size. Elaborate spires reached toward the heavens as if pointing the way to God. A beautiful cross rested on the highest pinnacle.

Lily tipped her head back to take it all in, then lost her footing and tightly grasped her uncle's arm.

He chuckled. "Best to keep your eyes forward."

She nodded and loosened her hold.

When they reached the arched front door, they found Aunt Helen waiting for them. "I can see you're already impressed." She pushed herself between her husband and Lily. "Come with me and I'll show you the interior."

"Take care of our girl," Uncle Stuart said. "I need to speak with Baxter, then I'll join you in our pew." He walked off without a word from Aunt Helen.

She took Lily by the hand, grinning like Alice's Cheshire cat. "The sanctuary is immaculate. And the pulpit has detailed carvings of Matthew, Mark, Luke, *and* John."

"How did the woodworkers know what those men looked like?"

Her aunt blinked rapidly several times, then waved a hand. "They simply knew."

And you *don't.*

Aunt Helen's confident air diminished for a mere moment. With a little laugh, she continued into the sanctuary.

As they walked, many folks passed by. They smiled and politely nodded. Lily did the same, while her aunt strutted.

Lily leaned close to her. "Why don't you introduce me to them?" she whispered.

"I'll present you when there's someone worthy of your acquaintance." Aunt Helen also kept her voice low, smiling amidst her words. "Mrs. Gottlieb, for instance."

The dear woman hastened toward them.

"But, I already know *her.*"

"That you do." Aunt Helen released Lily's hand and grabbed onto Mrs. Gottlieb's. "It's wonderful to see you."

"You as well." Mrs. Gottlieb beamed at Lily. "You're lovely, my dear."

"Thank you, ma'am." Lily graciously dipped her head.

The two older women chatted about some sort of upcoming women's supper, but Lily paid them little attention. Her eyes roamed the vast sanctuary, where folks kept pouring in. Hundreds could fit on the lower level and even more in the balconies.

As for the famed sculpted pulpit, its enormity alone had Lily mesmerized. It was as big around as the woodshed back home.

When she finally looked away from the carvings, her eyes came to rest on a young man. Though his appearance was nothing like Caleb—in fact, quite the *opposite*—she found him attractive. He didn't have one strand of his wavy blond hair out of place, and his facial features were carved as perfectly as the pulpit.

He wore a well-tailored black suit, similar to Uncle Stuart's. His unbuttoned coat revealed a sharp vest underneath. A gold chain dangled from the vest pocket and linked through one of its buttonholes.

Lily's breath hitched when his eyes met hers.

He grinned, pulled on the chain, and flipped open a watch. After glancing at it, he leaned close to a man beside him and nodded toward a pew. They both headed in that direction, but he paused and gave Lily a pleasant smile, then continued on to their seat.

"Oh, my," Lily muttered.

"Is something troubling you?" Her aunt stared in the direction she'd been looking. "Oh. I see . . ." She took hold of both Lily's arms and shifted her around to face her. "That boy isn't for you."

Lily nonchalantly tipped her head to one side. "What boy?"

Her aunt's eyes pinched into slits, reminding Lily of her ma. The two were definitely sisters. "The one who's gazing this way again."

Lily spun her head around. *Yep. He's lookin' right at me.* She turned to her aunt. "You know him?"

"Of course, I do."

Mrs. Gottlieb tittered. "She knows *everyone*, my dear." She patted Lily's hand. "I must leave you and take my seat."

"Don't you wanna sit with us?" Lily asked.

"Thank you, but no. You'll find we all have our favorite pew."
She wandered away and took a seat, three rows back from the
front.

Aunt Helen guided Lily to a pew on the opposite side, closer
to the back. Soon after they sat, Uncle Stuart joined them and
took his place on the other side of her aunt.

Lily folded her hands on her lap and sat poised as she'd been
instructed. Loud organ music startled her, but she soon found it
soothing.

"Lily noticed Zachary Danforth," her aunt said in a less-than-
pleasant manner. Though she spoke to Stuart, Lily easily heard her.

Her uncle leaned forward and peered around Aunt Helen,
looking Lily in the eyes. "Forget that boy. Hear me?"

Their behavior in the past had been odd, but this surmounted
it. "How can I forget someone I've not yet met?"

Uncle Stuart's eyes narrowed. "Every young woman in this
congregation has tried to catch his eye. He may be handsome and
wealthy, but he's not for you. There's someone else. You'll meet
him after the service."

Archibald.

"Is he here now?"

"Yes. But it's too late for introductions. The service is about to
start."

No sooner had he said it, and the organ played even louder.
Everyone stood.

Aunt Helen passed Lily a hymnal, flipped it open, and tapped
on the page. "Follow it as best you can. It will take time, but
you'll eventually learn it."

Lily nodded. Yes, she could learn anything if she set her mind
to it. If not, she wouldn't be standing here.

They sat and stood, up and down, over and over again. Some
of the singing sounded more like chanting. She'd never heard
anything like it. But, as strange as it was, the melody was quite

beautiful. Finally, during the sermon, everyone remained seated, much to Lily's relief.

Her mind wandered, as did her eyes.

Though she'd been told he wasn't for her, Zachary Danforth kept turning his head and looking her way. And of course, she couldn't help but admire *him*. From what her uncle had said, *all* the young women did.

If smart, she'd ignore every male who came anywhere near her for the rest of her life. Her heart would certainly appreciate it. Zachary was probably one of those kinds of men she despised. Handsome and enticing, but a devil below the surface. The sort of man who would take a woman's virtue and go on his merry way. Then again, hadn't Caleb done that very thing?

Just thinking it made her heart ache. She didn't want to believe Caleb was that type of man. If he'd simply been a wretch with no genuine feelings for her, she couldn't have fallen in love with him. Could she?

As for Zachary Danforth, unlike *Archibald*, at least his name sounded appealing. *And* he was a church-goer. A man with his soul in the proper place couldn't be *all* bad.

Mrs. Gottlieb had said *many* men would want to court Lily. If that turned out to be true, then why should she have to settle for some stranger her uncle had decided was the one for her? She should have *some* say in the matter.

Besides, the way Uncle Stuart had been acting lately, Lily could swear the man wanted her for himself. But if he ever laid a hand on her, she'd give him what for. A knee to the groin might suffice, though it would likely land her on the streets.

She hoped it wouldn't come to that. The next time he said something inappropriate, she'd speak her mind. It had to be done. As much as she disliked her aunt, no woman deserved having a husband whose eyes wandered.

Once again, Zachary peered over his shoulder, but this time received a nudge from the man beside him.

Must be his pa, settin' him straight.

Lily opened her fan and covered her mouth, so no one would see her grin. She had no idea where it had come from, but it felt good to genuinely smile.

Also in Zachary's pew were three women. Presumably his ma and sisters. Then again, Lily hated to assume things, but they favored each other and were probably related.

The preacher's loud voice boomed through the huge room. Sound carried well in this large church.

I should be payin' attention to him instead a worryin' over Uncle Stuart, Zachary Danforth, an' Archibald sumthin' or other.

Her life had become more complicated since she'd been allowed in public. She'd been set in a world of strangers with odd customs. But one that had become hers. She'd have to find a way to fit in, or be forever miserable.

Amen.

Chapter 14

Zachary had heard rumors about a niece who'd come to live with the Clarks, yet no one had uttered a word about her beauty. He'd not met a single woman who came anywhere close to her fresh, stunning appearance.

The confidence she carried enthralled him more so than her features. Though he had to admit, being able to admire a pretty face made life more enjoyable.

"Keep your eyes forward," his father muttered from the side of his mouth. "And pay attention to the sermon."

"Yes, sir." Zachary let out a long breath and stared at the preacher. Pastor Schaller spoke with authority and compassion— as well as remnants of a German accent—yet today, Zachary couldn't wrap his mind around any of the sermon.

The beautiful blonde some distance behind him held his brain captive.

When the service ended, he hastened from his pew in the direction of hers. He scanned the multitude of faces, yet she'd disappeared.

His father tapped him on the shoulder. "She's not for you, son."

He spun around. "Who?"

"My vision is by no means impaired." The man jerked his head toward the back of the church. "I saw you gawking at the Clark's niece. Yes, she's beautiful, but she's spoken for."

"But . . ." Zachary felt a tightness in his throat he'd never experienced before. "How can she be spoken for when she's only been here a short while?" Murmurs surrounded them, but he shut out every sound. He wanted to know more about the girl.

"Stuart Clark made an arrangement with Baxter Jones."

"What? He's too old for her."

His father laughed, then placed a firm hand on Zachary's shoulder. "Not Baxter. His son, Archibald."

"Good Lord," Zachary mumbled.

His father's eyes widened. "Remember where you are."

"I've not forgotten," Zachary whispered. "But how could Mr. Clark be so cruel? And why would such a lovely woman agree to marry Archibald?"

"As Shakespeare said more than once, love is blind."

"It would have to be where Archibald is concerned." The thought of that beautiful girl with Archibald Jones sickened Zachary.

His father held up a single finger. "Mind yourself. And for God's sake, be kind."

Jean Marie Hastings sauntered up beside Zachary. She was pretty in her own right and old enough for courting, but Jean Marie lacked brains. She couldn't carry on a conversation with a broomstick.

"Happy Sunday." She tittered and swayed back and forth like a little girl. "It's a pretty day."

"Yes, it is." Zachary smiled, which only amplified her giggles.

When he glanced at his father, the man rolled his eyes. "We need to go. Your mother and sisters are waiting."

Zachary gave him a curt nod, then turned to the girl. "I'm sorry, Jean Marie. I don't have time to talk. I hope you'll enjoy this *pretty* day." He cast his best smile, then walked away with his father, followed by Jean Marie's incessant giggling.

Once outside, Zachary found himself agreeing with her. The day was glorious. Although very warm, Zachary appreciated the clear blue cloudless sky. A perfect day for a swim.

Another more interesting shade of blue caught his eye; the back of the Clark's niece's dress. She stood beside Mrs. Clark, and they seemed to be waiting for someone. Perhaps *Mr.* Clark.

Zachary gestured to them. "Father, do you know the niece's name?"

The man gazed upward. "I'm trying to recall . . . it was some sort of flower." His brow creased, then he smiled. "Oh, yes. *Lily.* Fitting, don't you agree?"

"Yes. A gorgeous flower destined to be bound to a senseless cabbage."

His father firmly folded his arms over his chest and shook his head. "I hope the money I'm spending on your education will render more than this poor attitude. And since you're studying to be a doctor, you'll have to develop a decent bedside manner. Look at the good in people, not their downfalls."

"I *do* see good in people. And in her I see someone who deserves more than him."

"Someone like *you?*" His father huffed. "You've had your choice of more than a dozen young women in this congregation alone, yet you've shunned every one of them. What are you waiting for, Zachary? Your mother and I would like to see you married before your sisters. After all, you're the eldest and nearly twenty-two. Will you only be satisfied with a woman you've been told you can't have?"

"You don't understand, Father." Zachary peered at Lily. "I want a woman who stimulates me."

The man grunted.

Zachary butted against his shoulder. "Not the way *you're* thinking. But of course, that matters as well. I'm referring to intellectual stimulation. Something in her eyes tells me she has many important things to say."

"And she'll say them to Archibald Jones. Don't interfere."

"Why?" He splayed his arms wide. "They're not engaged. Or at least, it hasn't been formally announced. Until it happens, why can't I get to know her? It would trouble me greatly to discover that the perfect woman slipped through my fingers."

"No woman is perfect. Not even your mother." His father motioned to the waiting carriage. "As much as I want to see you married, I don't wish to damage my working relationship with Stuart Clark. He's invested in the union of his niece to the Jones boy."

They walked slowly to their ride. Zachary's mother and sisters were already inside.

"Invested?" Zachary asked. "How so?"

"All I can say is, if and *when* the marriage takes place, Stuart will have something new to export. People in the northeast, as well as overseas, enjoy fine tobacco. Baxter Jones has abundant crops and needs a means to ship them."

"And that's where Stuart Clark comes in. Right, Father?"

"Yes. The deal will be made when Baxter's unappealing son has a bride." He set one foot in the carriage, then looked over his shoulder and placed a finger to his lips. "Don't repeat any of this. Understood?"

"Yes, sir." Zachary glanced a final time at Lily.

He doubted she had any notion that her life had been so dreadfully manipulated.

* * *

Even Lily's fan didn't help beneath the blistering rays of sunshine.

"I'm burning up," Aunt Helen fussed. "What's taking Stuart so long?"

Lily shrugged. "I don't know. Why can't we wait in the carriage? David arrived ten minutes ago."

"We must wait here. Introductions are to be made."

"With who?"

Her aunt ignored her and kept fluttering her fan. It stopped abruptly. Her sour face changed completely and she stood tall, as if nothing bothered her one bit. "Mind your manners now, Lily. This is important."

Lily turned her attention to where her aunt had been staring.

Oh, my.

Uncle Stuart approached, along with two other men. The younger of the pair walked with his head down and trudged along, seemingly unhappy. Both men were finely dressed, though exceptionally fat. The strained buttons of their suit coats looked ready to pop. Truthfully, Lily had never seen such large men.

"Lily, my dear," Uncle Stuart said. "I'd like you to meet Mr. Baxter Jones, and his son, Archibald."

Archibald *Jones*? Not a difficult last name to remember, but if this man was to be her intended . . .

Lily's belly churned worse than before the service. It was just as she'd feared. She'd been groomed for marriage to someone no one else would ever want.

She'd been raised not to judge folks by their appearance, but she couldn't see anything appealing about Archibald. Maybe once he spoke, she'd find he was kind. Good-hearted. Possibly even *intelligent*.

She curtsied. "I'm pleased to meet you."

The older man nudged his son. "Say something. Miss Lily has greeted you."

Ever-so-slowly, Archibald lifted his head. "Hello." He tentatively smiled and revealed heavily stained teeth. His pudgy cheeks pushed up the skin under his eyes so much it nearly closed them, then his mouth snapped shut and his head dropped back down.

The poor man was not only unattractive, he had no confidence.

"We've asked Baxter and Archibald to join us for dinner this evening," Uncle Stuart said. "I'm sure you young people will enjoy getting to know one another. After all, Lily, you know very few people your age in St. Louis. Isn't that right?"

"Yes, sir." She folded her hands and prayed lightning would strike her down so she wouldn't have to carry on one more day. No such luck on a cloudless day.

"My boy loves Mrs. Winters cooking," Baxter said. "Don't you, son?"

"Yes. It's good." Archibald dug into his suit pocket and yanked out a handkerchief. He dabbed at his sweat-covered forehead, which drew Lily's attention to his hair. The shade of red reminded her of Lucas's hair. He also had similar freckles.

"We'll see you at six o'clock sharp," Aunt Helen said. "I've asked Mrs. Winters to bake a cherry pie for dessert. I know that's your favorite, Archibald."

He nodded a few times, but didn't speak.

A good thing. Lily didn't care to look at his teeth.

Mr. Jones stood tall. "It's been a pleasure meeting you, Miss Lily."

"Thank you. It'll be nice to see you again this evenin'." The words spilled from her lips. Her lessons in courtesy made her aunt and uncle happy, but she wanted to shrivel.

How had her life come to this?

The two round men waddled off, and Uncle Stuart took Aunt Helen's hand and led her to the waiting carriage.

Lily's feet didn't want to move. It wasn't until her aunt waved her over that she managed to budge from her spot on the church walkway.

When the horses began plodding along the road, Lily shut her eyes and leaned back in the seat.

"You did exceptionally well," Uncle Stuart said. "Everyone I spoke with was impressed by you."

Lily inched her eyes open and met his gaze. "I'm glad you're pleased."

He smiled almost too broadly. "Tonight, wear the dark blue dress."

"Yes, sir." She bolstered her courage. "Will I be left alone with him?"

Her aunt laughed. "Not yet. It wouldn't be proper."

Thank goodness.

At least one small prayer had been answered.

CHAPTER 15

August heat normally made Violet weary, but their small white church sat situated amongst trees that helped keep it cool. Something she felt grateful for. Perspiring bodies sitting tightly together in wooden pews offended her nose and often distracted from the sermon. Today, a nice cool breeze blew in through the open backdoor.

It had taken several harsh sermons from Brother Davis to get the parishioners right with each other. Some hard feelings lingered over which side of the war the cove families had favored. All in all, the reverend reminded them that they were all children of God and needed to put their differences behind them and love each other as Christians.

A good thing, too.

For two consecutive Sundays, Violet had hoped to see Gideon Myers. He'd fought with the Union army—the exact opposite of her pa. The previous week, she'd talked to Gideon's ma and was assured their family held no ill feelings toward them. But the dear woman told her Gideon wasn't feeling well. Violet hadn't felt comfortable prying, but assumed it had to be more than the common cold. Gideon hadn't been seen publicly since his return from the boarding house.

Violet wore her pretty blue floral-print birthday dress for today's service. Surrounded by mostly women and children, no one paid her much attention. Still, she sat tall in the pew.

Waiting.

Hoping.

Mrs. Myers slowly passed by. *Alone.* Not even her husband had come today. They'd both been poor-spirited after losing two of their sons in the war.

The dear white-haired woman hung her head low as she walked, and her shoulders slumped. The exuberant woman she'd once been no longer existed.

It broke Violet's heart. Every life in the country had been damaged by the war in one way or another.

As songs were sung and prayers were said, Violet stood and sat, exactly the way she should. But her heart wasn't in it—and not just from aching over poor Mrs. Myers. Though Violet knew it was wrong to attend church for the purpose of socializing and with the hopes of meeting a man, she couldn't help herself. Each day that passed, she further declined in age, making her chances of finding a man even harder.

After the final *amen*, she hastened from the pew. Her folks lingered behind with Noah, chatting up a storm with other parishioners. Her brothers stayed close to them, but she was determined to talk to Mrs. Myers again. This time, she'd be more persistent.

She slowed when she reached the wood steps, then carefully raised her skirt and descended.

Reverend Davis dipped his head. "Mornin', Miss Violet."

She in turn, slightly bobbed her head. "Mornin'. Fine sermon, Brother Davis."

"Thank you. An' what in particular stood out to you?"

She gulped. She'd not heard one word of the sermon and was simply being polite. In the past, he'd only greeted her and never asked questions.

That's what I get for goin' beyond 'mornin'.'

Her face heated and she prayed she'd not turned color. "The part 'bout God's never-endin' love, of course." It seemed safe to say. Whenever she *had* paid attention, he always preached on it.

He smiled and lifted a single brow. "Of course. I hope you have a pleasant day."

"You, too." She scurried away before he could pry any deeper, then spotted Mrs. Myers and hastened after her.

"Mrs. Myers!" Violet nearly tripped on a rock, but caught herself before she fell.

The woman stopped walking and faced her. "Are you all right? You almost took a tumble."

"Yes'm. I'm fine." She smoothed her skirt and lifted her head high. "How's Gideon today? Better, I hope."

His ma's face fell. "Some."

Violet chose to be bold and rested a hand on the woman's arm. "You can be honest with me. I've known Gideon most all my life. Can't you tell me what's truly wrong with him?"

Mrs. Myers glanced around them as if she feared being overheard. But no one was paying them any mind. "You know very well what's ailin' my boy. He lost a leg for God's sake."

"An' my pa lost an arm." Violet was determined not to lose her *nerve*. It had taken her pa a great while to overcome self-pity, but she knew it could be done, and she wanted to help Gideon. "The war was awful. But Gideon should be thankful he's alive. He's young an' has his whole life ahead a him."

"What kind a life can he have *maimed*?" Mrs. Myers' chin quivered.

Please don't cry. Violet stood tall. "A fine one."

Her words didn't help. Mrs. Myers dug into a satchel at her wrist and withdrew a hankie. She dabbed at her eyes. "I don't see how."

"*I* can help." The words easily tumbled out of Violet's mouth.

"How?"

"Me an' ma made some fine cornbread biscuits yesterday. An' you know Ma makes the best apple butter in these parts. I assume Gideon still has an appetite."

"Yes, but how—"

"I'll bring the muffins with me an' pay him a visit." Violet cast her best smile.

Mrs. Myers laid her palm to Violet's cheek. "Even as lovely as you are, I doubt he'll see you."

Violet tipped her head down. No one had called her lovely before—aside from that disgusting Sergeant Douglas, and *his* praise didn't matter one lick.

She took a large breath and boldly lifted her head again. "I can be rather persuasive when I wanna be. Lily taught me how. As you know, my sister never shied away from nothin'."

"Yes, I'm well aware. We all miss her. I was sad to hear she'd left the cove."

"I miss her more than anyone. She was my best friend." She pushed another smile to her lips. "So, what time would you like me to come by?"

"He might be hateful."

Lucas immediately came to mind. "I'm good at copin' with bad behavior."

"All right. Come by at two. I'll make certain he's dressed."

"Thank you. I'd rather not see him in his underwear."

The woman's eyes grew wide.

"Forgive me. But as you know, I have three brothers who run 'round in their drawers more often than I'd like."

"Three?" Her head drew back. "Oh. Yes, since Lucas is gone."

Violet let out a small giggle to cover her blunder. "That's right. 'Sides, little Noah ain't runnin' 'round at all. He ain't even walkin' yet."

"He will soon. That's more than I can say for *my* boy."

Once again, Violet brought tears to the woman's eyes. "I aim to change that. He got a crutch?"

"Yes. But he don't use it."

"Hmm. I reckon I got my work cut out for me."

Mrs. Myers blew her nose, then stuffed the hankie into her bag. "You'd best be prepared for disappointment." Frowning, the woman walked away.

"See you at two!" Violet called out after her.

A single wave over the back of her head was all Mrs. Myers afforded her.

Violet's ma tapped her on the shoulder. "What was that all 'bout?"

"Gettin' me a husband." Violet grinned, then reached for Noah.

Her ma passed him over. "A husband? You ain't considerin' the Myers boy, are you?"

"Course I am. He caught my eye years ago. Reckon he's still just as fine. An' he was always decent-actin'. Exactly the kind a man I need."

"A one-*legged* man," her ma grumbled. "You can do better."

Violet swayed with Noah, undaunted by her ma's poor attitude. "There ain't much pickin's 'round here. 'Sides, lookin' back now, I think Gideon had a fancy for me. I didn't understand it then, but becomin' a woman has changed how I see things."

Her ma's demeanor worsened. She scowled and shook a finger. "Becomin' a woman got your sister in trouble," she hissed in a whisper. "That Myers boy may be missin' a leg, but I reckon he's got all his other parts. You go chasin' after him, an' you're bound to get in a mess. That's how harlots behave. Decent women wait for callers to approach *them*."

Violet patted Noah's back, glad he couldn't understand a word they were saying. "Gracious, Ma. You shouldn't talk like that. Gideon ain't that kind a man. But if I have to wait for him to come callin', I'll grow old an' die 'fore it ever happens. I'd think you'd *want* me to find a husband."

Finally, her ma's hard features softened. "I do. But after what happened to Lily, I'm terrified. We all thought Caleb was decent." She brushed her hand along Violet's cheek. "You've always been my *sweet* girl. I don't want you hurt like your sister. Or for that matter, burdened with a man what can't provide for you."

Memories of the night Lily birthed Noah came to mind. Her ma had been harsh then, too. Made her watch the entire ordeal to teach her a lesson.

"I won't let myself be hurt, an' I know full well Gideon has the ability to keep up the farm. He's simply feelin' too sorry for himself right now to see it."

"I hope you're right. You've watched how your pa struggles."

"That's why I know I'm fit to help Gideon." She offered her best smile. "An' Ma . . . I promise not to show any affections till we're properly married. All right?"

Her ma nodded, then half-smiled. "That's good." She jerked her head in the opposite direction. "Your pa's waitin' at the wagon with the boys. He sent me to fetch you. 'Fore we get over to them, tell me how you aim to get Gideon Myers to propose."

Violet stood tall. "Good food an' plenty a smiles."

Her ma eyed her, then took hold of her hand and squeezed. "That's how I got your pa."

They remained holding hands all the way to the wagon.

* * *

Gideon lay flat on his back and tossed a canvas ball into the air. He had nothing better to do.

The summer heat sweltered the small cabin, so he wore next-to-nothing, trying to make it bearable. But every day that passed, he grew more miserable than ever. Something he didn't think possible.

He regretted coming home. He'd been better off dying on the battlefield.

The door swung open, and his ma trudged in. She glanced his way, then quickly turned her head. "You best be gettin' some clothes on."

"Why? I ain't showin' nothin' you haven't seen before." He rubbed a hand over his knee, now nothing more than a nub that led to emptiness. "Reckon you just don't like lookin' at *this*."

She grabbed an apron from a peg on the wall and put it on over her Sunday church dress. "Stop feelin' sorry for yourself. I'm tired a hearin' it."

"Tired a *hearin'* it? Try livin' like this."

She sadly shook her head. "Least you're livin'. Can't say the same for your brothers." She yanked out a pot from a bottom cupboard, then slammed it down on the stovetop. "I'm makin' soup. You hungry?"

"S'pose so." He tossed the ball again. High in the air, then straight back down into his hands. He hated himself sometimes for the way he kept hurting his ma. But he was sure she wished he'd been the one buried in the church cemetery. Not Ralph and definitely not Reuben. Reuben was her baby, Gideon the *middle* child. The one who'd always been overlooked. Till now. His folks had to stare at his deformed body every day.

His ma kept her back to him and chopped vegetables. "I meant what I said 'bout you gettin' dressed. I'm expectin' company in a couple hours."

"Company?" He inched upright on his bed. "Who's comin'?"

"Violet Larsen."

His heart thumped. "Violet? What the hell for?"

His ma whipped around faster than he thought possible and shook the paring knife at him. "Never use that kind a language! You know better!"

Yes, he knew better. But he'd heard much worse talk from the soldiers he'd served with. "Sorry, Ma. You just caught me off guard. Did you *ask* her to come?"

"No. She insisted." She returned to slicing up a carrot. "She wants to see you."

"Me? Why?"

His ma shrugged, but he believed her silence meant there was more to it than she wanted to let on.

Violet . . .

"I don't want her to see me like this." He'd never said anything truer.

When he'd left the cove to serve three years prior, he'd planned to come home and marry her. The image of her beautiful face had kept him going. But when he woke up in that hospital no longer a complete man, he swore he'd never burden *any* woman. Especially someone as sweet and good as Violet Larsen.

"I promised her you'd be dressed," his ma said. "So get to it."

"You mean to tell me, you let on that I lay 'round like this?"

"She has brothers. As she told me, she's seen her share of underwear."

"She said *underwear*? At *church*?"

His ma let out a small chuckle. Something nice to hear. "It was *after* services. But yes, she said the word."

Violet Larsen had grown up. No *girl* would ever speak of such things. "She as pretty as she used to be?"

"Prettier. She's become a woman."

He gulped. His ma said the very thing he'd thought. The last time he'd seen Violet, she was fifteen. Already well on her way to womanhood. But three years had surely done right by her.

He sat up and scooted to the edge of the bed, then bent down and rummaged through the bureau drawer beside it. He yanked out a pair of pants and a shirt. His blaring stub kept him from putting them on. "I don't want her here, Ma."

"She's comin' regardless."

"When she gets here, tell her to leave. I won't let her see me like this."

His ma sucked in air and puffed up, then let it out with a huff. "All right. But, do me the kindness of dressin' yourself anyways. I don't like lookin' at them underwear myself."

He breathed a sigh of relief. At least his ma had the sense to do as he asked. He tugged on the trousers—hating the way the one pant leg hung limp—then slipped his arms into the shirt and buttoned it up.

His ma peered over her shoulder and smiled. "Much better."

He lay back and once again tossed the ball.

His stomach rumbled. Soup would sure taste good—even on a hot day. And knowing he didn't have to worry about making an impression on Violet Larsen helped his appetite.

While he waited for the meal to be ready, he imagined what she must look like.

Of course she'd have long hair. Not so dark it would be called brown, but too dark to be blonde. If he remembered right, her eyes were sort of green, and she had a few freckles across her nose.

Her perfect, cute little nose.

She was shy, but obviously not so shy anymore. Heck, she'd been bold enough to say *underwear* out loud.

He smiled, recalling her pretty singing voice. She'd sing out real strong at Sunday services. "Ma? Does Violet still sing?"

"Course she does."

"That's good." He threw the ball so hard, it hit the ceiling. "Sorry, Ma. I'll be more careful."

Her head bobbed.

"She still thin?"

"Somewhat."

He sat up again. "What's that mean? Did she get *fat*?"

"Why you frettin' over her? You said you don't wanna see her."

He flopped back down. "I don't. I's just wonderin'."

Again, his ma's head slowly bobbed. "I'm goin' out to let your pa know the soup's 'bout ready." She left without saying another word.

Gideon shut his eyes and tried to form the best image possible of Violet Larsen. He'd lied to his ma. More than anything, he *wanted* to see Violet.

But if she saw *him*, she'd surely run away without giving him a second thought.

Of that, he was certain.

CHAPTER 16

Violet plodded along atop Stardust—so named for her unique coloring. Lucas always said the mare's dapple gray circles were ugly, but Violet thought she was the most beautiful horse in the cove. Best of all, she was gentle.

When they'd first gotten her, it had taken some doing to get Violet on her back. After years without a horse, she feared riding. But now, it came second-nature.

"Lily'd be proud a me." She stroked the horse's mane. "She told me to be bold, an' here I am on my way to set a man straight." She laughed softly, then a tinge of nervous fluttered her belly.

What if he is ugly to me?

She could tolerate harsh words, but not having seen him in more than three years, for all she knew, he might've become the violent sort. If he threw things, that wouldn't do. His ma had said he might be hateful, but she didn't elaborate. Hateful could mean many things.

She pushed onward and prayed she had Lily's strength.

Besides, she had another motive for going to the Myers'. For two weeks, she'd hidden a letter she'd written to her sister. She'd kept it under her mattress, but had tucked it inside her dress pocket and brought it with her. She even managed to scrounge a nickel for postage. Hopefully, it only weighed half an ounce and the coin would be plenty. But if it weighed a full ounce, she'd owe an extra penny. She hoped if Mr. Myers was traveling outside the cove soon, he might agree to take the letter with him and post it elsewhere. It was the only way to keep it secret from her folks. Then again, both Mr. and Mrs. Myers were respectable. They'd likely question her need for secrecy.

I might hafta come up with an infamous Larsen story of my own.

She shrugged. Story-telling was in her blood, and she couldn't deny it.

While holding the saddle horn with one hand, she clutched onto a basket with the other. Inside were a dozen cornbread muffins and a jar of apple butter. She brought plenty, so Gideon's folks could enjoy them, too.

At times like this, she was glad Lucas was gone. Otherwise, he'd have mercilessly teased her. But she hated to imagine what he and that horrid sergeant might be doing. As of yet, her folks hadn't gotten word they'd moved on to St. Louis. Since Violet wanted her letter to arrive before them, she welcomed their silence.

The Myers' cabin was about the same size as Violet's home. She wished they lived close enough so she could walk to see them. Granted, two miles wasn't out of the question, but riding Stardust made it easier.

Violet carefully dismounted, smoothed her blue dress, and took a huge breath. They didn't have a front porch, but rather well-set stones that had been formed into steps leading to the front door. She lightly rapped.

Seconds ticked by.

No one answered.

"Hmm . . ." She knocked again. A little louder than before.

Still, no one came, which made no sense. She'd timed her ride perfectly. It had to be at least *close* to two o'clock.

Mumbling came from the other side of the door, then it inched open, but barely enough to matter.

Mrs. Myers poked her face through. "He don't wanna see you." She spoke louder than necessary and with a great deal of earnestness.

It seemed to Violet that the woman behaved as she had for Gideon's benefit, so Violet decided to stand her ground. "I don't care. I'm here, an' I ain't leavin' till I see him."

The dear woman grinned. "I figgered you'd say that," she whispered.

Violet understood. Gideon's ma had done as he'd asked, but the sweet lady had hoped Violet wouldn't leave. "Is he dressed?" Violet said loudly, with just as much boldness.

"Yep."

Violet pushed the door open and stepped inside.

Mrs. Myers skillfully feigned annoyance and waved her hands in the air. "I said he don't wanna see you!"

"I heard you, but I didn't ride all this way, only to turn 'round an' go back home."

"Fine," the woman huffed, then jerked her head toward a bed against the wall on the far side of the room.

When Violet looked that way, all she saw was a mound of blankets.

She set the basket on the kitchen table and stomped across the wood floor. "Gideon Myers if that's you 'neath all them quilts, you'd best say hello!"

The mound shifted. Sadly, she could discern by the shape of it, the lack of his lower leg.

"Go away." His grumbled words were muffled by the layers of fabric.

"No. After all this time, I thought you'd *want* to see me. 'Sides, it's stiflin' in here. How can you even *breathe* under there?"

"Stop bein' a baby, Gideon," his ma chided. "Lower them blankets an' talk to the girl."

Little by little, his coverings dropped and exposed his face.

Violet held her breath. He'd become a man. Whiskers and all.

An' a handsome one at that.

His thick brown hair stood on end—thanks in part to the ridiculous blankets. Violet refrained from laughing. "Hey, Gideon." She smiled her best one ever.

He scooted up on the bed and leaned against the wall, then lowered the quilts to his waist, but no further. She understood why, and that was fine.

He dipped his head. "Hey, Violet. Why are you here?"

She gestured to the table. "I brung cornbread muffins an' apple butter. But I mainly wanted to see you." She peered into his deep green eyes, so much sadder than she'd remembered. "Want me to fix you a muffin?"

"I appreciate you bringin' them, but I just ate. Ain't hungry right now."

"That's fine. I'll leave 'em, an' you can enjoy 'em later." She cast another smile, wishing he'd return it.

"Thank you." Not even a glimmer of a smile.

His ma wandered over beside her. "I'm gonna go check on Haywood. Make sure he's all right. I won't be gone long." She shot a stern glare at her son, then went out the door.

"Mind if I sit?" Violet pointed at the far end of the bed.

"Reckon that's proper? What with my ma gone an' all?"

"Why, Gideon Myers, are you plannin' to take advantage a me?" She grinned, then laughed, but he remained stone-faced. "Heaven's sakes Gideon, I was teasin'. Don't you remember how we used to play? *Laugh?*"

"We was kids then." He turned his head and stared at the wall.

Violet grabbed a kitchen chair and placed it close to him. "Why's your bed out here an' not in your bedroom?"

"Pa brung it out, so I could be close to Ma durin' the day. She worried over me when she couldn't see me."

"So why not sit on the sofa? It can't be good for you layin' here all the time."

His head slowly rotated, and he faced her again. "You don't know nothin' 'bout it."

"Then tell me." It pained her to see him this way, but she had to be strong. It was the only way to help him.

"I'll *show* you." He yanked the blankets off his legs. "See this?" He patted the vacant spot at the base of his trousers. "You can't, can you? Cuz it ain't there. Damn rebels took my leg."

She stared at the empty space, praying some of his hostility wasn't aimed at her pa. "That they did." Though she'd never heard him curse before, she couldn't fault him for it, but she wasn't about to let him carry on this way. "Did they steal your heart, too?"

"Huh?"

She grabbed hold of his hand. He gasped, but didn't pull away.

"Yes, you lost part a your body, but not the important one. A leg don't make you who you are. It's your heart and soul that matter."

She tenderly rubbed across the back of his hand with her thumb.

His head rapidly shook, then he jerked away. "That's easy for you to say. You're beautiful an' perfect. I ain't."

If not for this horrible situation, his words would feel wonderful. And honestly, they felt darn good. But how could she make him see himself as she did?

"You're actin' the way my pa used to. Full a self-pity. I remember how confident you used to be. You told me how you wanted to have your own farm one day. Or maybe even raise cattle instead a crops. You had big dreams, not to mention a gorgeous smile."

"Can you see me chasin' cattle like this?" Again, he slapped the empty space. "Forget the boy you knew, Violet. He ain't here no more, an' neither is his smile." He rolled onto his side and faced the wall.

Violet refused to give up. "You're right. I *don't* see a boy. I see a handsome man. But one with an ugly attitude." She stood and went to the table, needing to put some distance between them. "I hafta talk to your pa, then I'll leave. Reckon *he'll* treat me more decent. As for you, I aim to come back t'morra. I want you to think on the way you've been actin'. If you're as hateful to me t'morra as you've been today, I won't come again. *Ever.* But I remember the good-hearted person you once were, an' I'm willin' to give you another chance."

Gideon grunted, but at least he didn't tell her not to come. It gave her a bit of hope.

His head slightly turned. "What do you need my pa for?"

"Sumthin' personal." Thinking of Lily, Violet jutted her chin high, grinned, and walked out the door.

That'll give him plenty to ponder.

She wandered to the tree where she'd left Stardust tied. Mr. and Mrs. Myers approached from the fields.

"Leavin' so soon?" Mrs. Myers asked, brows weaving.

"'Fraid so. Gideon's mood ain't all that pleasant, but I won't give up on him. I told him I'd come back t'morra. Hope you don't mind."

Mr. Myers shook his head. "Why do you wanna put yourself through all that? My boy . . ." He pointed at the cabin. "Don't know what to do with him."

"I hate to say it sir, but . . ." Violet hesitated. Maybe she *shouldn't* say it. "Well, that's the problem. You shoulda given him a swift kick in the tail months ago. Lettin' him wallow won't solve nothin'."

The man's head drew back. "He's hurtin'. I ain't gonna make it worse."

"Hurtin', yes. But he's made up his mind he's worthless. I don't believe that for a minute. He should be helpin' you work the fields."

Both his folks looked away, as if they were afraid to even try. But why?

She decided to push on. "It's awful you lost your other boys, but if you don't get Gideon on his feet, then you've lost him, too."

"On his feet?" His ma appeared ready to cry again. "You mean *foot*. What if he falls? Breaks his good leg?"

"You can't live life fearin' what *might* happen. At least let him *try*." Violet searched their faces, but couldn't see beyond their fear. "I'll help all I can." She withdrew the envelope from her pocket. "But, I hope you can help me with sumthin', too."

"A letter?" Mr. Myers asked.

"Yessir. It's to my sister in St. Louis. I have the money to mail it, but . . ." In this case, the truth might suffice. "I don't wanna give it to Mrs. Quincy. The letter's private, an' you know how she talks."

"So, why not have your pa mail it next time he goes to Sevierville?"

Story time. "Well, that's another issue. I don't want my folks knowin' 'bout the letter neither. I had some private things to talk over with Lily. If ma knew I wrote this, she woulda asked to read it." She looked into Mrs. Myers' eyes. "*You* have a sister. I'm sure you understand my meanin'. Don't you?"

The dear woman's eyes regained a bit of their sparkle. "You mention my boy in your letter?"

Violet placed her fingertips to her lips, then cut her eyes toward Mr. Myers and opened them wide. "If I tell you what I wrote, I fear I might embarrass myself."

The man took the envelope from her. "I'll post it for you. I hafta go into Gatlinburg in the next couple a days."

"Thank you." She dug into her pocket for the nickel, then extended it to him. "I hope it don't cost an extra penny."

"If it does, I'll take care of it. Anna tells me you brung corn muffins an' apple butter. That's worth more than a penny. An' if you can help our boy . . ." He patted Violet's letter. "Can't put a price on that."

She felt compelled to hug him, but didn't. After all, they weren't family. At least, not yet. "I'll do all I can. But like I told Gideon, if he's hateful to me t'morra, I won't come back again." She stroked Stardust's side, then stuck her foot in the stirrup and mounted. "Hope you understand."

Both his folks nodded.

Violet grinned. "I gave him some things to ponder. If he can only remember how we used to get along so well. I know he needs a friend. I'd like to be one again."

Mr. Myers waved the letter in the air. "Just a friend?"

Heat filled Violet's cheeks. "We'll see." She grabbed the reins and gave them a tug, then directed the mare down the dusty road.

If her woman's intuition served her correctly, Gideon would be a different man the next time she knocked on his door.

CHAPTER 17

Evie carefully fitted the net over Lily's hair. "So, tell me, is Archibald handsome?"

Lily pondered her words. "He has unique features." She smiled, hoping Evie wouldn't pry deeper.

"I admire men who don't look like they've been cut from the same cloth as everyone else. You're fortunate."

Lily pinched her lips together. The cloth Archibald had been cut from required more than one bolt of fabric.

"All done!" Evie chirped and patted Lily's shoulders. She then lifted a mirror from Lily's vanity and handed it to her. "Look at your hair and make certain it's to your liking."

"I doubt I need to. You always fix it just right." Regardless, Lily took the mirror and gazed into it, turning her head from side to side. "It's lovely, Evie. Thank you." She shifted her body toward the girl. "I'm curious . . . Mr. Jones implied they'd eaten here before. He said Archibald loved Mrs. Winter's cookin'. How is it you've not seen them?"

"It's an odd thing. They've dined here twice since I've been here, and the Clarks insisted I stay in my room. Usually, when they entertain, I help serve." She shrugged. "I suppose Mr. Jones and his son are private people."

Lily set the mirror aside and took Evie's hand. "Did my aunt ask you to stay in your room t'night?"

"Yes." Evie frowned, then her eyes glowed with a bit of mischief. "I'm so curious about your intended that I may sneak out and take a peek."

"*Don't*." Lily tightened her grasp. "I won't have you gettin' into trouble. But, I'll be honest with you. I know why they don't want you to see him."

Evie sat on the bed beside Lily. "Why?"

"Archibald Jones is *not* an attractive man. They might fear you'll say sumthin' inappropriate, or maybe laugh at him."

"I'd never do that. I may have been raised in an orphanage, but I was taught manners. Even before I met Mrs. Gottlieb." She peered into Lily's eyes. "I won't embarrass you. I promise."

"That's not what I'm frettin' over. I care 'bout you, Evie, an' I know how hateful my aunt can be when crossed."

"I'll be fine." Evie stood and headed for the door. "I'll go to my room for now. If I decide to take a peek at Archibald, you'll never know it. I can be quite light-footed."

She disappeared before Lily could say another word.

* * *

Though only five-thirty, Lily made her way downstairs, only to be met by Uncle Stuart, when she reached the bottom step.

He took her hand and helped her down the final stair to the floor, then raised her hand to his lips and kissed it in the same way he kissed Aunt Helen. "You're perfect." His eyes searched her face, and he drew her hand to his chest and held it there. "Don't disappoint me tonight." His fingers caressed her skin.

She yanked free of him, then quickly glanced around, praying they'd not been seen. "You have no right touchin' me that way." She kept her voice to a whisper, but intensified every *proper* word.

He tilted his head and smirked. "Oh, my dear, Lily. You misunderstood my actions."

"I am *not* ignorant." She internally smiled. Mrs. Gottlieb was right. Saying it like that sounded much better, and she definitely had her uncle's attention. "You've been lookin' at me in a way I'm well aware of. I know what you're thinkin'."

"Is that so?" His smirk transformed into a broader grin. "And what might that be?"

She swallowed hard and stepped closer, not wanting to raise her voice and risk someone other than him hearing her. "Your eyes tell me you want me in an un-Christian manner."

He licked his lips. "And how would a chaste young woman know of such a thing?"

Her heart raced. If she said too much, she'd be done for. "I've seen that look before."

"Truly?" He rubbed his chin. "From whom?"

Lily stood erect. "Soldiers. Ones who wanted to take what I wasn't willin' to give."

His eyes narrowed. "Did they succeed?"

"Heavens, no!" She slapped a hand to her mouth and again looked about. Fortunately, no one appeared.

"Good." He folded his arms. "I presented you to Baxter Jones as a virtuous woman. I pride myself in being an honest businessman, and if you'd been tainted, it would've been a misrepresentation."

"So, I'm a *product*? Like all the other items you transport?"

He chuckled. "No, my dear. You're exceedingly finer."

His arrogant demeanor disturbed her more than ever. "What's in this for you?"

He shook a finger in reprimand. "A good businessman never boasts of his dealings." He tapped the tip of her nose. "You'll benefit from this transaction. You'll never want for anything. Doesn't that please you?"

"I *reckon* so." She purposefully used the hated word.

He chuckled. "You're a sly one. Yet, I like you, Lily. And though I admit I enjoy looking at you, I'll never compromise you. I'm faithful to your aunt, so get those silly notions out of your mind. But please, give a man his pleasure. Allow me to look without criticizing the act."

She stepped back. "Fine. Go on an' look, but never *touch* me again."

"Very well."

Aunt Helen bustled in. Lily had never been happier to see her.

"You're radiant!" Aunt Helen grasped Lily's hands. "Archibald will be enthralled."

Lily glanced at Uncle Stuart, who merely smiled politely. "Yes, he will."

"They'll be here any minute." Aunt Helen's eyes darted over Lily's face, then she pinched Lily's cheeks. *Hard.*

"Ouch!" Lily rubbed the spots. "Why'd you do that?"

"For color." She studied Lily's offended skin. "And I succeeded. They're now a nice shade of red."

A loud knock shook the front door, sounding more like a battering ram than the tapping of the gold knocker.

Gerard appeared out of nowhere and went to answer it.

Aunt Helen grabbed Lily's arm and shuffled her down the hallway to the dining room. "I won't have you coming off as being over-eager. Archibald will have to work for his prize." She laughed, then rang a bell for Mrs. Winters.

Just as Gerard had emerged, Mrs. Winters came in before Lily could blink.

"Yes'm?" Mrs. Winters kept her eyes focused downward.

"Bring in the bottle of wine and five goblets." Aunt Helen shooed her away.

"Wine?" Lily continued to be stunned. "I've never seen you drink alcohol before. I didn't think you indulged."

"We drink wine for communion. This is no different. Besides, we're celebrating."

Thoughts of her pa tipping the jug came to Lily's mind. "You expect me to drink it, too?"

"Of course. It would be rude not to."

The idea didn't set well, and Lily turned away. How much more would she have to change her behavior?

"My dear girl . . ." Aunt Helen took hold of Lily's chin and made her look at her. "*Jesus* drank wine. It's not a sin to have one glass, but you mustn't *over*indulge."

"Yes'm." What she said made sense, yet Lily wasn't certain she'd even *like* it.

Multiple footsteps approached.

Aunt Helen stuck her nose high in the air. "I understand Archibald isn't the most desirable man," she whispered. "But he's far better than *any* mountain man."

You're wrong.

Lily donned her brightest smile. At least her thoughts were still her own.

Uncle Stuart walked in, followed by their two guests. Both men were dressed in the same suits they'd worn to church, and Archibald's eyes remained focused downward, yet differently than the way Mrs. Winters had done. She behaved in a way that seemed more like submission, whereas Archibald acted as if he didn't want to be here at all.

He looks as miserable as me.

Uncle Stuart directed them to their seats, then helped Lily sit, though he didn't touch her. He merely pulled out her chair. Seemed he'd listened to her. Maybe he feared she'd mess up his business transaction, so he'd decided to behave himself.

Mrs. Winters came in with the wine and poured five glasses. Aunt Helen took it upon herself to distribute them, while wearing her enormous *I'm so important* smile.

Lily daintily held the crystal goblet and waited to drink till the others had tasted theirs.

Once Aunt Helen took her seat, holding her own glass, Uncle Stuart raised his. "A toast to new acquaintances!"

"Here, here!" Mr. Jones clinked his goblet against Uncle Stuart's. Aunt Helen added hers, and even Archibald lifted his.

"Here, here," Lily said in her sweetest voice, then touched her glass to Archibald's.

His eyes popped wide, then he grinned.

So did Uncle Stuart.

She'd been taught well, and if she had to play this game, she would. If what Evie had told her was true, and Lily would be the heir to this estate, she could provide for her family back home. They'd never struggle for a meal again.

That alone could make this miserable endeavor well worth it.

* * *

Mrs. Winters outdid herself on the roast beef. She'd perfectly seasoned it, and of course, didn't burn it. But the food was the only bearable thing about the meal.

Lily had managed to drink the wine she'd been served, and she admitted she liked the taste. But the effects of alcohol on an empty stomach weren't good. She'd been light-headed until she'd eaten a few bites.

She behaved just as she'd been trained. She used the right utensils, said the proper words, and smiled at Archibald whenever he glanced her way. Which, to her good fortune, wasn't very often.

They'd been seated across from each other, so it would've been easy for him to look at her. Yet his eyes, for the most part, stayed on his plate, and he seldom spoke. His pa tried to encourage him, but it did little good.

Honestly, Lily pitied him. Something must've happened to make him this way. His eyes bore sadness.

She'd been curious about his ma and assumed she'd died. Divorce was unheard of, so maybe her loss brought on Archibald's pain.

"Well . . ." Uncle Stuart pushed his dessert plate away, then patted his belly. "After that fine meal, I'd like a smoke. Would you care to join me, Baxter?"

Archibald's head lifted. "A smoke?"

His pa leered at him. "Not for *you*. Not now."

Uncle Stuart stood, and so did Mr. Jones.

Aunt Helen jumped to her feet so fast, it startled Lily.

"Though I don't smoke," Aunt Helen said. "I believe I'll take a stroll in the garden to help my digestion." She wandered off.

Lily understood what was happening. They were about to leave her alone with Archibald. The very thing they said they wouldn't do.

Improper, my left foot!

She stared wide-eyed at Uncle Stuart, who merely grinned. "Archibald hasn't finished his pie," he said. "I'm sure you won't mind keeping him company while he does so. Will you, Lily?"

"Not at all." She poked at her own piece.

Ominous silence surrounded them the instant the others left the room. Even Mrs. Winters stayed away. She'd probably been told not to disturb them.

Archibald shoved a large bite into his mouth. His head stayed bent low, and his plump cheeks moved up and down as he chewed.

Lily couldn't bear the hovering quiet and needed to make conversation. "Is cherry pie truly your favorite?"

"Uh-huh." He kept chewing.

"Archibald?"

He swallowed, licked his lips, and looked at her. "Yes?"

"You don't wanna be here, do you?"

His eyes opened wide, then he leaned over his plate. "Shh. They might be listening."

Though he was right, why was he so concerned?

When he sat up straight, Lily noticed a bit of pie on the lapel of his coat. "I'm afraid you're wearin' some of your dessert."

"What?" He glanced down, adding more layers to his double chin, then grabbed his napkin and wiped at it. "I'm a mess."

"Those things can happen." She offered an encouraging smile, but he was too focused on cleaning off the globs of cherry to see it.

Changing the subject might help. "So," she said. "Do you like to smoke?" It would explain his discolored teeth.

"Yes. It calms me."

"Then I'm sorry my uncle didn't have you join them. 'Sides, you'd likely prefer conversin' with the men."

"What makes you say that?" He shyly lifted his eyes. "I'd rather be with you. But, I don't know why *you're* here with *me*."

What should she say?

Think before you speak.

"Well, we *are* similar in age, an' I'm sure we have other things in common. What are you, twenty-one, twenty-two?"

"I'm twenty-four."

"Oh. You've aged well." She gulped.

"What about you? You don't appear to be more than seventeen."

"I'm *nine*teen." She lifted her head high, then turned so he could see her profile. "Do I look older *now*?"

He laughed. A sound that actually warmed her. It seemed real, unlike everything else around her.

"Not much," he said. "But you're the prettiest girl I've ever known."

Her cheeks heated. "Thank you."

"Father says mother was beautiful when they first met."

Lily looked at him more closely. While speaking about his ma, he sat up tall and kept his head high. He appeared quite confident, so she decided to press him further. "And, what of her now? Was she unable to come t'night?" She'd taken a great risk asking.

"They didn't tell you?"

They? "You mean Uncle Stuart and Aunt Helen?"

He nodded.

"No. They said nothin' 'bout your ma." *Oops!* "That is . . . your *mother*." Again, her cheeks warmed, but for a different reason.

A large grin covered Archibald's face, but this time she found it endearing. "I like the way you talk. Even the way you said, *ma*. You're different than *anyone* I know."

She fidgeted with her pie. "Is that a good thing?"

"*Very* good." He glanced over his shoulder, then scooted his pie plate out of the way and leaned close. "Most of father's friends are stuffy," he whispered. "I feared you would be, too. But I was wrong." He leaned back and gripped the edge of the table with both hands. "Do you think we could be friends?"

Since they'd come this far, she chose to lay everything on the line. She had to know how much *he* knew. "Of course, we can. But . . ." *Deep breath.* "My understandin' is you're lookin' for a wife, an' my uncle has indicated *I'm* bein' considered for that role. Is that so?"

He released the table, lifted the tablecloth, and covered his head with it.

Strangest thing I've ever seen.

It appeared he was trying to hide from her. "Archibald? Are you all right?"

He eased his hands down to his lap, letting the table covering drop. His chubby cheeks had turned crimson. They'd both had their turn at embarrassment. "Why do people have to speak so openly?"

"I'm sorry."

"No. I didn't mean *you*. I was referring to the *adults* in the other room. Your uncle had no qualms telling you my greatest desire, yet he failed to mention the loss of my mother. If he couldn't reveal that detail about my life, why share my most intimate secrets?"

It took her several moments to process his words. He wasn't at all a simpleton, but rather a private person. "I think he was tryin' to prepare me."

"So, if you were aware of my inclination toward matrimony, why did you agree to see me? Every other girl I've shown interest in has run the other direction."

She couldn't tell him the truth. It would crush him. "I agreed so we could get better acquainted." At least this time he was looking when she flashed a broad smile. "Tell you what . . . Why don't we slow things down a mite an' get to know one another. You may decide I'm not suited for you."

"*I* may decide?" He placed a hand to his heart. "Are you saying you'd consider my courtship?"

She dabbed at her mouth with the cloth napkin. "I'm not ready to court just yet. But I welcome your friendship—and company." It wasn't a lie. Aside from her time with Mrs. Gottlieb, this was probably the most decent conversation she'd had since her arrival in St. Louis.

"That's almost like courting. Isn't it?"

"Almost. Not quite." She pushed her pie away, unable to eat any more. Though she liked him, she feared where all this would likely lead. Friendship was one thing, but taking on the role of his wife was something else entirely.

Archibald eyed her half-eaten piece of pie.

"Want it?" She pointed at it.

"If you're not going to eat it. I'd hate to see it go to waste."

She scooted the plate across to him. He devoured it in two large bites, then covered his mouth and belched.

"Oh, my," Lily muttered. "Feel better?"

"Forgive me. When I eat rapidly, it brings on gas."

"Then maybe you should slow down." She softly laughed and waved a hand. "You didn't offend me. My brothers' belches could raise the roof."

"Would you tell me about them?" He chuckled. "That is— your brothers. Not their belches."

He seemed honestly interested. "Only if you tell me about your mother."

"You mean, my *ma*?" He beamed.

"That's right." Lily laughed. "Your ma." She scooted her chair back. "Why don't we take a stroll, an' you can tell me all 'bout her."

He stood and straightened his coat, then extended his arm. Lily took it without reservation.

They wandered along the path around the house, until they reached the back courtyard. The gardener kept it pristine and lovely. Every evening, he lit the four tall lanterns positioned around a circular section of well-placed stones. Beautiful flowers and shrubs surrounded the flat rocks. Two wood benches faced each other on opposite sides of the stonework.

Lily had come here several times in the cool of the evening to read. She felt a bit like Alice herself—in a strange place like Wonderland, trying to fit in.

Archibald withdrew a cigar from his pocket. "Do you mind?"

"No. It's fine."

He lit the thing from one of the lantern's flames. As he puffed on it, he donned a serene expression.

It calms him alright.

He blew perfect circles of smoke into the air, then smiled. "So, what can you tell me?

"Excuse me?"

He took a seat on one of the benches. "Who are you, Lily Larsen? What makes you the person you are?"

Lily grinned. "Have you ever read *Alice's Adventures in Wonderland*?"

"No. I can't say that I have. Why?"

"Nothin' really. There's just this caterpillar you sorta remind me of."

"A caterpillar?" He laughed, then took another drag. "I've never been compared to such a small creature."

"He's unique." Lily sat beside him and positioned herself as she'd been taught. "*And*, he likes to smoke."

"A *smoking* caterpillar? That's a strange book you're reading. Perhaps I'll have to purchase a copy for myself. You've piqued my curiosity about this *caterpillar*, yet you've not told me more about *you*. That's what I truly want to know."

She shifted toward him and was about to speak, when a plump rabbit darted from one of the bushes, then raced away.

"Oh, my." She laughed. The timing couldn't have been more appropriate. "Did you see that rabbit?"

"Yes. But why are you laughing?" He inhaled more smoke, then blew it out in puffs.

"There's a rabbit in my book, too." She folded her hands on her lap. "But if you wanna know more 'bout me, if I was back home, that critter would've been supper."

His eyes widened. "I like rabbit. As long as it's cooked properly."

Aunt Helen probably wouldn't approve of her talking about this, but she no longer cared. "I know how to skin rabbits. I can trap 'em, gut 'em, and make a fine stew."

His head drew back, emphasizing his pronounced thick chin. "I'm impressed. What else can you do?"

Without thought, she rambled on about farming and how she helped tend her younger siblings. She told him about the beauty of the cove and the folks there.

He silently listened, all the while puffing away on his cigar. And though he had the vice, she knew she had his full attention.

She'd lost track of time. "Forgive me. I've not let you speak. Tell me 'bout your ma. Please?"

"Before I do, I want you to know I think you're incredible. I can't believe I'm sitting here with you having this conversation. I've not been so blessed in a great while."

"You're a blessin' to me, too, Archibald." She meant every word.

He extinguished his cigar and cleared his throat. "My mother died when I was only seven years old. The city suffered a cholera epidemic. More than five thousand people lost their lives."

"Five thousand?" She laid a hand on his knee in compassion, but when he gasped, she pulled it back. "I'm sorry 'bout your ma."

"Thank you. I remember clearly crying for days. Begging for her. Father appeased me—and himself—with food." He splayed his arms wide. "You can see the results. Grief brought me to this."

"Are you *still* grievin'?"

He sadly nodded. "Even after all these years. First, it was for her alone. But now, I grieve from loneliness of another sort. I have no friends. I love my father, but he doesn't *talk* to me. Not like this."

Her heart ached for him, and she peered straight into his eyes. "You have a friend *now*."

He shyly looked away.

They sat in silence for a while, then Lily began rattling on again about the cove. She told him things to cheer him. Tales about Mrs. Quincy and her meddling, but also about the way her brothers played charades.

Though it made her homesick speaking of it, it made Archibald smile again.

For the first time in a long time, she put someone else's misery before her own. Perhaps she'd made a step in the right direction.

CHAPTER 18

As Violet approached the Myers' cabin, Mr. Myers ran up to meet her. She had no idea he could move so fast.

"Is sumthin' wrong?" She dismounted and secured Stardust to a tree.

"No. Just the opposite." The man beamed. "This mornin', Gideon had me put his bed back in his room. I reckon you musta said sumthin' yesterday what prompted it."

Her heart leapt. "Has he been sittin' on the sofa today?"

"Yep. Fully dressed, too."

"Well, then." She lifted her face to the glorious sunshine. "Let's see what more I can accomplish with *this* visit."

"I'm headin' to the fields. You go on an' knock. Anna's expectin' you."

"What 'bout Gideon?"

The man laughed. "Figgered that was a given." He walked off, still chuckling.

Violet had feared coming here today, but all her anxious thoughts vanished.

He wants me here.

She boldly strode to the front door and knocked.

Mrs. Myers appeared almost instantly. "C'mon in." She stepped aside, so Violet could enter.

"It's fine to see you again, ma'am," Violet said, scanning the room. Her sight came to rest on the back of Gideon's head. His hair, perfectly combed.

"You, too." Mrs. Myers set her hand in the middle of Violet's back and nudged her toward her son.

Violet took the less-than-subtle hint and moved into the living area, while Mrs. Myers busied herself in the kitchen.

The interior of the cabin seemed a great deal larger with the bed removed. Violet casually wandered until she stood in front of Gideon. "Since you're up an' about, can I assume you gave some thought to what I said yesterday?"

He fidgeted with the cushions on the sofa. "Reckon so." Still, no smile.

"Well, we used to pick berries together. Do you recall *that*?"

"S'pose I do." He lifted his head and looked straight at her. "Why?"

"There's a gooseberry patch I passed on the road a ways back, burstin' with berries. It's a lovely day, an' I thought we could go gather some for your ma." Violet gazed beyond him. "Would you like that, Mrs. Myers?"

"That'd be wonderful." The dear woman's worrisome tone contradicted her words.

She doubts my ability to get Gideon off his rump.

Violet returned her attention to him. "If I remember proper, your pa loves gooseberry jam. So, how 'bout it? We can gather a bucketful, I'm sure."

Gideon grunted. "An' just how do you reckon I can pick them berries?"

"With your two hands, of course." She fisted her hands on her hips.

"How far down the road are they?"

She pondered his expression. Though he sounded a mite angry, he *looked* scared. She could cope with fear a lot better than anger.

"Not too far, an' they're close to the road, so we won't hafta climb up the mountainside."

"Good." He blew several bursts of air through his nose. "I ain't much on climbin' these days."

"Me neither. Honestly, I've never cared for exertin' myself more than I hafta."

Gideon chuckled, and Violet nearly dropped to the floor. She gaped at him, and he instantly sobered. If only she'd kept herself composed. For a moment, she'd witnessed an inkling of the old Gideon.

She grabbed the crutch from the corner of the room and extended it to him. "Need help gettin' up?"

"No. But first I gotta put on my boot. Can you bring it to me? It's settin' by the front door."

With a rapid nod, she hurried to retrieve it before his mood turned and he changed his mind. She leaned the crutch against the wall, then knelt in front of him, ready to put on his lone shoe.

He held up a hand. "Give it to me. I'm not an invalid."

She passed it over and stood. "Glad to hear you say that. You gave me quite the opposite impression yesterday."

Mumbling something she couldn't make out, he crammed his foot into the boot and laced it up tight. He jerked his chin high and motioned for the crutch.

His manners had certainly gone by the wayside.

She grabbed the crutch and held it close to her body. "Say, please."

"Huh?"

"You've been actin' rude. Demandin' an' such. So, kindly ask me for the crutch."

"No. You're the one who wants to go pick berries."

She soundly tapped her foot on the floor and glared at him.

"Fine." He huffed. "May I *please* have my crutch?"

His words held little sincerity, yet she was satisfied and grinned. "Yes, you may." She handed it to him. "I'll be kind to *you* an' carry the bucket."

Since she didn't want to see him struggle to stand, she went to the kitchen to get the container for the berries from Mrs. Myers.

It pained her to hear Gideon groan as he stood and steadied himself.

He hobbled slowly to the door.

His ma timidly followed him with her eyes. Violet stepped in front of her, blocking her view. "He'll be fine," she whispered. "He needs to do this."

The woman nodded, but Violet could tell she wasn't convinced. Her pained expression said otherwise.

Violet paraded to the door, bucket in hand, and opened it for him.

He made his way outside, proficiently using the crutch, much to her surprise. "You been practicin'?" She gestured to the thing.

"Some. It hurts my armpit if I'm on it too long."

"Why don't you pad it with some cloth? Maybe even a bit a cotton?"

He shrugged. "Didn't expect to need it."

They headed down the road at a snail's pace.

Violet bolstered her courage. "You don't hold my pa fightin' for the confederacy against me, do you?"

He grunted. "No. From what I understand, he was forced into it. 'Sides, we was all close long time ago. 'Fore the war . . ."

"I'm glad." More than he'd ever realize. It made it easier to talk about this. "Pa said most soldiers who lost limbs were given made-up ones. You know—made outta wood an' such. He didn't wanna mess with a wood arm, but I'd think a well-constructed wood leg would help you get 'round. Didn't them doctors offer one?"

"Yep." Another grunt. "It hurt to wear it. I didn't like it."

"Same way you feel 'bout the crutch, right?"

"Yep."

Violet didn't mind going slow, but his attitude disturbed her. Yes, she'd gotten him outside, however, his insides were horribly messed up. More so than his physical well-being. "Why would you think you don't need to use the crutch? Were you expectin' to lay 'round the cabin the rest a your life?"

"I dunno."

She stopped in the middle of the road. "What *do* you want, Gideon?"

He spun on his heel and faced her. His eyes shot fire. "My leg." The scowl he wore turned him into a complete stranger.

"Poor you." She glared right back at him. "When we was kids an' you used to chase me 'round, did you look down at your leg an' say, *Oh, leg, I love you so much. I couldn't live 'thout you . . .?*" She dramatized her words to the best of her ability.

His lip curled. "You're crazy. I'm convinced you've lost your mind. No one says dumb things like that."

"You're right, but I ain't crazy. I'm serious. How much did you care 'bout that leg 'fore it was gone?"

He rocked back and forth, leaning on the crutch. "Reckon I didn't think 'bout it."

"So, what you're sayin' is, it didn't matter one lick back then, so why should it now?"

He stepped closer. "Cuz it's gone! I can't do nothin' 'thout it!"

"But you're standin' right here in front a me, an' we're fixin' to pick berries. Ain't that *sumthin*?"

"Yes, but . . ."

She moved within inches of him. "But, what?" He'd grown quite a bit taller than the last time she'd seen him, and she couldn't recall them ever being this close.

He licked his lips, breathing hard. "Nothin'."

She hadn't realized just how warm it was. Till now. His breath mingled with hers, and drops of perspiration dripped down her back. "When did you decide to grow out your whiskers?"

"Um . . . I didn't. They got there all by themselves." His gaze penetrated hers.

She lowered her eyes, only to find herself admiring the rippled muscles of his arms. "You've grown up everywhere, Gideon."

"So've you."

Violet shut her eyes and took a step back. "We best be pickin' them berries. If we're gone too long, your ma will worry."

"Reckon so." He set off down the road.

Before following him, Violet took several deep breaths to steady her rapidly beating heart.

Though proud of herself for standing up to him and not letting him drown in self-pity, she doubted she could be so close to him again without touching him. He set off a fire in the pit of her belly that needed dousing.

Is this how Lily felt 'bout Caleb?

Violet finally understood why her ma had been concerned. Womanly feelings had never come out like this before. And the way Gideon had looked at her, she assumed he'd felt something similar.

Their childish ways had long vanished, replaced by something more *mature*.

She'd promised to hold back affection till marriage.

Hmm . . .

Since it took more than simple kisses to make a baby, then maybe she'd allow herself just a *little* affection.

But not today. Before any of that came about, Gideon needed to be in his right mind. If not, it would be meaningless, and she wanted something lasting.

I won't throw myself at him.

Regardless, she'd enjoy getting close to him. Picking berries had never been this much fun, and they'd not even started yet.

* * *

Gideon's leg had already begun to ache, but he wasn't about to let on to Violet that he hurt.

It was his own fault. He'd taken advantage of his ma's pampering and assured himself he deserved being bedridden. But what kind of life did he expect, staring at the same four walls every day, with his folks being his only company?

He found Violet a whole lot more enjoyable. Sure, she'd fussed, but it only meant she cared. Then again, she might simply feel sorry for him.

I don't want her pity.

He glanced over his shoulder. She'd stopped along the road and had her nose in a honeysuckle. He smiled, but didn't want her to see it, so he faced forward again. "Are we gettin' close?"

She hastened to his side. "Yep. Why? You gettin' tired?"

"No, but I figgered you was. Dawdlin' back there an' all."

"I wasn't dawdlin'. I was smellin' the flowers. You should take the time to appreciate nice-smellin' things."

The first *thing* that came to mind was Violet herself, but he wouldn't tell *her* that. When they'd stood face to face, she'd overwhelmed him. An urge to kiss her had crept in, but he'd never do it. He'd hate himself if he ever saddled a woman with the likes of his disability.

"Let's get them berries picked." He finally said the one thing he hoped wouldn't encourage her.

I shoulda stayed home. Told her never to see me again.

Violet pointed. "There they are." She grinned and headed for the bush.

"Careful a the thorns." He followed her—each painful step a brutal reminder of his limitations.

"They don't have many. Not like a rose bush." She reached in and plucked several berries, then dropped them into the bucket.

Like a gift from God, a long thick log lay close to the bush. Gideon painstakingly made his way to it and sat with a sigh. "Why don't you sit beside me an' pick. There's plenty right here. 'Sides, I can't reach the bucket."

"Perfect." She smiled, tucked her skirt beneath her, and perched next to him. *Right* next to him. "Reckon I *was* a mite tuckered out. This is nice." She turned her head and pursed her sweet kissable lips.

Stop thinkin' 'bout her that way!

He focused on the berry bush. "You've changed more than just your looks."

"I have?"

"Yep. You used to be shy. All girly an' meek. You remind me more a Lily now. She always said whatever was on her mind. An' she was never girly. Did things more like a man 'round your pa's farm."

Violet's shoulders slumped and she stopped picking. "Ain't quite sure how to take that. Maybe I *am* a bit bolder than I was before, but I've grown up." Her lip stuck out in a pronounced pout. "You don't like the way I am now, do you?"

He threw a berry into the bucket, then set it on the ground. "Why are you *really* here, Violet?"

She crossed her arms and looked the other direction. "Isn't it obvious?"

"Yep. I get it. You're helpin' the poor cripple to ease your Christian heart. Reckon you feel guilty for havin' two good legs."

"Oh!" She shook her fists in the air and whipped around. Her eyes pinched nearly shut. "Gideon Myers, you're a fool! I don't care 'bout your leg, or lack thereof. I care 'bout *you*!" She shot to her feet and returned to the road, then paced, mumbling.

No. She's lyin'. She hasta be.

"I don't want you to care! I ain't gonna spend my days worried 'bout no crazy woman. An' that's exactly what you are if you think you have feelin's for me."

She marched over to him and leaned close. "Don't even *try* to tell me what I'm feelin'! An' if you call me crazy one more time, I swear, I'll knock you off that log!"

"Is *that* what you wanna do to me?" He glared at her, finally witnessing how she truly felt.

"No! I wanna do *this*." She put her hands on the sides of his face and before he could utter another word, her lips were on his.

Dang!

She tasted as sweet as she smelled, but the pressure she'd put on him tumbled him backward to the ground, with her atop him. They'd not fallen far, but their precarious position brought out other more complicated feelings.

"Oh, Gideon. I'm so sorry!" She clumsily scrambled off him and got to her feet. "Did I hurt you?"

A laugh erupted from him, he hadn't expected. Nothing hurt but his pride. He struggled to get upright.

Violet knelt down and helped him. "*Are* you hurt?" Her brow creased and not a bit of humor lay in her features.

"No. But, I knocked over the berries." He stared at her beautiful face. "Why'd you kiss me?"

"Cuz I wanted you to know I ain't here outta pity. Truthfully, I'm bein' selfish."

She stood and held out a hand, then lifted him onto his foot. He teetered without the crutch, but she steadied him and guided him onto the log again.

He patted the spot beside him. "What makes you selfish?"

She brushed some dirt from her skirt and sat. "I don't wanna be with my folks forever."

"So, you see me as a way to escape. To help the poor neighbor who can't do for himself."

"Will you please stop sayin' things like that? I'm here cuz I wanna be. There's plenty a charity work to be had 'round here, an' if I'd wanted *that*, I'd be over at the Henderson's helpin' with their colicky twins."

Gideon picked at a piece of bark. "Least you don't hafta change my diaper." He nudged her shoulder, grinning.

She sat primly straight. "I certainly hope not." A giggle escaped her. "Forgive me, but the image your words put in my mind tickled me."

Maybe he'd been wrong about her. And if he wanted to be truly honest, self-pity was his greatest enemy. He himself caused all his troubles.

The most beautiful girl in all of Cades Cove—maybe even in the entire *world*—was sitting beside him. And she'd kissed him.

Would it be so wrong to try and make this work?

Though she stared at her lap, her cheeks rose high. Evidence of a bright smile.

He brushed his hand along the side of her face, and she gasped.

Slowly, she shifted toward him. "Are you done bein' hateful? Cuz I can't take many more of your angry words. An' if you want the girl you knew long ago, she's gone. We've *both* changed, but I don't reckon that's a bad thing." She grasped onto his hand. "If you're tryin' to make up to me, that's fine. But I don't want you playin' with my feelin's."

"I ain't playin'." He drew her into his arms and held her close. "Forgive me for bein' ugly. I've been so mad 'bout everythin'. The war. My brothers dyin'. Ma and Pa bein' heartbroke." He tenderly rubbed her back. "All that bitterness made me hateful. Then you came along. All rosy-cheeked an' lovely."

She sat up, but remained near. "I've been angry, too. What with Pa's troubles an' Lily leavin', it's been awful. Then I heard you'd come home, an' it gave me hope. I reckon we were meant to help each other. As I said, I'm bein' selfish." Her eyes gleamed with fresh tears.

"Don't cry, Violet. Please?"

"I can't help it. I'm not sad so much as I am thankful to be close to you. I've thought 'bout this a lot."

He stroked her cheek and smiled. "You thought 'bout knockin' me off this log?"

"No, silly." She fingered his beard. "I wanted to know what it'd be like in your strong arms, feelin' your warmth."

"Well, my warmth ain't such a good thing right now. It's one a the hottest days this year."

She moistened her lips and drew his eyes there. "That it is." Her eyes searched his, pleading . . .

"It won't be easy," he whispered, inching closer.

"I don't care." Her breasts heaved with labored breaths. "I'm up for the challenge."

He threaded his fingers into her hair and kissed her the way it should've been done the first time. Slow, steady, and with all the love he could pour out. By no means were they strangers. He'd loved her for as long as he could remember.

A pleasant whimper came from her throat. The sound brought unexpected chills, as well as desires he had no business thinking about just yet.

When they separated, her eyes briefly remained closed. He could look at her forever and never tire of the sight.

With a soft sigh, she bent over and picked up the bucket. "Reckon we best pick these berries fast as we can an' get back to your ma. We don't wanna worry her." She rubbed her fingers over his hand, then peered into his eyes. "I'm glad we've grown up, Gideon."

He kept his eyes locked with hers. "So am I." It might not be the way he'd planned his life, but if she was willing to be a part of it, even as he was, he'd find a way to make it work.

Her broad smile sent his heart soaring, then her head whipped around and she rapidly plucked berries.

He joined her.

For now, nothing more needed to be said.

CHAPTER 19

The sound of a cry popped Rebecca's eyes open, but it wasn't Avery.

Caleb's head thrashed from side to side atop his pillow. As far as she could tell in the dark, his eyes remained closed. "No . . ." he groaned.

"Sweetheart?" She gently shook his shoulders.

"Noah!"

Her head drew back. Who on earth was Noah?

"Caleb?" She patted his face. "Caleb, wake up. You're dreamin'."

He shot upright, breathing hard.

She eased up beside him and gently rubbed his bare back. "You're fine now. It was only a dream."

He bent forward and put his head in his hands, grabbing fist-fuls of hair.

He'd not been himself since that horrid visit from the Larsen boy and Vincent Douglas. Rebecca hoped after Caleb had finally told her about his ordeal posing as a woman, he'd be better. But for weeks, he'd not slept well.

His tossing about kept her up, too. Worse yet, even though they got little sleep, they rarely did much else in bed. Another month's flow had come and gone. She'd never conceive if things kept on this way.

She craned her neck and listened to see if Avery had stirred, startled by Caleb's outcry. Aside from his labored breathing, the house was silent.

"Sweetheart . . ." She dotted kisses across his shoulders. "Lay down an' tell me 'bout your dream. It might make you feel better."

With her guidance, he lay back onto his pillow. "I don't remember it."

She glided her fingers across his chest, then swirled them through the small patch of hair. "You said, *Noah*. Do you recall that?"

He trembled beneath her touch. She hoped she might be having an effect on him. After all, it wasn't cold in the room. But when she guided her hand lower, she found she was mistaken. Even so, she chose to offer some encouragement and gently stroked him.

"Don't, Becca. I can't. Not now."

Disappointed as usual, she pulled her hand to herself. "So, who's Noah?"

"Noah?" He rolled onto his side and put his back to her. "Like I said, I don't remember the dream."

"But you called out his name. You sounded afraid for him."

Caleb huffed a breath. "The only Noah I know is the one in the Bible. I musta been dreamin' 'bout the flood."

She let out a little laugh. "Maybe so." Not ready to give up, she pressed her body into his, then rubbed her hand up and down his side. "Since we're both wide awake, please, can't we love on each other? I need you, Caleb."

"It's too hot, Becca."

He *always* had an excuse.

She ached for him in many ways. Worst of all, each time he refused her, it chipped away at her heart. "You don't want me anymore, do you?"

He let out a long, drawn-out breath, then rolled onto his back. "Please don't start that again."

"I can't help it. I don't understand what's goin' on with you. You feel like a stranger, an' you hardly ever look at me. I fix myself up, tryin' to be pretty, but it's like you see right through me." She gazed heavenward, hoping for help to say the right things. "Most nights, I come to bed wearin' nothin', thinkin' it might spark your interest. Yet, I rarely get even a simple kiss, an' *I* usually have to initiate it."

She knew Caleb hadn't fallen asleep, but he didn't say a word —just kept breathing hard as if disgusted by her.

Though it pained her to say it, she had to know. "There's someone else, isn't there?"

"*No.*" He turned onto his side and placed a hand on her belly. "There ain't no one but you. I swear."

"Then, prove it."

"Huh?"

"Heaven's sake, Caleb. Do I have to *beg* you to make love to me?"

"But . . ." He flopped onto his back. "It's too warm."

I refuse to cry.

Naked, she hopped off the bed.

"Where you goin', Becca?"

"I don't know. Reckon I'll walk 'round the house till I feel better."

"But you ain't got no clothes on."

"You noticed?" She tucked her folded arms under her breasts and pushed them up. Though she assumed he couldn't see her, at least it made her feel more desirable.

"Course I did. I love how your soft skin feels against mine."

"Truly?" She knelt on the bed beside him and startled when his fingers crossed her breast.

"Lay down, Becca."

She happily obliged. Honestly, she felt a bit foolish thinking she could strut around the house in the dark. She might've tripped over something and broken a bone. Then, she wouldn't be good for anything.

Caleb's hand continued to roam—the very thing she craved.

She shut her eyes and relished it. He'd said *no*, but his actions indicated otherwise.

"I know I ain't been actin' right," he whispered and moved closer. "But, I *do* love you. The war messed me up more than I thought it did. I hate I'm makin' you suffer over my troubles."

She let her own hands freely wander and savored the feel of his capable body. "I'm here for you. That's what marriage is for. So two people can help each other through all the difficult times. But you've got to open up to me. Share what you're feelin'. All right?"

"All right." His warm breath dusted her cheek, and soon thereafter, his lips were on hers.

The hot night didn't trouble her, and somehow, she'd changed Caleb's mood. He'd stopped complaining about the heat and his kisses felt sincere. Perhaps, once again, she'd worried for nothing.

"Oh, yes, Caleb." She let her body sink into the soft bedding as he lay atop her.

* * *

Caleb shut his eyes and tried to erase the horrid visions from his dream. His infant son had been within reach, but he couldn't touch him. Whenever he'd tried, Noah drifted farther away. Dreams had a way of magnifying reality. They always seemed to grasp hold of his worries and slap him hard with the greatest of them.

Guilt returned him to his actual life and a wife he had no choice but to love.

He joined with Rebecca easily, yet every thrust was a betrayal. He hated lying to her. Noah's name had slipped out unintentionally, but telling her the truth about his son wasn't an option.

She softly moaned beneath him—a pleasant, sensuous sound.

He avoided doing this very thing, because every time he loved on her, he thought of Lily and hated himself for it. Now that he knew about Noah, he could never let her go.

Lucas may have told him Lily was *right as rain*, but Caleb knew better. She'd been made to give up their son.

An' me.

Lily didn't deserve that. She was good and kind. Strong and beautiful.

So beautiful . . .

He increased his pace. Rebecca's hands slid back and forth across his backside, occasionally squeezing. She was an exceptional lover—far better than he deserved. Everything she did felt good, but he shouldn't be enjoying it.

He breathed harder and harder.

God, how do I fix this?

Why would God help him at all? Even in his marriage bed, Caleb sinned.

"Oh, Caleb," Rebecca rasped. "This is what I've been wantin'. I love you so much . . ." She arched her back, then pulled down and away, bringing him with her. The skill she'd acquired in her movement sent him over the edge.

He exploded his seed within her, and Lucas's words haunted him.

You put a baby in Lily, then walked away.

"Oh, God!" Caleb folded down onto Rebecca. "Forgive me." He burst into a sob, but just as quickly, stifled it.

"Sweetheart." Rebecca stroked his face. "It's all right. I'm not upset with you any longer. This was perfect. *You're* perfect. An' maybe if we're fortunate, I'll conceive."

He buried his head into her shoulder. If she knew what he'd truly begged forgiveness for, she'd despise him. His list of sins had grown and kept on building. Even now, if he'd created a child, he'd done it wrongfully.

He wanted to run. But he had nowhere to go.

CHAPTER 20

Gideon couldn't help himself. Though he'd not stepped foot in a church since before the war, he couldn't keep his attention on the preacher. He kept shifting his eyes two pews back, to where Violet sat with her folks.

I should be sittin' beside her.

He hadn't seen her since their berry picking—or more importantly, their first kiss—six days ago. But a moment hadn't passed that he'd not thought of her. Even in his sleep, she floated through his dreams like a beautiful angel.

His ma kept patting his good leg, as if she wanted to make certain he truly sat beside her. Or maybe she did it because she was nervous about his intentions. She'd nearly cried when he told her he planned to attend worship, then burst into a sob when he let on that he planned to ask Violet's pa if he could court her. God should've been his reason for coming to church, but Lord help him, he just had to see Violet again. Regardless of whether or not her pa agreed to his proposal.

Whenever Gideon glanced her way, she coyly smiled. But when he looked at her pa, he didn't seem so happy.

I don't care. I'm gonna do what hasta be done.

The instant Brother Davis said his final amen, Gideon got up, ready to tackle the task at hand. He'd taken Violet's advice and had his ma sew a pad for his crutch. It helped, yet he still had to regain his strength. Months of lying around in bed had weakened his muscles. His good leg had to work twice as hard, and though the crutch helped a mite, he had a long way to go. Violet inspired him to succeed. She was worth every worry that gnawed at his insides.

He hobbled as fast as possible down the aisle and over to the Larsens. "Mr. Larsen, sir?"

The wary-eyed man faced him. "Yes?"

Violet peered over her pa's shoulder, questioning with her own eyes. She firmly held her baby brother in her arms. Gideon easily pictured her cradling *their* children. A vision that made him smile and briefly forget his purpose.

"*Yes?*" Mr. Larsen said again with more earnestness.

Gideon cleared his throat. "I'd like a word with you, sir."

"I'm listenin'."

Too many folks encircled them, and Gideon needed privacy. "Mind if we talk outside?"

"Nope. Don't mind at all." The man laid a hand on his wife's shoulder. "'Scuse us, Rose. Sounds like men talk needs to be had."

As Gideon made his way from the church, he felt Violet's eyes on him. He did all he could to walk as tall as possible. Though impaired, he needed her to see him at his best.

When they reached the front steps, her pa stopped. "Need help gettin' down?"

"No, sir. I can manage." He proved himself and capably mastered the three steps.

They shook the reverend's hand in turn, then moved on to a place where no one else was about.

Mr. Larsen folded his arms and stood stone-faced. "What's on your mind?"

Gideon swallowed hard and forced himself to breathe. "Your daughter, sir."

His head drew back. "Which one? I got two."

"Well—Violet, sir. I thought—"

The man chuckled. "I'm foolin' with you, son." He patted Gideon's back. "Go on an' breathe. Reckon I know what's truly on your mind."

"You do?"

"Course I do." He leaned close. "I was young once. You shoulda seen Rose when we was young. So purty, she made my heart beat outta my chest. Violet favors her. More so than Lily." Smiling—*thank goodness*—the man stood tall again. "So, go on an' spit out what you wanna say."

"I—I know I only got one leg, but I wanna court Violet. With your permission, of course."

Mr. Larsen's serious expression returned. "What in tarnation does your leg hafta do with courtin' my daughter? I can see you only got one, but that don't matter. Boy, you gotta get over puttin' that leg 'fore anythin' else."

"Well . . . I thought you might think it would keep me from providin' for her—that is if things move on, an' we end up . . . well, you know . . . marryin' an' all." Heat rushed into Gideon's cheeks and he wavered on his crutch.

"Ain't marriage the reason for courtin'? Or were you simply wantin' to get my daughter alone whenever you please?"

"Yes. I mean, *no*! That is . . . I aim to marry her, if she'll have me. Far as bein' alone with her, I know it ain't proper till we say our vows." Beads of sweat formed on Gideon's forehead. He reached into his pocket for his handkerchief, then dabbed at his face.

"From my understandin', you was alone with her pickin' berries. Seems to me we best get this here situation in line. You can court her . . ." His eyes narrowed. "But do right an' marry her 'fore you do much else. Get my meanin'?"

Gideon gulped. "Yes, sir." Once Gideon got beyond the man's harsh tone, his approval of their courtship sunk in. "Yes, sir!" He hugged Mr. Larsen, then quickly released him and stepped back. "Sorry. But you've made me a very happy man."

"Go on an' see Violet." He chuckled. "Know that's what you've been waitin' for."

"Thank you, sir." Gideon moved faster than he thought possible and made his way to her.

* * *

"Ma," Violet said from the side of her mouth. "It looks like Pa's bein' hateful. No. Wait. He's smilin' now." She let out a relieved sigh and swayed with Noah.

"Stop your frettin'. Mark my words, the boy's askin' to court you. Good thing, too. I won't have you endin' up like your sister."

Violet cuddled Noah closer. "We've talked 'bout all that, Ma. I told you, you don't have nothin' to worry 'bout."

"Nothin'? I seen how your cheeks glowed when you came home from pickin' berries. Reckon more than pickin' happened."

"Ma!" Violet glanced around at all the parishioners exiting the church. "Hush. You don't want folks hearin'."

"You're right." She reached for the baby. "Give 'im to me. Can't have *you* holdin' him all the time. Folks'll think he's yours."

Violet reluctantly passed him over, but Noah immediately fussed.

Her ma patted his back and hushed him, but he kept reaching for Violet. She'd bonded with him the way Lily should have. He was most content in Violet's arms.

"Oh, my goodness," Violet muttered. "Gideon hugged Pa. Never thought I'd see that."

"Your pa musta said *yes*."

Isaac wandered up beside them. "Said yes to what, Ma?"

"Your sister's acquirin' a beau."

"Huh?" Isaac's face puckered. "She's already got plenty a bows. Wears 'em in her hair every Sunday."

Horace grabbed Isaac by the arm. "C'mon. I just seen a big ol' turtle down by the pond."

Their ma huffed. "You boys go on, but don't get wet. Hear me? We'll be headin' home soon as your pa's ready."

"Yes'm." They raced away.

Her ma followed them with her eyes. "I'll be glad when Noah can go off with his brothers. It'll make things easier on me."

Violet had to bite her tongue. If she said what she wanted to, she'd likely get slapped. Fortunately, Gideon was heading their way. She needed the distraction.

He beamed like the sun. A very good sign.

"Hey, Violet," he said and dipped his head. "Mrs. Larsen." Another polite dip.

"Mornin' Gideon," her ma curtly said. "Reckon I'll take Noah an' go talk to Harriet Quincy. She's been fussin' at me ever since I birthed this boy. Says I'm too old to be havin' babies. I'll show her what for." She strode away before either of them could utter a sound.

Violet inched closer to Gideon. "Forgive my ma. She used to be kind, but she's gotten harsher with age."

"Can't be easy startin' over with a little 'un, bein' on in years. Reckon she has every right to be cranky." He nervously looked around, then eased his hand closer to hers. "Your pa agreed to let me court you. After last Monday, I figgered you'd be open to it. Was I wrong?"

Her heart thumped. Every awful thing her ma had said went right out of her mind, replaced by thoughts of Gideon. If she could, she'd kiss him right here and now. "Course you wasn't wrong. It's what I've been hopin' for." She cautiously brushed her fingers over the back of his hand, making certain to hide the action from the sight of others.

He trembled and wavered on his crutch. "I wanna see you as often as possible, but it ain't easy for me to get 'round. I ain't ready to ride no horse yet. Maybe in time. For now, I'll ask Pa if I can use the wagon. Come fetch you for supper. How'd that be?"

"I'd like that. Then, when Isaac sees you, we can explain what a beau is. He thinks it's just sumthin' I put in my hair."

Gideon ran his hand along the back of it. "Like the purty blue one in there now."

His touch sent chills to every inch of her body. She decided to put her attention elsewhere. "You're gettin' 'round quite well on that crutch. I see you made the pad I spoke of."

"You're blushin', Violet."

"Can't help it," she whispered. "I keep thinkin' 'bout that old log by the gooseberry bush."

"The log makes your cheeks turn red?" The playfulness in his eyes reminded her of the old Gideon. It warmed her through and through.

She lightly smacked his arm. "You know full well what I mean."

His expression softened. "Yep. I've been thinkin' 'bout it, too." Their eyes locked. "I'll come by an' fetch you at five. All right?"

"I'll be ready." The desire to kiss him grew even stronger. Something she didn't think possible.

"Violet!" her pa called out and waved his arm. "Time to go!"

"I'll be right there, Pa!" She worked her lower lip and stared at Gideon. "See you later."

"Bye." His fingers once again brushed hers.

She ran toward the waiting wagon, before she did something she shouldn't.

CHAPTER 21

Evie paced beside Lily's bed. "You honestly like him?"

"As a matter of fact, I do." Lily followed Evie's movement with her eyes. "Archibald Jones is likely the kindest person I've met here."

Evie shook her head back and forth. "But he's so unappealing. Will you willingly marry him?"

Lily patted the spot beside her on the bed. "Please sit. You're wearin' me out just watchin' you."

"Sorry." Evie plopped down.

She'd confided in Lily that she'd spied on Archibald at dinner last Sunday, and after that day, she'd been beside herself worried over Lily and the arrangement her uncle had made with Mr. Jones. She'd come to Lily's room daily, questioning her intentions. And since Archibald was coming by himself for a private dinner tonight with Lily, Evie had become relentless.

She took Evie's hand. "You need to stop frettin' over me. It's nice you care, but I've accepted what's been laid out for me."

"Only because I told you about the inheritance. Isn't that right?"

"Partly." She released Evie and looked toward the window. "It would ease my mind knowin' my family would be provided for." With a heavy sigh, she faced Evie again—someone she now called *friend*. "Aunt Helen an' Uncle Stuart have been kinder to me lately. An', if it makes you feel better, I've not yet agreed to marry Archibald. We're simply gettin' to know one another. Once I found out 'bout how his ma died from cholera, it's made me understand who he is. Eatin' excessive amounts of food has been his means to cope with her loss. Well, that an' smokin' up a storm."

"I've been told everyone who lived in St. Louis in 1849 lost someone in the cholera epidemic. It was a horrid thing. Not long before you arrived here, the city struggled with another outbreak. Your aunt and uncle stopped going out for a time. They didn't even go to church."

"I wasn't aware. Are folks still dyin' from it?"

"From my understanding, it's under control. But diseases are unpredictable. The city put together a Board of Health to come up with ways of improving sanitation."

"That's good. I s'pose big cities can afford such things."

"If I'm not mistaken, Archibald's father is on the board. He has a vested interest, what with losing his wife as he did." Evie frowned. "I know you're sympathetic toward Archibald, but all that aside, why'd you let him smoke while you were in the courtyard together? Proper men don't do that in a lady's presence."

"I wanted to help him. He told me it calms him."

"How do you tolerate the smell?"

Lily hadn't thought about it much. "Reckon it didn't bother me, bein' outdoors an' all."

Evie giggled. "You said that word."

"I did, didn't I?" Lily lifted her hands in the air and shrugged. "I s'pose since I've gotten so comfortable talkin' with you, my old habits slip out. I'll try an' do better."

"It's all right. Honestly, the way you talk has never bothered *me*." She stood and moved toward the door. "You best be getting ready for dinner. Archibald will be arriving in thirty minutes."

"Evie?" Lily carefully pondered her words.

"Yes?"

"Will you think badly of me if I marry him?"

Evie's frown deepened. "No. But I'll *feel* badly for you."

"Because he's so unappealin'?"

She shook her head. "No. Because you'd be marrying him for the wrong reasons. People should marry for love, not money, or status, or to make their aunt and uncle happy."

Lily stared at her lap. "Things don't always work out the way you think they should."

"Don't you want to be in love, Lily?"

Without thought, Lily hugged herself. "What I want doesn't matter anymore." She lifted her eyes to find confusion on Evie's face, but then it turned to something more understanding.

Evie stood taller. "We do what we have to, don't we?"

Lily nodded and Evie walked away.

* * *

Lily had had several enjoyable meals with Archibald, but he told her he wasn't ready to sit with her at Sunday services. She couldn't have been more relieved.

A sense of vanity had crept in—or something like it. Maybe just simple pride. She enjoyed spending time with him privately in her home, but if they were together in public, folks would assume she was attracted to him. She *liked* him, but it would take a miracle to find him desirable. And though what other people thought shouldn't bother her, for some reason, it did.

September had arrived, yet the unbearable heat remained. She'd been told they were having unusually warm weather. No matter how hard she fluttered her fan, it didn't cool her. At least she'd worn her lavender dress. The three-quarter-length sleeves and light cotton fabric helped a bit.

Almost every member of the congregation looked as if they'd rather be up to their necks in the river than enduring the close proximity of so many bodies.

Uncle Stuart leaned across Aunt Helen and tapped Lily's knee. "Archibald didn't come today, nor did his father. They don't cope well with the heat."

Lily smiled and politely nodded. Uncle Stuart had been behaving himself lately and the simple tap didn't bother her.

Aunt Helen pushed him upright. "Please, Stuart. I can scarcely handle the warmth of my own body, let alone yours."

Frowning, he scooted over several inches.

The congregation stood for the opening hymn, and Lily caught sight of Zachary Danforth. He hurried up the aisle to his regular pew, and as he'd done in the past, glanced over his shoulder and smiled at her.

Why couldn't God have put Archibald's kind heart into Zachary's attractive body?

Shame on you, Lily. Looks ain't everythin'.

She chided herself.

Aren't. Looks aren't *everythin'.*

It seemed silly to worry about having proper verbiage in her thoughts, but Mrs. Gottlieb's teaching constantly lingered.

She, too, was absent today. Aunt Helen informed Lily that Mrs. Gottlieb had gone out of town to visit her sister-in-law for a few weeks. Lily's lessons had been put on hold. And honestly, Lily thought they'd be done by now. But next week, they were starting up again.

Aunt Helen had nearly burst a seam raving about a surprise for Lily. She'd be taught something completely *thrilling*, as her aunt had put it. Lily didn't have an inkling of what it might be, but tried not to think about it. For Aunt Helen to be so excited, it had to be horrid.

The woman nudged her. "Why aren't you singing?" she whispered from the side of her mouth.

Lily'd been so lost in her thoughts, she'd stared at the hymnal without seeing it. "Sorry."

Aunt Helen pointed to the verse, and Lily found her place. She didn't sing out, but moved her lips enough to satisfy her aunt.

Because of the wretched heat, Pastor Schaller shortened his sermon. The church rapidly emptied. Aunt Helen had never walked so fast, and Uncle Stuart hastened at her heels. Lily wasn't nearly as energetic and took her time.

"Hello."

The low, smooth-sounding voice stopped her from taking another step. She turned and found herself face to face with Zachary. He stood similar in height to Caleb—almost a full head taller than her. Now that he was close, she discovered he not only *looked* fine, he smelled incredible.

Cologne?

She refrained from sniffing him. Remembering to be *proper*, she composed herself and straightened her posture. "Hello."

He grinned. "I've not had the pleasure of an introduction, which I feel is quite a shame. I noticed you weeks ago."

"Yes. I noticed you noticing." She cast her most sophisticated smile. "An' you are . . .?"

"Zachary Danforth. And *you* are Lily Larsen." He bent toward her. "I asked," he whispered.

Why did her cheeks heat even more than the rest of her body, which had spiked in temperature just by being close to him?

His head slightly tipped to one side. "You're blushing. Did I embarrass you?"

She flipped her fan open and fluttered it. "I don't embarrass easily. It's blisterin' hot in here."

"That it is."

Members of the congregation worked their way around them, casting curious eyes as they passed.

Zachary grinned and bowed his head, acknowledging several of them.

He lightly touched the back of Lily's arm and moved closer. "We're bound to start gossip. Does that trouble you?"

"Lutherans gossip?" She tried to ignore the way he'd made her skin tingle. "An' I thought y'all were above that."

His chest dramatically rose and fell. She feared she'd offended him.

"The way you talk . . ." His mouth hovered so close to her ear, his heated breath covered it. "I can't explain how it makes me feel. I could listen to you all day."

"I doubt my aunt an' uncle would approve."

He took a small step back. "You're a grown woman. You should be allowed to make your own decisions as to whom you converse with."

"You're extremely forward. Aren't you, Mr. Danforth?" Her heart thumped hard and her throat tightened. Why was he having this effect on her? She'd not felt this way since . . .

Caleb.

"Mr. Danforth?" Zachary smirked, but not in an unpleasant way. "You'd best call me Zachary, or I shall have to call my father over so you can converse with him. As for being forward, I wanted to meet you the first time I saw you. But, I was told you're spoken for. I assume it's an arrangement your aunt and uncle orchestrated?"

The church had almost emptied, leaving the two of them practically alone—aside from Matthew, Mark, Luke, and John. Any moment now, her *dear* relatives would be searching for her. She wanted to carry on this conversation as long as possible. "Why do you think the Clarks would plan my future?"

"Are you saying you're *not* spoken for?"

She jutted her chin high. "I'm a grown woman. You said it yourself. I make my own decisions." *What am I doin'?*

His smile grew and made him even more pleasant to look at. "I'm happy to hear it." He quickly scanned around them, then stared straight into her eyes. "Are you allowed in the city unaccompanied?"

She gulped, with a firm understanding of his intentions. "I've never cared to venture out, aside from my instruction with Mrs. Gottlieb. But there are times when my aunt and uncle are preoccupied, an' I doubt they'd miss me." She must be crazy even thinking about doing this, but it felt wonderful making her own choices again. "What do you have in mind . . . *Zachary*?"

The pleasure on his face grew the instant she said his name. "Have you been to Lafayette Park?"

"No, I haven't."

"I'm surprised. It's not far from the Clarks' residence. It's within walking distance. I'd love to show it to you."

"All right." She swallowed hard. "When?"

"Lily!" Aunt Helen's sharp bark destroyed the moment. "We've been searching everywhere for you!"

"Sorry, Aunt Helen." Lily gestured to Zachary. "Mr. Danforth an' I were talkin'."

"I can see that." She smiled at him, but it was the ugliest one Lily'd ever seen. "Good day, Zachary. Lily, say goodbye to Mr. Danforth."

Lily curtsied. "Goodbye, Mr. Danforth." She searched his eyes. She'd most definitely not seen the last of him.

Zachary dipped his head. "Miss Larsen."

Aunt Helen grasped onto her arm and almost dragged her from the sanctuary, then hustled her along the pathway to the waiting carriage. Once there, her aunt yanked open the door and shoved her inside.

Lily stumbled onto the seat, almost into Uncle Stuart's lap.

He chuckled as she sat, but when Aunt Helen got in and closed the door, the laughter ended.

"What were you thinking talking to that young man?" she hissed.

"Are you sayin' I'm not permitted to speak to whomever I please?"

Aunt Helen pointed a finger in her face. "You know very well what I'm saying. You've been promised to Archibald Jones. Zachary Danforth is a bachelor who's known to have a wandering eye. You cheapened yourself by talking with him. Now everyone in church will think less of you."

Lily sat tall. "That's plum silly. He was bein' polite. He introduced himself to me, which I appreciated. You've only acquainted me with a handful of parishioners. Shouldn't I get to know *everyone?*" She glanced across the seat at Uncle Stuart, who smugly shook his head.

"I won't have you tarnishing our good name," he said. "We've gained the respect of the members at Trinity. How do you think Archibald will feel when he hears you've been chatting with Zachary Danforth?"

"The way you're talkin', you'd think I'd been *kissin'* on the man. What's wrong with a bit of pleasant conversation?"

"Pleasant?" Uncle Stuart's steely gaze dug deep. "*How* pleasant?"

Lily threw up her hands. "Why do I even try to make you happy? I've done everythin' you've asked me to do. I won't have you chastisin' me for simple conversation."

Uncle Stuart frowned and turned to Aunt Helen. "It seems Mrs. Gottlieb neglected to instruct her in appropriate interaction with young men. Speak to her about it and have her set Lily straight."

"Of course." Aunt Helen shook her finger in Lily's face. "Don't converse with Mr. Danforth again."

Lily looked away and said nothing. Though her thoughts raced faster than a frightened rabbit, she had no fear of her demanding relatives. A spark of her former self had been ignited by Zachary Danforth. She'd nearly succumbed to being fully manipulated by her aunt and uncle, but her life was too important to be set in stone by someone else. Rich relative or not.

Yes, she'd made choices that brought on more pain than she could scarcely bear, but she'd survived. If this was the life she had to live, then she wanted it to be the best possible.

If Zachary could fill the hole in her heart, why not let him try?

After all, she wouldn't be betraying Caleb. He'd made *his* choice.

But . . . Noah held her back. Maybe Zachary would be understanding—accepting of what she'd done. Perhaps he'd be willing to help raise her son.

Stop!

She'd gotten way ahead of herself. First, she needed to get to know him. Accomplishing that would be a grand task in itself.

And what about Archibald? She'd grown to care for him as a dear friend. The last thing she wanted to do was drive him into a deeper depression.

CHAPTER 22

Lily had to admit, the clothes her aunt had purchased for her were exceptional. Not only the dresses, but her nightgown as well. Made of the softest silk, it lay against her skin like the most delicate rose petal.

She pulled back the corner of her blanket, but a knock on her door stopped her from getting into bed.

"Evie?" Lily moved toward the door.

"No. It's Stuart."

Wonderful.

She pressed herself against the door, fearing he might try to open it. "I'm not dressed."

"I have something for you."

She didn't trust him one bit. "What is it?"

"A letter." His less-than-cordial tone disturbed her, but the idea of finally getting mail made up for it.

She stood behind the door and opened it a sliver. Just wide enough to fit an envelope. "Why'd you wait till now to bring it?"

"Helen's not aware it came," he whispered. "I waited until she fell asleep."

"Why?"

He pushed the letter through the small space. "If she'd seen it, she would've read it. I know you think little of me, but I'm an honorable man. The letter is addressed to you alone, and I respect your privacy."

Stunned, Lily took it from his hand and expanded the opening enough to see his face, though she kept herself concealed behind the door. "I—I don't know what to say. I appreciate it, that's for sure."

He stood tall. "Regardless of what you believe, I'm not a beast."

"Thank you." She started to shut the door, but he stopped her.

"There *is* one thing I require."

Course there is. "Yes?"

"Swear to me you won't pursue Zachary Danforth."

No wonder he'd made a kind gesture. He had other motives. "I'm not fond a swearin' 'bout anythin'."

"Lily." Cold as ice. "Continue your relationship with Archibald, or future correspondence won't receive the same courtesy given to the letter in your hand. Do you understand?"

"Perfectly."

"Very well. Good night, then." He strode off down the hall.

She clicked the door tightly shut, went back to her bed, and turned the wheel on the lantern to increase the output of light.

She'd managed to avoid swearing to something she doubted she'd uphold, and yes, she'd continue to see Archibald Jones. That wouldn't be difficult. Especially since she liked his company. For now, she'd appeased her uncle and not dug herself into a hole.

Casting all other thoughts aside, she opened the envelope and withdrew the letter.

Her heart ached. Simply seeing Violet's fine penmanship made Lily homesick. With a sad smile, she read silently to herself.

Dear Lily,

Home is miserable without you here. Please do not feel badly, but I had to say it. Every day, I miss my best friend.

Her sister's proper sentence structure would please Mrs. Gottlieb, but it wrenched Lily's heart. She clutched the letter to her breast and pushed away tears. She wouldn't have them clouding her vision and obstructing her ability to read.

I am not sure how much I should say, but my heart is leading me to tell everything. This will not be easy for you to hear, but it is important.

First, you should be happy to know that Noah is well. He is growing every day, babbles almost nonstop, and crawls everywhere. Pa put up a gate at the base of the stairs, because the silly boy tried to follow Isaac and Horace to their room. Noah will surely walk any day now.

There is no need to fret over him. We all keep an eye on your boy.

You also no longer have to worry that Lucas might physically harm him. But I fear there are worse things Lucas may do, because he knows the truth about Noah.

Lily couldn't breathe. She set the letter aside to compose herself. If Lucas knew the truth, he'd be even *more* inclined to hurt Noah. But since Violet had said not to worry, Lily lifted the letter and kept reading.

Lucas tried to use his knowledge to make all of us to do anything he asked. Of course, Pa would not stand for his behavior. He told Lucas to leave, assuming he would learn his lesson and come back home. Sadly, Pa was wrong. While Lucas was gone, he met up with Sergeant Douglas. You surely recall the disgusting man Pa hit over the head with a shovel.

"An' the one who touched *you* inappropriately," Lily mumbled.

You will be surprised to learn that Captain Ableman's widow hired Sergeant Douglas to search for Callie. They want to find her so they can prosecute her for the captain's death. Lucas is helping the sergeant and proudly taking the widow's money.

Of course, they are venturing on a wild goose chase. Lucas is using the situation for his own benefit. Worse yet, Lucas told the sergeant that Callie sent you a letter posted in Waynesville. They left the cove to go there and question folks about her.

Lily clutched her stomach. "Caleb."

What did Lucas think he could accomplish by exposing such things? It didn't take her long to grasp the obvious. Lucas had found a way to make a living without working.

She quickly found her place again.

While talking about the letter with our folks, Ma told the sergeant she no longer has it and that you do. She went on to say that the letter was likely destroyed. The sergeant believes you still have it and stated that young women keep all their correspondence. How he knows that, I am not certain. As far as I am concerned, the man is ignorant in regard to women.

He asked where you were, and Ma told him. I understand why. It would not be smart for her to lie about that.

They plan to seek you out in St. Louis. I know you probably have the letter, and you also have the sense to tell them you don't, but they will still come to question you. Ma told him all Callie said in the letter was she was fine, but would not be returning to the cove. If you tell him the same, all should be well.

I hope and pray this reaches you before they do, so you will not be caught off guard.

I have pondered the best means to send this, and my intention is to give it to Mr. Myers. I see him and his wife weekly at Sunday services. One day, I hope to see Gideon, too, though he has not attended worship since he came back to the cove.

No doubt you remember my fondness for him. His brothers died in the war, and Gideon lost a leg, but you and I both know life goes on after the loss of a limb. I hope to help him. I am trying all I can to have your strength.

Ma, Pa, and the boys are well. They also miss you. Ma and Pa rarely speak of it, yet I see it in their eyes. On the other hand, Horace and Isaac talk about you all the time.

I'm proud to say that Pa keeps working hard. Mrs. Quincy is letting her grandsons work with him in the fields. Hopefully by October, he can hire a few other hands who can help sow the wheat. No matter who comes, I know I will never see anyone who cared about the farm as much as you did.

I pray for you every day. I hope you are eating as you should, and also that you are happy. It cannot be easy living with Aunt Helen, but perhaps Uncle Stuart is kind and makes living there bearable.

Please write and tell me everything. It would be best if you send the letter inside another one, and address it to Mrs. Myers, with no return address, of course. She is gracious and is well aware Mrs. Quincy is a busy-body, known to spread rumors and pry into other's mail. Aside from that, I do not want Ma to interfere with our correspondence. I will do what I can to earn Mrs. Myers' trust. She has known me forever, so I feel she will be understanding.

As I said, I pray for you, but I need your prayers, too. I hesitated telling you any of this, because I know you have your own troubles. This will surely add to them. However, if you had been caught unaware by the arrival of Lucas and the sergeant, it would likely have troubled you more. At lease now, you will be prepared.

I fear for our brother. I do not know how his heart turned so cold. I reckon he needs our prayers more than anyone.

I love you dearly,

Violet

Silent tears trickled down Lily's cheeks. She'd never cared to be so far away, but now, she *hated* it. Violet needed her. They all did.

Panic covered her and brought on a cold sweat. If the sergeant and Lucas confronted Caleb . . .

"Lawdy," she mumbled. "I have more than enough troubles right now, I can't worry myself over that."

If she fretted even more about everyone back home, her brain might burst right along with her heart.

Ping!

Lily gasped. Something had struck her window and startled her from her dismal thoughts.

Before she could move to explore it, something else hit the glass. Any harder, and it might break.

She gazed into the darkness. A small flicker of light caught her eye. It came from the branch of a nearby tree.

Though a mite nervous about what she might find, she raised the window to get a better look.

Oh, my goodness.

Her anxious feelings vanished, replaced by excitement. She'd know that grin anywhere. Zachary Danforth perched in the branches like the bears back home. He held a candle in one hand that illuminated his face. She wasn't certain what he'd thrown at the window, but he'd definitely gotten her attention.

Though she wanted to laugh, she stifled it. Coming across like a silly girl wasn't an option. Not if she wanted to make any sort of decent impression on the man.

She leaned out into the open air, then quickly covered herself, remembering her simple nightgown.

He'll think I'm shameless.

"What are you doin' here?" she whispered as loudly as she could.

He blew out the candle, then climbed a bit higher, putting him only ten feet or so away from her.

"Isn't it obvious?" He, too, whispered, yet she heard him plainly.

Her heart rested in her throat. "You're a fool, Zachary Danforth."

"At least you dropped the *mister*. But please, stop the formality." He inched across the limb, even closer.

"*Don't.*" She held up a hand. "The branch is gettin' too thin. You'll fall an' break your neck."

He released the limb and held both hands to his heart. "You care." Even in the dark, his bright smile gleamed, but then he teetered, gasped, and grabbed onto the branch.

Her breath hitched. "Get down from there this instant." She wanted to scream it at him, yet had she done it, it could've woken the entire household.

"Not until we confirm our outing. Are you able to join me in the park tomorrow?"

One thing was certain. His persistence was an admirable trait. Her mind spun. "How on earth did you know which room was mine?"

"I have my ways." He sat taller. "Now, please, answer my question. Are you able to see me tomorrow?"

"I'm meetin' with Mrs. Gottlieb t'morra. But . . ." *I hope this works.* "I can ask David to take me to the park after. I'll tell him I have a hankerin' to walk. I doubt he'll question me. He never says much a anythin'. I could likely be there 'round three. Will that do?"

Silence.

She craned her neck to see him better. He hadn't fallen from the tree. His dark silhouette remained mingled with the leaves. "Zachary?"

"Yes?"

"You didn't answer me."

"Sorry. I was mesmerized listening to you speak."

She rolled her eyes. "Are you goin' to be one of those wretched men I should run away from? Tell me now an' save me the trouble."

"Wretched?" He laughed. "I compliment you, and you consider me *wretched*? I'll have you know, I'm one of the most honorable and loyal men you'll ever encounter."

Honorable. The word her uncle had recently used. She wasn't convinced. "The very thing a cad would say."

"Now I'm a *cad*?" Another laugh. "Please. Allow me the opportunity to prove myself. There's a large concrete post with a domed spire at the entrance to the park. I'll wait for you there."

"What if David sees you?"

"If it would ease you, I can hide behind the trees."

"It would." Truthfully, she doubted anything could calm her thumping heart. Then, or now.

"Very well. Tomorrow at the park. Three o'clock." He scooted farther away, then shimmied down the trunk of the tree, reminding her of Lucas.

She blinked, and he was gone.

Heart still pounding, she blew out a long breath and shut the window. She preferred leaving it open, but Aunt Helen had fussed about disease being carried on the night winds. A silly notion. However, since learning about the cholera epidemic, Lily abided by her wishes, ridiculous as they might be.

After dimming the lantern, she lay back atop her bed and shut her eyes.

A mixture of confusing emotions troubled her.

The prospect of getting to know Zachary pleased her, yet simultaneously brought on guilt. If she allowed herself to care for someone else, would it cheapen what she'd felt for Caleb and what they'd done? And would it be *proper* to bring any man into her troubled life?

She certainly *liked* Zachary. He made her laugh, and God forgive her, but he was far more pleasant to look at than Archibald. She doubted it was sinful to enjoy admiring a handsome man.

Surely not.

Odd he'd arrived just after her heart had been so tormented over Violet's letter. He'd lifted her out of her gloom, and she was glad for that. She had an overabundance of despair. Joy was a welcome change.

* * *

Zachary couldn't stop smiling. Not only had Lily agreed to meet him in the park, he'd seen her scantily clad. A sight he wouldn't soon forget. The light that had flickered behind her from the lantern in her bedroom illumined the image of her perfect form.

He hadn't lied about being mesmerized. The lilt in her accent boiled his blood. That, combined with her womanly figure . . .

I can hardly bear it.

Although uncomfortable in his lower extremities, he managed to hurry home. Fortunately, twenty long blocks capably cooled him down.

As quietly as he could, he opened the back door. This time of night, everyone should be sleeping, therefore they shouldn't hear the slight creak.

He tiptoed across the wood floor.

"Zachary."

His father's gruff tenor stopped him cold. "Yes, sir?"

"Come with me." He jerked his head toward his study.

Zachary followed him into the room and the man shut the door behind them.

"Sit." His father pointed at a chair, then sat in another across from it.

"Is something wrong?" Zachary feigned nonchalance and casually took the seat.

"You're impossible. Of course, something is wrong. You're sneaking around like a criminal."

Zachary smiled and leaned back. "I did nothing I should be sorry for."

The man eyed him warily. "I know you. I was told you were speaking to the Clark's niece after worship. You're chasing after her, aren't you?"

"Me?" He held a hand to his heart. "Father, I've never had to *chase* a woman."

"Oh, yes. I'm aware. They fall at your feet." His sarcasm came through clearly. "I specifically told you Lily Larsen is spoken for."

He thrummed his fingers on the arm of his chair. "Did you see her tonight?"

Zachary had never lied to the man, but briefly considered it. "Yes." Maybe his father could help. "I saw her. But—"

"I don't want to hear it."

"Why? She's a grown woman. I find her extremely attractive, and if I'm not mistaken she reciprocates those feelings."

"Have you forgotten the arrangement made with Baxter Jones?"

"How could I?" Zachary shuddered. "Thinking of her with Archibald turns my stomach."

His father gave him a warning glare.

"Why can't I get to know her and decide if she's worth my pursuit?"

"Worth your pursuit?" The man grunted. "Listen to yourself. I didn't raise you to be arrogant."

"No, you brought me up to be honorable. *And* truthful. I have a deep feeling about her." He patted his chest. "Way down in my heart. She could be the one. And if I find it to be true, can't you offer her uncle a similar arrangement? Perhaps help with his finances. Guide him into some proper investments. Maybe even wave some money under his nose."

His father's mouth twitched from side to side, his silvery mustache along with it. "I've never seen you so earnest. Why *this* girl?"

"I don't know." He smiled just thinking about her. "When I see her, feelings arise unlike anything I've experienced before."

"Mmm, hmm." The man crossed his arms. "Mind those feelings. That young woman is untarnished. It's crucial she remain that way."

"Father. I won't do anything inappropriate. I swear it."

"You're not going to let this go, are you?"

"No." Zachary sat up tall. "I've arranged to see her tomorrow. I'm showing her the park."

"Without an escort?"

"Perhaps a pigeon or two." He grinned, hoping his father would appreciate his humor.

The man stood, without a trace of a smile. "I can't say I approve, but you're an adult now. I'd like to see you married before your sisters. However, I doubt that will happen. I'm expecting a visit from York Hasselbeck any day now. I believe he intends to ask for your sister's hand."

Zachary rose to his feet, grinning a bit broader. "I think York wants more than Ursula's *hand*."

"Exactly. The very reason a wedding must be expedited." He wrapped an arm around Zachary's shoulder. "Please, mind yourself. Treat Lily with respect."

"I will. And if I choose to pursue courtship, can I count on your help?"

His father let out a long breath and remained expressionless. "Yes. You're my only son. I expect you to carry on the family name. Truthfully, I'm pleased you've finally found someone you feel is worthy. However, I wish to God she wasn't related to the Clarks. Helen can be so . . ." His face contorted.

Zachary laughed. "No need to say it. I know exactly what you mean."

They patted each other on the back, then parted ways.

Zachary went to his room, satisfied. At least, *somewhat*.

Thoughts of Lily drifted through his mind, until he managed to fall asleep.

CHAPTER 23

Violet rapidly moved her undergarments up and down the washboard.

Her ma stood a short distance away, hanging a freshly washed sheet over the clothesline. She pulled a clothespin from her mouth and secured it to the fabric. "He propose yet?"

"No. Heaven's sake, Ma. We've only been courtin' a week."

"Far as I'm concerned, it's high time he gets to it." She fisted her hands on her hips and gazed upward, then shielded her eyes from the sun. "I'll be glad when it cools down a mite." She jerked her head toward the cabin. "Go check on Noah. Reckon he's napped long 'nuff."

Violet handed her the damp clothes. "What'll you do once I get married an' move out? Who's gonna help with Noah then?"

"I raised all a you. I can manage the baby myself."

"But you ain't done none of it yet. I change him, feed him, an' rock him when he cries. I'm more his ma than you are."

The woman's eyes shot fire. "Don't go sayin' such things. Just cuz I let you tend him, don't mean I ain't able. I love that boy."

"So'd Lily."

Her ma slapped her hard across the face. "I don't wanna hear that. Now, go an' see to your *brother*."

"Yes'm."

As much as Violet loved her folks, sometimes they made it awfully hard to care about them.

She trudged into the cabin, downhearted. But the instant she saw Noah's adorable grin, her spirits lifted.

Wide awake, he gurgled and kicked his feet.

After she changed him, she carried him to the rocker and held him close. "Your ma loves you. Never forget that."

She'd almost told Gideon about Noah, and someday she would. Now that they were courting, she didn't want to keep any secrets from him. Once they married, she wanted their life together to start out right. And hopefully, it would stay that way. Someone had to change the wayward course the Larsen family had set.

Weeks had passed since she'd sent Lily the letter. By now, she should've received it. Violet had neglected to tell Mrs. Myers that she suggested Lily send any correspondence between them to her. Even though it hadn't been said, she assumed Mrs. Myers wouldn't mind. After all, as she'd indicated before, sisters needed to be able to communicate privately.

Violet needed to hurry up and finish the laundry so she could get ready for supper with Gideon. He'd be coming at five to fetch her.

She had to be careful whenever Isaac came around them. He'd gotten comfortable with Gideon and had nearly spoken about Caleb. Fortunately, Violet stopped him before he said something he shouldn't and turned the course of the conversation. Later that night, she reminded Isaac that Caleb was a secret that must be kept.

Time flew right along with her thoughts. It wasn't easy contemplating a way to say what needed to be said.

Unlike the previous week, her family paid little mind to Gideon's arrival. He shuffled Violet off into his wagon soon after, then drove the horse extra slow.

Violet kept her hands folded in her lap. "We keep goin' at this rate, an' we'll be late for supper."

"Ma's expectin' us late."

"What?"

Gideon stopped the horse in the middle of the road, then shifted on the seat and faced her. "Ma's gonna have supper ready at six. I told her I needed some time with you first." He took Violet's hand and scooted closer.

His proximity had her melting into the woodwork. "Reckon this is wise?"

He grinned. "We're courtin'. Folks expect to see us together."

"But we're unaccompanied. An' the look in your eyes tells me you have sumthin' more on your mind than talkin'."

They'd managed to steal a few kisses since the first ones on the log, and each one grew stronger. She couldn't take much more without throwing herself at him.

"I have *lots* more on my mind than talkin'." His eyes penetrated hers. "That's why I gotta do this."

She gulped. "Do what?"

He held her hand firmer. "Violet Larsen, will you be my wife?"

Yes, she expected this eventually, but . . . "We've only been courtin' a week. Ain't it too soon for marriage?"

His head drew back. "Is that a *no?*"

"A no? *No.*" She rapidly shook her head. "What I mean is . . . Course I wanna be your wife. But . . ."

"There's a *but?*"

She frowned and silently nodded.

"Ah, hell." His shoulders slumped. "I thought for sure you'd be happy as a lark. Now you're frownin' an' look more like your ma."

She smacked his arm. "Don't say that."

"Well, you do." He crossed his arms. "So, what's this *but?* Go on' an' spit it out, so I can stop frettin'."

This was harder than she'd imagined. Yet she wouldn't agree to a marriage proposal unless he knew the truth.

She grabbed onto his hand to ease him, and perhaps herself as well. "There's things 'bout our family you hafta know. Secrets we've all sworn to keep. But if I'm to be your wife, I don't wanna hold nothin' from you."

He eyed her suspiciously. "I'm glad to hear it, though you got me a mite worried. Your pa some kind a government infiltrator or sumthin'?"

"That's an odd thing to say. But, no. It ain't Pa. Well, not exactly. It's more 'bout Lily." Violet's stomach turned flip-flops. She trusted Gideon, but it didn't make this any easier.

"Lily? Sumthin' happen to her in St. Louis?"

"No. What happened is why she had to go there." The words didn't come out quite right, but she hoped she made sense. She tightened her grasp.

His thumb moved over her skin. "I'm listenin'."

Like water flowing from a broken dam, she spilled out everything about Caleb, Lily, and Noah. She even told Gideon about Sergeant Douglas and how he'd touched her and made her feel sick inside. Lastly, she revealed how Lucas was with the sergeant looking for Callie. Someone who didn't exist.

Gideon didn't interrupt at all.

She poured out her heart and soul to him, and his eyes never once lost their love for her.

Telling him freed her. A weight she'd carried for a long time had lifted. Though she missed Lily, Violet finally had someone to talk to. Someone who truly cared.

* * *

Gideon sat without moving, taking in every word that spilled from Violet's delicate lips.

"The letter I had your pa mail to Lily," she said, "told her 'bout the sergeant an' Lucas plannin' to come to St. Louis to talk to her. I had to warn her."

"Lawdy be, Violet. You wasn't lyin' 'bout family secrets." His mind spun, trying to process so much information. One thing stood out more than the rest. "If I'd a been there when that man had his hands on you . . ." He tightened his fists. "No one has the right to touch you like that."

She laid her hand against his cheek. "He didn't hurt me."

"Yes, he did. *Inside*. I could tell when you spoke 'bout him." He set his hand atop hers and cradled it to his face. "I won't never hurt you, Violet. I'll only touch you how you want me to."

"You're nothin' like him. When we're married, you can touch me any way you please, an' I won't mind. I *want* your hands on me."

He swallowed hard. The images she'd created weren't easy to dismiss.

"So," he managed to squeak out. "You're sayin' *yes?*"

"Long as you haven't changed your mind, now that you know our secrets. I love Noah with all my heart, an' I get angry with my folks for sendin' Lily away an' separatin' her from her baby. If Lily ever returns, an' folks here learn the truth, our family name will be shamed. It's sumthin' you'd best be prepared for if you align yourself with me."

He circled her with his arms, drew her to his chest, and caressed her back. "I love you, Violet. Always have. I'm willin' to take on whatever might come our way."

She raised her head to face him straight on. "It could get ugly."

"I don't care. Long as you're by my side. You've been worryin' over secrets, an' I've been frettin' over my leg. Reckon we can overcome *anythin'.*"

"Together." She lit up with a bright smile.

Gideon wasn't certain how much time had passed. They'd likely be late for supper, but he doubted his ma would care. Right now, he could only think of one thing. Her sweet mouth begged for it.

The kiss he gave her started in his heart and spread to his lips. He consumed her very essence and didn't want to let go.

When they parted, they said nothing. Just stared at each other.

His heart pounded. "We best be plannin' a weddin'."

"Yep. An' *you* best be thinkin' on how you'll ask my pa." With a playful smile, she cuddled against him.

Asking Mr. Larsen for Violet's hand shouldn't be hard. After all, he'd survived asking to court her. Marriage was already an assumption.

He snapped the reins and headed toward home. A place he hoped she'd share with him. The sooner the better. It would take some doing, but he'd work it out. He'd satisfy her selfish wish—as she'd put it—to no longer live with her folks. He prayed she wouldn't mind residing with his.

Chapter 24

For some unknown reason, Aunt Helen purchased another new gown for Lily. This one, an emerald green. Lily appreciated that it didn't have a scratchy collar like the others. In fact, it had a scooped neckline and exposed more flesh than Lily thought appropriate, but Aunt Helen assured her it was fashionable. She also claimed she had more surprises once Lily returned home from Mrs. Gottlieb's.

Lily should be excited about what might be waiting for her, but Zachary captivated her thoughts. Anxious described her best. She looked forward to spending time with him, but feared they'd be caught.

For now, she needed to turn her attention to whatever Mrs. Gottlieb had in store for her.

David grasped her hand and helped her from the carriage.

"Thank you, David. I'll be waitin' for you to pick me up just before three."

"No need to wait."

"Huh?" Would he ruin all her plans?

"Once I settle the horses and carriage at the livery, I'll be joining you."

She gaped at him, then snapped her mouth shut. The action was highly improper.

He laughed. A sound she never expected to hear. "I assume your aunt neglected to tell you."

"Um . . . That's right."

"Well, then. I won't be the one to spoil the surprise. You go on. I'll see you shortly."

He hopped up onto the driver's seat and popped the reins. She stood and watched him leave, feeling more befuddled than ever.

The only way to get answers was to ask Mrs. Gottlieb.

Lily hurried along the pathway.

She hadn't even knocked, when the door swung open.

"Oh, my dear!" Mrs. Gottlieb hugged her. "I've missed you."

"I've missed you, too."

Mrs. Gottlieb took her by the hand. "Come inside. We have so much to do today. I hope you wore comfortable shoes."

"I'm wearin' the ones I always wear."

"They'll have to do." She bustled Lily down the hallway and into a large room they'd never entered before. A piano stood in one corner. Otherwise, the space was void of any furnishings.

"Am I learnin' to play the piano or sumthin'?" Lily studied Mrs. Gottlieb's mysterious expression. "Don't tell me you're gonna make me sing."

"No, my dear." She tittered. "*Dance*. Today you shall learn to waltz."

"Waltz? I've heard a that dance, but no one back home ever did it. Why do I need to learn it?"

"For the ball. Didn't Helen tell you?"

"Aunt Helen likes to keep secrets." *It runs in the family.* "She didn't say anythin' 'bout a ball."

"Well, you had to have expected it." Mrs. Gottlieb wandered across the room and sat on the piano bench. "You remember the sentences I sent with you, don't you?"

Each and every one of the lines Mrs. Gottlieb had sent home with Lily had come into use. Except one.

"I remember. I assume the one you want me to quote is, *the ballroom filled to capacity. Gentlemen in fine clothes bowed to their intended partners and the ladies curtsied in reply.*" Lily leaned against the piano. "Shall I also assume I'll be doin' my share of curtsyin'?"

"Yes. And Archibald, bless his heart, will be forced to bow. Though I fear more for his capability as a dancer than how he bends at his abundant waistline."

Lily covered her mouth to hide a grin. "Bless his heart is right. He's actually very kind. I've grown fond a him."

"Truly?"

"Yes'm. He's smart and quite funny when he wants to be. It's a pity he doesn't look finer. Perhaps dancin' will improve his health *and* his waistline."

Mrs. Gottlieb smiled, then gazed beyond Lily and stood. "Come right in, David!"

Lily turned and faced him. For the first time ever, she actually took him in. He wasn't bad looking. She assumed he was at least thirty, but he'd aged well and had retained all his dark hair.

Mrs. Gottlieb crossed to him. "David will be your partner, Lily. He's an exceptional dancer." She guided him to Lily's side, then placed his hand in hers.

Lily stared at their joined hands. She'd frequently touched him while getting in and out of the carriage, but this felt a bid odd.

"You must touch," Mrs. Gottlieb said. "It's required in the waltz."

David stood so close, Lily heard him breathing. He was only a few inches taller than her, so they seemed well-suited to dance together.

Mrs. Gottlieb returned to the piano. "This is what a waltz sounds like." Her hands gracefully moved over the keys and created the most beautiful sound.

Lily found herself swaying to the comforting tune. "It's nice."

"David," Mrs. Gottlieb said, while she continued to play. "Show her a basic step."

Without hesitation, David positioned Lily's left hand on his shoulder, and kept hold of her right hand. He then extended their joined hands outward. *His* right hand rested on her waist.

Hmm . . .

He nodded toward the floor. "Your first step will be back on your right foot, then forward on your left." His eyes lifted, questioning her understanding.

"All right."

"Good. All you need to do is follow my lead. The waltz is a simple one, two, three. Feel the music and move with it." He smiled and held himself rigid, while his head bobbed rhythmically with Mrs. Gottlieb's playing. "Ready?"

"Uh-huh."

"I'll give you an encouraging nudge when it's time to move." He inhaled deeply. His head continued to bob and his lips mouthed *one, two, three, one, two, three,* over and over again.

When he *nudged*, she stepped back on the wrong foot and he stepped on her toe. "Ouch!"

He closed his eyes and shook his head. "Step back on your *right* foot, not the left."

"Sorry. I got it now." She found herself bobbing and counting just like him. As for Mrs. Gottlieb, she simply kept on playing.

This time, Lily stepped correctly.

The music moved her and David's able guidance kept her going. When he released her hand and guided her into a turn, she felt like a princess from a fairytale. She giggled when he pulled her back in and kept on dancing. The song ended, and David slowed her to a halt.

After a brief pause, Mrs. Gottlieb started a different tune. Though another waltz, it was slightly faster.

David tipped his head to the side. "Do you believe you're up to this?"

"Yes, I do." With confidence, she stood perfectly straight.

David nudged her into motion. The more they danced, the brighter he beamed.

When the music stopped, Lily pouted. "That was so much fun. Can we do it some more?"

"Yes," Mrs. Gottlieb said. "After tea." She faced David. "Thank you. You've never disappointed me."

He bowed. "Lily is a fine student. One of your best." After a nod to Lily, he walked out of the room.

"Don't worry, dear." Mrs. Gottlieb took her hand. "He'll be back. He's not fond of tea. Besides, we need some time alone to talk."

They strolled arm in arm to the tearoom. Lily hadn't lied when she said she'd missed the dear woman. She enjoyed her company and her wisdom.

Once they'd fixed their individual cups to their liking, they sat at the window seat.

"You play beautifully," Lily said.

"Thank you. And you *dance* exceptionally well. You never cease to amaze me."

Her praise always sent warmth across Lily's skin. "Thank *you*. So, when's this ball s'posed to happen?"

"The twenty-second of September. We have three weeks to perfect your skill. And I'm pleased to hear you're fond of Archibald Jones, because I believe your uncle intends to announce your engagement at the affair."

Lily nearly spewed her drink. She choked it down, then dabbed at her mouth with a napkin. "Engagement? We ain't even courtin'."

Mrs. Gottlieb's eyes grew wide. "Excuse me?"

In her distress, Lily's verbiage had slipped. "I'm sorry, but I'm not ready for an engagement. Are you certain it's their intention?"

"Yes. Helen's inviting everyone imaginable. She wants it to be the event of the year." Mrs. Gottlieb swirled her hand through the air. "Maybe even the decade." She grinned and sipped her tea.

"But . . ." Stomach churning, Lily set her cup down.

"I believe I understand why you're so troubled." Mrs. Gottlieb's brows drew in. "Helen told me you spoke to Zachary Danforth and said you were quite taken with him. Is that so?"

"Yes, I spoke to him, after he approached me. But, I didn't do anythin' outta line. He was nice."

"Do you know *why* men speak to women?" Mrs. Gottlieb pursed her lips.

"To get acquainted?"

"Yes, but they have *other* intentions. Men *desire* women. I assure you, I've never met a man who can simply be a friend to a woman. They always want something more. That is why it's best to have *woman* friends. Especially once you're married."

Lily thought about all the men she knew. It scared her a bit, but she feared Mrs. Gottlieb was right. And since she was being honest with herself, there was no doubt in her mind Zachary wanted to be more than friends.

She smiled at Mrs. Gottlieb. "I can say without reservation, I consider Archibald my friend an' nothin' more."

"He sees *you* otherwise."

"You mean, he *wants* me?"

"Of course, he does. He may be large and unattractive, but he's still a man with desires just as strong as one who's handsome. And you, Lily, are a beauty. How could he not want you?"

The images forming in Lily's mind were highly disturbing. "I don't love him." She lowered her head and stared at her lap.

"But you *like* him. That's a start." Mrs. Gottlieb tucked two fingers under Lily's chin and lifted her head. "He'll be good to you. Of that, I'm certain. He's a gentle soul with a loving heart."

All the joy Lily felt while dancing had vanished. She doubted she'd do nearly as well once they started again. Her spirit was no longer in it.

* * *

Lily waited at the corner while David fetched the carriage.

She'd done her best that afternoon dancing with him, but her heart weighed her down. The thought of being engaged to Archibald Jones had made her miserable.

Zachary.

He might be able to lift her spirits again. After all, he'd done it before.

David pulled up with the carriage, then hopped down to help her in. "Are you all right, Miss Lily?"

"I'm fine. Just tired."

"You worked hard today. I'll get you right home."

She'd nearly forgotten her plan. "Oh. *No.* Tell you what . . . I'd really like to walk a bit. I was told Lafayette Park is lovely. Can you drop me there?"

"Alone?"

"Yes. Truthfully, I feel like I could use a little time by myself."

He studied her face. "Mrs. Gottlieb told you about the plans for your engagement, didn't she?"

Tears pooled in Lily's eyes. "Yes. I wasn't aware you knew as well."

"I've known for a while." He gazed at her with such pity, she believed he truly cared. But if he was like all other men, did that mean *he* wanted her, too? "Miss Lily. Don't marry him, unless it's what you want."

She wiped at her eyes with her sleeve. "What I want hasn't mattered for a very long time." She took his hand and stepped up into the carriage.

He hesitated in the doorway. "I'll take you to the park. But please, think about what I said." He shut the door.

His sincerity seemed real. She had to believe not all men were lecherous. David had never attempted to compromise her. He'd never even *looked* at her inappropriately. Either he didn't care for women, or perhaps he had someone special in his life. She'd never asked. Of course, up until now, they'd barely spoken.

She slowed her breathing and forced her tears to stop. Soon, she'd see Zachary and didn't want him to notice she'd been crying.

Chapter 25

Well past three o'clock, Zachary paced behind several large trees. This foreign predicament stumped him. No woman had *ever* kept him waiting.

The clip-clop of horses' hooves stopped him. He darted behind the largest oak and peered around it.

Yes!

The carriage stopped at the park's entrance. The driver hopped down and opened the door, then helped Lily to the ground.

Wearing green, she'd blend in perfectly with the trees and grass. Perhaps that was her intention.

His heart thumped. The anticipation of being near her had his blood pumping hard.

He waited without moving until the carriage was well out of sight, then eased out from behind the tree.

Lily strolled toward him, head high. "Why, Zachary Danforth. What brings *you* here?"

He'd willingly play along. Though no one was in sight, she seemed to have the need to pretend they'd merely bumped into each other. "Hello, Miss Larsen. It's fine to see you. I decided I needed some fresh air. What about you?"

"*I* felt the need to walk." She sidled up beside him. "Truthfully, I'm spent," she whispered. "I've been dancin' all afternoon."

"Dancing?" He let out a slight laugh, then reality slapped him. "Oh, yes. The ball."

They walked side by side along the pathway. "You know of it?"

"Everyone does. Your aunt's been boasting about it." He kept his face forward, but shifted his eyes toward her. "I was told they plan to announce your courtship to Archibald Jones."

She stopped and laid a hand on his arm. "Courtship? That's what you heard?"

"Yes." She'd never appeared so distraught, and if he wasn't mistaken, she'd been crying. "What's wrong, Lily?"

She turned away from him. "You heard wrong. They're plannin' on announcin' our *engagement*."

No.

He tried to keep calm. "That's ridiculous. Courtship always comes before an engagement. Have you agreed to . . . *marry* him?" He choked out the word.

"Heavens, no." She stood tall, jerked her shoulders back, and sniffled. "I won't cry. But I get so angry at times. I feel like my life's not my own."

He gently turned her to face him. "Then do something about it. Go to your uncle and tell him how you feel."

"It won't change things. I don't know what he has invested in this, but I have a feelin' money's involved. Somehow, he's benefitin' from this arranged union."

Though Zachary promised his father he wouldn't tell, he couldn't keep this from Lily. After all, the Clarks truly were manipulating her life. He couldn't just stand by and watch her suffer. "I know about the arrangement."

"You do?"

He nodded and guided her to a wrought iron bench. "Let's sit."

She took her seat daintily, like the flower she'd been named for. "What do you know?"

Since they were in public view, he kept a good distance from her on the bench, even though no one was presently in sight. "Your uncle will gain a new export for his shipping business. Mr. Jones has an abundance of tobacco to be shipped overseas."

"So, I'm his pawn? A means to gain more business?"

"Yes. Baxter has been desperate to find a bride for his son. Seems the man wants an heir." *Just like my father.*

"An' I'm merely the vessel to carry it." She lowered her eyes.

It tore at his heart seeing her this way. "You're far more than a vessel. What do *you* want, Lily?"

She moistened her lips. He'd kissed many women, but had never wanted to kiss anyone more than he wanted to kiss Lily at this very moment.

"I . . ." Her entire body lifted and she met his gaze. "I want you to tell me all 'bout yourself. I don't care to ponder anymore 'bout Archibald, the ball, or my hateful relatives. Fill my mind with other things, Zachary."

No wonder she'd enamored him. He hadn't met a woman with her strength before. "Very well. However, once I'm finished, you must reciprocate."

She gave a single nod, and he could swear her eyes held a bit of uncertainty, but he wouldn't fault her for it. Her life was more complex than it should be. He intended to change that.

He shifted his body sideways, rested one arm on the back of the bench, and faced her. "Were you aware I'm a medical student?"

"No." Her eyes lit up. "That's quite impressive."

"I attend St. Louis Medical College. Fortunately for me, I've been on summer recess. Classes resume next week. I'm glad I was able to meet you here today. If we'd waited any longer, it wouldn't have been possible."

"Then it's good you came to my window when you did."

A sight I'll never forget. "Yes, it is. It's a shame we weren't acquainted at the start of my break, and though I'll miss having ample time to relax, I enjoy school. You see, I want to help people. Discover new medicines and cure diseases. You know . . ." he leaned toward her. "*Simple* things." He grinned.

She let out a soft laugh. "Back home, I learned how to make poultices from my ma—my *mother*." Her cheeks reddened. "The Cherokee Indians were right smart 'bout such things an' passed on their knowledge."

He finally understood why she'd been sent to have lessons with Mrs. Gottlieb. Lily had obviously been retrained in proper English. Still, everything she said—regardless of her brief slip—endeared him. "Did you ever have the need to use that knowledge? Patch up wounds?"

"A few times." She fidgeted with her skirt. "Tell me more 'bout *you*."

"Well, let's see . . ." *What would impress her further?* "I have two sisters. You've likely seen them at church."

She nodded. "They're pretty. So's your . . . *mother*." She readjusted her position on the bench and folded her hands on her lap.

"Pretty *annoying*." He laughed, and she grinned. "But, truthfully, I'm fond of them. Especially my mother, of course. And, I enjoy being an older brother. Father has relied on me over the years to watch out for them. But now that they're practically grown, it's become more difficult. Any day now, Father expects Ursula's beau to ask permission to wed her."

"I hope for her sake she loves the man."

Zachary searched Lily's sad eyes. "She does. They've been courting a full year. My parents had hoped I'd marry first, and I believe that delayed York's request—her *intended*, York Hasselbeck. But, I feel they're tired of waiting for me to find the right woman."

Lily swallowed hard and kept her eyes locked with his. Exactly where he wanted them.

"It's hard for me to understand," she said in the softest voice. "I'd think you'd have your choice of any woman you want. Surely you've met *someone* who suits you."

"Not until recently, but that particular woman is already spoken for."

Her eyes widened, then shifted downward.

He inched a bit closer to her. "You understand what I'm saying?"

"Of course, I do. But, why me?"

He couldn't help but chuckle. "That's the very thing my father asked me."

Her head popped right up. "You told him you have feelin's for me?"

"Yes. Though I believe he realized it the first Sunday you attended services. I couldn't keep my eyes off you."

She folded her arms and lifted her chin high. "How could you feel sumthin' simply by lookin' at me? You know nothin' 'bout me."

"A man can tell a great deal by the way a woman carries herself. And, the more we converse, my feelings deepen."

"Would you feel the same if I was poor-lookin'?"

He brushed a finger along her rigid chin. "But, you're not."

She turned away.

"Lily. Is it so wrong to enjoy gazing at someone beautiful?"

Her eyes slowly shifted toward him again. "No. I confess I've found pleasure doin' that very thing. I'd be lyin' if I said otherwise." She blinked ever-so-slowly, and once more moistened her lips. The act tortured him.

"So . . ." He glanced about to make certain they were alone, then moved even closer. "Have *you* been admiring *me*?"

"Yes." Her breathing quickened. "But what good does it do? What with Archibald Jones ready to escort me down the aisle?"

"What if *I* asked to court you?"

Still breathing hard, she clutched a hand to her breast. "You want to?"

"Oh, yes."

"How? My aunt an' uncle would never approve. An' Archibald would be crushed."

Zachary rubbed his chin. "You actually care for him and how he might feel?"

"Yes. He's a kind-hearted man. I don't wanna hurt him."

"Do you want to *marry* him?"

"No." She closed her eyes and shook her head. "Definitely not."

"Then I'm afraid, you'll either have to hurt him or harm your-self."

She rapidly blinked a few times, then stared at her hands, primly folded on her lap.

Though he'd not known her long, he could tell her thoughts were spinning fast. "As for the Clarks," he went on, "My father can use his influence to sway your uncle to see things our way. I'm sure you're aware my family doesn't lack for money. I'm not bragging about it—after all, our wealth has been handed down from several generations—but it needs to be said. It affords me a fine education, and it also gives leverage in private matters when needed." Her focus had remained downward, so he lifted her chin. "Lily. Wouldn't you rather dance with *me* at the ball?"

She tilted her face into his touch. "*Can* you dance?"

"Yes. I'm quite accomplished. I'd show you here, yet I fear we'd attract attention. The squirrel in that tree behind you already has his eyes on us."

Finally, she smiled again. "I don't know what to say. You hardly know me."

"Something I intend to change. Courtship should allow that very thing." Their faces were so close, he could easily kiss her, but not now. It was too soon. Even so, her eyes begged for it. "I shan't kiss you today, though I want to."

She gulped. "It's probably best you don't."

He took hold of her hand and caressed it. Her skin wasn't as soft as others he'd held—an indication her life hadn't always been easy. It heightened his curiosity. "In time. First things first. I don't want you to worry yourself over any of this. I'll set your life on its proper course."

"Bein' courted by you?"

"If it's what you want. Do you, Lily?"

She glided her fingers over his. "I do."

He brought her hand to his lips, kissed it, then stood. "We best be on our way home. Can you meet me here again Wednesday? I know it's soon, but my days of leisure are limited."

"Your education is important." She remained seated, but kept her eyes on his. "I'll come Wednesday. I'm sure I can find a way to be here."

"Good." He smiled and gestured in the other direction. "I realize we didn't see much of the park. Perhaps next time we can accomplish it. For now, why don't you stay on the bench for a few moments, while I leave. Until things are settled, I'm sure you'll be more comfortable walking out alone."

"I would. Thank you."

He bowed his head, then strolled away.

"Zachary!"

Lily's loud cry stopped him. "Yes?"

"Thank you. For *everythin'*."

He understood. "Trust me. All will be well." Once again, he dipped his head and left.

He and his father had a lot to discuss.

* * *

Lily's confused heart should've calmed some, but Zachary's declaration of affection had the opposite effect. Though eased a bit about the prospect of *not* having to marry Archibald, the overwhelming desire to be close to Zachary tore her in two. Likely because she'd experienced intimacy and knew how pleasurable it was. That alone tormented her.

Her shameless desires were that of a harlot. Weren't they? Then again, from what she understood about those kinds of women, pleasure had little to do with their reasons for coupling with men. Like Uncle Stuart, money was the driving force.

She trudged along the road, wishing she could walk away her frustrations. Why couldn't she simply allow herself to be happy about Zachary's willingness to help her out of her ordeal?

"Cuz it only creates new troubles," she muttered.

The feel of his hand on hers lingered, as did the idea of kissing him. He was clean-shaven, just like Caleb had been when they'd shared their first kiss. She'd never cared for the feel of whiskers. Whenever her pa had given unshaven kisses, the prickliness of his rough facial hair irritated her cheek.

Caleb had perfect lips.

The image of his body entwined with hers popped to the forefront of her mind. Warmth spread throughout her, and her heart raced.

I want that again.

Not only did she crave physical closeness, she wanted to be loved. *Wholeheartedly.* Cherished by a man who loved her and her alone.

A man like Zachary had to have had his share of kisses. But being a Godly man, he was certainly chaste.

Honorable, just as he'd said.

Now she had a larger problem. Unless she revealed the truth about herself to Zachary, she'd not feel right carrying their relationship further.

How do I tell him?

She opened the front door and walked inside.

"Lily!" Aunt Helen stormed across the floor. "Never again go unaccompanied to the park! What were you thinking?"

"Did David tell you he took me there?"

"Of course he did, and I scolded him for doing so." She fisted her hands on her hips. "You're to go to Mrs. Gottlieb's and come straight home. Is that too complicated for you?"

"No, Aunt Helen. But please don't fuss at David. He only did what I asked. I wanted to walk an' clear my head. The park seemed a nice place to do it."

"David Carrington does what *I* say, not what *you* tell him to do. *I* am his employer. If he wasn't such a valuable employee, I'd dismiss him over this."

Lily tenderly laid her hand on her aunt's arm. "I'm sorry. Truly, it was all my fault."

"Well, you must make up for it." Aunt Helen calmed and *almost* smiled. "Go clean yourself up, and I'll meet you in your room shortly. Before David upset me, he informed me you capably waltzed. That pleases me. And as I promised, I have another surprise for you."

"Thank you. I enjoyed dancin'. I haven't been grateful enough for all you've done for me. You've given me opportunities I never would've had back home."

This time, Aunt Helen *did* smile. "You're correct. And . . . you're welcome." She whipped around and walked away as fast as she'd entered.

Whether or not she'd keep that smile was a different matter. Especially after Zachary did *whatever* it was he planned to do. Lily feared once that happened, all hell would break loose.

She continued on to her room to freshen up and wait for her aunt. She'd worry later about her troubled heart and what *might* happen.

If only she'd met Zachary before Caleb.

No sooner had she scrubbed her face and hands, and her aunt paraded in. A turquoise blue garment lay draped over her arm.

"Another dress for me, Aunt Helen?" Lily's wardrobe was already full.

"Yes. But this one is special." She laid it out atop Lily's bed.

Lily stared at the thing. "It seems to be missin' some fabric 'round the neckline. More so than the dress I'm wearin' now. Does it have a separate collar?"

"No. It's exactly as it should be. But, in order to have this gown fit you properly, you must wear this." Aunt Helen extended an odd-looking item with strings dangling from it.

"What's that?"

"It's a corset. I assume you've not heard of these."

I am not ignorant. "Actually, I have. But I've never seen one. Why would I need it? It looks . . ." She fingered it. "*Painful.*"

"You'll wear it while you dance. It will help you stand straight and tall, and it will enhance your figure. This dress is your ball gown. It's designed to be worn with a corset. You must appear at your very best for Archibald."

"Only Archibald? From my understandin' most a St. Louis has been invited to the ball."

Her aunt beamed. "Only the important people. And yes, you'll be making an impression on all of them. So, you must practice wearing the corset and gown. It will take some getting used to. After dinner, I'll send Evie up to assist you." She headed toward the door, but stopped and grinned. "Eat very little. It will make the experience of being bound less painful." She flitted away.

Lily doubted she could each much anyway, so it didn't matter.

She ran her hand along the gown and caressed the beautiful silky fabric. The neckline and sleeves were decorated with white lace, and the full skirt would look lovely pushed out by crinolines. Lily would float across the dancefloor.

But who will I be floatin' with?

She lifted the corset and studied all the hooks and laces. It was hard to the touch and not at all flexible. She couldn't comprehend how it would fit on her body. And why enhance her figure? All her womanly parts held their own.

Caleb never complained.

She dropped down onto the bed, then flopped backward.

Though the dress Aunt Helen had surprised her with was lovely, all it accomplished was to add another worry to Lily's confusing life.

CHAPTER 26

"This can't be good for you." Lily held onto the doorknob, while Evie pulled the corset strings tighter. "Stop! I can't breathe, and this thing's squishin' me."

Evie didn't loosen her hold. "Stand upright."

Lily released the knob, stood straight, and twisted to face Evie.

With her fingers entwined in the strings, Evie stared at Lily's bosom. "I see what's wrong. You need to reach under your breasts and lift them. They're supposed to rest *above* the corset."

Lily's cheeks heated. Though she wore a chemise beneath the wretched device, it still seemed odd to be showing so much of herself—even to Evie. "It's so tight, I can't get a hand under there to fix 'em."

"I'll loosen the laces enough so you can adjust yourself."

So humiliatin'.

Lily faced away from her. The instant the garment loosened, Lily bent down, reached under her chemise, and lifted each breast above the rigid corset. Once she stood upright again, Evie tightened the strings.

"Lawdy," Lily mumbled. Yes, the garment made her stand straight and tall, just as Aunt Helen said it would. As for enhancing her figure, Lily hadn't seen her breasts so round and full since nursing Noah.

"Much better," Evie said, smiling. "Archibald will be beside himself. Go look in the mirror."

Lily felt as if a board had been tied to her back. Dancing in this silly thing would be nearly impossible. No wonder Aunt Helen told her to practice wearing it.

Stiff and utterly uncomfortable, she faced the mirror. "This can't be right. I'm indecent." Her mounded breasts filled the mirror.

"This will help." Evie lowered the gown over Lily's head and buttoned up the back. "You see. You're stylish. It's what all the ladies wear to balls and other fine affairs."

"If my ma saw me like this . . ." She turned from her reflection, unable to bear it. The gown was gorgeous, but her eyes kept shifting to her bare flesh. "She'd call me shameless. Dressin' like this will only put improper thoughts in the minds of men. Why would Aunt Helen want me paradin' 'round this way?"

"Because . . ." Her aunt appeared in the doorway. "It's fashionable. You look lovely, my dear. Now, pull your shoulders back and let me see you walk."

Lily did as she asked. "I'm not too graceful, an' I need my crinolines."

"Don't worry about those right now. I promise, you'll improve. Practice every night. Once you've mastered walking, you shall take the garment to Mrs. Gottlieb's and dance in it. By the night of the ball, I'm certain you'll be exceptional." Aunt Helen nodded to Evie. "Thank you for assisting her. After you help her *out* of the dress, leave her be. She needs her beauty sleep."

"Yes'm." Evie curtsied and Aunt Helen walked away.

"I'm glad she told you to get me out of this thing. My ribs are achin'." Lily bent at the knees, while Evie lifted the gown up and over her head. When she loosened the corset strings, Lily let out a relieved sigh.

Evie giggled. "You truly are beautiful in the gown. I understand why you're uncomfortable, but you'll be the envy of every woman at the ball."

Lily rubbed across her chemise, trying to soothe the places that had been pinched by the corset. She had creases in her skin right atop her ribs. "I've never wanted anyone to envy me. Wish you could go in my place."

"I'll be serving. That's *my* place." Evie headed toward the door. "Get some rest. You'll feel better in the morning." She smiled and left.

Lily crossed the room and shut the door. She'd been tempted to tell Evie about Zachary and their meeting in the park, but for now, it was probably best left unsaid. Hopefully, she wouldn't have to keep it a secret for long.

* * *

Lily slept more soundly than she had in weeks. Dancing had expended all her energy.

She woke, feeling refreshed, and honestly looked forward to more dance lessons. At least she didn't have to wear the corset and gown. Not yet, anyway.

She leisurely dressed, went to the kitchen for a bowl of oats, and chatted with Mrs. Winters. The sweet woman was more inclined to talk when Aunt Helen wasn't there, but Lily could tell she tiptoed around any sort of discussion about Archibald. Lily preferred it that way. She'd rather keep such things to herself.

After eating and thanking Mrs. Winters for the meal and conversation, Lily still had time to spare. She strolled outside and tarried along the pathway, then went all the way down the walkway to wait for David.

Surprisingly, the carriage had already arrived, even though she was early. David always came at exactly eight-thirty. When she'd left the house, it was only eight-fifteen. Odder yet, he was nowhere to be seen.

The horse stood almost motionless, with its nose in a feedbag. *Hmm . . .*

Lily decided she'd rather sit in the carriage and wait for David, than stand on the road watching the horse eat.

She grabbed the door handle and opened it.

"Oh, my!" She slammed it shut again.

Without asking or being told, she'd discovered David did indeed like women. In addition, she now knew why Evie had made the comments she had. Lily had stumbled onto a scene of passion she'd not soon forget.

Embarrassed didn't come anywhere near to how she felt. She considered hastening back to the house, but since David would soon need to drive her to Mrs. Gottlieb's, she chose to wait.

Loud mumbling came from the interior of the carriage. It rocked side to side and soon the door opened again.

Evie stepped out. She smoothed her dress and ran her fingers through her hair. Moments later, David exited as well.

An uncomfortable silence followed.

Evie deflated. "Lily, I'm sorry you saw that."

Lily turned in her direction, but kept her eyes gazing upward. "Me, too." From the corner of her eye, she caught David tucking in his shirt. "I won't tell, if you two are worried at all 'bout that. I assume the Clarks are unaware of your . . . *feelin's* for each other?"

David stepped closer. "I love Evie. I want to marry her, but we haven't found a way just yet. We've been saving our funds so we can buy a house."

"That's right," Evie said. "We're putting away all we can. We don't want the Clarks to know about us, because we doubt they'd approve. Once we're married, I plan to leave my employment. They rely on me. I'm worried they'll try to interfere."

"They will." Lily finally managed to look her in the eye. Her embarrassment had subsided into pity. "It'll be difficult for Aunt Helen to find someone she can boss around like she does you." She turned to David. "An' you, too. She should appreciate *both* of you more."

"You're kindhearted." David frowned and stared at the ground. "Even when we have enough money and Evie gives notice of her intentions, I fear they'll relieve me of my position out of retribution for taking her away from them."

"I'm sure someone else will employ you."

"Hopefully." He smiled at Evie. "All I want is for the two of us to be together. We'll make it work somehow."

Lily nodded. "So, for the time bein' you sneak off whenever you can?" She offered them both a smile. "It's kinda romantic. But, you should be careful. What if it'd been Aunt Helen who opened the carriage door 'stead a me?"

Evie placed a hand over her heart. "I would've died. Right then and there."

"Well, just remember that. Now, you best go on inside—to the *house* that is. Your hair is all messed up. Better fix it 'fore Aunt Helen sees you."

"Thank you, Lily." Evie locked eyes with David, then mouthed *I love you* and hurried away.

David's head bent low. "You must think very little of me."

"No. You're wrong." She understood more than he'd ever know. "I can tell you mean it when you say you love her. But please do right by her an' marry her as soon as you can."

"I will." He slowly lifted his head. "She's all I've ever wanted. I fell in love with her the first time I saw her. But, she was too young then."

"An' now, she's not." Lily moved toward the carriage door. "I'm happy for the two of you. Real love's not easy to find."

David smiled, then wiped his brow with a handkerchief. After tucking it back into his pocket, he opened the door, then took her hand and helped her in. "Are you ready to dance?"

"Yes." She folded her hands and stared at the seat across from her as he closed her inside.

She shut her eyes and took slow, steady breaths. Moments ago, heated passion had filled this small space—similar in size to the burrow on the side of the mountain in the cove.

Caleb's an' my burrow.

She touched her fingers to her lips and recalled the feel of his. Nearly a year and a half had passed since they'd been together, but the memories remained fresh.

Evie had said women would envy Lily at the ball, yet Lily envied Evie. Though the sweet girl might think her relationship with David had complications, it came nowhere close to Lily's. Evie and David would one day be together. Lily didn't have that luxury. At least, not with the man she loved.

I hafta learn to love someone else.

She'd learned many other things, so how much different could this be?

The time had come to let Caleb go.

She'd tried before, but hadn't truly committed herself. Yet she knew without a doubt, it was the only way she'd ever be happy again.

She inched her eyes open and sat taller. Soon, she'd be in David's arms dancing, with his secret hovering over them. It helped to be able to set aside any worries that he might *want* her —as Mrs. Gottlieb indicated all men did.

David would be her friend, whether Mrs. Gottlieb believed it possible or not. Archibald would also remain her friend and nothing more. Zachary, on the other hand, was bound to be someone far more important in her life.

An excited shiver ran down her spine.

Letting go of Caleb had benefits. Not only did the prospect of a new, meaningful relationship thrill her, but the thought of mending her broken heart did wonders for her soul.

I can make this work.

She parted the curtain and peered outside. Clouds overhead indicated rain. The carriage moved along at a steady pace, and her heart beat right along with it.

CHAPTER 27

Caleb rapped on his ma's hotel room door. "Ma, it's me. You in there?"

She opened the door wide, scowling. "I'm here. Why are *you*?"

He peered beyond her, into the room. "I'm lookin' for Becca. You seen her?"

His ma soundly tapped her foot, then waved him in.

He recognized her foul mood, and his gut instantly churned. Just like it had when he was a boy, knowing he'd done something wrong and expecting a spanking. But that boy was long gone—as were his ma's physical reprimands. However, the verbal assault he believed she'd reign down on him would be much harsher and harder to bear.

Trouble was, he couldn't figure out what he'd done to make her angry. His guilty conscience assumed the worst.

The second he stepped in, she pushed the door shut. "I swanee, son. When are you gonna learn to take proper care of your wife?"

"What's that s'posed to mean? Is she here?"

"She was. She left 'bout fifteen minutes ago. I managed to stop her cryin', but she's a mess. Swears you don't love her." She stood within inches of him. "What did you do? You been hittin' her?"

"Course not! I'd never strike her or any woman. You know me better than that." He dropped down onto the edge of the bed and put his head in his hands. "Comin' here was a mistake."

She cuffed the back of his head. "Stop your whinin' an' tell me what you done."

"Dang, Ma. There ain't no need to hit me." He sat up tall and smoothed his hair.

"Don't be usin' that language 'round me." She took the place beside him. "Sometimes I feel I don't know you no more—usin' foul words an' such. An' whenever I see you, you rarely smile. You mope like our old coon dog used to when he was near death. It makes no sense. You're married to the finest woman in North Carolina, you've got a beautiful daughter, an' a well-producin' farm. What more do you want, Caleb?"

"I'm tryin', Ma. Really, I am."

She threw up her hands. "What's there to *try* for? You've got it easy. Rebecca loves you with every part of herself, yet she comes here cryin', swearin' you must have another woman locked away somewhere." Large puffs of air hissed out her nose. "Do you?"

"*No.*"

Her eyes pinched nearly shut and she leaned in. "You sure 'bout that?"

"Heaven's sake, Ma. When would I have time? I work from sunup till sunset. It ain't easy runnin' that farm by myself."

Her foot kept tapping the floor. An obvious sign she believed he was hiding something.

He pulled his shoulders back. "What did Becca tell you?"

"That it's like pullin' teeth to get you to love on her. She's all tore up cuz her flow came again. She wants more babies. I'd think it wouldn't be all that difficult."

Caleb gaped at her. "She said all that? Ain't nothin' private no more?"

"Sweetheart." She patted his leg. "Rebecca an' I have talked 'bout everythin' for a very long while."

"Seems so."

Her pat turned into a gentle rub. "I feared for you when them men came to town lookin' for *Callie*. I was sure Rebecca would see into the truth. An' maybe she has. I think she believes there's more to your relationship with Lily Larsen than you let on. It might help if you go on an' tell her the truth. Tell her that yes, you cared for Lily, but it was a passin' thing. An' that once you saw *her*, Lily was forgotten."

"I can't tell her that."

"Why? She'd have more respect for you if you were honest."

He rubbed his temples to help his pounding head. "I ain't even been honest with you, Ma." He'd grown tired of the lies. Maybe she'd understand.

"Do what?" She pulled her hand to herself and scooted several inches away.

"I ain't right, cuz I done wrong. I can't live with myself like this."

Her face paled. "You're scarin' me, Caleb. What did you do?"

His shoulders slumped and he closed his eyes, unable to watch her reaction when he spilled his guts. "Not sure where I should start, but you gotta know, all along I only wanted to do what was right. But no matter how hard I tried, I kept makin' everythin' worse."

"Stop carryin' on so, an' get to tellin' me."

"I was with Lily longer than I said. I lived with her family for eight months. Long enough to develop deep feelin's for Lily. As I told you from the start I *loved* her."

"Yes, you did. An' I reminded you, true love grows with time. Even eight months ain't long enough to know *real* love."

"You're wrong." He stared straight into her eyes. "I *still* love her. That's why I'm worthless to Becca."

"That's plum silly! I know you ain't been seein' that woman. You've never left Waynesville to visit the cove. It's a three-day ride."

"She's in *here*, Ma!" He thumped his chest.

"Well, get over it! You're bound to a wife by God *an'* the law. You have the responsibility of a child, an' eventually more. Get your head on right or you'll ruin everythin'."

"I can't!" He jerked to his feet and wandered to the window. Raindrops pelted against the glass.

"Why? I guarantee *she's* moved on with her life. Probably has a man an' child by now. Why waste away pinin' over someone who'll never be yours?"

He whipped around and faced her. "Because she had my son!" He dropped to the floor, covered his face, and burst into sobs. Saying the words drove it in hard.

He gasped when his ma's hand grasped his shoulder. "How do you know this?"

Pain squeezed his broken heart. He rocked back and forth, but couldn't utter a word.

His ma positioned herself on the floor beside him and wrapped an arm around his shoulder. "Caleb. Tell me how you know."

He sniffed and wiped his eyes with his sleeve. "Her brother, Lucas. He told me."

"He could by lyin'. We *know* he's lyin' 'bout Callie."

"No. I have no doubt it's true." He sucked in air. "I had her, Ma. Even if we didn't make a baby, I shoulda gone back to her. I was wrong to marry Becca."

Her features hardened. "Then, why did you?"

Once again, he covered his face in shame. Telling her the rest would be much harder. "It was the only way to make things right. 'Sides, you pushed us together. All that talk a the Bible sayin' men should marry their brother's widows. What choice did I have?"

"You're a man. Don't go blamin' your decision on me, an' especially not on God. What were you makin' right? Seems to me, the only choice you had was to make things right by Lily. You took her chastity. Shame on you for that! An' if there *is* a baby, then I have a grandchild I ain't never gonna see. You've broken my heart!" Her chin quivered and she looked away.

He leaned against the wall, defeated. "What 'bout *my* heart? Every day I hafta carry this inside me. I have a son I can't see, a woman I ain't allowed to love, an' a wife who thinks I hate her."

"It's your own fault!"

"You think I don't know that? I *had* to marry Becca! It was the only way to make up for Abraham!"

His ma stared at him as if he was a stranger. "Abraham? What 'bout my boy?"

Numb, Caleb pushed on. "Remember how I was wearin' them Union trousers when I came here?"

Without a trace of expression, she kept on staring, barely nodding.

"They were his. I stripped 'em off his dead body. I killed him, Ma. But, I swear I didn't know it was him, till it was too late. We was all fightin', an'. . . How could I a known—?"

"Stop." Her hand shook as she lifted it in front of him. "I can't take no more." She pushed herself up from the floor, went to the wash basin, and poured water into it from the pitcher. Methodically, she went through every motion. Absent of all feeling. She splashed water on her face, then stumbled back onto the bed.

Caleb got up and crossed to her, and she curled into a ball.

"Ma?" He sat down and laid his hand on her arm. "I wanted to tell you when I got here, but I couldn't. I've carried this guilt so long it's been killin' me inside. I don't know what to do . . ."

Ever-so-slowly, she rolled onto her back and gazed up at him. "The past is the past." No trace of a smile, or a frown. Still completely emotionless. "You've confessed your sins, now you best get on with your life. Don't ruin Rebecca's by tryin' to atone for all you done."

He fought back more tears. *I'm too old to be cryin' like a baby.* "Do you hate me, Ma?"

"Oh, Caleb." She smoothed her hand across his cheek. "When you hurt, I hurt. It's the pain a ma bears. I could never hate you. An' I know how much you loved your brother. You woulda never pulled that trigger, if you'd seen his face. I don't doubt that for one minute."

He took her hand and cradled it to his heart. "I'm so sorry. But I'm afraid to tell Becca the truth 'bout any a this. When we got married, I told her I'd never had a woman before. I can't go to her now an' tell her there's a child."

"There *might* be a child. Much as that boy lies, you can't take his word for gospel. The only way to know for certain would be to go lookin' for the child yourself. But you ain't gonna do that. Hear me?"

"Yes'm."

"Becca don't need to know any a this. You can make up for it by lovin' her. An' I mean *deeply* with your entire heart. She deserves that from you. So does Abraham."

Abraham.

Caleb had let him down by not being the husband Rebecca needed.

He searched his ma's eyes. "So, you've changed your mind 'bout me bein' honest with her?"

"Course I have." She sighed and sat up. "How was I to know the extent of your lies? Good lord, Caleb. Best for you to just hush 'bout all of it. Never breathe another word of it to a soul. You an' I will carry this burden together." She opened her arms and motioned him into her embrace.

He held her and drew strength knowing he was no longer alone. It eased his heart and unburdened his soul.

She rubbed his back the way she had when he was a boy. "It's gonna be fine, son. I promise."

He rested his head against her and closed his eyes.

For the first time since he'd set foot in Waynesville, he had hope. As she'd said, *the past is the past.*

Even if he did have a son, he wouldn't be allowed to raise him. And maybe she was right—the boy didn't exist.

Lily had gone on with her life, so he had to stop looking back and move forward.

"Ma? Do you know where Becca went?"

"Yes. She's gone to the cemetery."

"In the rain?"

She sadly nodded.

"An' Avery's with her?"

"Course she is. Go fetch 'em, Caleb. Take 'em home an' love 'em like there's no t'morra."

"Yes'm." He stood and headed for the door. "You gonna be all right?"

"Right as rain." She pushed an unconvincing smile onto her lips.

Right as rain.

The exact way Lucas had described Lily. And for all Caleb knew, she very well could be.

I'll never know for sure.

He walked out the door—the first step in moving forward. He needed to grow up and face his responsibilities. After all, his beautiful wife had been more than patient, and she'd waited long enough.

He sped from the hotel and ran the entire way to the cemetery. Fortunately, the rain had let up and had become a misty drizzle. The warm temperature made the air heavy. By the time he reached the graveside, he was almost out of breath.

He found Rebecca standing over Abraham's grave, clutching Avery close.

Tears of a different kind filled his eyes. "Becca?"

Her head lifted, but she didn't face him. Avery, on the other hand, stretched out her arms.

He rushed to them and took his daughter. She cuddled against his chest, but her ma kept her distance.

"Why are you here, Caleb?" Rebecca's voice sounded gravelly —full of pain.

His words stuck in his throat. He stared at his brother's grave, wishing things had turned out differently. "I've told you I'm sorry so many times . . ." Though he spoke to Rebecca, his words were also meant for Abraham. "But I haven't known how to make things right."

Rebecca finally turned toward him. "That's what I don't understand. For the life a me, I can't see anythin' wrong with our lives. We don't lack for nothin', 'cept maybe the love we need."

"We got plenty a love," he whispered. "I just ain't good at showin' it." He stroked her damp hair. "I wanted to make Abraham proud a me. But all along, I never measured up to him. I *can't*. He was good an' decent, an' he took care a you as he should."

She shook her head and hung it low, but said nothing.

"Since the day we was married," he went on. "I've been wallowin'. Feelin' sorry for myself for this, that, an' the other." Tears trickled onto his cheeks, but these had nothing to do with self-pity. "I wanna start over. Will you give me another chance?"

She looked up into his face, then cupped her hand to his cheek. "I've never stopped hopin' things would improve, an' I won't give up on you. You're my husband an' always will be." She wiped away the tears that had mingled with a few scant raindrops. "Stop comparin' yourself to Abraham. I know how much you loved him. So did I. But we have to move on."

She turned her attention to Avery and kissed the top of her head. "She loves you. You're the only pa she knows. An' honestly, you're the only husband *I* know. The few days I had with Abraham were scarcely a speck of time in my life. I expect many *years* with you."

"But . . ." He pointed at the grave. "How can I—?"

"Stop." She rose up on her tiptoes and kissed him. "Let it all go. You said you want to start over, so today, we will."

He gazed into her beautiful eyes, and she smiled.

No, he didn't deserve her, but God help him, he intended to love her from this day forward.

He placed his hand behind her head, bent down, and kissed her thoroughly.

Avery giggled.

"Let's go home," he said and jerked his head toward the road.

"Gladly." Rebecca put her arm around his waist and they walked out together.

His family.

His home.

CHAPTER 28

Zachary leaned over and braced his hands against his father's desk. "You agreed to help me. You've *never* gone back on your word before."

The man folded his arms and sat back in his chair. "I'm not now. I said, it won't be *easy*. Everyone attending the Clark's ball expects an engagement announcement. It's all the talk. Of course, young women are tittering over the fact that lovely Lily is aligning herself with Archibald."

"It's not right!" Zachary pounded his fist on the desktop. "They mock her behind her back. She doesn't deserve any of it."

"I agree. She's an exceptional girl." He gestured to the chair across from him. "Please sit. You're making me nervous."

Zachary dropped onto the seat. "So, what can we do? How do we fix this?"

A loud squeal from the hallway drew their attention.

"Ursula," his father muttered.

She burst through the door, flew across the room, and flung her arms around him. "Thank you, Daddy!" She kissed his cheek, beaming.

Their father took her hand and patted it. "You're welcome, my dear. I'm certain York will be a fine husband."

Her green eyes sparkled. "Mother and I are spending the day going over wedding plans. She's hired a seamstress to make my gown. All my dreams are coming true!" She cast a sideways glance at Zachary. "I'm sorry you won't be walking down the aisle before me. But I'm glad you understand that York and I don't wish to wait any longer. For all we know, it could be *years* before you ever say your vows."

With a giggle, she whipped around and headed toward the hallway, her red curls bouncing with her. "This is the happiest day of my life." She blew a kiss to their father, then flitted away.

The man shook his head. "Happiest day of her life," he muttered. "This wedding will cost me a fortune. As you know, your mother will want the best of everything."

"Of course. I'd expect no less." Zachary sighed. "Her comment about *me* didn't help matters. I don't intend to wait *years* before I take a bride."

"Yes. Back to the matter at hand." He soundly tapped a finger on the desk. "I'll speak to Stuart Clark. As you suggested, I'll offer some sound financial advice. And . . ." He grinned and leaned in. "As you know, my future son-in-law was recently given a significant stake in his father's textile business. I can use my influence to guide him into using Stuart's shipping services. What newlywed wouldn't want to please his father-in-law?"

"You make it sound simple. I thought you said it wouldn't be easy."

"The hard part is going to the Clark's. Hopefully, I won't have to speak to Helen. She grates on my nerves."

Zachary's heart thrummed. "When will you go?"

"So eager." The man chuckled. "I have time today. Will that suit you?"

"Yes. Thank you, Father." He stood and headed for the door. "I'm supposed to meet her in the park this afternoon. I'd like to give her good news."

"Slow down. I'll do what I can. I can't guarantee Stuart will be agreeable."

"He *has* to be. For my sake."

Zachary hurried into the hallway and up to his room. He needed to ready himself for Lily.

* * *

Lily slumped into the carriage seat. "Sometimes, I despise that woman."

"Miss Lily," David stood in the open doorway. "She's my employer. She *harshly* instructed me to bring you straight home from Mrs. Gottlieb's. As I said, I can't take you to the park. I'm sorry." He stepped back and shut the door.

Just when she'd decided to pour her heart into pursuing Zachary Danforth, Aunt Helen snuffed out her fire. What would he think when she didn't arrive?

Reckon he'll assume I don't care.

Maybe it was for the best. She and David had danced almost nonstop. Her chemise had soaked up her perspiration, but she doubted she smelled like roses—or lilies for that matter. She'd be far from appealing. Still, she didn't want him to believe she'd intentionally missed their outing.

The carriage jerked to a stop. Within seconds, David opened the door and extended his hand. "Please don't look so sad, Miss Lily."

"I can't help it." She sluggishly got up from the seat and let him help her to the ground.

"I know why you wanted to go to the park." He kept his voice low.

"You do?"

"Yes." He put his face close to her ear. "Zachary Danforth approached Evie at the market the other day. He swore his intentions with you are honorable and begged to know which room was yours, so he could speak with you. I hope you can forgive her, but she told him. And . . . I saw him waiting for you at the park on Monday. But I promise, I didn't tell Mrs. Clark."

"So, that's how he knew . . ." She stood a little taller. "It seems we all have secrets to keep, don't we?"

"Are you angry?"

"No. I'm just frettin' over Zachary."

David smiled. "You care for him, don't you?"

"Reckon I do." She grinned, but it instantly became a frown. "I feel awful 'bout Archibald, however. He's a kind man. I don't wanna hurt him."

"I have a feeling he'll understand. And so will Zachary when he finds you absent from the park. From what Evie tells me, he's quite taken with you."

Even on the warm day, Lily's cheeks heated. "Seems there's a lot of that goin' 'round." She nudged his arm. "I'm glad I'm finally gettin' to know you, David. Evie's a fortunate girl."

"No, I'm the lucky one." He strode away and hopped up onto the driver's seat. Grinning, he popped the reins and drove away.

Lily stood and watched him for several moments, then headed for the house. A part of her wanted to be defiant and hasten to the park, but it would only cause more trouble for her *and* David.

Before she stepped inside, an odd sound greeted her. It reminded her of a cross between a howling coyote and a wounded dog. Unpleasant to say the least.

She quickly went in. The sound pitched even higher.

Gerard approached her, shaking his head. "I'm glad you're home, Miss Lily. Mrs. Clark wishes to speak to you." Another wail.

Lily questioned him with her eyes.

"That's your aunt. She's extraordinarily forlorn."

"It sounds like she's dyin'."

"Not *that* forlorn." He peered down his nose at her. "You've upset the apple cart. You'd best fix it."

"Huh?"

"Go to her." He snapped his head high and walked away.

Lily's stomach rumbled, but not from hunger. Then, it struck her. Maybe Zachary had something to do with it. He'd said he wanted to put her life on the right course, but if that was what troubled Aunt Helen, his action had caused damage to an apple cart. Lily didn't even know the Clarks had one.

She crept toward the parlor in the direction of Aunt Helen's wailing, then peeked around the door.

Her aunt sat on the chaise with a frilly handkerchief in her grasp. Uncle Stuart paced beside her.

This ain't gonna be fun.

Her uncle caught her eye and motioned her in. "We've been waiting for you, Lily."

She gulped and took slow steps forward. "Sumthin' wrong?"

Another wail—almost a shriek.

"Please, Helen," Uncle Stuart grumbled. "Stop. It's not as bad as you think."

That's good to hear.

"But I won't be able to show my face," Aunt Helen whimpered. "Everyone will think I'm daft."

"Why? In my opinion, all has worked out for the best."

Lily simply watched them talk, wishing all the while someone would tell her what had happened. "What's worked out for the best?"

Her aunt leered at her. "You should be happy. You're getting exactly what you wanted. Spoiled girl!"

"I don't understand." *At all.*

"Have a seat." Uncle Stuart gestured to an overstuffed chair.

Lily eased into it and folded her hands on her lap.

"I had a visitor today," Uncle Stuart said. "Thomas Danforth. I'm sure you're aware he's Zachary's father."

Lily's heart thumped hard. "Yessir."

"It would seem you've captured the boy's attention. He's asked —through his father—to court you."

Aunt Helen whimpered and sniffled.

Lily could barely breathe. "He did?"

"Don't act so surprised!" Aunt Helen snapped. "You've been leading the boy on. Acting shamelessly in church."

"Shamelessly? I *talked* to him."

Her aunt held up a finger. "Don't get smart with me."

"Helen, please." Uncle Stuart pressed a firm hand on her shoulder. "Let me deal with this."

"Fine." She dabbed at her eyes with the hankie, then jutted her nose high.

Uncle Stuart moved close to Lily. "Are you agreeable to a courtship with the Danforth boy?"

She glanced toward her aunt, who kept her head turned in the other direction, then faced her uncle. "Yessir. I am."

"Of course, she is," Aunt Helen grumbled. "Every girl in the city wants him. Why *she* had to catch his eye is beyond me."

Uncle Stuart chuckled. "Helen, my dear, the way you're be-having reeks of jealousy. You should be happy to know our niece will be courted by one of the finest bachelors in St. Louis. Would *you* have chosen Archibald over Zachary?"

"No, but—" Aunt Helen waved the handkerchief in the air. "How do we save face? Archibald Jones will remain unwed, when everyone expected a glorious engagement party in his honor. I shall have to cancel it."

"Why?" Uncle Stuart lit a cigar and took several puffs. "We can have the ball and announce the courtship of Lily and Zachary. There's no need to abandon our plans."

"But what of tonight's dinner? Archibald is coming to see Lily, and—"

"And Lily can let him down easily. Isn't that right, Lily?"

"Oh, my." She sat up tall. "I don't wanna hurt him."

Aunt Helen grunted and rolled her eyes.

Uncle Stuart blew a ring of smoke. "He's never asked permission to court you. Yes, it was an understanding I had with his father, but nothing has been set in stone. Therefore, you don't have to *break things off* with him, so to speak. I'd suggest you tell him of your affections for Zachary and let him know I've agreed to *that* courtship. Archibald has been turned down before. He's used to it."

"That won't make it any easier." Just thinking about it caused Lily's heart to ache. "He's a nice man."

"A man requires more than *nice* to snare a bride."

Lily stared at her lap and built up courage. "Uncle Stuart?"

"Yes?"

She rose to her feet and approached him. "How did Mr. Danforth change your mind 'bout your plans for my future?"

"I've told you before, a good businessman never boasts of his dealings." He smirked and wandered from the parlor, puffing on his cigar.

The minute he was gone, Aunt Helen got up and moved within inches of Lily. "Count your blessings. At least you won't have ugly children." She scowled and left Lily alone.

It didn't seem right that her aunt would be hateful over this arrangement. But since she'd bragged about the engagement party and the *event of the year*, she probably blamed Lily for embarrassing her.

Once Aunt Helen and her negativity were far away, Lily felt something else.

I'm gonna be courted by Zachary Danforth.

Somehow, he'd done as he'd promised.

Her belly fluttered and tingles crept across her skin. An uncontrollable smile emerged.

I'm gonna be courted by Zachary Danforth!

Her ears perked up to the sound of the loud front door knocker. Gerard's footsteps crossed the floor.

Though muffled, she could tell he was speaking to another man. She crept toward the hallway to see who'd come.

Zachary?

His eyes shifted and met hers, and he beamed. The most gorgeous smile in the country.

"Mr. Danforth." Uncle Stuart strode across the entryway and extended a hand. "I assume you've come to see Lily?"

"Yes, sir." Zachary shook her uncle's hand and Gerard walked away.

Uncle Stuart looked over his shoulder. "Lily, you have a guest. You may take him to the courtyard. After all, it's the proper place for courting, wouldn't you agree?"

"Yes, Uncle Stuart." She floated toward Zachary, light as air.

He extended an arm and escorted her outside. All the way to the courtyard, they walked without speaking. Once there, they perched on a bench. The very spot she'd shared with Archibald not long ago.

"You weren't at the park," Zachary said, taking her hand.

She trembled from his touch. "I wasn't allowed. But, it doesn't matter anymore, does it? You fixed everythin', just like you said you would."

"Yes, I did." With his free hand, he stroked her bare arm. "You have chill bumps, Lily. Why's that? The weather's quite warm."

"You know very well why."

"Do you enjoy my touch?" He drew invisible patterns on her skin.

"More than I probably should." Her heart beat harder and harder. She fought every urge to touch him.

"My sister's getting married. Hopefully soon. You see, *if* we decide we care for one another, our courtship could very well lead to a proposal. My parents can manage only one wedding at a time. So, you and I have a while to discover more about each other." He brushed his hand along her cheek. "I have a feeling I'm going to appreciate everything about you."

She swallowed hard and licked her lips, only to have his fingers trace around them. "You torture me, Lily."

She turned her head. "We can't show affection here. For all I know, Aunt Helen's watchin' us."

"Do you *desire* affection?"

"Yes." She panted out the word.

"Then we shall find a way to be alone."

Not a good idea. "I'm afraid of what could happen. I mean—"

"I won't compromise you, if that's what you fear. That will be left for our wedding night, and something I'm sure we will both find agreeable. But, I'd like to kiss you—hold you in my arms. Is that too much to wish for?"

"No. I'd like that, too."

"Good. Because I doubt I can refrain from tasting your lips."

Warmth spread throughout her body. If they didn't change the conversation, she'd likely melt into the ground. "I hafta tell Archibald 'bout us t'night."

"I see." Zachary folded his arms. "I feel sorry for him. You're going to break his heart, you know."

"Don't say that. It's hard enough tryin' to figure out how to tell him."

He once again took her hand. "It's best to do it now. He'll understand." He lifted her hand to his lips and kissed it, lingering on her knuckles. "If your aunt *is* watching, I want to leave her with a little something to rant about."

"You're horrid, Zachary." She lightly smacked his leg.

"Am I?" He leaned close. "Then why do you want to kiss me?"

"Stop. You're not makin' this easy."

"Good. I intend to make you *very* happy." He stood and extended his arm. "I'll return you inside for now. It'll give you time to compose yourself and find a way to tell Archibald our news."

She sighed and rested her hand at his elbow. They meandered slowly along, and honestly, she didn't want him to leave. Then again, if he stayed, she'd only want him more. A dangerous thing.

He left her with a simple bow, but one accompanied by twinkling eyes.

She wasn't certain how he'd manage to be alone with her, but he'd accomplished everything else he'd said he would. The man had smarts. Exactly what he needed to be an accomplished doctor.

If things proceeded as they possibly could, her future might be that of a doctor's wife.

Oh, my.

She needed to pen a letter to Violet. Finally, Lily had something worth sharing.

After I see Archibald.

Once she'd completed that task, she hoped she'd be calm enough to write.

CHAPTER 29

Why'd he hafta bring flowers?

Lily smiled graciously at Archibald and took the bouquet from his hand. "These are lovely. Thank you."

"I picked them from our garden. They're calla lilies, but I assume you already know that."

She grinned. "Yes, I'm quite familiar with all kinds a lilies. But I don't believe I've ever seen *any* lily this beautiful."

"I'm looking at one now." His cheeks reddened, but he kept his eyes on her.

He's not makin' this any easier.

She coyly tilted her head. "You're too kind. You hungry?"

"Yes. However . . ." Smiling, he patted his belly. "Since I met you, I've trimmed down some. I doubt you can tell, but I've not been indulging as much."

I hate myself. "I'm proud a you." She linked her arm into his. "I'll walk with you to the dining room, then I'll take these flowers to put in some water. All right?"

He nodded, and they walked together down the hallway.

When she left him to search for a vase, she nearly ran out the back door. She'd never accomplish telling him what had to be said without hurting him, and the way her stomach churned, she swore she might vomit.

Her aunt and uncle had made themselves scarce. Oddly, for once, she would've appreciated their company. Uncle Stuart might have been kind enough to help ease the heavy blow. Then again, Aunt Helen would've gloated, enjoying Lily's misery.

Best they're gone.

Evie appeared out of nowhere, likely spying again. "I'll put those in water for you." She grabbed the lilies. "You all right? You look dreadful."

"How can I be all right?" She pointed at the flowers. "Archibald's one a the kindest men I know. I wish I didn't hafta do this."

Evie tenderly rubbed Lily's arm. "Think about Zachary, and you won't have any difficulties. Your life will be so much better with someone you love."

"I never said I loved Zachary."

"You don't have to. I can tell by looking at you whenever you speak of him. He had the same expression when I saw him in the market. The two of you will make the handsomest couple." She gave Lily a gentle shove. "Go on now. Mrs. Winters is ready to serve."

Lily trudged from the kitchen and returned to the table. Archibald had already taken a seat, but when he saw her, stood.

She waved a hand. "No need to get up for me."

"You're a lady. It's appropriate." He waited for her to take a seat, then sat again.

Mrs. Winters came in carrying a platter of food. "Would you like me to serve, or would you rather do it yourselves?"

Archibald's brows lifted, and he questioned Lily with his eyes.

"Why don't you leave it here?" she said. "We can portion it out. Thank you, Mrs. Winters."

The dear woman set the large platter at the center of the table, bowed, and walked away.

"It looks delicious," Archibald said, rubbing his hands together. "I *love* chicken." He nabbed a leg and bit into it. He used no utensils, just plain old fingers.

Perfect.

At least *something* could be done without difficulty tonight.

Lily scooped up some carrots and beans, then grabbed her own piece of meat. Moments later, Mrs. Winters brought in a basket of fresh-baked biscuits. She grinned when she saw Lily holding the chicken leg.

Lily bit into it and chewed. "It's wonderful, Mrs. Winters." She shouldn't have spoken with her mouth full of food, but maybe it would lessen Archibald's opinion of her and make it easier to let her go. "Just how I like it. Crisp an' well-seasoned."

Archibald nodded his agreement and kept eating.

"Thank you," Mrs. Winters said. "Do you need anything else, Miss Lily?"

A rock to hide under? "Strawberry preserves for the biscuits?"

"Coming right up." She scurried away.

Archibald flipped his napkin open and wiped his mouth. "I'm glad it's only the two of us tonight. I feel *comfortable* with you."

"You, too. I appreciate you know how to eat chicken like it should be done. I think it's silly to try an' eat it with a fork."

He laughed. "When I try, the pieces end up on the table."

"Me, too!" She laughed along with him, but immediately felt like crying. She sucked in air and slouched.

He set his napkin aside. "Is something wrong?"

She closed her eyes and silently bobbed her head.

"Are you ill?"

"Sorta." She forced herself to look at him. "I'm makin' myself sick, worryin' 'bout how to tell you sumthin'."

His features shadowed over. "I can probably guess what it is." He blinked methodically several times, then sighed. "You don't care to see me anymore, do you?"

The hurt on his face stabbed right into her heart. "Well . . . not exactly. I mean . . . I consider you my friend, an' I'd like to always be that to each other." She worked her lower lip.

"But . . .?"

Just say it.

"I can't have you courtin' me."

He stared at his plate, no longer eating. "I never asked to."

"I realize that, but the ball—"

"Is an affair I've been dreading. I don't dance. I find *walking* a great accomplishment. I've been making *myself* sick with worry over how to tell you I don't care to attend. I'd be made a fool."

She'd been so concerned over how *she'd* look and how well *she'd* dance that she'd neglected to consider *his* feelings. "You're no fool. But what 'bout our engagement? I was told it'd be announced that night."

"Yes. Once again, our lives are arranged by our elders who think they know what's best for us. I care for you, Lily, and if you ever had feelings stronger than friendship for me, I'd be the luckiest man on earth. But I've never—for even a *moment*—thought that would happen. You deserve better than me."

She scooted her chair back, went around the table, and pulled out the chair beside him. She sat, facing him. "Any woman who'd have you to love her would be fortunate. You're smart, you've got an amazin' sense a humor, an' you're kind."

"But, your feelings go no deeper than that of a friend." He took her hand and squeezed. "It's all right, Lily. You must stop fretting or you'll prematurely wrinkle. Don't ruin your lovely face." His eyes met hers. "What would Zachary think if you grew old before your time?"

Her heart sunk into her shoes. She stared at him unable to think of a thing to say.

"Rumors travel *loudly*," he said. "And, I have very good eyes. I noticed the two of you staring at each other at church. You're well-suited. Much more so than you and me."

She swallowed the lump in her throat. "So, you've had your suspicions for a while now, haven't you?"

"Yes. The very reason I didn't want to be here that first night. Then, when we got acquainted, I found I liked you. A *lot*. I wanted to get to know you better, and I'm glad I did. You're an exceptional woman. Not only beautiful, but you've got a caring heart. Something this world needs more of."

"Is it cuz a Zachary that you didn't ask to court me?"

"Partly. I wanted to get a real sense for what *you* desired. *Your* wishes and dreams are more important than what someone tells you to do. If Zachary Danforth can make you happy, then I want that for you."

She circled his massive neck and hugged him. "I still want us to be friends. All right?"

"For now. Once you become engaged, it will no longer be appropriate."

She sat back, and though she *should*, she honestly didn't feel any better. "Is your pa angry?"

"He doesn't know yet. But, I'm certain he's heard the rumors. He may come beating on your uncle's door soon, but I'll do what I can to make him understand this was my choice. I only want what's best for you." He took her chin in his hand. "Now. Why don't you go back to your seat and finish eating? When we're through, we can take a stroll in the courtyard for old times' sake. I finished *Alice's Adventures in Wonderland* and would like to discuss it with you. I finally understand your *caterpillar*."

She'd never read that book again without thinking of her dear Archibald.

She placed a hand over her belly. "My appetite's gone."

"Stop fretting, Lily. I've freed you. From here on out, your life is your own. Make the choices you wish." He peered deeply into her eyes. "Go on. I'm dying for a smoke. Until you finish your meal, I won't be able to satisfy *my* craving." He winked.

She begrudgingly stood and returned to her place, feeling a bit like a scolded child. But, in a good way. He'd handled her with a tenderness she hadn't expected, yet it shouldn't have surprised her. From their first conversation, she'd discovered he had a heart of gold.

Archibald grabbed a biscuit and Mrs. Winters came in at the perfect moment with the preserves. He smeared a large glob onto the biscuit, then popped it in his mouth.

Lily picked at her food. He'd said he'd freed her. She'd been given the right to make her own decisions. As the thought sunk in, she sat a little taller.

If rumors had been flying in regard to Zachary and her, then Archibald wasn't the only one who'd noticed their attraction to one another. Maybe things would work out as she hoped. She prayed Zachary would be as kind and understanding as Archibald.

The things she had to tell her suitor would require him to be the most sympathetic and forgiving man ever. It was a lot to hope for.

CHAPTER 30

Violet held Gideon tight, not wanting to let go. "With each wagon ride from my place to yours, we take longer an' longer gettin' there." She trembled from the way he nuzzled her neck. "An' this is the very reason why."

"I can't help myself. You smell so good." His lips slid along her skin till they reached her mouth.

They'd found the perfect place along the road for this. It was a point where the path bended enough so that their wagon couldn't be seen from either direction. They also had the benefit of trees that hung over the road from both sides.

"We need to set a date," she rasped between kisses. "Soon."

He pulled back, then gave her a light peck on the tip of her nose. "Least your pa agreed. I reckon after what happened to Lily, he an' your ma both wanna rush this along."

"Yep." She placed a hand against his chest. His heart pumped hard beneath her touch. "The more we kiss, the firmer my understandin'." She fingered his beard and peered into his eyes. "I can't wait to have your child. You'll be the best pa, an' I aim to love our babies so much they won't never wanna leave home. An' there ain't gonna be no lies. Only honest-to-goodness lovin'."

"That's a lotta love." He smiled, then his body slumped. "'Bout that home . . ."

"What 'bout it?"

"Well . . ." He fiddled with the reins. "I know you don't wanna live with your folks no more, but for now, reckon we'll hafta live with mine."

She laughed. "Course we will. We can't afford our own place just yet."

His eyes widened.

The look he wore tickled her, and she laughed harder. "You was worried 'bout tellin' me, ain't that right? Is that why you've been delayin' our nuptials?"

"You're amazin', Violet Larsen!" He grabbed her and rocked her back and forth. "I've lost more night's sleep over this than I can count." Laughing, he took her face in his hands. "I don't deserve you, but I thank God for you!"

The kiss that followed wasn't at all passionate, but she saw it as a good thing. They had plenty of time for that later.

He sat taller than ever and snapped the reins. The wagon jerked so hard, she had to grab onto him to keep from tumbling out. Maybe he'd done it on purpose.

They arrived at his folks' cabin even before they were expected. A big change from the usual. She got out of the wagon, grabbed his crutch, then went around to his side and handed it to him. Every week, he'd gotten better at maneuvering proficiently with it. She could tell he'd gotten stronger.

They walked inside. Though *he* already belonged, she felt it, too.

"You're early," his ma chimed. "Everythin' all right?"

"Yep." Gideon went up beside her and kissed her on the cheek. "We talked 'bout livin' here after the weddin'. Violet's fine with it."

The dear woman turned to her and opened her arms.

Violet went into her embrace. "Can I call you Ma?"

Mrs. Myers sniffled. "Course you can. It'll be wonderful havin' you here." When they separated, she wiped her eyes with the edge of her apron. "Won't it, Haywood?" She looked beyond Violet to the living room, where her husband sat reading a book.

He set the book aside and eased onto his feet. "Best news I've had in a great while." He went to Gideon and patted his back. "I ain't never been prouder. Time to start workin' on our weaner house, I reckon."

Violet giggled. "You have one?" Though she understood his meaning, it still sounded funny. Many folks in the cove set aside a place to wean newlyweds, but built it close enough so they could help with the family farms.

"Yep. Ain't much, but it'll give the two a you some privacy." He pointed over his shoulder. "It's a one-room cabin back yonder. Built it for storage, but with a woman's touch, it'll suit you right fine."

Violet grabbed onto her future father-in-law and hugged him. "Sounds perfect." Blushing, she released him and went back to Mrs. Myers. "Will you help me fix it up?"

"Glad to. But first, we gotta decide on a weddin' date." She ran a hand along a cloth calendar that hung on the wall. "Saturdays is best. How 'bout the twenty-ninth a September. That'll give us three weeks to make the arrangements, an' we can have you two married 'fore the cold sets in."

Three weeks, an' I'll be a bride.

Nervous excitement flooded over Violet and her head felt light. She fluttered her hand in front of her face to help cool her. "That works for me. What 'bout you, Gideon?"

He teetered on his crutch—his eyes held something other than joy. It was more like *fear*, but she thought he'd overcome all that.

She put her arm around him. "What's the matter?"

"I—I just can't believe it's really gonna happen." His eyes teared up. "I ain't never felt this kind a happiness, an' I don't right know what to do with myself."

Violet nestled against his shoulder. "Simply love me an' never stop."

"That'll be easy." He kissed the top of her head.

His folks didn't say a word, merely watched, smiling.

"Oh!" His ma's outburst made them both jump.

"What's wrong?" Gideon asked.

"Nearly forgot." She dug into her apron pocket and withdrew an envelope. "This came for you today, Violet. It was addressed to me, but when I opened it, I saw this here other envelope with your name on it. Reckon it's from your sister, but the outside don't have no return address." She handed the letter to Violet, chuckling. "Haywood said Mrs. Quincy was beside herself when he picked up the mail. We'll have fun keepin' her guessin'."

"Thank you!" Violet clutched the envelope close to her heart. "I'm dyin' to read what she has to say, an' I sure have more to tell her myself. Guess I'll be writin' my own letter t'night. Will you mind postin' it for me Mr. Myers?"

"Soon, you can call me Pa. Course I don't mind."

Violet hadn't felt this loved in a great while. "All this excitement nearly made me forget we should be eatin' by now. Y'all are probably starvin'. Anythin' I can help you with, Mrs. Myers?" She giggled. "*Ma?*"

"I was just finishin' up. Why don't you go on an' read that letter, while I get the food on the table?"

"You're too kind." Violet hugged her, then looked toward the front door. "Mind if I go outside?"

"Course not. I understand you'll wanna read it alone."

Violet took hold of Gideon's hand. "Will you come with me?"

"Don't you wanna read it by yourself, like Ma said?"

"No. I'd like you to hear it."

"All right then."

They went out the door, followed by smiles from his folks. She helped Gideon situate two rockers, then they both sat.

Gideon leaned toward her. "You sure you want me here?"

"Yep. I told you everythin' there is to know 'bout Lily. I wanna share this with you. I doubt she'll say anythin' that'll embarrass you."

"Hope not." He rubbed his chin. "If she's gonna be my sister, I wanna be able to look her in the eye."

"You're so silly." Violet pulled the letter from the envelope and smoothed the paper. "I wish she could be here for our weddin'."

"Ain't possible, is it?"

Violet shook her head. "Oh, well. Least we have the good fortune of mail service. Regardless of Mrs. Quincy's nosiness."

Gideon sat back in the rocker and folded his hands atop his belly. "Go on, then. I'm curious as can be."

"All right." She cleared her throat. "Dear Violet. Today has been the most unusual day I have had since my arrival in St. Louis. My hands have finally stopped shakin', allowin' me to write this letter. I am glad because there is so much to tell. It is hard to know where to start.

"First, I appreciate the letter you sent. Ma an' Pa have yet to write. Sometimes I feel they don't care 'bout me. I know it's not true, but I also know the farm is doin' well enough that they can afford postage. They have no excuse other than their bitterness toward me an' the trouble I brought on our family." Violet stopped and sighed. "Wish she'd stop bein' so hard on herself." She returned to the page. "I thank God for you, Violet. Though your letter shared some difficult things to digest, the love you put in it was evident."

Violet paused again and glanced over at Gideon. He smiled warmly, then gestured for her to continue.

"As of yet, Lucas has not arrived. I assume I shall see him any day now. At least I am prepared for his visit an' that of the sergeant. Of course, I will tell him I no longer have the letter. Truth be told, I kept it, but I have contemplated burnin' it. My heart has ached so long, pinin' for Caleb, an' even more so for Noah. I am glad he has you to look out for him. I hope you tell him every day that his ma loves him."

Violet wiped tears from her eyes. "Sorry, Gideon. But this is so hard . . ."

"Wanna finish it later?"

"No. I'll be fine." She inhaled a long breath through her nose, then picked up the page and blew the air out again. "I am happy to hear you are followin' your heart an' pursuin' the Myers boy." Violet lifted her eyes and gazed at him over the top of the page. He grinned, then beamed. "I always liked Gideon, an' yes, I remember you goin' on an' on 'bout how handsome he was an' what a fine husband he would be."

Gideon reached over and placed a hand on her knee. His tender gesture said more than words, yet it put a lump in Violet's throat that made it hard to keep reading.

She rubbed over his hand, patted it, then refocused on the letter. "I will be prayin' that everythin' works out for you. You deserve the finest man in the cove, an' I'm quite certain Gideon fits that description."

He puffed up and lifted his chin high, but before she could blink, he slouched down again. "She know 'bout my leg?"

"Course she does." Violet pursed her lips. "You see. It don't matter. It has no bearin' on the kind a person you are or your outstandin' qualities." She gave him a quick peck on the cheek, then returned to the letter.

"As for me . . . my goodness. Where do I start? You said you hoped Uncle Stuart was kind and would make up for Aunt Helen's lack of human decency. Well, you did not use those exact words. I added my own." Violet giggled. Lily had a unique way of putting things. "Yes, he is nicer than her. Most of the time. However, he is a schemer. He had made arrangements for me to marry the son of a rich tobacco farmer. I have been taught everythin' proper. How to talk, walk, dress, an' even dance."

Violet reread the final sentence to herself. "She's dancin'?" She stared at Gideon. "That's sumthin' I'd like to see. She used to kick up her heels at the barn dances, but I can't imagine her doin' anythin' like that 'round Aunt Helen."

"Hmm." Gideon's brows dipped together. "What do you s'pose was wrong with her walkin' an' talkin'? I don't recall her ever havin' trouble with *that*."

"They must do it a lot different there." She quickly found her place, anxious to know about the prospective husband. "When I met my intended, I found him to be very nice, yet I feel nothin' more for him than friendship. Meanwhile, durin' the time he an' I were gettin' acquainted, I met someone special. His name is Zachary Danforth. He is a medical student an' a member of my church. I am attendin' a Lutheran church with Aunt Helen an' Uncle Stuart. It took some gettin' used to, but I kind a like it. Good thing, too. If things progress as I hope, I will be walkin' down the aisle in that very church. Zachary asked permission to court me, an' Uncle Stuart granted it."

Violet slapped the letter onto her lap. "I thought for sure she'd never get over Caleb. An' now, if she marries this Danforth boy, she won't be comin' back here. How can she do that? What 'bout Noah?"

"Why don't you finish readin'? She might say."

Violet sadly nodded. "My heart is torn in two, an' I am not sure what to do. I know Caleb has moved on with his life, an' I need to carry on with mine. If I can find love with another man, I want to grab onto it an' hold on tight. I am tired of all the lies, an' I intend to tell Zachary 'bout Caleb an' Noah."

Gideon groaned. "That ain't gonna go over well."

"No, it ain't." Violet was almost afraid to keep reading. "If Zachary is the kind of man I believe him to be, he will understand. Hopefully, he will be willin' to help me raise Noah. If that happens, I intend to travel with him to the cove an' bring Noah back with us. He is my son, an' no matter what Ma an' Pa might say, I want him in my life."

More tears. Violet couldn't stop them. "I am scared to death, but I know I cannot marry Zachary unless he knows everythin' 'bout me. If he loves me, whatever I tell him should not make a difference. Please keep the prayers comin'. I surely need them. All my love, Lily."

Violet folded the letter and returned it into the envelope. "Mercy . . . Thank goodness Mrs. Quincy didn't get her hands on this, or the cove would be abuzz with all kinds a gossip."

Gideon slowly got to his feet. "I'm glad our lives ain't as complicated as hers. I swear to you, Violet, I don't have no secrets. There anythin' *you* need to tell *me*?"

"I've told you all there is to tell. All I can say now is, I love you Gideon Myers, an' I'm thankful I have you to share this with. I couldn't bear it on my own. I'm terrified for Lily. We can *both* pray for her. All right?"

"Yep. I'm happy to."

She kissed his cheek, then motioned to the door. "We best go in."

"Ma's gonna know you've been cryin'."

Violet wiped her eyes. "I reckon she'll understand. She's well aware how much I love my sister."

When they went in, supper was waiting. They took their places, said grace, then quietly ate. His folks didn't pry for information, they simply accepted her tears and showed her love.

Violet couldn't ask for anything better.

Chapter 31

Lily stood in front of Evie, knees trembling. "Are you sure I look fine?"

"Except for the scared-out-of-your-wits expression, you're lovely." Evie pushed a wayward strand of Lily's hair into place. "It's only dinner. I'm sure Zachary's parents are as kind as he is."

"An' his sisters?"

"Of course. They could be *your* sisters someday, so I hope you'll like them."

Lily had received a message by private courier two days prior. Zachary had invited her to dinner at his home, so his family could meet her. Since they were courting, it was expected, but Lily couldn't convince her upset stomach that the evening would come off without complications. It had become her way of life.

She wore the emerald green dress that she'd worn to the park. She thought Zachary liked it, and she wanted to make a good impression on his family. If she wore the high-collared ones, she might scratch at her neck all night and lead them to believe she had a disorder. Not a good thing.

"C'mon, now." Evie took Lily's arm. "David will be waiting for you."

Lily grinned. "Reckon you'd like to go with me to my waitin' ride?"

"I thought you'd never ask." Evie radiated love for the man.

They paraded down the stairs together. Unfortunately, Aunt Helen was waiting at the bottom.

She flitted her fingers at them. "What's this? Have the two of you become joined at the hips?"

"No'm." Evie stopped cold. "You go on, Lily. I have work to do." Before Lily could respond, Evie spun around, lifted her skirt, and hurried up the stairs again.

Aunt Helen proudly jutted her chin. "I don't know what's gotten into that girl." She leered at Lily. "Likely, your bad influence."

Lily took the final steps to the bottom and approached her aunt. "Why do you hafta be so hateful all the time? You must prefer havin' folks dislike you."

"Those who are important *adore* me." She pursed her lips, then studied Lily. "Do well tonight. Make a mess of *this* arrangement and you'll be out on the streets."

Her threats didn't intimidate Lily. "I know how you feel 'bout me. I've tried to love you, but you make it impossible. Reckon I'm not *important* enough."

"*Reckon.*" Aunt Helen shuddered. "If you speak that way to the Danforth's, they'll see you for what you are."

"An' what's that?"

"A vulgar mountain girl." She cocked her gray-haired head.

"I pity you." A lump formed in Lily's throat. "Ma told me when you was little, you were a happy child. Seems bein' proper ruined you. I won't let that happen to me. Long as I live, I intend to be kind."

Her aunt didn't waver from her uppity stance. The way she pinched her lips formed deep wrinkles in her skin, making her haggard.

"Has growin' old been so painful?" Lily whispered. "Made you jealous a me? Is that why you behave so badly?"

"Jealous?" She folded her arms over her chest. "Look around you. I have everything. One word from me, and you'd have nothing."

"Appears to me, *you're* the one with nothin'. I'd rather have a heart full a love than a house full a *things*." Lily pushed away tears. Knowing her aunt would never understand real love, broke Lily's heart. "If you'll excuse me, David's waitin'."

Lily left her standing in the middle of the floor.

Someday, she'll be a very lonely old woman.

Lily paused at the door and looked over her shoulder. Uncle Stuart was nowhere in sight.

It seemed Aunt Helen was already alone.

* * *

The carriage stopped and David opened the door.

Lily gaped at the house in front of her. "You sure this is the right place?"

"Yes. This is the Danforth home. Spectacular, isn't it?"

Lily knew they had money, but didn't expect this. "It's twice the size a Aunt Helen's."

David grinned and extended his hand. "Are you getting out so you can go inside, or would you rather just gape at it?"

Before she could answer, she spotted Zachary hurrying toward them. His radiant smile lifted away all her worries.

"Let me," he said, nodding at David.

"By all means." David stepped aside and Zachary reached out to Lily.

She took his hand, grabbed on tight, and stepped to the ground.

"I'll return at eight to carry you home," David said.

Lily dipped her head. "Thank you."

"Enjoy your evening." David nodded to both of them in turn, then climbed up onto the driver's seat and drove away.

Lily linked her arm through Zachary's. "I was nervous till I saw you. Now, I believe I'll be fine."

"You *are* fine." He scanned her from head to toe. "So beautiful."

"Thank you. So are you." She grinned and he laughed. The evening had started off perfectly.

She should be accustomed to wealth by now, but whenever she ventured into a new place like this, it overwhelmed her.

Folks in the cove had suffered miserably during the war and struggled for survival. If she'd lived in St. Louis all her life, she might not understand what it meant to want for something. Everyone needed to know, not all things came easily. It might make them appreciate what they had.

No sooner had they walked through the front door, and his youngest sister sauntered up to them. "I'm Olive." She held her nose high, similar to the way Aunt Helen did. "I'm sixteen, but father says I act much older."

"I'm happy to meet you," Lily said, smiling.

Olive studied her. "Zachary hasn't brought a girl home in a long while. I didn't like the last one. Maybe I'll like you."

"I hope so." Lily shifted her eyes to him, begging for help.

"Olive," Zachary sternly said. "Lily's our guest, and *I* happen to like her a great deal. So please, mind your manners."

"Hmph." Olive spun on her heels and walked away.

Lily tightened her grasp on Zachary's arm. "That didn't go well. Sorry."

"It's not your fault. She's at a difficult age. Father won't let her be courted yet, and she's envious of Ursula." He faced Lily straight on. "Please don't judge me by my sisters. All right?"

"I won't. I have a brother who's nothin' like me. If you judged me by *his* behavior, you'd likely high-tail it in the opposite direction."

He chuckled and shook his head. "I love the way you express things. You'll have to tell me more about him."

"Eventually." She shifted her eyes downward. "There's plenty to tell."

"Hmm. Now you've really piqued my interest." He stroked her cheek. "I want to know *everything* about you."

She pushed a smile on her lips. "The very reason for courtin'."

His eyes rested on her mouth. "Yes. *That* and more."

She understood desire, and it flowed from every part of him. What troubled her more were the feelings he brought out in her whenever he looked at her. Especially the way he was gazing at her now.

"Aren't your folks waitin'?" she whispered.

"Yes." He sighed, then smiled. "I adore you. I could stand here with you all day and not tire of being with you."

"Well, we have lots of time to spend together. But we best not keep them waitin'. They might decide *they* don't like me. It seems I already have my work cut out for me impressin' your sister."

Laughing, he held out his arm.

Once again, she took it and walked with him down a long hallway. Wonderful aromas met them as they entered a large dining hall.

She recognized his folks from church. When they saw her, they crossed the room and approached them.

Mrs. Danforth donned a genuine-looking smile. "Welcome, my dear." She kissed Lily's cheek—something utterly unexpected.

"Thank you. I appreciate the invitation."

Mr. Danforth stood tall, right beside his wife. "We're happy to finally meet you. Forgive us for not making your acquaintance at worship. As you know . . . your uncle . . ." His brows wove.

"There's no need to apologize," Lily graciously said. "An' yes, I *do* know. But all is well now, isn't it?"

The man grasped onto her hand. "Yes, it is."

Mrs. Danforth cast an even brighter smile.

Lily glanced at Zachary, whose eyes filled with pride. He guided her to a chair at the table and helped her sit.

Olive paced at the other side of the room with her nose in the air. Eventually, her neck would ache keeping it up so high. Lily might have won her folks over, but the girl would be a hard nut to crack. She eventually took her own chair, flipped open her napkin, and sat as if she had a board strapped to her back. Almost as if she were wearing a corset, though she wasn't. The young girl had little to enhance.

Mrs. Danforth sat beside her husband. She darted her head about as if searching for something lost. "Where are Ursula and York?"

"We're here, mother." Zachary's other sister hurried into the room with a tall, dark-haired man at her heels. They both appeared a bit flushed.

Olive giggled, but immediately stopped when her ma shot her a sharp glare. It reminded Lily of her own ma.

Zachary reached under the table, took hold of Lily's hand, and squeezed. His mere presence had her heart racing, his gesture made it pound.

Two women in crisp white uniforms brought in the food. They didn't say a word, and their faces bore no expression. Either they were miserable, or they'd been taught to behave that way.

Steaming platters filled with roast beef and vegetables were set in the center of the table.

Thank goodness it ain't chicken.

Lily was also grateful for Mrs. Gottlieb's instruction. She knew exactly what to do with her napkin, which utensils to use, and the appropriate direction to pass the food. Not having it served by the help was an extra benefit. She could choose the size of her portions.

All would be well, if she wasn't asked too many questions.

"So . . ." Mr. Danforth looked right at her. "I know you're not from St. Louis. Your lovely accent depicts another location. I've yet to learn where you lived prior to your arrival. Why don't you tell us about your home?"

His kind remark eased her. She briefly closed her eyes and envisioned her dear cove. "I'm from a small town in Tennessee called Cades Cove. It's the most beautiful place you'll ever see—a lush valley surrounded by the spectacular Smoky Mountains. Trees galore, an' more wildlife than you can imagine."

"It sounds wonderful," Ursula said. "It must've been hard to leave it behind."

"It was. But my folks wanted me to have the chance for a better, more fulfillin' life. When Aunt Helen agreed to take me in, they were quite grateful."

"Are you happy here?" Mrs. Danforth asked.

Lily glanced at Zachary. "I am *now*."

Her comment brought smiles to everyone there, with the exception of Olive. The girl rolled her eyes and picked at her food.

The meal progressed with much lighter conversation. Fortunately, most of it centered around Ursula and York's upcoming marriage.

Lily startled when Zachary rested his hand on her leg. And when he moved it back and forth in a caress, she nearly crumbled to the floor. Though well-hidden beneath the table, she feared being discovered. It didn't help matters when she broke into an unladylike sweat.

He must've sensed her discomfort. He brought his hand out from under the table and focused on his dessert.

Once he'd finished eating, Zachary laid his napkin on his plate. "I'd like to show Lily the rest of the house. The grounds as well." He turned to her. "Would you enjoy that?"

"Yes. Thank you. As long as your folks don't mind."

"Why should we mind?" Mrs. Danforth said. "It will give the two of you some time alone to chat."

Olive tittered and was reprimanded again.

Lily looked around the table at the folks that could one day be family. Aside from Olive, she believed she'd be welcomed here.

Zachary scooted his chair back, then helped Lily to her feet. They wandered from the dining room with no objections. The rest of his family stayed seated, talking.

Zachary put an arm around Lily's waist and escorted her down the hall. "You know, once we're well out of sight, we'll be the subject of conversation."

"Yes. I assumed so." She, in turn, encircled his waist with one arm. "Olive doesn't care for me. I can't imagine what she might say."

"Olive doesn't like *anyone*. Even herself. She fusses endlessly about her *ugly* freckles. We've all told her they're cute, but she won't hear it. As I said, her age warrants her poor disposition."

"*I* have freckles."

"Yes, you do. And on *you*, they're lovely."

She gave him a sideways glance. Why did he always seem so focused on her appearance? She wanted him to care for *her*, not simply her looks.

He guided her to a tall, double-door. "I have something special to show you." He jiggled his brows, then swung the door open.

They entered a room with the highest ceiling she'd seen yet. Just like at Mrs. Gottlieb's, the room had no furnishings, except for a large piano and several cushioned benches along the walls.

Zachary fanned his arms. "Our ballroom."

"It's incredible." She gestured to the piano. "Do you play?"

"No. But I can *hum*." He faced her and bowed. "Miss Larsen, may I have this dance?"

She giggled, then curtsied. "Certainly, sir."

He held her similarly to the way David did when they waltzed. However, he drew her in much closer. They had no open air between them.

"You're makin' it difficult to concentrate on dancin'," Lily said.

"Forgive me." With a grin, he increased the space. "Now then, show me what you've learned."

He hummed a one, two, three tune, then gently nudged her into motion. She followed his lead without a single stumble. They twirled around the floor as if floating on air. Maybe her light heart had something to do with it.

After several circles around the room, he stopped and pulled her against him. "I told you I'd manage to get you alone."

She could scarcely breathe. "Are you sure we are? Olive may be lurking behind the piano."

"I'm certain. I locked the door when we entered."

Knowing what was coming, she moistened her lips.

He grinned. "You want a kiss as much as I wish to give it. Don't you?"

"Would you think less a me if I said yes?"

"Nothing could make me think less of you."

I hope you mean that.

She shut her eyes and waited for the contact she craved. His lips pressed to hers—lightly at first—then he covered her mouth fully and deepened the kiss.

She wrapped her arms around his strong body and pulled him firmly to herself. He let out a wonderful moan that increased the rate of her heartbeat.

"Oh, Lily." His mouth searched hers, then continued down her neck.

"Yes, Zachary." She threaded her fingers in his hair, desiring so much more than kisses.

His hands moved along her waist. Though she should be ashamed for wanting them to roam further, she couldn't help herself. Being with him brought back memories of a time she cherished. She'd been free and loved. And now—because of Zachary —her freedom had been renewed. She'd finally begun to make her own choices again.

As her heart thumped in rhythm with the sound of his labored breaths, it affirmed her greatest need.

I wanna be loved.

His mouth returned to hers. They kissed over and over, heating the enormous room.

Breathing hard, he took her face in his hands. "You've been kissed before. Haven't you?"

She shut her eyes and nodded, not wanting to lie. "But none as fine as yours. I believe you've had *your* share of kisses, too."

"Not like these." He devoured her with another, then stepped back and held his hands in the air. "We have to stop." He put his back to her. "I won't shame you."

She moved up behind him, put her arms around his body, and rested her head on his back. "You're a good man. I feel safe with you. You haven't offended me in any way."

He grabbed her hands and kissed them, then faced her again. "I wish I'd met you long before Ursula and York made their plans."

She sighed. "I wish I'd a met you several *years* ago."

"Years?" He caressed her cheek. "That's an odd thing to say."

She wasn't ready to tell him her reasons. "Well . . . years ago, I doubt you'd have had so many kisses. Maybe I woulda been your first."

"And I yours." He tapped the tip of her nose. "But, none of that matters. I chose to court you, because it's you I wish to pursue a lasting relationship with. I'll be kissing no one else."

"Neither will I."

He took her hand and pressed it over his heart. "I anticipate many more kisses and eventually, even *greater* passion." He looked upward, grinning, and shook his head. "If I can bear it. You may give me heart failure."

"Good thing you're a medical student. You can learn how to prevent that."

He cast a sideways smirk. "You make me *so* happy." He raked his fingers into her hair. "Why don't we take a stroll in the garden? The evening air has cooled, and I believe we'd both benefit from it."

"All right." She knew it was for the best. They needed to ward off temptation.

She'd not yet decided she loved the man, though her body craved him. There was nothing at all right about that. Love should come first.

Caleb had ruined her.

Hopefully, Zachary could redeem her.

CHAPTER 32

Zachary paced outside his father's office door, struggling with what to say.

He's a man, he'll understand.

He rapped on the door, then entered. "A word, Father?"

The man lifted his eyes from his papers. "I heard you in the hallway. I wondered how long it would take you to knock." He gestured to a chair. "Come sit and tell me what's troubling you."

Zachary made certain the door was shut tight, then he sank into the fine leather seat.

He'd been courting Lily almost two weeks. During the day, he'd do all he could to keep his mind on his studies, but in the evenings, he'd visit with her. Whenever he managed to get her alone, he'd struggle to keep his hands to himself. There had to be a reasonable solution.

"You look wretched," his father said. "Are you ill?"

He met his gaze. "Yes. *Love*sick."

The man chuckled. "I see. So, what's the problem? The courtship appears to be progressing as it should."

"It is. But until Ursula says her vows, I can't say mine. Waiting won't be easy."

His father's eyes narrowed. "Are you saying what I think you are?"

Just tell him. "I want her. In every way possible. Whenever we're together, my needs . . . *rise.*"

"I'm sure they do." He smirked and withdrew a cigar from the wooden box on his desk. "Would you like one?"

"No." Zachary tightened his fists. "You shouldn't enjoy my misery."

After lighting the cigar, his father's expression became something more sympathetic. He casually puffed. "Are you unable to ease those needs yourself?"

"Good heavens, Father." Zachary looked at the floor. "*No.*"

"So, you require a woman to do it for you. Am I right?"

"*Yes.*" He stared at the man. "Of course. But until I marry Lily, I won't have her that way."

"As it should be. However . . ." He blew a plume of smoke over their heads. "Are you aware there are two kinds of women?"

"I always thought there were many more than that. What are you getting at?"

"There are women you marry, and those you don't. *They* are the two kinds of women. Lily will make a fine wife and bear your children. She'll be faithful to you and I imagine enjoyable as well. As for the other kind, their sole purpose is to satisfy the desires of men."

Zachary leaned toward the desk. "Are you referring to . . . *prostitutes?*" He whispered the word.

His father laughed. "You're twenty-one years old. Don't act like you've never considered them. Don't you remember the first time we discussed the Bible story that told how a prostitute named Rahab helped Joshua destroy Jericho? You wanted to know what the word meant. And I told you. You seemed quite intrigued."

"Of course I was intrigued. I'd recently discovered girls. But I know aligning myself with a woman like that isn't right. I'd never consider it."

"Why?" His father took a long drag, then blew it out.

"Because—because I know I should wait to lie with my wife. Not some . . . *whore*." He glanced over his shoulder to assure himself the door remained shut. "How could you even suggest it?"

"You asked for a solution to your dilemma. I gave it."

"You'd condone such a thing?" Zachary scooted his chair closer to the desk and set his hands atop it. "Have *you* done it?"

The man grinned. "There was a brief period prior to marrying your mother, when I found myself in your predicament." He leaned back, still smiling. "Alexandria was her name."

Zachary gaped at him, then snapped his mouth shut. "And you never once felt guilty for being with her?"

"There was no need. I paid her for a service. It's perfectly legal. And until you're bound by marriage to one woman, why not take advantage of it?"

Zachary had always respected his father's advice, but something about this didn't feel right. "What of disease? I've studied the effects of promiscuity. There are none more promiscuous than harlots."

"My son, the medical student. Yes, disease is a risk. However, if you choose the proper *harlot*, it's not an issue."

"I wouldn't know where to find one." Zachary's throat dried.

His father got up from his chair and came around the desk, then leaned against it. "There's a steamboat that stays moored on the riverbank. The *Evening Star*. Only true gentlemen are allowed on board. You must be properly dressed and pay a fee upon entering." He extinguished his cigar. "The women aboard are exceptional."

"How do you know this?" Fearing the answer, Zachary's heart thumped.

"Since you're a grown man, I'll speak openly. You see, after Olive was born, your mother decided she was done bearing children. Whenever I tried to touch her, she'd push me away. Her rejection nearly destroyed our marriage." He stood tall and adjusted his collar. "She encouraged me to find another means. The odd thing is, she's never complained about the lack of intimacy in her own life. She seems satisfied with simple affection. I, however, am not."

"You're saying, you *continue* to use the services of those women?"

"Every now and then. My needs aren't as strong as they were when I was your age. But, I do understand how you feel. Once in a while, I find it enjoyable."

Zachary couldn't digest all he'd been told. It sat in his gut like a rock. He thought he knew his father and never expected this. "How do you keep from being caught? Or seen *going* there for that matter?"

"Well, your mother knows, so that alone eases me. But you can be certain, if you ever went there and saw someone familiar, you'd never speak of it. Neither party would want to let on where the other had been seen."

"Have you come across men there that you know?"

"Many times. And I have great respect for them."

"But . . ." Zachary's frustration grew the more they spoke. "Isn't it a sin?"

"Everyone sins. That's why we go to church." He returned to his seat behind the desk. "I've never claimed to be a saint. I'm merely a man. If you decide to go there, I won't fault you for it. And Lily will never have to know. You can choose to remain faithful after you're married. And perhaps, she may end up like your mother one day. She'll send you away to find affection elsewhere. At least then, you'll know what to do."

Zachary eased onto his feet, but had no idea what to say.

"You're pale, son. Go find something to eat. It might make you feel better." His father lifted a paper from the desk and began to read.

Food wasn't what Zachary needed. He had a lot to consider and trudged into the hallway.

His mother wandered toward him. "Are you all right?"

He looked into her face. So lovely, and up until now, he presumed *innocent*. His parents were like strangers. "I'm fine. Actually, I'm a little tired. I think I'll go to my room."

She pressed her hand to his forehead. "I hope you're not coming down with something." With a kiss to his cheek, she smiled and walked away.

Zachary continued on to his bedroom. He flopped onto the bed and gazed upward.

I can't do it.

He'd fallen in love with Lily. Lying with another woman wasn't an option. It didn't matter that the act was legal or biblical, it didn't feel honorable.

He'd reign in his desires and douse his needs. It was the only solution.

* * *

Lily shut her eyes tight, while Evie placed the ball gown over her head. Though she faced the mirror, she didn't want to see her image. The corset did as it should, but what would Zachary think?

Their passionate kisses of late answered her question. As she'd told Evie before, her appearance in a corset would only put improper thoughts in the minds of men. She knew exactly what Zachary would be thinking.

God help her, but she *wanted* him to think it.

Her mind should be solely on thoughts of pure love, but her body had other ideas. Maybe her ma was right about her, and the devil had taken hold. She needed to remember what was important. Desires of the flesh were fleeting, but honest-to-goodness love would last forever.

Truthfully, she wanted *both*.

"I can't dance nearly as well wearin' this thing." Lily finally looked at her reflection. "It cuts into my ribs if I bend at all."

"Well, I can say without reservation, you're beautiful. Zachary will be pleased."

"You said that 'bout Archibald." Lily sighed. "How things changed."

"You sound sad. Do you miss him?"

"Some. Archibald an' I had great conversations. It's different with Zachary."

Evie giggled. "A lot less conversation?"

Lily swatted her arm. "You should talk. Remember, I saw you an' David in the carriage."

"Yes. And you've never let me forget it." She gazed downward and cupped her hands over her belly. "Miss Lily? I know I can trust you . . ."

"Course you can." Lily placed a hand atop hers. "You're with child, aren't you?"

"Can you tell?" She smoothed the fabric of her dress. "I didn't think I was showing yet."

"You're not. Least, not enough for anyone to see it. Somehow, I just knew." Lily looked her in the eyes. "You an' David need to get married soon as you can. That baby's gonna need both a you."

"We want to. We've almost got enough money saved, but I'm scared about giving my notice. I fear Mrs. Clark will be mean as a snake when I tell her I'm leaving."

"She's mean regardless." Lily rubbed Evie's arm. "Do what's best for you, David, an' your child. Don't mind Aunt Helen. All right?"

Evie bobbed her head. "You best get downstairs. The music's starting."

Lily fanned her turquoise skirt and walked toward the door. "Wish me luck. I fear either I'll fall, or worse yet, pop out a this dress."

Evie covered her mouth, wide-eyed. "I'll be down soon to serve."

"Mind that baby in you. Don't lift anythin' heavy. Hear me?" Lily left her, hoping she'd pay mind to her request.

The Clarks had hired a five-piece orchestra for the affair. As Lily descended the stairs, the music surrounded her. She'd been told they played more than just waltzes, but she'd bide her time and wait for the right song before she ventured onto the floor. Of course, she wouldn't do much of anything till Zachary arrived.

Gerard stood by the door. He opened and closed it more than once, while Lily made her way to the bottom of the staircase. Men in black suits and women in a variety of colors filtered in. She caught the eye of one particular gentleman, who stumbled upon seeing her. A woman, she presumed to be his wife, kept him from falling face-first to the floor.

Most all the ladies wore dresses like hers. Low-cut and enhanced with their stylish undergarments. The very thing Lily was already cursing. She huffed when she saw a few women without corsets. Apparently, they weren't a requirement.

Maybe Aunt Helen wanted her to be tortured.

Likely.

Lily moved to the side of the entryway to wait for Zachary.

"Good evening, my dear." Uncle Stuart crept up behind her and peered downward. "You look . . . *marvelous.*"

She wanted to slap his face and flee back up the stairs. "I'm uncomfortable. I feel like a caged animal."

"Caged?" His brows creased, then he laughed. "Oh. I understand. Trust me. Every man here appreciates your discomfort." He jerked his head toward the front door. "Especially that one."

Thank goodness.

Zachary had arrived. "'Scuse me, Uncle Stuart. My beau's here." She hurried away.

Lily's heart thumped in a good way, and for a while, she forgot the pain. Aside from Olive, all of the Danforths had come. Zachary had told Lily that Olive would be staying with a friend for the evening. His ma felt she was too young for the affair.

Lily's cheeks warmed when *Mr.* Danforth eyed her. Yet she couldn't fault *any* man for noticing her. Not like this.

As for Zachary, he seemed to be having difficulty breathing.

His pa nudged him. "Why don't you escort the lady to the ballroom?"

"Yes, sir." Zachary extended his arm, and Lily took it. They paraded across the floor, then down the hallway to join the party.

The music grew louder.

"I'm glad you're here," she said, tightening her hold.

He lifted her hand to his lips and kissed it. "You take my breath."

"I noticed." She jutted her chin high, grinning.

Once in the ballroom, Lily caught her aunt's eye. Aunt Helen gave a quirky smile, then flitted away and fawned over all the other *important* people. Her obnoxious loud voice carried above the music.

"Fruit tea?" Evie extended a tray filled with beverages.

Lily took one. "Is that heavy?"

"No." Evie shyly looked down. "I'm fine."

"Good." Lily grabbed another cup and handed it to Zachary. "I had some a this earlier. It's quite tasty."

Evie wandered off to serve other guests.

Zachary took a sip. "Mmm. Very good."

Lily drank hers in several gulps, then set the cup on a side table. "That's 'bout all I can have t'night. I certainly can't *eat*. Not in this dress."

"It's a shame. But I must say . . ." He moved his mouth close to her ear. "You move me."

Perfectly timed, a waltz began.

"Well, then," Lily took his drink and put it beside hers. "Let's dance."

Smiling, Zachary guided her to the center of the floor. Once there, he quickly swept her into the proper hold. They gracefully moved across the floor. Her skirt swooshed along with the music and they didn't make a single misstep.

She hadn't smiled so broadly in a great while. And though she'd not known him long, she believed she'd fallen in love. The way he kept looking in her eyes affirmed he bore deep feelings for her. They shared mutual desire, but without a doubt, there was more to his affections.

They danced until her feet hurt. She'd even managed something he'd called a foxtrot. Thankfully, Zachary was an accomplished leader. She merely followed him.

Out of breath, she held onto his arm. "Let's go sit in the courtyard for a spell."

He didn't argue. Laughter and loud conversation followed them outside. Everyone seemed to be enjoying themselves, including Aunt Helen. But, she was in her element and bragging up a storm.

Lily sat on the bench, rigid as ever. "This has been the best night of my life. I can't recall *ever* havin' so much fun."

He took the place beside her. "I'm glad to hear it. Hopefully, we'll have many more like this." He shifted on the seat and faced her. "Lily, if I said I love you, would you believe me?"

Her heart raced. She'd longed to hear the words. "Reckon so. But, you don't know me too well. I wanna believe you truly care, but part a me fears your feelin's are just. . ." How could she say it?

His eyes searched hers. "Just what?"

She swallowed hard. "Physical attraction. Maybe even a little bit a *lust*."

He traced her lips with the tip of his finger. "I'd be lying if I said I don't want you. But what I feel goes beyond that. I swear to it."

Their eyes locked. "I have the same kind a feelin's for you. I'm sure it's love, but it's the *other*, too."

"You *want* me? Like *that*?"

She nodded.

He grabbed onto her hand and held it to his chest. "I wish now more than ever I'd met you sooner. Waiting won't be easy. You see, you've taught me something I didn't know. I never thought a woman could feel the same desires as a man."

"Is it wrong?" She felt like crying. Her past had tarnished her mind more than she'd ever thought.

He pulled her close and held her. "No, it's not wrong, and I'm thankful it's *me* you want. It's simply not the right time."

She tipped her head back and studied his handsome face. "I need to tell you some things, but not tonight." She flattened her hand against his chest. "*Do* you truly love me, Zachary?"

"I do."

Her chest constricted. "I love you, too." Just saying it scared her to death.

He bent down and kissed her lightly on the lips. "Being together will be worth waiting for."

She caressed his cheek, but said nothing.

CHAPTER 33

She loves me.

Zachary twirled Lily around, then pulled her into his arms. They'd taken the dancefloor alone, after her aunt announced their courtship. Everyone watched them move, smiling and applauding, but Zachary kept his thoughts on Lily's proclamation of love. Her declaration of desire also spun through his mind. How could it not?

"Aren't they a handsome couple?" Mrs. Clark bellowed.

More applause.

Zachary caught his father's eye, along with an approving nod. Since their private conversation, Zachary had struggled with his opinion of the man. He still respected him, but would always wonder where his father might be, on night's he wasn't home. Zachary also had a hard time looking at his mother without pity. Yet, she seemed completely happy.

I don't understand.

His eyes shifted from Lily's, and moved further down. A great mistake. The sight before him piqued his desire. He longed to bury himself between her rounded breasts.

Stop!

He peered into her face. She worked her lower lip and her eyes slowly blinked. Something about her actions told him she'd been aware of his thoughts. He placed his cheek to hers. "Shall we take another respite in the courtyard?"

She moistened her lips and nodded.

Once the song ended, he bowed to the crowd. "If you'll excuse us, we need a bit of air."

Mumbled remarks followed them out the door, but no one objected.

He took Lily by the hand and led her behind the house. After glancing about to be certain they were unseen, he pulled her body against his and kissed her deeply.

She let out a soft whimper, then grasped onto him—with more strength than he expected from a woman—and fervently kissed him. Breasts heaving, she rapidly unfastened the top buttons of his shirt, pushed it open, and glided her lips across his bare chest with even more kisses.

"Lily. What are you doing?"

She said nothing, simply lifted her eyes. Kiss by kiss, she worked her way up to his neck. When she once again reached his lips, she put her hands in his hair and held his head tight, then devoured his mouth.

His heart raced, and his body begged for more.

"I love you," she whispered. Her hand moved inside his shirt. She caressed his chest, all the while kissing him.

He'd been frozen by her actions, but his hands came to life. Without thought, he cupped her breast and gently felt her.

A soft moan escaped her, and she pushed him backward against the exterior wall of the house.

How could they continue this way?

He brought his hands to himself. "We'll be found," he managed to say between her unstoppable kisses.

"No. Everyone's enjoyin' themselves. They won't bother us." She laid her head on his chest. "Hold me, Zachary."

He wrapped his arms around her. "I'm sorry for touching you that way. But your actions made me lose my senses."

She lifted her head, frowned, and refastened the buttons. "Forgive me. Reckon I lost my senses, too." She blew out a slow breath. "We should go back in. It's best we start doin' more talkin' than kissin'." She stepped away from him. "When you come for dinner on Tuesday night, I have some things to tell you. *Important* things."

"I'll be here at my usual time. I may be tired from schoolwork, but I can always listen to you." The change in her behavior concerned him. "Are you angry with me?"

She rushed back into his arms. "No. Never think that."

"Then, what's wrong?" He gently rubbed her back.

"I'm a little scared. That's all." She nestled against his neck.

"Don't be. Everything will be fine."

Still frowning, she jerked her head toward the house. "C'mon. The music won't be playin' forever. Let's go dance once more 'fore you hafta go."

"Only if you'll smile for me."

She jutted her chin high and did so. "Better?"

"Much."

They returned indoors. His emotions whirled faster than he and Lily had moved on the dancefloor. One moment they'd been passionate and on fire, and the next, they'd been thoroughly doused. Maybe his intimate touch had truly angered her.

I must control myself.

He stood back and watched her wander over to Evie to get another drink. She gulped it down, and her face flushed a beautiful shade of red.

Thoughts of her kisses and her hands on him reignited his internal fire. Only one thing could squelch it.

Many people had already left, but he and Lily had their last dance. It was a slow waltz, but it didn't decrease the rate of his heartbeat.

He told her goodnight and followed his parents out the door. When they neared their carriage, he grasped onto his father's arm. "Go on without me. I need to walk."

The man eyed him. "Are you certain?"

"Yes." He looked him straight in the eye. "I may be a while." Fortunately, his mother and sister had already gotten into the carriage with York. "Tell mother not to worry about me."

His father smiled and patted him on the shoulder. "Very well." He gazed upward. "Is that the *evening star* I see?"

Zachary's throat closed up. "Yes. I believe it is."

Another pat. This time on the back. The man leaned close. "Ask for Caroline. She's young and someone I've not had. It's best that way." He strode away without saying anything more, yet too much had already been said.

Zachary couldn't utter another syllable if he'd wanted to.

The riverfront wasn't far, yet he questioned every step. He argued with himself, believing on one hand it was the only way to keep from compromising Lily. On the other hand, it felt like a betrayal. Even so, he kept putting one foot in front of the other.

He easily found the right steamboat. The words, *Evening Star,* were surrounded by fully illumined lanterns. Dressed as he was, he looked like a gentleman, and he always carried money. Although uncertain of the amount he needed, he assumed he had plenty.

His knees shook as he walked across the dock to the boarding plank. The boat lightly lilted, swaying with the motion of the river.

Music came from the interior. A simple piano playing happy tunes.

Zachary could scarcely breathe.

A man greeted him with a simple bow of his head. "Two dollars," he said and held out his hand.

"That's all?"

The man grinned. "For now. What you do inside determines the rest." He smirked.

Zachary handed him the money, and the man waved him in.

Heavy smoke hovered low. Zachary had been inside many steamboats, and this one was no different. The main room was decorated like an elegant parlor filled with tables and chairs. In the corner, the piano player swayed with the music he created. Men played cards and tossed dice, glasses clinked together, and the scent of alcohol was evident.

Zachary spotted several women dressed similarly to the way Lily had been clad. Their bosoms rounded above their gowns.

It wasn't easy imagining his father here.

Why am I here?

A man tapped him on the shoulder. "What's your pleasure? Gambling? Whiskey? Or are you here for a woman?"

Zachary gulped. "Caroline?"

The man grinned. "Good choice. Ten dollars." He wiggled his fingers.

Fortunately, Zachary had enough money. He dug into his pocket, then gave it to him.

"Go up those stairs." The man pointed at the stairway on the opposite side of the room. "She's in number eighteen. Be sure to knock first. She might be occupied."

"Thank you." Zachary feared his knees might buckle.

The man studied his face. "Don't worry. She doesn't bite." He nudged him, then wandered off to another *customer*.

That's all this is. A business transaction.

If he believed *that*, he wouldn't feel like throwing up.

He did all he could to avoid making eye contact with any of the men there. God help him if he saw someone from church.

Somehow, he made it to the stairs. He grabbed the rail and ascended one slow step at a time.

All the doors on the upper deck were numbered. He slowly forced himself down the corridor to find number eighteen. The sounds coming from behind every closed door had an effect on him. Similar to the sight of Lily's bare flesh.

I'm such a sinner.

But, if it was a sin, why was it legal?

He stood taller and kept going. Within moments, he faced number eighteen. His hand shook as he lifted it to knock, then the door burst open, and he stumbled backward.

A *boy* came out, tucking in his shirt. He appeared younger than Olive.

"Sorry," the redheaded youth said, smirking. "Didn't mean to scare you." He jerked his head toward the room. "She's sumthin'. Best I ever had." His already wide grin broadened. "Reckon I tuckered her out. I've learned how to keep it up for a real long time." He laughed. "Have fun."

Speechless, Zachary gaped at the young man. The boy's accent —though not as refined—reminded him of Lily.

The boy hurried off, and Zachary couldn't move. The door remained ajar and he caught sight of the woman within. Bare breasts and all.

No. I can't!

He whipped around and ran down the hall, passing the redhead. He nearly stumbled down the stairs, but kept going.

I'm not that kind of man!

He sprinted all the way home.

He passed his father as he raced up to his room. The man questioned him with his eyes, but Zachary didn't want to speak to him. He'd never felt so ashamed of himself.

He slammed his door shut and swore he'd never tell a soul about what he'd seen. He prayed he could forget it.

CHAPTER 34

Lily hadn't slept a wink. She could use a good nap, but her tormented mind wouldn't allow it. Ever since the ball, her thoughts had troubled her to the point of making her sick. She couldn't eat, let alone sleep.

The ball had been more fantastic than she'd expected. She'd laughed, danced, and felt more joy than should be allowed. Maybe that's why she was paying this horrid price. She didn't deserve that kind of happiness. Not with her past hanging over her.

Until she told Zachary everything, her heart wouldn't rest.

She'd nearly lost all control that night behind the house. She'd come close to ripping the poor man's clothes off. And when he'd touched her . . .

She laid a hand to her breast and sighed. His intimate contact had reignited many pleasant memories. Yet unlike Caleb, Zachary had put a stop to her advances. A very wise thing.

Why am I like this?

Had being raised to be strong made her fearless with men?

All she knew for certain was that she enjoyed being in Zachary's arms, and she was fairly confident she loved him. At least, she cared more for him than anyone since Caleb.

Caleb was real *love.*

She tipped her head back and breathed in the fall air. The scent of autumn leaves reminded her of the cove. The temperature was perfect in the courtyard, but she needed to dress for dinner and prepare herself for the dreaded conversation with Zachary.

Reckon I should wear black.

It was nearly impossible to expect a positive outcome from their talk. All she had to hold onto was his declaration of love for her. Hopefully, it would be enough.

"Lily!" Evie hurried toward her. "There's someone here to see you." She brightly smiled. "Two men, actually. One says he's your brother."

Lucas.

Though Lily had expected him for some time, she'd been so caught up in other things, she'd forgotten him.

I don't need this right now.

"Lily?" Evie tapped her shoulder. "Did you hear me? Your brother's here to see you. He's quite the charmer. He actually brought your aunt a gift, and she's bubbling all over him. I rarely see her so thrilled."

Lily quickly composed herself. "Where are they?"

"In the parlor. Mrs. Clark invited them for dinner. Won't it be wonderful to have Zachary meet someone in your family?"

Lily clutched her stomach. "So, Lucas is bein' *nice*?"

"Yes." She tipped her head. "Is that uncommon?"

"He's gone through a rough spell as of late." *I'm bein' too kind.* The little devil definitely knew how to deceive. Even so, Lucas was still her brother and she had difficulty speaking poorly about him. "I'm gonna go wash my face, then I'll be down to see them. All right?"

"Of course, it is. I'll let Mrs. Clark know you're coming." Evie bustled away.

Lily returned inside and trudged up to her room. She had no doubt the man with Lucas was Sergeant Douglas, and she assumed they'd come to question her. But if Lucas was cozying up to their aunt, he probably had other motives.

All the face-washing in the world couldn't wipe away her worry. After putting on her high-necked blue dress, she donned her best smile and descended the stairs.

Low voices came from the parlor. She bolstered her courage and walked in.

"I'm glad you're finally joining us, Lily," Aunt Helen said, in her sing-song voice. "Your guests have been waiting." She took Lily's hand and guided her in front of the pair seated on the sofa.

She barely recognized her brother. He wore a fine suit and had his hair stylishly cut. He'd not grown any whiskers—likely *couldn't*—and his freckles stood out more pronounced than ever.

He looked up at her and grunted out a laugh. "You're quite a sight." He fingered her dress, then smiled at Aunt Helen. "You made a lady outta her. That's an accomplishment."

"Yes." Aunt Helen laughed. "Fortunately, I had help."

Sergeant Douglas rose to his feet and eyed Lily up and down. "Lucas understated your fete, Mrs. Clark. You created a masterpiece. You're lovely, Lily." He took her hand and kissed it.

Lily's skin crawled. She stepped back from him as far as she could. "You shouldn't a done that."

"For heaven's sake, Lily," Aunt Helen scolded. "His action was that of a gentleman. Mind your manners."

Lucas sniggered.

"Forgive me," the sergeant said and bowed. "Miss Lily is correct. Though we met on a previous occasion, it's been a great while since we've seen each other. I'd forgotten she doesn't care to be touched."

Aunt Helen waved her hand. "That's silly. She recently learned to dance, which required her to be touched by more than one man. I've never known it to bother her."

Lily crossed her arms. "Dancin's different." She met Lucas's gaze and received another gloating smile.

What are you up to?

Aunt Helen looked from her to Lucas. "I'm surprised the two of you didn't embrace. If I recall, don't mountain folk like to hug? Aren't you happy to see each other?"

Lucas stood, but didn't go anywhere near Lily. "I'm not a boy anymore. I'm a man. It ain't right to be huggin' on my sister."

Aunt Helen put an arm over his shoulder. "It warms me to hear you speak. I believe it's because it reminds me of my youth." She jiggled her wrist in the air. "Thank you for the splendid gift."

Lily covered her mouth to keep from gaping. Not only had her aunt not scolded him for speaking improperly, but it looked as though he'd given her a *gold* bracelet. No wonder she was being nice.

Lucas puffed up tall. "You're welcome, Aunt Helen. Figgered it was right to bring you a present, bein' related an' all."

She spun and faced Lily. "You could learn a thing or two from him." She released Lucas and sauntered across the floor. "I'll leave you all to talk. Let me know if you need anything. I'm going to speak with our cook to make certain she has prepared plenty of food."

Lily *had* brought her a gift, yet it seemed she'd forgotten about it. Probably because Aunt Helen thought the necklaces were her rightful property and didn't see them as anything but that. Lily wished her ma had never parted with the jewelry. Aunt Helen had more fineries than anyone needed.

Once her aunt left the room, the air chilled. Lily shivered.

"Why don't you sit?" Sergeant Douglas motioned to a chair, then returned to his own seat. Lucas followed him like an obedient puppy.

"Why'd you come, Sergeant?" Lily sat. This horrid situation along with lack of sleep and food had weakened her knees.

"I'm no longer a sergeant. You may call me Vincent." His eyes rested where they shouldn't. "You've *blossomed*, Lily." Lucas chuckled and nudged the man. "St. Louis suits you."

"I'm doin' what I can to fit in." Thank goodness they'd not arrived days ago and attended the ball. She wouldn't want the lecherous man to see her in *that* gown. "But I'm a mite confused why the two a you are here, an' *together*."

"Don't pretend you didn't expect us." Vincent keenly studied her. "I'm sure your mother warned you of our arrival. Told you to destroy a particular letter? Hmm?"

"I haven't heard one word from my ma. Seems my folks have forgotten 'bout me."

"But, you didn't act surprised to see us. *Someone* must've told you we were coming."

"Yep." Lily jutted her chin. "Evie. You know, the housemaid. She said you was here."

Vincent grinned and leaned back, then crossed one leg over the other. "I remember you well. You're the sly one." He shook a finger. "I have a feeling there's more to it, but I'll play along. Your brother and I are searching for the mountain woman, Callie."

Lily glared at Lucas, then turned her attention back to Vincent. "Why? She ain't here." All her proper training went by the wayside. She'd transformed into her old self, simply by being in their presence.

"We realize that," Vincent said. "Lucas told me you received a letter from her, and your mother confirmed it. I assume you still have it."

"Nope. Lost it while I was travelin' here. Not sure *what* happened to it."

"Can you tell me what Callie said in the letter?"

She shut her eyes and envisioned every word Caleb had written. Each painful part that changed her life. "She said . . ." Lily once again looked at her brother. His arrogance sickened her. "She said she'd arrived safely in Waynesville, an' wouldn't be comin' back to the cove. But she assured me, she was fine." Tears threatened, but she'd never cry in front of them.

Lucas sat up straight. "See, Vincent. There's nothin' more to it. We came all this way for nothin'."

The man kept his eyes on Lily. "You're sure there wasn't anything more in the letter that might help us?"

"Why are you lookin' for her?"

Vincent grunted. "You were there that night. You know full well she killed Captain Ableman."

Lily got up and moved toward him. "An' she had every right. He was tryin' to have his way with us." She hovered above him. "If I'd a been able, I woulda done it myself." She breathed hard and glared at Lucas. "Why are you helpin' this man? Don't you remember what he done to Violet?"

Lucas got to his feet and stood within inches of her. "I remember. An' I also recall her sayin' she *liked* it."

Lily smacked his face. "Stop lyin'!"

"What's going on here?" Aunt Helen strode across the floor and grabbed Lily's wrist. "Why'd you strike him? Have you lost your mind?"

"My sister," Lucas said. "Has always enjoyed hittin' me. Makes her feel important."

The hateful woman tightened her hold. "Apologize this minute."

"No. He had it comin'."

Aunt Helen hissed air through her nose. "Mr. Douglas, I'm sorry for my niece's rudeness. We've done all we can to teach her proper behavior. And you . . ." She cupped Lucas's cheek with her free hand. "You poor young man. Your life in that wretched cabin must've been horrid. Thank goodness you've aligned yourself with someone decent. I hope you both can overcome this ordeal and enjoy sharing dinner with us. Mrs. Winters assures me we'll have plenty to eat."

Lily struggled to break free from her grasp. "You're hurtin' me!"

Aunt Helen didn't let up and dug her sharp fingernails into Lily's skin. "Good. It serves you right for harming your brother." She stuck her nose high in the air. "Have you finished your business with my niece, Mr. Douglas?"

"I believe so. I'm afraid she knows nothing of use to us."

"It doesn't surprise me." She leered at Lily. "Go to your room until dinner, at which time I expect you to give your brother a full apology." With a slight shove, she released her. "Go on."

Lily wanted to scream. Instead, she hurried from the room and raced upstairs.

Her wrist throbbed.

No sooner had she gone into her bedroom, and Evie walked in behind her. "What happened down there? I heard yelling."

"I'm so angry right now I could spit!" Lily rubbed her sore wrist.

"Why?" Evie's brows wove with worry, and she pointed. "Is that blood?"

The place Lily had been rubbing was smeared with red. She went to the wash basin and added fresh water, then put both hands in, carefully cleaning the wound. "Aunt Helen truly hates me."

"She did *that*?"

"Yep. Reckon *I* shoulda given her a gold bracelet."

Evie laid a hand on her shoulder. "Should I get something to wrap your wrist?"

"No. It'll be fine. I've had much worse." She faced her dear friend. "T'night might get ugly. If sumthin' happens an' I'm sent away, I want you to know I'm glad we met. An' please . . ." Lily fought back tears. "Marry David soon. Your child needs his name. No matter how hateful Aunt Helen can be, it won't come close to how you'd feel if you had to birth a bastard. It would ruin your life."

Evie's chin quivered. "I'm scared for you, Lily. I don't understand any of this."

"Don't fret over me. I learned a long time ago how to take care a myself. Now, go on an' help Mrs. Winters 'fore Aunt Helen comes lookin' for you."

"All right." She hugged Lily, then sped from the room.

CHAPTER 35

Zachary chose to walk to the Clarks. He'd been doing a great deal of it lately. Mostly, to clear his head. He'd had difficulty concentrating at school, and he'd avoided speaking to his father about the night at the boat. At least the man hadn't pressed him.

Lily stayed at the forefront of his mind. He hadn't stopped wondering what she so earnestly wished to speak to him about.

He'd been pleased with himself for not going through with his intentions to bed Caroline. He'd resisted the temptation. If he could do that, he could overcome anything. No matter what Lily had to say, he'd meet it with confidence.

He wore a comfortable gray suit and carried a bouquet of wild geraniums he'd picked along the way.

Gerard answered the door and Zachary went inside, feeling quite at home. However, on previous visits, Lily had greeted him in the entryway.

"She's in her room," Gerard said without feeling, then sighed. "She's once again upset her aunt."

"Oh. Is she all right?"

"Mrs. Clark is beside herself. But that's not uncommon."

"I was referring to Lily."

The butler looked toward the ceiling and shook his head. "Of course, you were." Dry as ever. "Miss Lily will improve her lot in life if she can learn to control herself. I hope you're aware what a handful she can be." The dour man walked away, leaving Zachary a bit stumped.

What did she do?

Voices neared from the hallway. Zachary casually folded his arms and waited. After all, he couldn't go up to Lily's room and look for her.

He gasped and nearly crumbled to the floor when the red-headed boy from the *Evening Star* appeared with another man. Without thought, Zachary dropped the flowers.

The redhead met his gaze, then smirked.

Although Zachary's father had told him he'd come across other men he knew from the steamboat, he'd said he respected those men. This brazen boy didn't strike Zachary as someone to be esteemed. But why was he here?

Worse yet, what if the boy told Lily where they'd seen each other?

Mrs. Clark walked with them. She had her arm linked in the older man's, who stood at the boy's side. She broadly smiled. "Good evening, Zachary. Come meet our guests. They'll be joining us for dinner."

He swallowed hard and crossed to them. The older man extended a hand, and Zachary shook it. "I'm Zachary Danforth."

"Vincent Douglas." The man nodded to the youth. "And this is my associate, Lucas Larsen."

Larsen?

Zachary stared at the boy.

"Lucas," Mrs. Clark said, "is Lily's brother and *my* nephew. He and Mr. Douglas traveled a long way to speak with her. Sadly, she misbehaved and I sent her to her room."

You did what?

She smoothed a hand over Lucas's head. "Lucas, dear, Mr. Danforth is courting your sister. Unlike her, he has manners."

Lucas chuckled, but Zachary feared it had greater implications than a reaction to his aunt's remark. "You're her beau?"

"Yes, I am. I'm extremely fond of your sister. There's no one like her."

"Nope. There ain't. She's quite a prize." He twisted his mouth from side to side. "She told you much 'bout herself?"

"Well—"

Rapid footsteps descended the stairs. Zachary turned to find Lily practically tripping down them. She hastened to his side. "Someone should've told me you were here."

He took her hand. "Yes. I brought flowers, but I'm afraid I accidently dropped them."

Gerard was scooping them up with a broom and dustpan.

"It's all right." Her eyes held fear. "I see you met my brother."

"Yes. Just now." He shifted his gaze to the boy, whose smirk never left him. Why Mrs. Clark fawned over him made little sense. Especially since she was always so short-tempered with Lily.

His aunt wouldn't be so gracious if she knew where he'd been Saturday night.

This had to be the notorious brother Lily had spoken of. However, no scandalous sibling would make Zachary abandon her.

Mr. Clark joined the uncomfortable gathering. "Why are you all standing here? Mrs. Winters is ready to serve." He eyed his wife, who hadn't released Mr. Douglas.

"We're coming, Stuart. I was showing our guests the courtyard." She sauntered past Zachary, with their *guests,* and soon disappeared from view.

He let out a relieved sigh, pleased to be alone with Lily, who kept a tight grip on his arm.

"You're trembling," he whispered. "What did she do to you?"

Lily held up her wrist. "Tried to squeeze the life outta me." Her skin bore small red cuts, freshly made. "Used her fingernails to make a point."

"But, why?"

"I slapped my brother." She kept her voice to a whisper, but her words grew in intensity. "That man with him is horrid. He touched my sister in an improper way. Lucas shouldn't be with him. They're up to no good."

Zachary believed it. Although he'd not seen him, he assumed the older man had been with Lucas at the boat. "Why's your aunt being so nice to him? Is she blind?"

"He gave her a gold bracelet. He's suckin' up to her. Sumthin' I'd *never* do." Lily placed her hand against Zachary's chest. "There's a lot you need to know. I pray they leave after we eat, so I can tell you everythin'."

He encased her delicate hand inside both of his, then drew it to his lips and kissed it. "I'm here for you. I hate seeing you so frightened."

"I'm more *angry,* than I am scared." She stood on her tiptoes and kissed his lips. "I don't deserve you, but I'm glad you're here."

"Right by your side. I promise."

He escorted her to the dining room, where everyone else was already seated. They took their places. Her brother sat in the chair directly across from him. His presence alone made Zachary uncomfortable.

He must think I'm as lewd as he is.

Zachary wished he'd never gone to that wretched steamboat.

Silence hovered over the table.

Roasted pork and potatoes were served, along with some kind of greens and beets. Zachary could barely eat a bite, but he pushed the food into his mouth regardless.

Lily's ragged breathing didn't help. He'd never seen her so out of sorts.

"So, Lily." Lucas waved his fork in the air. "Why ain't you asked 'bout Noah?"

Lily's body went rigid. "Don't talk with your mouth full, Lucas."

"Noah?" Mrs. Clark said. "Isn't that Rose's most recent child?"

"Yep." Lucas tapped the fork on the table. "My littlest brother. Lily was right fond a him. Weren't you?"

"I love *all* my brothers." Lily's face had gone ashen.

"Even me?" Lucas sneered. "That why you slapped me, cuz you love me so much?"

Mrs. Clark cleared her throat. "Now, now. Let's be civil."

Lucas smiled at her. "But Lily ain't apologized."

Zachary reached under the table and gently rubbed Lily's leg to calm her. He could swear heat poured from her body.

"I don't intend to," she said. "Not when he made light of what that man did to Violet." She pointed at Mr. Douglas. "I don't know why I hafta be at the same table with him. He's a scoundrel an' has no business here."

Mr. Douglas sipped from his water glass. "A scoundrel? My, my. Your vocabulary has certainly improved, Lily." He nodded at Mr. Clark. "I assure you, sir. Our business here is honorable. We're searching for a woman who committed murder."

"Murder?" Mr. Clark smoothed the front of his suit. "And how is my niece involved?"

"The woman sent her a letter. I hoped Lily might still possess it."

Mr. Clark's brows creased. "Why would a murderess correspond with Lily?"

"They were fond a each other," Lucas sniggered. "Closer than any two women should be, if you understand my meanin'."

Zachary snapped his head to the side and questioned Lily with his eyes.

She rapidly shook her head. "He's lyin'. It was nothin' like that."

Lucas grunted. "Then why was you kissin' on her? I seen you."

Mrs. Clark's eyes nearly popped from their sockets. "Good heavens." She fanned her face.

Mr. Douglas grinned. "I had no idea, Lucas. Why didn't you mention this before? It sheds a whole new light on our case." He leaned across the table toward Zachary. "Were you aware of Lily's tendencies?"

Zachary held up his hands. "Stop this! I won't have you speaking about her this way. She's a decent woman."

Lucas leaned back in his chair. "How long you known her?"

"Long enough."

Lucas shook his head and laughed. "Reckon you don't know much a anythin'. I could tell you all kinds a stories."

Lily shot to her feet. "Hush, Lucas!" She grabbed Zachary's hand. "Come with me. I don't wanna be here." She practically dragged him from the room.

"Have fun tellin' him all 'bout Callie!" Lucas called out after them.

By the time they reached the courtyard, Lily was sobbing. Zachary guided her to the bench and held her.

She clutched onto him and buried her face against his neck.

"Shh . . ." He stroked her hair to soothe her.

She sat upright. "I ain't never done nothin' with no girl. Lucas is lyin'." Her poor English didn't bother him, and her tear-streaked cheeks broke his heart. The distress she was under obviously broke down her reserve.

"So, tell me about Callie. I want to know the truth."

She wiped her eyes with her sleeve and sniffled. "Yes, I was kissin' on her, but Callie wasn't a woman, she was a man named Caleb."

"What? But—why would anyone think she was female?"

With a huff of exasperated-sounding air, she faced forward. Her eyes stared off somewhere, no longer on him. "Back 'fore the war ended, soldiers was comin' to our cabin all the time. They'd help themselves to everythin'. Food. Livestock. Whatever they wanted. Some a the women in the cove were helpless, what with their men gone fightin' an' all. Them soldiers took advantage."

He put a hand on her leg, but she pushed it away. "Please, Zachary, just let me finish."

He'd wanted to give comfort, but he abided by her request and set his hands on his lap. "Go on."

"We took in a wounded soldier named Caleb. Pa dug a bullet outta his shoulder. It took him a while to heal, an' once he did, he stayed on an' helped with the farm. But he couldn't go out as a man, or he woulda been seen an' captured. More than likely, killed. So, I gave him one a my dresses, an' he wore it an' a bonnet whenever he went outside."

Zachary's heart wrenched, knowing very well where this story led. "You fell in love with him, didn't you?"

Her head slowly bobbed. "We was plannin' to get married after the war ended. But then, Captain Ableman came—the man who was shot. He came up on us in the barn. He thought Caleb was a woman an' he wanted both a us. Said we could have us a real good time." Her hands tightened into fists, and her eyes closed.

"So, Caleb shot him. Right?"

"No." Her body jerked and she cried. "I was so scared the captain would find out he was a man. I didn't know what to do. He'd only seen Caleb from the back, but he kept gettin' closer. An' then, a shot rang out, an' the captain fell. I seen Lucas standin' there holdin' Pa's gun. He saved Caleb an' me, but he ain't been the same since. He's doin' all he can to hurt our family." She covered her face with her hands and bawled.

Zachary rubbed his temples. His head pounded. "If there's no Callie, then why is Lucas traipsing around the country searching for her?"

"Cuz Ableman's widow is rich. She's payin' my brother an' Mr. Douglas to bring Callie to justice. Mr. Douglas is none-the-wiser."

"So, tell him the truth. Tell him Lucas killed him."

She sat up, shaking her head. "I can't. If it weren't for him, Caleb would probably be dead, an' I would've been defiled. 'Sides, as wretched as he is, he's my brother. He done it to protect us."

Zachary pulled a handkerchief from his pocket and gave it to her. She soundly blew her nose.

There was more to her story he needed to know. "What became of Caleb? The war's been over for a while now. I assume you still love him."

Lily had stopped crying, but breathed heavily. She kept her eyes on the stones at her feet.

"Do you?" Zachary dreaded her answer.

"Yes. But, he married someone else."

He swallowed the stone in his throat. "Why?"

She grabbed onto his hand. "It's too complicated, an' it's not important. You're in my life now, an' that's all that matters."

"Not if you love *him*. There's no room in your heart for me."

"But, there is. Since I met you, I've stopped thinkin' 'bout him. But . . . I can't let go a Noah."

"Your brother?"

Tears trickled down her cheeks. "My *son*."

Zachary clutched his chest and inched away from her. This changed everything. The sympathy he'd felt for her vanished, replaced by disgusted betrayal. "What kind of woman are you?" He slowly got to his feet. "Your brother was right. I don't know you at all."

She burst into another sob. "Please, don't say that. I wanted to tell you the truth, but I didn't know how. I thought if you truly love me, you'd understand."

She reached for him, so he backed farther away. "Your uncle has been peddling used wares. How dare he!"

"He doesn't know. No one here does. Zachary, please. Sit down. You hafta let me explain."

"I've heard all I care to. I finally understand why you were throwing yourself at me. You're no better than one of the whores on that riverboat!"

"Don't say that!" Her chin quivered out of control, making her ugly.

"My father told me there were two kinds of women, but I believe now that there are three. Those you marry, those who sell themselves, and ones like you. You pretend to be pure to snag a rich husband, then lay with him only to set the trap. You disgust me!"

"But, that's not what happened. I loved Caleb, an' I love *you*. Don't punish me for what happened in the past."

"Punish you? You're exactly like your brother. As far as I'm concerned you can both rot in hell. I saw what type of man he was before I even came here tonight. He'd been with a prostitute and was bragging about his *accomplishment*."

"How'd you see him with a woman like that?" She sat fully upright and studied his face. "Where were you?"

"I have no qualms telling you the truth. I went to a steamboat called the *Evening Star*, known for its fine prostitutes. I feared my desires would cause me to compromise you. I thought dousing them in the arms of a professional could help me overcome them and wait to have you. To be able to take your innocence on our wedding night."

He grunted, sickened by the thought. "Because I thought I loved you and didn't want to betray what we had, I didn't follow through. After seeing your brother and being repulsed by him and the half-naked woman in the room waiting for her next customer, I bolted. I ran home covered in guilt. And what for? A woman who's already tarnished." He spit out every word, wanting to be free of her.

Guilt no longer plagued him, and his heart held no love for her. "When the Clarks know about this, you'll be on the streets. No one will have you." He glared at her. "I'll let you continue your game with your brother, because I don't want to be involved with either of you. I shan't see you again."

He stormed away. Not even her tears troubled him any longer.

He marched into the house and went to the dining room. "A word, Mr. Clark?"

The man stood and gestured to the hallway.

Zachary glanced at Lucas. A satisfied grin covered the boy's face. The impish youth held a secret over Zachary's head that he'd no doubt reveal if crossed. Though Lucas was a murderer, Zachary washed his hands of all the Larsens.

Let the law discover his sins. I won't reveal them.

Zachary was disgusted with himself for being so deceived and manipulated. It seemed Helen Clark had every reason to despise her niece. If Mrs. Clark knew what was good for her, she'd disown the entire Larsen family.

CHAPTER 36

If only Lily could curl up into a ball and die.

She lay on the bench and sobbed. Zachary hated her. Her aunt hated her. Maybe she even hated herself.

How could *love* bring her to this?

Zachary had been so angry, he hadn't seen into her heart. Yet if he had, he would've found falsehoods there, too. She'd been lying to *herself.* She didn't love Zachary—not like she loved Caleb. Zachary had been his replacement—the best she thought she could do.

I'll never be right.

Time passed and darkness set in. The last place she wanted to go was into the house, but soon it would be too cold to be outdoors.

"Lily!" Her aunt's hateful tone startled her, but she didn't budge.

In mere seconds, the woman hovered over her. "I knew from the start you'd be trouble, but I never expected this! You've tarnished our image! Shamed us beyond repair!" She grabbed Lily's shoulders and forced her upright. "I'll be writing to your mother and I intend to tell her what I think of her. How dare she send you here!" Her aunt fiercely shook her.

Numb, Lily said nothing.

"You will not step a foot inside my home again. Hear me?" The woman gave a final pronounced shove and released her.

Lily sat tall and jutted her chin. "Fine."

The woman smacked her across the face. "Nothing about you is fine. I spent hundreds of dollars on you—a despicable, tainted woman. I want you to leave *now*. Thank God I'll no longer have to endure having Stuart gawk at you, then touch me and look right through me. You're a sinful, ugly girl, and you placed improper thoughts in his mind." She yanked Lily to her feet. "Now, get out!" She pushed her down the pathway.

Lily stumbled, but kept on going.

Her eyes were so full of tears, she couldn't see the path in front of her. She wiped them away, only to have them cover her eyes again.

When she reached the front gate, she dropped to the ground and leaned against the brick wall.

She gazed toward the heavens. "God, what do I do now?"

He had every right to abandon her like everyone else.

"Lily?" Evie's gentle hand rested on Lily's shoulder.

Lily grabbed her hand and hugged it to her cheek. "Oh, Evie. What do I do?"

The sweet girl sat beside her and extended the satchel Lily had brought with her when she'd arrived. "I got this from your room and put everything in it I knew was yours. I wish I could've taken some dresses, but your aunt would've missed them." She pulled Lily into her arms. "I heard everything. I'm so sorry. I know you, Lily. You're not the horrid person they're making you out to be. How'd you ever give up your baby?"

Sobbing, Lily laid her head on her shoulder. "My folks made me. I miss him so much. . ." Unstoppable tears flowed.

"Shh . . ." Evie smoothed her hand along Lily's hair. "David's coming to take you somewhere safe."

"Where? No one wants me."

"It's called Water's Rest. The people who own it help women like you. I knew another maid who got herself into some trouble. She went there. She said the owners are kind. I know they'll help you."

Help me?

Lily's dear friends had answered her prayer. She should've remembered God never abandoned anyone.

She lifted her head to the sound of the approaching carriage. "Don't let Aunt Helen know you done this. All right?"

"We won't. And Lily . . . David and I are getting married next week. I'm turning in my notice."

"Good." Lily pressed her forehead to Evie's. "You understand now everything I said. Don't you?"

"Yes." She kissed Lily's cheek. "Now, go on. Before someone finds us here. I'll never forget you, Lily." She helped her stand.

Lily hugged her tight, then opened the door to the carriage. David remained high in the driver's seat, waiting.

The instant she sat, the carriage jerked. He drove it faster than ever. Thank goodness the streetlights had been lit.

Her tears streamed. There was no stopping them. She felt worse than when she'd arrived. This was a new kind of pain. Her shame would be known to everyone in the city, thanks to Aunt Helen's ranting.

There was something to be said for silence. She should've listened to her folks and kept her past to herself. By telling Zachary the truth, Lily's life had taken an even uglier turn.

She scratched at her neck. The stiff, white collar irritated her skin, so she ripped it off, no longer caring how fine her dress looked.

She leaned back and shut her eyes. Maybe her broken heart would burst and her suffering would be over.

* * *

Lily shifted uncomfortably.

Where am I?

The last she recalled, she was in the carriage on her way *somewhere*.

Her eyes ached. Simply opening them was a chore.

"You're awake." A soft, sweet-sounding voice loomed over her. "I thought you'd sleep forever."

Lily eased into a seated position and rubbed her puffy eyes.

The girl gently grabbed her hand. "Try not to rub them. I'll get you a cool damp cloth, so you can wash them. Tears can be very cruel to the eyes."

Lily blinked several times and tried to bring her into focus.

"I'm Amorette," the girl said over her shoulder, as she poured water into a bowl. "And we were told your name is Lily. Is that right?"

"Yes." Lily cleared her scratchy throat. Now that she could see Amorette plainly, the girl was lovely. Her dark shiny hair flowed all the way to her waist, and her defined facial features were those of an angel. "Where am I?"

"Water's Rest. Mr. Carrington brought you to us." She dipped a rag into the water, wrung it out, then returned to Lily's side and perched on the edge of the bed. "Here. I'll let you do it."

Lily took the cloth, then shut her eyes and pressed the cloth against them. It helped. "Thank you." She scooted up higher on the bed and leaned against the wall. "I don't remember bein' brought in."

Amorette looked at her with pity. "You'd fallen asleep in the carriage. Mr. Carrington carried you inside. He didn't want to leave you without saying goodbye, but he feared for his fiancée and left."

"Are you the *owner* here?"

She giggled. The softest-sounding one Lily had ever heard. "I'm only fourteen. My parents run Water's Rest. I told them I wanted to be the one to tend you. My heart broke when I heard what had happened. You know—the reason Mr. Carrington brought you."

Lily's shoulders dropped and she stared at her lap. "So, you know 'bout me."

"And your baby." She laid a hand atop Lily's. "Your heart's been torn in two. We want to help fix it."

"How can you? I ain't got money. No one wants me, an'—"

"*We* want you. You can stay as long as you need to."

The small room Lily occupied held little more than the bed, along with a small table where the water basin sat. Though comfortable, it was a far cry from what she'd had. Even so, she was thankful to be here.

The door opened and a petite older woman entered.

Amorette beamed. "She's awake, Mother."

"*Oui.* I can see that." The woman's heavy French accent surprised Lily. Her daughter showed no trace of it.

As the woman approached, Lily saw their resemblance. Her ma was as lovely as her daughter.

"I am Francine Waters." She smiled graciously. "Are you feeling better, Lily?"

"I'm confused. What is this place? An' why do you want me here?"

Francine put a hand on Amorette's shoulder. "Please go and tell your father that Miss Lily is awake. I need to speak with her privately."

"Yes, Mother." Amorette rose from the bed. "I'll come back later. You may want someone *younger* to talk to." She grinned.

Her ma playfully smacked her rump as she left the room. "Amorette is a good girl, but she loves to tease."

"She's kind. Sumthin' I ain't seen much of lately."

Francine sat on the bed in the spot her daughter had been. "Mr. Carrington shared your dilemma. It was important for us to understand why he believed our services would benefit you. After all, most women here are those trying to escape a life of selling themselves. You are not like them."

"You mean, prostitutes? Y'all help them?"

"*Oui*." Francine pulled her shoulders back. "I once was one of *them*."

Lily gaped at her, then snapped her mouth shut. "But, you have a husband, an' a daughter. How'd that happen?"

"It is a long story for another day. I only told you of my former life to assure you things will get better. Sadly, people scorn women who lay with men who are not their husbands. Sometimes, it is the only way a woman can put food in her mouth. Or —as it was for you—a woman might give herself to a man expecting matrimony. Love often prompts deeper desires that turn what resides in the heart into something physical. That is what happened to you, no?"

"Yes. I loved Caleb so much. Was it wrong to want him that way?"

"Wrong? No. It is human."

"But I've ruined my life. Everyone hates me."

Francine took Lily's hand and tenderly rubbed across it. "You are wrong. We will help you get back on your feet. Eventually, you will have to decide what you want. For now, you must rest. I can see in your eyes that you have not slept in days. I doubt you have had much to eat. After you sleep, I will introduce you to the others here."

"Prostitutes?"

"*Oui*. Some are. But they are *women* first. Like you and me."

Lily had no idea what was in store for her, yet anything was better than being with the Clarks.

Francine tapped a single finger to Lily's forehead. "You are thinking too hard. Do not be afraid of what is to come. I could tell from the way Mr. Carrington spoke of you that you have a good heart, broken though it may be." She patted the pillow. "Lay down and sleep. I will check on you in a few hours."

Lily had to admit, her eyes were still heavy, as well as sore. She scooched down under the covers and lay back.

Francine took the cloth, rewet it, then placed it on Lily's forehead. "*Dormez bien*, Lily."

"What's that mean?"

"Sleep well." Francine walked out and shut the door behind her.

Thoughts tumbled through Lily's mind like boulders in a landslide. It took her quite a while, but eventually she replaced ugly thoughts with pleasant dreams.

CHAPTER 37

"I do!" Gideon yelled the words.

"Well then," Brother Davis chuckled. "You may kiss your bride."

Gideon looked out at all the folks gathered. The same faces he'd seen every Sunday since he'd started coming to church again. His ma was crying, but he knew they were happy tears. As for Mrs. Larsen, she just clutched her Bible to her chest and kept her eyes closed.

He preferred looking at his wife.

Wife.

He faced her again, then wiped some wayward tears from her eyes. They, too, were the happy kind. He had no doubt of that.

She wore no veil, and her wedding dress was the same floral print she'd been wearing to church. But she'd never been prettier.

Her brows lifted. "Gideon," she whispered. "You're s'posed to kiss me now."

It seemed odd to do something so intimate in public, yet everyone who got married was required to. So, he leaned close and gave her a gentle peck.

Applause broke out.

His cheeks were so hot, he assumed they glowed. He shuffled closer to Violet, and she linked her arm through his. They made their way down the long center aisle and outside into a downpour.

He'd been told rain on your wedding day meant good luck. He saw it as a means to get drenched, cold, and likely become ill. But, since they'd vowed to care for each other in sickness and in health, at least he was assured Violet would stay by his side.

Truthfully, he never questioned it for a minute—regardless of the vows. She'd proven her love by her persistence. She'd never *once* given up on him.

They rushed to their wagon to go home. Folks filtered out of the church and hopped into their own buggies.

Mrs. Larsen came up to the side of the wagon beside Violet, holding little Noah. She held a hand above her eyes, keeping the rain from trickling into them. "You be good to my girl. Hear?"

"He's gonna be wonderful, Ma." Violet cupped the baby's head. "Get him outta the rain 'fore he gets sick."

Mrs. Larsen held the child tighter. "I know how to tend my son. Now go on. Don't be worryin' 'bout us no more. You got *your* life to live, an' I got one less mouth to feed."

What an awful thing to say.

Isaac and Horace ran up and gripped the backboard.

"You better come visit," Isaac said and stomped his foot in a puddle. "I'm gonna miss you."

"Me, too," Horace said. "Who's gonna work our letters with us?"

"You know your letters just fine." Violet smiled at them. "But I'm countin' on you to teach Noah. All right?"

They bobbed their heads in unison.

The rain came down harder.

Gideon's folks hurried over and climbed in. "Let's get on home. Cake's a waitin'."

"Cake?" Isaac said, eyeing his ma.

"We gotta get home. Noah needs a nap. You don't need no cake."

"But, Ma." Violet leaned toward her. "Mrs. Myers is expectin' all a you at her place. She's givin' a reception. I told you all 'bout it."

"The weddin' was important. Feastin' on cake ain't."

Gideon witnessed a transformation in his new bride. Her happy spirit had been crushed. "Mrs. Larsen. Mind if we take the boys with us? They can have some cake, then I'll bring 'em home to ya."

Mr. Larsen took his time wandering over. "I want cake." Seemed the rain didn't bother him. He held his face up to it, grinning.

Violet sat taller. "So, you're comin', Pa?"

"Course I am. Ain't every day my daughter gets married." He pointed at the back of the wagon. "Mind if the boys ride with you?"

"Fine by me," Gideon said.

Isaac and Horace scrambled in.

Mrs. Larsen didn't look one bit happy. She marched to their wagon and climbed in holding Noah. She sat rigidly, unmoving.

"Forgive my wife," Mr. Larsen said. "She's been a mite disagreeable lately. Ever since that telegram from her sister."

"It's all right." Gideon patted his shoulder. "Violet told me. I hope you hear from Lily soon. Not knowing where she is must be hard on all a you."

The man frowned and nodded, then pushed out a smile. "Let's think 'bout happy things today. Have cake an' celebrate."

This time, he moved a lot faster and joined his wife.

"C'mon, Gideon," Horace said. "We're gettin' soaked!"

Violet cuddled against him. "He's right. My dress is gonna stick to my skin."

Gideon blew out a breath. Up until now he'd managed to think about everything *but* her skin. However, tonight, he'd see more than he feared he was ready for.

* * *

Violet turned around and grinned at her brothers. Yes, they were all getting soaked, but they didn't have far to go.

She couldn't fault her ma for being grumpy. After all, the woman had always handled frustration that way. She only wished for this one day, her ma could *try* to be happy.

She faced forward again. "I'm tryin' not to worry 'bout Lily. I know that eventually she'll write an' tell me what happened. But I still hurt for her. I wish she had someone as wonderful as you to love her."

"We'll keep them prayers goin'." He gave her a quick kiss on the cheek, accompanied with her brother's sniggers. "Lily's strong," he whispered. "But we both knew if she told that Danforth fella 'bout Caleb, it wouldn't be good."

Violet cuddled his arm. "I'm glad I can talk to you 'bout it all. Pa don't know I told you everythin'. He believes I just let on that Lily an' Aunt Helen had a disagreement, an' Aunt Helen kicked her out. Reckon it's best he thinks that."

"Reckon so." He patted her leg. "Soon as we get home, get into sumthin' dry, all right? Can't have you gettin' sick."

"I will. An' I have sumthin' special for later." She peered into his eyes and he almost veered off the road.

She giggled. "Best we talk more about *cake*." She said the word as loudly as she could.

The boys cheered.

They arrived at the Myers' cabin followed by five other wagons. Some of the folks from church declined to come due to the nasty weather, but they had plenty of people to fill the small house.

Mrs. Myers passed around towels, and everyone took turns drying themselves in front of the fire. Mr. Myers stoked it up nice and high. Though no one looked like they were in their Sunday best any longer, they didn't seem to mind. Matted wet hair or not.

Some of the folks brought gifts, while others promised to drop something by later. Violet appreciated each and every one. She especially liked the quilt Brother Davis's wife had made.

But all she could honestly think about—aside from worrying over Lily—was her new husband. If she wanted to give him a night to remember, she'd best get her mind right and think *only* of him. Besides, Lily wouldn't have it any other way.

She always wanted me to be happy.

Noah sneezed.

Violet rushed over to him. Her ma held him, but gave him little regard.

"Ma," Violet felt his clothes. "He's still wet. Ain't you got sumthin' dry to put on him?"

"No. But he'll be fine. 'Sides, we'll be goin' soon. Won't we, Buck?"

"Reckon so. The boys got their fill a cake."

That they did. They wrestled on the floor, full of energy.

Violet's mind spun. She found a large dry towel and extended it to her ma. "Why don't you get Noah's clothes off an' wrap him in this? It'll help some."

She held out the baby. "You do it. I know you want to."

"I do." Violet rushed into Gideon's old room and quickly stripped the wet garments from Noah. "Someone's gotta look out for you. I wish I could keep you."

She thoroughly dried him, then wound the towel around his body. She found an old piece of rope she used to secure it. He looked odd, but at least he was dry *and* happy. He smiled and held his arms up, reaching for her.

She lifted him and cuddled his sweet little form, then swayed back and forth. "You're so precious."

"You two make quite the picture." Gideon's words warmed her through and through.

"Thank you." She kissed Noah's chubby cheek. "One day, we'll have one of our own." Unable to stop them, tears came. "I hate givin' him back to Ma. I won't be there to look out for him. What if sumthin' bad happens?"

Gideon moved close, teetering on his crutch. "You can go over there as much as you like an' check on him. Least he won't be too far away."

"But winter's comin'. I won't be able to go when the snow gets too heavy."

Noah patted her face, then sneezed again. She grabbed his tiny hand and kissed it.

"You gotta give him to your folks." Gideon cupped his palm over Noah's head. "Your pa's a good man. He won't let nothin' happen to him. I know he loves this boy, an' your ma does, too. She's just strugglin' with things right now."

"Violet! Gideon!" Mrs. Myers called out. "Folks is leavin'!"

"We best go out an' say our goodbyes," Gideon said.

Violet sadly nodded. She held Noah close and walked into the main room. Her ma stood close to the door, waiting. Violet forced her feet to move and took Noah to her.

"He looks plum silly," her ma muttered.

"Yep. He does." Violet took her *Lily* stance and jutted her chin. "But he's dry."

Her pa passed them, chuckling. "C'mon boys, let's go home." Horace and Isaac raced to his side.

They left, as did the rest of their guests. Fortunately, the rain had let up. Noah would remain dry all the way to the cabin.

An odd silence hung in the air with everyone gone. That is, everyone but those who lived there. Mr. and Mrs. Myers meandered around, picking up dishes and sweeping up bits of cake.

Gideon stood in the doorway to his bedroom rubbing his beard. "Well, then. Reckon we best get over to our place. I'm dyin' to see what you done to it."

Violet's heart danced. She and her mother-in-law had worked hard fixing up the small cabin. They'd told Gideon he wasn't allowed to see it, till now.

"Yes," Mr. Myers said. "You two go on. We'll finish up here."

Gideon gave a quick nod. "Thanks, Pa."

"He started a fire for you," Mrs. Myers said. "Should be nice an' cozy in there."

"Thank you, Ma," Violet said.

Gideon hobbled across the floor and waited for Violet to join him at the front door. She grabbed the lovely quilt from Mrs. Davis, and they silently walked out together.

Their feet, and the tip of his crutch, got covered in mud on the way to their cabin.

"There's a rug on the front porch to wipe our shoes," Violet said. "Can't have dirty floors."

"Nope."

They reached the tiny porch and proceeded to clean their footwear, then Gideon scraped the end of his crutch across the rug. "That should do."

Violet grasped the doorknob.

"Sweetheart?" Gideon stopped her from opening the door. "I know it's custom to carry you in, but I can't."

"I'm well aware. But it don't matter none." She stroked his cheek. "Want me to carry *you*?"

"That ain't funny. You'd drop me, then we'd both be good for nothin'."

She pressed her body to his and moistened her lips. "Then let's just walk in, so we can be good for *sumthin'*."

His head rapidly bobbed.

She pushed the door open. "Now, close your eyes. I'll guide you in."

He did as she asked. Her heart thrummed. She prayed he'd like what they'd done.

"Okay." She positioned him in the center of the room. "You can open your eyes now."

* * *

Gideon's heart pumped hard. He inched his eyes open and took in their home.

"Well?" Violet worked her lower lip. "You like it?"

He faced the bed. Large enough for the two of them. The covers had already been pulled back. Violet laid the Davis's quilt at the end of the bed and gave it a pat. "Well?"

He gulped. "It's perfect. Just right for the two of us."

She hugged him. "I think so, too."

The old wood stove had a single eye, but they'd likely be eating at his folks' place, so she wouldn't be doing much cooking on it.

He grinned at the frilly window coverings on the only window in the room. "Your doin's or Ma's?" He wiggled his finger at the drapery.

"Both. Course, once winter comes, I'll be puttin' a heavy quilt over it to keep things warmer."

A table with two chairs had been positioned close the stove. Aside from that and the bed, the only other furniture were a couple old chairs, in need of new upholstery.

He looked at the floor. "I changed my mind. You deserve a finer house than this."

She nestled against him. "We're startin' with next-to-nothin', but it don't matter. We got love. That, an' a little food now an' then, is plenty."

"I wanna give you more."

"We'll get there. In time." She gestured to the bed. "Sit down an' get comfortable, while I change. An' since this cabin is only one room, you'll either hafta watch me or close your eyes."

"For now, I'll close 'em. I wanna be surprised." He shut his eyes tight.

With them closed, he concentrated on other things. The fire crackled and popped. A wonderful aroma filled the small space. "You cookin' sumthin'? Smells like apples."

"There's a pot a cider brewin'. Your ma thought we might get thirsty."

"Smells good." He gulped. His folks would know what they'd be doing tonight. It bothered him a bit having them think such things.

The fabric of Violet's dress ruffled close to his ear. His heart beat even faster, knowing she was undressing.

He unbuttoned his shirt. "It's gettin' a mite warm in here."

"I'm glad. Reckon it's gonna get chilly later on." She knelt beside him. "All right. Open your eyes."

He slowly lifted his lids, greeted by Violet's bare shoulders. "Lawdy." He ran his hand down her soft arm. "You cold? You got chill bumps."

"Only cuz you're touchin' me like that. Ma made this gown for me. Least she did sumthin' nice."

"You're beautiful. You could be wearin' a flour sack and you'd still make my heart thump." He shifted his eyes down her body. The thin fabric revealed everything beneath.

"Kiss me, Gideon." She lay back on the pillows and reached for him.

He gladly did as she asked.

Their kiss turned into something more.

He recalled her saying she wanted his hands on her, so he let them wander.

She boldly pushed his shirt open. "You got too many clothes on."

I can't do this.

He sat up, moved to the edge of the bed, and put his head in his hands.

"Gideon?" She rose up and got behind him. "What's wrong? Don't you wanna be with me?"

"Course I do. But . . ." He slapped a hand against the bed. "I don't want you to see my leg. An' I'm worried I won't be able to . . . to do things right."

"Reckon I won't know the difference. I ain't never done it." She rubbed his back, then dotted his neck with kisses. "Show me your leg."

"I can't."

She hopped from the bed and pushed on his shoulders, sending him onto his back.

He tried to sit up again, but she shoved him back down. "What are you doin', Violet?"

"Takin' charge. You won't, so I will. Cuz I want a baby, which means I gotta get your britches off."

He gaped at her, but her bluntness set him on fire.

Fearlessly, she unbuttoned his trousers then yanked them down and tossed them aside. Not wanting to see her reaction to his stumped leg, he closed his eyes again.

He gasped when she caressed the tender spot. "It's scarred, but it don't look bad." She knelt beside him on the bed. "So, if you'd like . . ." She eyed his drawers "I can strip off them underwear, or you can do it yourself. Either way, they hafta go."

"When did you get so bold, Violet?"

"Lily taught me everythin' I know. Well—not *everythin*'. Some of what's to come, you an' I will learn together." She cuddled into him and ran her hand over his bare chest. "Let's get under the covers, an' see what happens." She unfolded the quilt from the preacher's wife.

"Um . . . Violet?"

"Hmm?" She smoothed the colorful blanket, then folded it down at the top and fluffed the pillows.

"You wanna do things with *that* coverin' us?"

"Well, it's gonna get a mite cold in here. Even with the fire. An' since this was a weddin' gift, I thought it'd be nice to use it on our first night together."

"But . . ." He scratched at his beard. "It was made by Brother Davis's wife. Ain't it holy or sumthin'?"

She giggled. "You're the silliest man ever there was. Now get your tail under here an' give me a proper weddin' night." She lifted the edge of the quilt and slowly batted her lashes.

Heart thumping again, he happily obliged her. What else did he have to fear? He had no qualms about her seeing *other* parts of his body. He had nothing more to be ashamed of.

They quickly freed themselves of every single garment, and Gideon soon found out that a partially missing leg didn't inhibit lovemaking. He'd gained the strength needed to stay atop her and move.

His beautiful wife opened her heart and body to him. He loved on her with all of himself, and thanked God for the wonderful angel He'd sent to bring him back to life.

They had babies to make, and Gideon figured they'd managed a very good start.

CHAPTER 38

"Miss Lily?" Amorette rapped on her door, then eased it open.

Lily sat on her bed, staring into nothingness. Even after six days at Water's Rest, she ached too much to do anything more. "Yes?"

"You have a visitor. Can you come to the common room and meet with him?"

"Him?" *Zachary?*

Maybe he'd had a change of heart.

"Yes, it's a *him*." Amorette cast her lovely smile. "And though I think his request is a little strange, he said to tell you your *caterpillar* is here."

Lily thought she was done crying, but tears bubbled up. "I'll be right there."

Amorette softly giggled. "I'll tell him." She shut Lily's door.

Lily dug into her satchel and withdrew the hand mirror Evie had so kindly included. It wasn't hers, but she doubted Aunt Helen would miss it.

I look a sight.

She touched a hand to her haggard-looking face. Her puffy eyes had aged her, and her hair needed grooming.

"I'll hafta make do." She ran a brush through the tangled locks, then braided it the way she used to when she lived in the cove.

Francine had kindly given her another dress. This one was brown and not very attractive, but it didn't matter. *Nothing* mattered any longer.

But if that were true, then why was she so eager to see Archibald?

She hastened to the common room, passing several new acquaintances. Shirley, the runaway, and Hazel, the prostitute. They were both nice, but horribly troubled. Lily fit right in.

Archibald was easy to find. He sat on the large sofa and nearly filled it. The dear man's presence moved her to another kind of tears.

Though compelled to hug him, she knew he wouldn't want it, so she sat in the chair across from him and tucked her legs in the way she'd been taught. "I can't believe you're here." She placed a hand to her heart. "How'd you know where to find me?"

The pity in his eyes made her look away. She didn't deserve it.

"Mr. Carrington told me where you were. I heard what happened with Zachary, and I had to come."

"Makes no sense. You must think I'm horrid."

"Not at all. Why should I?"

She faced him. "Cuz I'm sure you've heard *all* the rumors by now." Defeated, her body folded into itself. "Archibald, I confess. I had a baby an' I was never married."

"I know." He gave a tender smile, then scowled. "Your aunt has told everyone I know about her *sinful* niece, and how you shamed them. She raved about it in *church*. She's trying to get pity, but I think her actions made her appear cruel. You're part of her family. She should've been more understanding."

His passionate rant touched her, but she could tell he wasn't finished, so she silently waited, while tears pooled in her eyes.

"As for Zachary . . ."

She held her breath.

Archibald hissed out air and tightened his plump fist. "All he had to do was to accept you for who you are and love you. Instead, he chose to break your confidants. He told your secrets to people he *knew* would spread gossip like wildfire. He purposefully hurt you, and I despise him for it."

She leaned toward him and took his hand. Her chin quivered, and her tears streamed. "I should've chosen *you*."

He tenderly stroked her skin. "If you had and you'd told me what you revealed to him, I would've loved you regardless. Because I know you. I know your *heart*. You're a rare gem, Lily Larsen. A woman any man would be blessed to love."

She sniffled. "No man will have me. Not now."

"I wish *I* could. But I can't. For one thing, I don't want you anywhere near those people from church who'd look down their noses at you and torment you for the rest of your life. In addition, Father has forbidden me from pursuing you. He'd make our lives miserable. But most importantly, I know you don't love me. Your heart belongs to someone else."

"Someone I can't have." She wiped her eyes, but it did little good. "My caterpillar . . ." She sucked in air, studying his sweet face. "I'm in wonder*hell,* an' I don't know where to go from here."

He shook his head and smiled. "At least you haven't lost your sense of humor."

She burst out crying again. He was much too kind.

"Lily?" He patted her hand. "If you could go *anywhere*, where would it be?"

She shut her eyes and pondered it, but it didn't take long to decide. "The mountains. Somewhere close to my son. I know my folks don't want me livin' with them, but if I could be near Noah, maybe I could manage to see him."

Archibald dug into his pocket. "I want you to have this." He extended a wad of bills. "You can use it to get you there."

"No." She held up her hands. "I won't take your money. I'll work this out myself."

"But—"

"I said, no. I appreciate it. But like I said, I got myself into this mess, an' I aim to get out of it. *Somehow.*"

He stuffed it back into his pocket. "I wish you'd change your mind. I have plenty to spare."

"Well . . . you *can* help another way."

"How?"

She prayed this would work. "Reckon you can hire Mr. Carrington? I imagine Aunt Helen's fired him by now. Evie, too."

Archibald grinned. "I already did. *Mr.* Carrington, that is. *Mrs.* Carrington is settling into their new home."

"They got married?" Lily's heart danced. "Evie told me they were goin' to, but I feared sumthin' would stop it from happenin'. Well, some*one*. Namely, Aunt Helen."

"They were wed yesterday. It was a quiet ceremony. I was their witness."

"But—how did you know he'd need a job?"

"As I said, I went looking for you and found him. He was almost as forlorn as you. It felt good to make things better for him. *And* his lovely new wife."

She shook her head. "You never stop amazin' me."

"One more thing . . ."

"I can't take much more, but go on." All her tears had dried. Knowing at least *someone* would be happy lifted her spirits.

"Your brother left the city. I heard he and Zachary had some sort of altercation, and soon after, Lucas and the man he travels with left. He's not well-liked."

"Do you mean Zachary, or my brother?"

Archibald chuckled. "Both, I *reckon.*" He grinned, but instantly sobered. "I know you cared for Zachary, and though he shamed you and *I'll* never forgive him for it, I'm certain his life will go on unscathed. You have no need to concern yourself over him."

She grasped onto his hand and squeezed. "You truly are a dear friend." She blew out a long breath. "I'm glad Lucas is gone. Not sure where he's off to, but anywhere far from me an' my son is a blessin'."

Several other folks wandered into the room. Archibald looked nervously about.

"You don't hafta stay," Lily said, then leaned close and lowered her voice. "I know some a the women here aren't what you'd call *respectable*."

"They're getting the help they need. I'm glad of that, but yes, they make me a bit uncomfortable." He shrugged, then cast a tender smile. "I didn't come alone. But the person with me doesn't wish to be seen. She's in my carriage. Will you come out with me to see her?"

"Evie?"

"No." He pushed himself up from the sofa. "And don't worry, it's not your Aunt Helen." Smiling, he extended his arm.

Lily got to her feet and took it. They received more than one confused stare, but she ignored them. Maybe Mrs. Winters had come.

Water's Rest faced the Mississippi River. A cool breeze blew over the water, rippling the waves. Lily paraded with her escort to the waiting carriage. She beamed when she saw David in the driver's seat. He grinned and tipped a top hat. A fine, fancy new look.

Lily gave a slight wave, then went to the door Archibald had opened. He helped her enter, but remained outside.

Lily's heart leapt. She sat, facing Mrs. Gottlieb. And just like that, her tears returned.

"Oh, my dear." Mrs. Gottlieb opened her arms.

Lily flung herself across the seat and into her embrace. "I thought I'd never see you again."

"My poor, poor girl." The sweet woman rubbed Lily's back. "I hate what happened to you."

Lily sat up, but didn't leave her side. She sniffled and blubbered like a baby. "You don't hate *me*?"

"Certainly not. In all my days, I've never met a young woman with such a big heart." She gave Lily a loving pat on the cheek.

Lily picked at the ugly brown material of her dress. "I know I look awful an' a far cry from the proper woman you made me, but I don't have fine things anymore."

Mrs. Gottlieb grabbed her hand and held it. "Clothes are not what make a woman attractive. Yes, your eyes are swollen and your hair needs some attention, but none of that matters. I understand heartbreak. You mustn't torment yourself over your appearance." She sighed and shook her head. "I wish you would've told me about your son. I may have been able to guide you into a more favorable outcome."

"I *couldn't* tell. My folks told me to keep it to myself. But when Zachary—"

"I know. You wanted a clear conscience before you carried on your courtship." Another sigh. "We women bear guilt on our sleeves. We have to tell all or *die* inside. Men, on the other hand . . ." She fluttered her fingers. "Never mind. We won't talk about men. I'm concerned about *you*. Where will you go? You can't stay here forever."

"I wanna go home. I don't belong here. I miss the cove."

"Well. If that's what you wish, then do it. Talk to Mr. Waters. He and his lovely wife may have the solution to your problem. I've been told of other women they've relocated."

"Relocated?"

"Yes. You see, when a woman gains the reputation of being . . ." She twirled her hand through the air. "What's the word?"

"A prostitute?"

"I suppose that will do. A *prostitute*." Her expression soured. "I don't like the way it sounds. Regardless, those kinds of women can't reestablish themselves in communities where they're known for lewd behavior. So, the Waters have found work for them elsewhere. Reputable work. Not the lying-in-bed sort."

Her bluntness tickled Lily, but she was in no mood to laugh. "Reckon they have sumthin' for me? In the Smokies?"

Mrs. Gottlieb chuckled. "*Reckon*. My dear, you're slipping."

"Sorry."

"I forgive you. You've been through Hades. And yes, I believe they can help you."

"How do you know so much about them?"

"I pride myself in charitable giving. I donate regularly to Water's Rest. My life has been spent helping young women, including the less fortunate."

Lily leaned against her, wishing with all her heart *she'd* been her ma. "I'm sorry I let you down."

"Stop. I don't want to hear any more of that." She gently pushed Lily to an upright position. "Get yourself on your feet and stop the pity party. It doesn't become you. Along with your loving heart, you're strong. You have many more years of life left. Make the most of them."

"Yes'm."

"That's my girl." She framed Lily's face with her hands. "And when you get wherever you're going, you must write and let me know you're well. I insist."

"I will." Lily took her hands and held them both. "What are you gonna tell Aunt Helen? She'll be mad if she knows you're bein' nice to me."

"Helen Clark doesn't need to know everything. Why do you think I'm hiding in this carriage? I love you, Lily, but I have to live my life here. I don't have the luxury of going on adventures. You do."

"Adventures . . ." Lily liked the sound of that. "I love you, too. You taught me so much."

"You are *not* ignorant."

Surprisingly, Lily laughed. Mrs. Gottlieb had taken away all her pain. At least for now.

She kissed the woman goodbye, then exited the carriage.

Archibald helped her to the ground. She hugged him tight—like embracing a big bear.

The time had come to have a heart-to-heart talk with Mr. and Mrs. Waters.

* * *

Lily sat primly in a chair across from the owners of Water's Rest. Francine, the former prostitute, and Luke, the one-time steamboat captain and preacher's son. When Lily had heard the story of how they'd met, she'd been amazed. She'd never have believed two such unlikely lovers could be so happily paired.

"So . . ." Luke folded his hands on top of his desk. "You'd like to live in the Smoky Mountains, or somewhere reasonably close?"

"Yes, sir. Can you help?"

"*Oui.*" Francine sat regally tall. She held herself as if she'd been trained by Mrs. Gottlieb. Maybe she had.

Lily fidgeted with her skirt. "Do you have work for me? What do I need to do? I mean—how can I get there? Wherever it is you're gonna send me."

Francine laughed and Luke shook his head.

Lily's cheeks heated. "Sorry, but I just wanna get on with my life. Y'all have been kind, but it's gonna be winter 'fore we know it, an' then I'd be stuck here till spring. An'—"

"Slow down," Luke said, holding up his hands. "We'll tell you everything."

Lily twisted her fingers into knots. The *adventure* waiting had her anxious.

"You will travel by steamboat," Francine said.

"Wait a minute." Lily waved her hands. "I heard them boats are for—you know—*prostitutes*. I don't want no one thinkin' I'm one a them." Once again, her face heated. "Not that there's anythin' terrible 'bout y'all, but . . ."

Francine smiled so sweetly. Completely unoffended.

Lily's shoulders slumped. "I reckon I'll be quiet an' let you finish."

"*Merci.*"

Luke quietly chuckled, then gestured for his wife to continue.

"As I said," Francine went on, "you shall travel by steamboat—one *without* prostitutes—to Tennessee. From there, you will hire a carriage driver to take you to Asheville, North Carolina. It is the best we can do."

"Asheville? Ain't it close to Waynesville?" Lily's throat dried.

"*Oui.* Will that be difficult for you?"

"No. Long as I can be nearer to my son, I'll be happy. What'll I do there?"

Francine nodded at Luke, who pushed a document toward Lily. "This letter explains everything. We were contacted by a man named Arthur Jacobson. He's aware of our program and requires a nanny. His wife suffered an accident that has crippled her, and their four children need tending. You'd not only be helping with the children, you'd be required to assist Mrs. Jacobson."

"In what way?"

"Personal care, such as assistance with bathing. The dear woman can't walk. Mr. Jacobson has tried to care for her himself, but he's spent."

Lily's hands shook. "Why me? Can't they find someone closer? Other family maybe?"

"Do you want to decline his offer?" Luke eyed her curiously. "I thought this would be an answer to your prayers."

"It is. I like children an' all, an' I don't even mind the idea of carin' for Mrs. Jacobson. But . . . it makes no sense that they'd bring in a stranger."

"Tell her," Francine said. "She must know, so she'll understand."

"I agree." Luke leaned across the desk. "Mr. Jacobson's sister was a soiled dove in the war. It's what they called prostitutes. She died at the hand of a drunken soldier. When Mr. Jacobson learned of our shelter here, he wanted to help in any way he could. He feels if his sister had had a place like this to go to, she might have lived. He's been donating funds to us for a great while. When his wife had her accident, he decided to contact us to see if we could find someone suitable. Someone who needed a chance for a new life. I believe you, Lily, are the perfect fit."

No longer trembling, she rubbed her hand over her heart. "When do I leave?"

Francine laughed. "You are in a hurry again, *no*?"

"Yes, I am."

"Then, pack your things," Luke said. "There's a steamboat bound for Chattanooga in two days."

Lily's heart pattered harder. "But—how do I pay for it? I don't got nothin'."

"Oh, but you do," Francine said. "*Plenty.*"

"How?"

"Your dear friends. Mr. Jones and Mrs. Gottlieb."

"No. I told Archibald I don't want his money."

Francine cast her sweetest smile yet. "He did not give it to *you*. He gave it to Water's Rest, as did Mrs. Gottlieb. It is only fitting we pass it on to you. They love you. It is how it should be."

Lily jumped up from her chair and hugged her. "Thank you." She faced Luke. "An' you, too. Someday, I hope I can make up for all this somehow. You've been awfully good to me."

"Everyone deserves a second chance," Luke said. "We all make choices in life that have lasting effects. Whether good or bad. And sometimes, when we're down, we need help getting up again. That's why *we're* here."

Francine sighed. "Several years ago, we ran a home for orphans, but then we saw a greater need. The state was more than willing to help the children, but no one wanted to bother with wayward women. And now, we are happy helping *you*."

Lily squeezed Francine's hand. "Thank you. Or I should say, *merci*."

"*Tres bien!*"

"What's that mean?"

Francine stood and faced her. "Very good. Now, go and get your thoughts together. We will see you later for dinner."

Lily curtsied. For some reason, it seemed appropriate.

She walked outside and wandered toward the river. Steamboats lined the shore. She wondered which one would take her to Tennessee, but whichever it was, she'd go with her head held high.

If someone like Francine could change her life, find love, and raise a child, Lily had no doubt she could do the same.

As Mrs. Gottlieb reminded her, she was strong, and she was *not* ignorant.

BOOKS BY JEANNE HARDT

The River Romance Series:
Marked
Tainted
Forgotten

From the Ashes of Atlanta

A Golden Life

The Southern Secrets Saga:
Deceptions
Consequences
Desires
Incivilities
Revelations
Misconceptions
Redemption

He's in My Dreams

The Smoky Mountain Secrets Saga:
Whispers from the Cove
Hushed into Silence

For more information about Jeanne's books,
check out the links below:

www.facebook.com/JEANNEHARDTAUTHOR
www.jeannehardt.com
www.amazon.com/author/jeannehardt
www.goodreads.com/jeannehardt

CPSIA information can be obtained
at www.ICGtesting.com
Printed in the USA
LVOW11s0227201217
560343LV00003B/199/P